A Thief's Revenge

Douglas Skelton has published numerous non-fiction books and crime thrillers. He has been a bank clerk, tax officer, shelf stacker, meat porter, taxi driver (for two days), wine waiter (for two hours), reporter, investigator and local newspaper editor. He has been longlisted for the McIlvanney Prize six times, most recently in 2025. Douglas has contributed to true crime shows on TV and radio and is a regular on the crime writing festival circuit.

Also by Douglas Skelton

A Company of Rogues

An Honourable Thief
A Thief's Justice
A Grave for a Thief
A Thief's Blood
Ship of Thieves
A Thief's Revenge

Other novels by Douglas Skelton

Blood City
Crow Bait
Devil's Knock
Open Wounds
The Dead Don't Boogie
Tag – You're Dead
The Janus Run
Thunder Bay
The Blood is Still
A Rattle of Bones
Where Demons Hide
Children of the Mist
The Hollow Mountain

DOUGLAS SKELTON

A Thief's Revenge

canelo

 Penguin Random House

First published in the United Kingdom in 2026 by

Canelo, an imprint of
Canelo Digital Publishing Limited,
20 Vauxhall Bridge Road,
London SW1V 2SA
United Kingdom

A Penguin Random House Company
The authorised representative in the EEA is Dorling Kindersley Verlag GmbH. Arnulfstr. 124, 80636 Munich, Germany

Copyright © Douglas Skelton 2026

The moral right of Douglas Skelton to be identified as the creator of this work has been asserted in accordance with the Copyright, Designs and Patents Act, 1988.

All rights reserved. No part of this publication may be reproduced or transmitted in any form or by any means, electronic or mechanical, including photocopy, recording, or any information storage and retrieval system, without permission in writing from the publisher.

No part of this book may be used or reproduced in any manner for the purpose of training artificial intelligence technologies or systems. In accordance with Article 4(3) of the DSM Directive 2019/790, Canelo expressly reserves this work from the text and data mining exception.

A CIP catalogue record for this book is available from the British Library.

ISBN 978 1 80436 736 0

This book is a work of fiction. Names, characters, businesses, organizations, places and events are either the product of the author's imagination or are used fictitiously. Any resemblance to actual persons, living or dead, events or locales is entirely coincidental.

Cover design by Henry Steadman

Cover images © Shutterstock.com

Printed and bound in Great Britain by Clays Ltd, Elcograf S.p.A.

Look for more great books at
www.canelo.co | www.dk.com

In memory of Struan Adam

1

London, 1724

Jane Burton wasn't young. She had never been beautiful, she knew that, but she had been comely enough to attract the attentions of men with ease. That had been her downfall. Certainly, an abiding thirst for gin had contributed to her decline, but an ability – no, a need – to draw men to her was what had ruined what had once been a comfortable, if often painful, life. Her father had been a fellmonger, a dealer in sheepskins in Hungerford. God-fearing, he was, which was something she never understood. Why fear God? Shouldn't he be loved? Anyway, her father, Zachary Burton, tried to instil in her that fear of the Almighty, usually with the back of his hand or the swish of a birch twig. When he found out that she had been entertaining a farm labourer up against an oak tree, he used his clenched fists not to beat the fear of God into her but to beat the devil from her. Had he known that there had been a steady succession of young men, and old men, who'd had many bouts of devilish entertainment with her against that aged bark, then he might have taken down his fowling piece and despatched her to hell there and then. She had tried to argue that if God didn't want them to partake in such activity then He shouldn't have made their bodies so compatible. That line of reasoning provoked a more enthusiastic response from her father, this time using a heavy leather belt that left long welts on her flesh, all the while reciting verses from scripture. It was following that session of intense religious instruction that she reached the conclusion that if she didn't leave the house on her own two feet, then she'd leave feet first. She didn't bid farewell to her mother, who had not only stood by and witnessed the abuse but had actively spurred her husband on.

She had no idea where she was going; she let those still-living feet take her east, and eventually pitched up in London, where the skills she had learned up against that tree in the west stood her in good stead.

Only, this time, she turned coin from it. The flower of her youth soon wilted, thanks to the ministrations of too many men and a superfluity of gin with which she tried to burn away what was left of her conscience. For though she had never thought of her lusts as sinful, she had been instructed in scriptural strictures to such a degree that she believed to use her body so in return for cash was most sinful indeed. She still bore no fear of God, but she did fear that He would turn his face away from her because of her transgressions.

She learned a new skill that added to those transgressions. Men paid for a tupping, pressing her against walls up back alleys, her skirt around her waist, their breeches at their knees, thrusting and huffing until their desires were spent. It was while they were so engaged, she all the while encouraging them with many guttural cries (forced) and even curse words (often not forced), that she realised that their attentions were on the immediate sensation, and not on their purse, which nestled in a coat pocket, said positioning of which she was already aware, having insisted on being paid up front. It was an easy thing to lift that purse as they bucked and heaved, and secrete it within a special pocket under her dress. By the time they noticed it was gone, she was long away in the maze of alleys and lanes.

A buttock-and-file they called her on the streets. Swift-Finger Jane. While the cull dipped his wick, she dipped his pocket. The benefit of not being comely meant that she easily merged with the other girls, and if the culls came looking, they couldn't with ease pick her out.

But one man picked her out. He wasn't like the others. He wasn't even a cull – well, not one of hers, anyway. He had lurked in the shadows of an alley off Holborn, watching as she guided a fellow to a wall and lifted his purse as he rutted. What he'd been doing all alone in the dark she knew not, but he followed her, and when she felt his hand on her shoulder, she thought she was destined for the Whit or the Clink and then for Tyburn. When she turned, she was met with a tall cove, dressed all in black – hat, coat, boots. And he had a kerchief wrapped around his nose and mouth. She'd cried out when she saw that, her hand automatically clutching the purloined purse through the material of her dress as if to protect it.

'I have no interest in that,' the man said, and she heard the laugh in his voice. 'That's yours as far as I'm concerned.'

Her other hand reached for the dagger she had concealed under her short jacket, but he gripped her wrist, reached in with his free hand and plucked it from its hiding place. He studied the blade closely. 'A nasty piece of steel, that.'

'A woman has to be able to defend herself in these streets.'

'This would certainly do the trick, if you know how to use it.'

'I know how to use it, you ain't no cause for worrying.'

'I try not to worry. It's not good for the digestion.'

She'd sidled closer to him, the prospect of making further coin overcoming her initial fear. 'What is it you wish, me 'ansum?'

Another laugh as he pushed her away a little. 'I have no interest in that, either, though thank you kindly for the offer.'

She dropped all warmth from her tone. 'Then if you don't want a tup and you don't want my purse and you don't want to arrest me, then unhand me, and let me be on my way.'

'There is a service you can do me.'

'What sort of service?'

He said nothing further at that point. He dragged her to the end of the alley up by Saffron Hill and wordlessly guided her from lane to lane until they reached a dingy passageway with a reputation for being the haunt of cutthroats.

'I doesn't have no wish to go there, my lover,' she said, drawing back.

'But I wish you to go there,' he said.

'I won't.'

'You will, or it's to the magistrates you will go for stealing that man's purse.'

'You can't prove nothing.'

He sighed. 'His name is Benjamin Rawlins, he's a shoemaker from St Giles and you took every penny he had. He will press charges and the magistrates will frown most deeply upon you.'

She jutted her chin in a defiant manner. 'How can you know who he is?'

'I know him.'

She thought upon this. 'I think you tell a tale to pressure me to do your will.'

'Very well,' he said, tugging her away again. 'Let's to the Sessions House and see who the magistrate believes.'

She drew back. 'Wait, we can discuss this, friendly like.' She cast her eye to the mouth of the passage. 'That is a most evil place.'

'You will be perfectly safe.'

'People has died in there. Their throats cut. There was a girl molested most brutal just last week. She died today.'

'I know.'

'And yet you wishes me to walk in there?'

'I do.'

She hesitated, her fingers tightening on the hard lump of the stolen purse. The man's claim that he knew the cull she had just tupped could be false, but his eyes above the mask shone with a confidence that she didn't like. She wondered if she had been somehow lured into this, that he had engaged the man Rawlins – if that was his name in truth – to engage her, tup her, and allow her to lift his purse while this one waited in the dark of the alley to follow her.

'Why does you need me to do this?'

'The why of it needn't concern you.' He reached into the pocket of his coat and produced a pouch of his own. 'But if it makes you feel better…'

She reached for it, but he jerked it away.

'It's yours once you do as I say,' he said.

She had little choice. Her arm dropped away and she turned towards the passageway. 'It's of little use to me if I'm dead.'

'You will walk from that place unharmed and considerably better off. On that you have my oath.'

There was that confidence again. She sighed.

'I am to simply walk into that passage?'

'To the end and then return.'

'And where will you be?'

'Close.'

Jane studied the dense darkness. 'You're touched in the head, you are.'

'That's been said before.'

'Will you give me back my blade? In case I must defend myself.'

'No, I don't think I shall.'

'Why not?'

That laugh again. It was actually a very nice laugh, but she saw nothing to amuse her. 'I'm touched in the head but I'm not stupid.'

'You think I would use it on you?'

'I know you would. Now, time is pressing and the night wears on. Is it a short walk through yonder passageway, and earn this pouch, or a trip to the magistrates' court and earn a walk to Tyburn?'

She drew a deep breath. *Life is nothing without risk*, she thought. 'To the end and return, correct?'

'Correct.'

'And you will give me that there bunce?'

'Correct again.'

Greed overcame her caution so, shaking her head and mumbling complaints over the madness of it all, she began to walk into the passageway, shooting a glance over her shoulder at him just before she entered. The alley was wider than she had first believed, and darker, though she hadn't thought that possible. When her eyes grew more accustomed to the gloom, she began to make out doorways on either side, and piles of what seemed to be baskets and barrels piled here and there. She stopped when she realised that anyone could lie in wait behind them, or skulk on the other side of those doors. She looked again at the opening to the alley, hoping to see the masked man still watching her, but he was gone.

Walk to one end and back, he'd said. You'll be safe, he'd said. What sort of jest is this?

She decided to return. Damn him and damn his purse...

A man's figure loomed before her from behind a pile of barrels. She gasped, stepped back, bumping into another man. She wondered where he had hidden, then saw a sliver of light cutting through from a partially open door to her left. It slanted onto the side of the man's face, revealing one eye that was milky and a mouth twisted into a grin that revealed stubs of blackened teeth. She had been with many unattractive men, but from that half-lit glimpse even the word 'ugly' didn't begin to describe him.

'Hello, lass,' he said, his accent Scottish. 'What would you be doing in this gloomy place, then, all on your own self?'

'Wee lass, all alone in such a lonely lane,' said the other one. He was Scottish also. She half turned to face him, but couldn't see him at all clearly; she'd wager he was no prize.

'Just making a short cut,' she said, hoping they didn't ask her destination because her mind had frozen and she was unsure as to where this passageway led.

'Short cut, is it?' Ugly spoke again. 'You'll be paying the toll, then.'

'What toll?'

'For using this lane, lass. Ae body pays the toll.'

A thought occurred that she should reach within the folds of her dress and give them the pouch she had recently lifted, but it was a fleeting one. She had worked hard for that bunce and was damned if she would hand it over.

'There's no toll here,' she said, looking beyond him for sight of the masked man.

'Aye, there is. See, lass, this is our lane, ye unnerston? We collect a toll frae all who use it after dark.'

She wished she had her blade, for then she would give them a toll they wouldn't forget. She silently cursed them for being rogues. She cursed the masked man. The bastard was working with them, luring her with promise of coin, sending her in so they could have their fun. She cursed herself for being so gullible. She thought herself wise to the ways of these streets, but she had been fooled by a smooth-talking cove with a bag of silver.

'I have no money,' she said.

A finger plucked at the button of her coat and she jerked back, only to bump again into the man behind her. They crowded against her till she could feel their rancid exhalation on her face. She was used to the odour of body and breath, but this was particularly disgusting. 'Ye sure and certain o' that?'

A hand snaked over her blouse, down her hip. Men had touched her many times but this time she screamed, tried to break away, then she felt cold steel at her throat and a voice whispered, 'Still yourself, lass, or we'll slit you, by God.'

She stilled herself. The blade didn't move. The hands did, though; she felt them on one thigh then the other, finally closing against the solid bulk of the pouch.

And then…

'Gentlemen, I do believe the lady has had enough of your attentions.'

His voice. The masked man. She opened her eyes to see him standing nearby, a dark figure even blacker than the gloom around them. He must have hidden himself in the shadows and moved silently.

'This isnae none of your concern, stranger,' said Ugly. 'Get yoursel' gone.'

'I think not.'

She felt Ugly shrug and then whirl, the blade slicing high, but a pistol cracked and the blade clattered on the ground, the man falling with it. Jane felt something wet spray over her. The second man swore and pushed her out of the way, his hand reaching for his own weapon, but then he stopped, gagged as if something choked him and slumped to the side. In the dim light from the open doorway Jane thought she saw something liquid glistening at his throat, but then the masked man's shadow fell over him. He replaced his pistol in his belt, then wiped the knife blade off on the breeches of the nearest dead man. He extended a hand to draw her away from them. She wrapped her coat more tightly around her, a deeper cold than that of the air seeping into her body.

Her voice trembled as she spoke. 'You used me as bait, you bastard.'

'I did.'

'Why?'

He dropped to one knee and began rifling the men's pockets, finding a thick purse on each. 'Because for three nights I've paraded up and down this passageway and they didn't bite. I realised I was using the wrong lure. They weren't only robbers, they were men who took their pleasure from fear and believing themselves more powerful. I wasn't the type of mark they desired. I needed someone such as you.'

He stood and she reached out for one of the pouches, but he snatched them both away from her. 'Ah-ah, these are mine.'

'They could have killed me.'

'No,' he said, and there was a finality in that one word that made her understand that she was never in any danger of death.

'You're still a bastard,' she said.

'As a matter of fact, I am,' he said, then held out the purse he had shown her earlier. 'But I'm a bastard with coin.'

She snatched it away, feeling its weight with professional ease. The two purses he had taken from the Scots seemed heftier, but she was satisfied. He was already walking back the way he had come and she shouted after him, 'I don't know your name?'

He stopped, turned back, tipped his black hat. 'Just call me Paladin.'

Then he resumed his exit from the passageway and into the street. She watched him go. The Paladin. She had heard of this cove but didn't believe him to exist. And yet, there he was. She hefted the pouch again, deciding that it had been worth it after all, and stowed it beside the other in her skirt. When she looked up again, the man was gone, as if the darkness of the city streets had swallowed him. She wondered who he was. She wondered why he did what he did. She wondered if she'd ever see him again, for she might be willing to further act as bait.

And when she saw another man, also in black, step from a heavily shadowed doorway opposite the opening of the passageway, she wondered if the Paladin knew he was being followed.

2

Gabriel Cain savoured the brandy. The anticipation of the action, and then its delivery, was a stimulant, but once it dissipated he enjoyed the warmth of the alcohol as it coursed through him. The nightly business of the Black Lion played out in front of him, his table and chair being against a wall at the back where he had plain view of both the entrance to Drury Lane, and the doorway leading to the kitchen and through it to a rear exit. There was a third door, but that led not only to the stairway leading to the private rooms upstairs but also another leading to the alley behind the tavern. He sat among the noise and revelry but was a man apart from it. Later, he would retire to the room above where he knew there were games of chance afoot, for the purses he had liberated from those two cutthroats in the lane were crying out to be put to good use. Until then, he would relax a while, enjoy the brandy, let the excitement of his blood abate. And wait.

The two men entered the tavern from separate doorways. The tall one, his garb black as the night outside, came from Drury Lane, the smaller one from the kitchen, his blue coat a little brighter but ill fitting, as if he had taken it from someone whose build was even slighter than his. Cain was immediately aware of their focus upon him, and he eased one hand below the table to cock his unspent pistol. He didn't know what business they had with him, whether friendly or otherwise, but his old mother had always told him that a man who was prepared for any eventuality was a man who would never die of surprise.

They made directly for his table, their arrogance evident with every stride. Cain recognised them as two of Jonathan Wild's newer recruits but didn't know their names. They liked to call themselves thief-catchers, but they were nothing more than thieves themselves, using the threat of arrest and incarceration, even execution, in order to gouge a share of illicit proceeds for their boss. They were very much at home in this tavern and a number of the revellers avoided their gaze, lest eye contact might result in them stopping at their table. But they needn't have worried, for the men's attentions were fixed very firmly on Cain.

'Gabriel Cain,' the man in the blue coat said, his smile friendly and malevolent at the same time. Cain wondered how he did that.

He inclined his head a little. 'Guilty as charged.'

'Oh, Mr Griffin and me knows that, doesn't we?'

Cain glanced at the taller man, whose right hand rested lightly on the sword in his scabbard. He had never met the man in black, but he had heard of him. William Griffin, once a king's guard, until he fell out of favour. Some said because he had taken his duties of protecting the royal person too far when he performed a security check on a young maid that fat George had been eyeing for himself, that check involving a mutually agreed intimate examination of her naked body. Others said that he had remonstrated with some nobleman too enthusiastically when that particular lord had shown a serving girl considerable disrespect. It was possible that both stories were true, for Griffin was known to be something of a swordsman, not only in a brawl but also in the bedroom, and Cain could see why. He was a handsome fellow, and if Cain had been that way inclined he might have been interested in an intimate grapple himself.

That made his companion Sebastian Bartholomew Knapp who, like Cain, was a child of the Rookery streets, and yet had aspirations so above his station that he insisted on using three names. He hadn't been born with the Sebastian, but had added it himself because he believed it sounded sophisticated. Individually, these men were dangerous. Together they were downright diabolical.

Cain was going to enjoy this.

'How can I assist you, gentlemen? You may have noticed that I am taking my leisure at the moment—'

'The Thieftaker General sent us.'

Cain always had to stifle the urge to laugh whenever he heard of Wild's grandiose, but entirely unofficial, title. 'Does Mr Wild have concerns over my wellbeing? As you can see, I am most hale and hearty.'

'For the moment,' said Griffin, his tone almost refined, but humour sparkling in his eyes. Another tale told of him was that he was of noble birth, if on the wrong side of the blanket, and the man who had sired him had paid for an expensive education. Cain, whose own education had been entirely self-administered, thought that lazy.

He affected a worried frown. 'I sense discord between us, gentlemen. Whatever could be the cause?'

'We knows what you has been about,' Knapp said, expecting him to respond, but when none came was taken a touch off guard by having to amplify. 'By that, we means your activities in the street.'

Cain continued to maintain his silence, but a smile began to play.

'I saw you,' Griffin said, completely unperturbed. 'This very night, with that doxy and those two Sawneys.'

'Ah,' Cain said, not surprised at all. 'I have a Scottish friend who, were he here, might take exception to the use of such a term for his countrymen.'

Knapp sneered. 'Well, he ain't here and ain't been for many a year.'

'And even if he were, he would worry me not,' Griffin added.

'We is here about you, Gabriel Cain,' said Knapp. 'Them two gallow birds on the low toby in that alley ain't the first you've robbed.' He tutted. 'A thief robbing other thieves. It's immoral, is what it is.'

Cain's smile broke free. 'You must converse with your superior concerning that, for he's been at the doing of it for many a year.'

Knapp's eyes narrowed and his voice thinned. 'We doesn't like you insulting Mr Wild in such a manner.'

'Really? Well, which manner of insulting him do you prefer? Please let me know, for I am keen to please you.'

Knapp swallowed, forcing his temper to subside. 'He wants his due.'

'Finally, you get to the point. And what makes Mr Wild of the opinion that he is due anything?'

'He says that if you doesn't cough up, then we is to arrest you and march you to the Sessions House at Newgate immediate.'

'Where you will be charged with theft,' Griffin added.

'Thank you for clarifying,' Cain said, 'but I had worked that out for myself.'

'Mr Wild would then use every power at his disposal to ensure that you take the Tyburn Walk,' Knapp said.

'In other words, a judge would be bribed to pronounce the death penalty, correct?'

Neither Knapp nor Griffin confirmed. They didn't deny, either. Cain had no desire to ride the three-legged mare, but he also had no intention of playing Wild's game. He drained his brandy glass and stood up. Knapp stepped back, but Griffin's hand merely tightened on the hilt of his sword.

'Take your ease, Bill,' Cain said. 'I have no intention of instigating any boisterous activity here. I believe we three should take a walk to see Mr Wild, where he and I can discuss the matter over a glass of wine like civilised gentlemen.'

Knapp sneered. 'You isn't no civilised gentleman, Gabriel Cain, despite your airs and graces and your fancy way of speaking. You're a rat from the gutters of the Rookery, like me. Highwayman you may have been, but a highwayman is still a common thief, though he be called gentleman of the road.'

'All true, Bart.' Cain was gratified to see Knapp bristle at his purposeful use of the diminutive form of his given name, rather than his adopted one. 'Nevertheless, I believe Mr Wild and I can reach some form of agreement that would be acceptable to us both without any recourse to the courts. What do you think, Bill?'

'I think if you call me "Bill" once more the courts will be the last of your worries.' Griffin's tone remained reasonable, even amused.

Cain was all innocence. 'Why? Don't you like it? I do apologise. Do you prefer Willie?'

'Griffin will suffice.'

'Griff, then? That has a manly timbre to it, don't you think? The very hearing of it would send lesser men to the nearest hole to hide.' Cain adopted a dramatic pose, both hands out, fingers splayed, one shoulder down, his eyes darting to and fro. 'Watch out, Griff is about! Malefactors beware!'

Griffin's eyes deadened for a moment, then warmth crept back and he laughed. 'I was warned about you, Cain, that you would try to goad me.'

Cain's hand flattened on his chest. 'Me? Goad?'

'It won't work. Had Mr Wild given me orders to harm you, then you would even now be bleeding out on the sawdust. But no such order was given. We either get his garnish or we convey you to the Sessions House, those were the choices. He has no interest in having converse with you – he has more important things to do.'

'Ah yes, betraying all your friends does take up a great deal of time, it's true.'

Knapp decided he'd been left out of the conversation too long. 'Which is it to be, Cain? The coin or the courts? Or do you and Mr Griffin here have at it? There's innocent folk around us and some will get hurt.'

Cain looked around him, knowing well that there were some not so innocent folk around them, but wishing to involve no one else in this private matter. He retrieved his hat from where he had hung it on the back of the chair. 'Then let us to the Sessions House, boys, for I have no money to give you.'

Knapp frowned. 'What of the money Mr Griffin saw you take from those two Sawneys?'

Cain affected a sorrowful expression. 'I regret to say that I lost it at the tables in the private room above.'

Knapp was astounded. 'Already? We were only a few minutes behind you.'

'Long enough, alas, for a poorly considered wager to divest me of all but the necessary with which to purchase that brandy.' He gestured towards the empty glass on the table. 'And even that has gone. And so, we must take our business to the lawyers and hope that justice will look kindly upon my sinful soul. Allow me to lead the way.'

Griffin laid a hand on his chest to prevent his passage. 'Let's have your weaponry first.'

Cain's hope that they would forget to disarm him had been slim, but he was reluctant to divest himself of protection. Nevertheless, his desire not to engage in any form of violence within the confines of the tavern still held, so he reached under his coat to produce his pistols and sword, then set them upon the table, allowing Knapp to pick them up.

Griffin eyed the weapons. 'What of the knife you took from the doxy?'

Cain feigned a sudden remembrance and slipped his hand behind him to pull from a sheath the dagger he'd taken from the woman outside the alley. 'Well remembered.'

Knapp took it from him and, glancing to Griffin, jerked his head. 'Best make sure he's clean.'

Cain stepped back and raised a hand to ward Griffin off as he made to search him. 'I'll not have your hands upon me. I give you my word of honour that I am picked clean of ordnance, and that should be satisfactory.'

Knapp smiled. 'There is no honour among thieves, so Mr Griffin here will pat you down and that'll be the final of it.'

Cain sighed heavily, but held his arms out and allowed Griffin to run his hands down each side of his body, checking his pockets, sliding his fingers under the coat to inspect his waistcoat, his belt, then continued downwards on the outside of his legs, poking into the tops of his boots, then up the inside to his groin.

Cain flinched. 'Have a care, Griffin. Your touch would not make your fortune at even the lowest of buttocking shops.'

Griffin snorted, his humour showing again. 'Unlike you, I have not the inclination to pay for a woman's attention in any brothel, or street corner.' He straightened. 'He's clean.'

'There,' Cain said. 'Now that the proprieties have been observed, shall we go?'

Griffin waved him ahead and Cain made for the door, his head high, ignoring the curious, amused and fascinated eyes that had followed the entire encounter.

If you think this was a show, he thought, *then you should see what I plan for an encore.*

3

After the heat from the fire and the press of bodies within the tavern, the night air was damnably cold. Cain fastened his thick coat to ward off the chill embrace. 'We walk, I assume?'

Knapp smirked. 'Doesn't you like a bit of exercise?'

'I welcome it. The night may be somewhat raw, but a stroll will be most pleasant, especially as my liberty is in peril and this may be the last chance I will have to enjoy such activity.'

He turned south on Drury Lane and walked at a brisk pace ahead of the two men, Knapp having to break into a near run to keep up with the taller men. 'Slow down, Cain,' he demanded.

Cain picked up speed. 'Don't you like a bit of exercise?'

'Bastard is attempting to flee,' Knapp said, his breath already ragged.

'He won't escape,' Griffin said, making Cain smile. He had no intention of escaping. He was only searching for the right place and waiting for the right time.

'Slow down, damn you!' Knapp said.

Cain kept the pace steady until they reached the bottom of Drury Lane, where it narrowed before emerging onto the Strand near to the newly constructed St Mary le Strand Church. It was in the confines of this Little Drury Lane that Cain stopped. It was deserted. This was where he would spring his surprise.

He turned, taking off his hat while holding up his free hand, then slowly reaching into his pocket. 'I make for my kerchief, Griffin,' he said. 'I admit that our rapid perambulation has caused me to perspire more freely than is fitting in a gentleman.'

Griffin smiled. Knapp sneered. 'I says it before and I says it again now, you is no gentleman, Gabriel Cain, no matter how many fancy words you use. Now, push on, and this time not so swift, my legs weary.'

Cain wiped the brim of his hat with his kerchief. 'They are little legs, to be sure, and somewhat spindly in those stockings and shoes.'

Knapp shot a look down, turning his foot inwards so he could see his calf. 'There ain't nothing wrong with that, damn you.'

'As long as you're happy with them. All the same, my advice would be boots. They can obscure even the most disappointing of calves.'

Knapp's temper snapped and he stepped forward, tossing Cain's weapons aside and reaching for his own pistol. 'Damn you, I won't stand for this—'

'With those little spider shanks, I'm surprised you can stand at all.'

Knapp jerked his arm free and advanced on Cain. 'I'll save the hangman the trouble.'

As soon as he was close enough, Cain snatched his own dagger from where it was secreted in the brim of his hat and buried it deep into the little man's upper arm. He cried out, reeled away, dropping his pistol and allowing Cain to reach for it. All was going to plan.

'I wouldn't.'

Cain raised his head, his fingers inches from the fallen weapon, to see Griffin aiming a pistol at him. That was not in the plan.

'Drop the knife,' Griffin said, and Cain complied.

Knapp whined about his arm as he kicked himself along the ground with his heels.

'I knew you had something in mind,' Griffin said, his tone conversational.

'I didn't know you had a pistol,' Cain said. 'I understood you much preferred the blade.'

'I do prefer the blade, but these are dangerous times and a man must move with them.'

'Put a ball in him,' Knapp ordered. 'Bastard deserves it.'

'Mr Wild might not like that,' Cain said, not terribly fond of the odds in this game. They were not in his favour. Fear rippled from his belly to his chest, to his throat.

'Mr Wild will care not a jot,' Griffin said. 'Let's be honest, if we take you to the courts, you are as good as dead. This way it's quicker. More merciful, I'd say.'

As he raised the muzzle slightly higher, Cain held out both hands as if he might catch the ball. He'd seen something behind the man that called for a little more time. A figure approached, slowly and silently. 'Wait, let's discuss this a little longer.'

'There's been too much talking,' Griffin said.

'You forget the coin I took from those two in the alley.'

Even Knapp, who remained prostrate on the ground, inspecting his wound, perked up at this. 'You said you lost it at the gaming table.'

'I hate to make you think the less of me, but I lied. However, I have hidden it in a safe place and it will be yours if you let me go.'

The figure was closer now. Cain couldn't make out who it was, but he was glad to see him.

Griffin was not convinced. 'We're not interested.'

'It's a tidy sum.'

'We're still not interested.'

'Now, hold, Mr Griffin,' Knapp said, struggling to his feet. 'If there's profit in this for…!'

And then he saw the man closing in on them and cried out. Cain threw himself across the narrow divide towards Knapp as Griffin half turned to face the new challenge, but the dark figure had already swung the butt of a pistol and cracked him across the jaw. Knapp screamed as Cain jabbed his clenched fist into his arm, squeezing a further burst of blood from the wound. Griffin had spun away under the force of the blow, but righted himself and was attempting to level his pistol at the newcomer but came face to face with the muzzle of the man's weapon.

'I've no quarrel with you, friend, so I'll thank you to drop that barker.'

Cain smiled broadly when he recognised the Scottish burr, even though he hadn't heard it for six years. 'Jonas,' he said.

'Gabriel,' said Jonas Flynt, shooting a quick glance at him from under the shadow of his wide-brimmed hat. 'Good to see you, even under these circumstances.'

4

They sent Knapp and Griffin on their way, the former still muttering oaths and imprecations but the latter accepting his being bested with professional equanimity, even though his cheek sported a sizeable welt. There was little doubt that should they ever cross paths – or swords – in the future, then he would seek some form of redress. Satisfied that no further action would be taken by either of them, at least not that night, Flynt and Cain repaired to nearby Wych Street and the White Lion Inn, which despite its name was no more pristine than the Black Lion.

A bottle of brandy was purchased with a small portion of the proceeds of the encounter with the two Scotsmen, retrieved from a special pocket sewn into the back of Cain's coat at the nape of his neck, obscured by the thick collar and the pony-tailed sweep of his long blond hair. Swift-Finger Jane was not the only one who was nimble with needle and thread. They settled themselves in the corner, weapons within easy reach. They did this unconsciously, with no ceremony, for that was the way of men such as they.

They fell into each other's company with equal ease, despite having been apart for so long. When Cain last saw his friend, he was on a jetty on a tropical island in the West Indies. He thought it fitting that they should come to this particular establishment, as it was here that he had once reappeared in Flynt's life after some time away. Cain could not say for certain if he had frequented the White Lion himself since that day, there being no lack of hostelries in London offering liquor, women and gaming. To his eye it had not changed. It was still a wide space, crammed with tables and patrons, the light low, the smell of ale and roasting meat and burning logs filling the air, the cheap candles belching tallow fumes, pipes being smoked, women offering themselves for a fumble and a tumble, a fiddler scratching away at some Irish jig in the corner.

Flynt had changed, though. His garb remained black, as did Cain's, save for the white shirts they both wore. It was his face that had transformed. Where once he had been clean-shaven he now sported a beard, flecked with grey, but with a bald streak where a scar ran from below his left eye down to his chin. His hair was also greyer than previous and longer, tied back from his face with a red ribbon.

These changes were evident to anyone, but Cain also saw something others might not. Flynt's eyes bore a far deeper sadness that had not been previously present. Cain was aware of the source.

He raised his glass and spoke their customary toast. 'To good times and bad times.'

Flynt hoisted his own. 'And those in between.'

They drank deeply and were silent for a few moments before Cain laughed. 'By God, I missed you, you Scottish bastard.'

'And I you, you cockney laggard.'

Another custom dispensed with. Cain poured a second measure and swallowed his whole. In truth, he still had not recovered fully from the terror he had experienced when he thought Griffin would do for him. It was not a sensation to which he was overly accustomed, for it was usually he who manned the other side of the pistol. There had been times, most certainly, when he had felt that throat-clutching terror of imminent mortality, but they were few. Had Flynt not appeared when he did, then he without a doubt would at that moment be lying dead in Little Drury Lane.

'Who were those men?' Flynt asked, having not touched his second drink.

Cain banished the remembrance of his weakness. 'Envoys of Jonathan Wild.'

That raised Flynt's eyebrows. 'He's still active? I thought someone would have done for him by now.'

'Still active, still as twisted as ever. When they finally do for him, they will have to screw him into the earth.'

Flynt smiled. It did nothing to relieve the torment in his eyes.

'Do you wish to know of young Jack Sheppard?'

The smile died. 'I know of Jack,' Flynt said, and by his tone it was clear to Cain that he would discuss the young man no further.

'Wild's men,' Flynt said. 'Did their visit have anything to do with those two low toby individuals you hushed earlier this evening?'

Cain, in the process of pouring himself a third drink, paused. 'You were there?'

'I was.'

'I didn't see you.'

'I didn't wish to be seen. You also didn't see that tall fellow who followed you from the alley.'

Cain poured the brandy, set the bottle down and waved his hand dismissively. 'Oh, him I saw. I knew he was on my tail. Griffin may be a master of the blade but his skill as a shadow leaves a lot to be desired.'

Another thin smile from Flynt. 'You put that woman in danger.'

'Swift-Finger Jane puts herself in danger every time she dips a cull and makes off with his purse. I at least gave her enough coin to keep her happy for a week or two.' He sipped his drink this time. 'Anyway, she was never in any peril. I was close by at all times. My own shadowing skills are most accomplished.'

Flynt spun the glass on the tabletop. 'And the Paladin?'

Cain sat back in his chair. 'You were close enough to hear?'

A twitch of an eyebrow was all the response Flynt made.

Cain's smile was rueful. He should have known Flynt was so close. 'The cognomen was lying fallow in your absence. I gave it new life.'

The soubriquet had been bestowed upon Flynt some years before without his knowledge or his consent by Madame de Fontaine, a sometime agent of the French, or anyone else who paid her. It was both an act of mischief on her part and an attempt to undermine his work for the Company of Rogues, unwilling employee though he might have been. By creating the persona of the Paladin, a knight protecting the poor and the downtrodden, she might have brought him out of the half-light in which he had to operate in service of Colonel Nathaniel Charters. The fact that, by happenstance rather than intention, he often had come to the aid of others who could not aid themselves was something that Charters accepted, albeit grudgingly, for there were times when Flynt's more altruistic tendencies merged with the more practical needs of the security of the nation. Cain had cautioned Flynt before on that side of his nature, for it was a tendency he didn't share. Looking at his friend across the table, he saw Flynt was well aware of that simple truth.

'And yet you use it to fill your own pockets.'

Cain laughed. 'Even a knight errant has expenses, Jonas. And I only thieve from those who have thieved.'

He expected Flynt to make some comment, even display some disapproval, for though he had himself been a thief, he often had odd notions of morality quite unbecoming in men of their stripe. It was one of the things that made Cain cleave to him in friendship. Even a black-hearted rogue such as he needed some measure of decency in his life, and his friendship with Flynt had forced him to participate in adventures that were not solely rooted in self-interest. No comment came, however. Flynt was silent for a moment, as if lost in his own memory.

'What of the Company of Rogues?' he asked finally. 'Did you return to the fold?'

'I did,' Cain said. 'Charters pays well, and in truth I had no appetite for taking to the heaths once more. Sitting for hours on horseback in the cold is not fitting for a man of my years or temperament.' He pointed to the brandy. 'A game of chance, a bottle, a warm fire, an even warmer wench, is all I need now.'

'And he still holds that bogus assault and robbery over your head?'

Unbeknownst to either of them, Charters had extorted their labours by threatening them each individually with a charge of robbing the coach of a duchess and her young lover.

'I have assured him that he has no call for such devices,' Cain said. 'With you absent, he had need of a man with my particular talents, as long as he was willing to pay considerably more than the King's Shilling. Anyway, the duchess was stricken by a fever and with her went the only credible witness to the crime, the lover being a young man of somewhat capricious temperament and suspect morals.'

Flynt cocked an eyebrow. 'You make judgement on someone with suspect morals?'

Cain's own morals were virtually non-existent, except when it came to his friendship with Flynt. 'I make no judgement, merely state a fact.'

Flynt fixed him with a steady gaze. 'And what of your other, more lucrative, work?'

Cain knew that to which he referred. Flynt had long suspected that he was the Wraith, a killer of men for hire. Cain had denied it but Flynt persisted.

'I understand that individual, if he ever existed, has retired from the field.' He pushed the conversation away from that subject. 'The good Colonel Charters will be most interested to learn of your return.'

'If he does learn of it.'

'Come, Jonas, you know he has eyes and ears everywhere. God may move in mysterious ways, but I'd wager they are known to Charters in advance. That said, he isn't the man you knew.'

'How so?'

'I'm certain you will see for yourself right soon, but he lost his fortune in the collapse of the South Sea Company. He retained dominion over the Company of Rogues only thanks to Robert Walpole, who ensured he had funds sufficient to weather the storm. Did news of his return to power reach you in the colonies?'

'News did reach us on the other side of the world,' Flynt said, his smile diluting the sarcasm. 'He had been seeking ways to ease back into the King's good graces when I left. I understand the South Sea scandal greatly aided him back into the heart of government.'

'Aye, he had managed to avoid being drawn too deeply into the frenzy of buying and selling of shares that was the business of the South Sea Company, which was a house built upon sand. When it collapsed, many people lost their fortunes, Charters being one. Walpole, though, was immune both financially and politically. Not that he is above the greed that drove the frenzy, of course, but he somehow managed to emerge relatively unscathed, unlike many government ministers and even members of the royal entourage, including the King's mistresses. Walpole became the steady current amid the troubled waters and he regained the King's trust, though old George still doesn't care for him overmuch.'

'So if Charters is in his debt, that means he is now Walpole's man.'

'Well, with Walpole's star back in the ascendant, he would've danced to his tune anyway, but aye, the financial support does make Charters more beholden to him.'

Cain watched Flynt ponder on this development, wondering what was so obviously on his mind, but knowing that when – or if – he wished him to know, he would tell him.

'And were you tempted to invest in the South Sea frenzy?'

'I was invited to participate in the buying of shares in not just the South Sea Company but many of the smaller concerns that sprang up. You wouldn't believe how many curious, addle-brained schemes clamoured for anyone with a penny to their name. I watched people

I'd believed to be level-headed risk their livelihoods on pieces of paper and promises of return that never came. The world was truly mad.'

'But you didn't share that madness?'

'A touch, I confess, but truly it was like giving somebody else your money and letting them game with it. I pulled away from the affair in time. A roll of the dice, a turn of the cards at the tables are of sufficient excitement for me.' Cain paused to refill his glass. 'While word winged its way to the colonies, news also reached us from across the ocean.' He sipped his brandy. 'It was writ in a pamphlet of a pirate captain by name of Flint who was, shall we say, making waves.'

'Yes, I heard of such, too.' Flynt remained casual. 'But his name was of a different spelling to mine. He uses an *i* where I am *y*.'

Cain didn't believe this attempt at diversion. '"The scourge of the Spanish Main" is the phrase the pamphleteer used.'

'Yes, he has made a name for himself.'

'He keeps his own counsel, the text claimed, but commands devotion from his men. And remains little more than an ocean-going will-o'-the-wisp. Something of a phantom.'

Flynt caught the humorous but ironic tone in Cain's voice. 'It sounds like the author was given to some hyperbole.'

'Is this Captain Flint not so elusive, then?'

'They certainly haven't caught him, but then, I understand he targets only other pirates and the occasional Spanish treasure ship when their military has made itself a nuisance to British colonists.'

Cain considered this, then said, 'So he thieves from thieves?'

Flynt's half-smile returned, but his eyes remained untouched. 'Something like that. And he does so under letter of marque from the Governor of Nassau, with the full backing of the colonial governments. At least, so they say.'

'I think I might like this Captain Flint, who uses the *i* instead of the *y*. He seems to be a rogue after my own heart.' Cain made a show of studying his face. 'How came you by the scar?'

A short pause before Flynt said, 'I thrust when I should have parried.'

'You were lucky your head was not split in two.'

'That thought did occur to me.'

'And what of the man who marred your pretty face?'

'He lived to regret his actions.'

'Not for long, I'll wager.'

Flynt didn't amplify further. Instead, he abruptly changed tack. 'Have you heard from Cassie?'

Cain paused. 'She is well.'

'You've seen her?'

'Whenever I am sent north on Charters' business I call upon her.'

'When were you there last?'

'Oh, perhaps four years ago. There was a little bit of trouble from Jacobites and I was despatched to Edinburgh to garner intelligence.'

'She lives with my father and her mother?'

'She lives alone, still in that apartment above the shoemaker's shop.' Cain knew what was foremost in Flynt's mind regarding the woman he had loved since boyhood. 'And even though you will not ask, I will tell you that she has never formed any liaison with another man. And that includes me.' Cain paused again, knowing they had reached the truth behind Flynt's presence. 'She still grieves, Jonas.'

When Flynt dipped his head, it was obvious that he also still mourned the loss of his son, murdered in the Indies before his eyes. Cain waited a moment before asking his next question.

'Why are you home, Jonas?'

Flynt's head rose again, his eyes sheening but no tears falling. 'Daniel Hawke,' he said.

'Did you never find him?'

'Not yet.'

5

New York, three months earlier

The man's agonised screams rent the air but Flynt ignored them, for there was work to be done and he had not the leisure to tarry.

Another scream, accompanied by a cheer, and this time he paid some attention to the chair at the corner of Pearl and Whitehall Streets, a makeshift sign beside it proclaiming its owner as an Operator of the Teeth. He was a strong man, bearing no look of a learned practitioner of any medical art, and was perhaps a farrier by trade. Around him milled sailors from the ships berthed in the docks and soldiers on leave from Fort George, all mingling with townspeople and servants examining the goods on offer from traders who had come from Brooklyn and beyond to hawk their bread and fish and garments and pots and pans. The dentist, his hat askew upon his head, with one knee pinned down the young man who had complained of a toothache that was like to burst his head open. He had already submitted to loosening the offending molar with hammer and chisel, but was now unwilling to submit further to the prospect of relief. Onlookers cheered as his clenched jaws were forced to gape, a set of pliers clamped firmly around the tooth and the dentist proceeded to twist and pull to facilitate extraction. The strain was evident on his face, as was the agony of the patient, who howled and gurgled and who would have pushed the dentist away had not two of his friends immobilised his arms and pinned him to the chair.

Flynt returned his attention to one man who had paused to smile at the discomfort of another human being but who now broke away to saunter among the crowds, stopping to examine goods and wares while exchanging a word or two with the trader. At one point he engaged in conversation a young woman carrying a basket of apples. By her blushes, Flynt could tell he had made some kind of carnal suggestion to her and she walked away quickly. The man smiled again and walked on.

A gargled cry followed by another cheer from the cluster of witnesses to the oral exploration caused Flynt to glance back. The pliers were being held aloft, a bloody tooth clenched within their jaws, and the dentist was accepting the congratulations from all sides as though he were an actor taking his bows. The erstwhile patient was bent over the arm of the chair, thin ribbons of blood streaming onto the street. Flynt was grateful that his own teeth gave him little discomfort and resumed his study of the man he had come here to see.

It was a warm August day, and the breeze from the East River failed to cool the air, yet the man displayed no sign of wilting in the heat. He was tall and gangly and he dressed well, his brocade doublet lined with silk, matching the material in his pristine white hose, setting off the red velvet of his cloak. His head was adorned by a powdered wig that draped down the back of his mantle, his gold-braided cocked hat tucked under one arm. He carried a Malacca cane with an ivory handle, which he tapped on the ground as he walked. He was a gentleman and displayed all the arrogance of the wealthy. Here was a man who was comfortable with himself and aware that most of those around him were poorer than he, and therefore that made him better than they. His treatment of the young apple seller was indicative of his belief that he was above any form of social niceties.

Flynt intended to prick that pomposity.

The man entered the doorway to one of the red-brick houses erected when the island of Manhattan was a Dutch colony. Flynt gave him a few minutes, for he knew why he was visiting that particular house and that particular room, because previous inquiries had informed him of his activities. He needed this gentleman at his most vulnerable and so he gave him time.

He crooked a finger to a tall young man lingering beside a stall of cooked meats.

'What's the plan, Cap'n?' the young man asked once he had joined him.

'You and Israel stand by that doorway.'

John Silver motioned towards a smaller, sallow-faced youth who squatted on the ground nearby, twirling a knife in his hand. Israel Hands was too fond of that blade and many times Flynt had urged Silver, the only individual to whom the lad paid any heed, to keep him in check. Israel bore no affection for Flynt. The knowledge that Flynt had been present when his father was killed didn't warm the boy to him. Flynt wasn't responsible for the man's death, but he knew the boy suspected him of it. He would have had the young man banished from his crew long since had it not been for Silver, who constantly defended him.

'Ain't you wishing us to accompany you up them stairs?' Silver asked.

'I'll do this alone, John, thank you.'

Israel had hauled himself to his feet but still held the knife. 'Is we heading back to the *Walrus* now?'

The boy was uncomfortable in the press of humanity.

'Not yet. Sheathe that blade,' Flynt ordered. 'Do not draw attention to us.'

His expression sullen, Israel slid the knife under his shirt out of sight.

'You might be needing us, Cap'n,' Silver said. 'You doesn't have no notion of what you might meet.'

Israel sniggered. 'Cap'n's got a doxy awaiting up there, I'm thinking, Long John. He don't need no assistance from us.'

Flynt had first met John Silver when he crossed the Atlantic. He was mate to the ship's cook and was known to him only as Barbecue. It was only later he discovered his given name was John Silver, just before he and Israel had left Nassau in the Bahamas to go pirating with Captain England. They had seen action around Madagascar before they returned to the Caribbean, where Flynt was acting for the colonial governors to help stamp out what remained of the Flying Gang, the confederation of pirates that had once ruled the island of New Providence. The two joined his crew. John had grown into a tall, strapping young man, so had been dubbed Long John.

'Stow it, Israel,' Silver said. 'You know the cap'n is here on business, not personal.'

He was the only person who was allowed to speak to Israel Hands in such a manner. Anyone else would have been met with a black look and perhaps the reappearance of the knife.

'Remain by the door,' Flynt said. 'Dissuade anyone from entering.'

'How does we do that?'

Flynt was already crossing to the doorway. 'Persuasion,' he said, his next words aimed at Israel. 'But gently.'

Once beyond the doorway, Flynt ignored the doors leading to left and right and headed straight to a wooden stairway, knowing where he was going. They had followed this man for a week and this was the only visit he made from his fashionable home at the Foot of Wall Street without his two bodyguards, because his activities here were not something he would wish his wife to know. Her family stretched back to when Dutch traders bought Manhattan from the Lenape tribe for a handful of trinkets and were so well established that they remained when the British took over Manhattan. She was wealthy enough to buy the island back from the Crown. She was unaware of his activities here but others were, and Flynt had spoken to them.

The door he sought was to the right of the top of the stairs and he eased his pistols, Tact and Diplomacy, from his broad belt, then listened at the door. He could hear panting and the creak of a bed. He could simply have knocked, but he needed to make an entrance and it had to be dramatic. He took a step back and slammed one foot just under the handle. The door crashed open and he stepped over the threshold, both pistols held high.

The man threw himself from where he had been rutting on top of a red-haired woman, who attempted to hide her ample proportions behind a thin sheet. The man sprawled on the floor, the sight of Flynt causing his mouth to open and close like a landed fish. He realised he was naked and covered his genitals with both hands. One would have been sufficient and even then would have had room to spare.

'Don't get up,' Flynt said, one pistol aimed straight at the prostrate man, whose shock finally gave way to bluster.

'This is an outrage, sir! How dare you burst in here!'

Flynt kicked the door closed again with one heel. 'Shut up and listen.' The woman edged across the bed, the sheet barely concealing her charms. She was either careless with how she held it, or she was proud of her shape. 'Madam, please be so good as to stay where you are. My business is with your gentleman caller, and once transacted I will leave.'

She gave him a nervous smile, but the obvious sincerity of his tone allowed her to relax. She sat back against the headboard and watched.

The man struggled to rise while continuing to do his best to cover his modesty. 'Good God, sir, this is an outrage—'

'Aye, so you said. And I said to stay down.'

The man was now kneeling, but he stilled. 'Do you know with whom you trifle, sir?'

'I do, but in case you've forgotten your name, you are Sylvester Lewis, merchant, banker, and, eh —' Flynt waved one pistol in the general direction of the woman on the bed — 'adulterer.'

That seemed to infuriate Lewis. 'I am no adulterer!'

'I do believe your wife might take a different view.'

'Tupping a doxy is no adultery,' Lewis insisted.

Flynt smiled. 'I have some friends outside. Shall I send one to fetch your good lady and we can see what she makes of this? It won't take a moment.'

Lewis swallowed, the bluster and rage leaving him. 'Who are you, sir, that you presume to interrupt my leisure?'

'Who I am is immaterial.'

'Then if this be robbery, my purse is there among my clothes. Take it and begone.'

'I'm not interested in your money, Lewis.'

A puzzled frown creased Lewis's forehead. 'Then what?'

'Daniel Hawke. I would know of his whereabouts.'

'I know of no such person.'

Flynt sighed, took two swift steps and swung Tact against the man's cheek, sending him sprawling onto the floor again. The woman gasped and Flynt gave her an apologetic shrug. She returned it as if she had merely been surprised at the suddenness of the act, not shocked at its vehemence. She settled back again, one arm crooked and propping up her head, the sheet sliding down further.

Flynt didn't have time to admire the view. He returned his attention to Lewis, who was face down on the boards, weeping.

'Let's try again, shall we?' Flynt said. 'Where's Daniel Hawke?'

'I know no Daniel Hawke.' The man's voice was muffled against the floor.

Flynt stuck Tact back into his belt, then stooped, grabbed Lewis's hair and jerked his head back. Lewis cried out, but it was cut short when Diplomacy's muzzle was rammed none too gently into the base of his skull.

'I'm not in the mood for nonsense, Lewis. I know you and Daniel Hawke are confederates. I know you've bought goods from his family, from his father and then from him. I know he was in New York recently. I wish to know where he went from here.'

'I know not!'

'That,' Flynt said, cocking the pistol, 'is unfortunate.'

'London!' Lewis blurted. 'He sailed for London.'

Flynt felt like cursing. 'When?'

'Just two days ago.'

Flynt knew the truth when he heard it. He released his grip suddenly, allowing Lewis's face to slam into the floor. He'd been chasing Hawke across the Thirteen Colonies and the islands of the Indies for six years. Each time he'd come close, the man slipped through his grasp. Now he'd done it again.

'What business does he have there?'

'He doesn't inform me of his—'

Flynt placed his foot on the back of the man's head and applied some gentle pressure, pushing his face into the boards.

'The Fellowship!' Lewis's voice was muffled and nasal. Flynt removed his foot, and the man turned his head to rest his cheek on the floor. 'He sees the Fellowship.'

'Lord Moncrieff?'

Lewis rolled a little, but it was more in surprise than a bid to escape. 'How did...?'

'Never mind how I know of him. What does Hawke wish to see him about?'

This provoked a rueful smile. 'Can't you guess? You have been harrying him for so long and he wishes you halted.'

That was to be expected. 'It will do him no good,' Flynt said. 'Where does he lodge when in London?'

'We're business acquaintances, not bosom friends. I don't have intimate knowledge of his movements while abroad.'

Flynt raised his foot again.

'There's a lady he pays attention to,' Lewis said hurriedly. 'A widow woman, whose lawyer husband left her in fine financial condition.'

'Name and address?'

For a brief moment it was clear that Lewis considered denying further knowledge, but a glance at Flynt's boot convinced him that way lay more pain. 'Inglis, Melanie Inglis. All I know is that she lives in Lincoln's Inn Fields.'

Sensing the truth of it, Flynt committed the name and location to memory.

Lewis was sobbing again. 'You'll be killing me now, I expect.'

Flynt had already returned his other pistol to his belt. 'You've told me what I need to know. I've no cause to kill you.'

'But it's what you do, isn't it? Kill?'

Flynt's gaze flicked to the woman; concern clouded her eyes once more. 'If I have reason.'

'You'll be Jonas Flynt,' Lewis said through the tears.

Flynt didn't reply.

'Dan told me about you. How you blame him for the death of your son.' Lewis twisted round to lie on his back, his weeping subsiding. He touched the blood seeping from where Flynt's pistol had broken the flesh. 'You've left a trail of death in your search for him.'

'Only when I had reason.'

Lewis sensed his life was saved and his arrogance returned. 'Pirates. Merchants. Criminals. You've had them executed or you've killed them yourself.'

Flynt had been ruthless in his pursuit. Thanks to his father, Toby, Daniel Hawke had a vast network of accomplices across the eastern seaboard. People the family had dealt with, worked with, traded with, made rich while enriching themselves. There had been some Flynt questioned who had not been as malleable as Lewis. It had not ended well for them. As for the pirates, most of them were brought to justice under the authorisation bestowed upon him by Woodes Rogers, when he was Governor of New Providence Island, and co-signed by the Governors of Virginia, Jamaica, and New York. Those deaths were at least legal. Others, not so much.

Lewis managed a sly smile. 'You'll never get to him – you must know that.'

'I'll get him.'

'He is protected, don't you understand? By men who you can't hope to vanquish. You may be the dreaded pirate hunter, but you are still nothing but a cheap thief. You—'

Flynt lashed out with the sole of his boot and silenced him.

6

Covent Garden never truly slept. Yes, at the end of the day, when the patrons were gone, the merchants and porters of the market on the square packed up their stalls, trundled their barrows and drove off in carts, but the piazza and surrounding streets still buzzed with another kind of commerce, when the fruit market became a flesh market. Taverns offered liquor and warmth and companionship of either sex, women in the streets and alleyways promised a momentary salve to the pressures of life, while for those who preferred their coitus to be conducted in more comfortable surroundings than a threepenny upright against a wall or column, there were brothels of standards high and low.

In King Street on the north-west corner of the piazza, Mother Grady's elegant townhouse was of a higher class than many. Flynt stood among Mr Inigo Jones' colonnades staring across the square towards the familiar door, at the lights in the windows, ignoring the looks and offers of a sexual adventure from the bobtails and bunters who wandered by. He couldn't bring himself to walk across the cobbles and knock upon that door. Some years before he had also been rooted on that very same spot, wishing to make the crossing but unable to do so.

The front door opened and he tensed, wondering if it would be she, but it was only a cull taking his leave. Flynt was gratified to see Jerome holding the door open and bidding him goodnight. He was glad he remained as the house bully, watching over the women who worked there. He was a big fellow, kindly and capable. Jerome watched the gentleman descend the steps to the street and walk off in the direction of Bedford Street, then scanned the piazza. For a brief moment, he hesitated, as if he had seen something, but then closed the door.

Flynt heard a footfall behind him but didn't turn. He knew it was Cain, who had followed him after they parted in the White Lion.

'Have you seen her, Gabriel?'

'A few times.'

'Is she well?'

'She is.'

Flynt fell silent, staring at the window on the first floor. Belle St Clair was one of the many guilts he carried.

Cain moved to his side and followed his gaze. 'She's not there, Jonas. She gave up the house, oh, maybe a year or two following Mary Grady's death.'

Before he left for the Indies, Mother Grady had confessed to Flynt that she had only months to live. Belle St Clair had already been made a partner in the house, already freed of the slavery into which she had been born.

'She still owns it,' Cain said, 'still has a large share in its revenues, which remain considerable, but she no longer lives there.'

In his mind, Flynt saw her again, standing in that very room on which his eyes were fixed. It was the last time they had been together and her expression was sorrowful.

Go, Jonas. You will return, or you will not. I will be here, or I will not. Go now. Do what you have to in order to protect Cassie and her son.

Your son.

A fine job he had made of that.

'Where is she?'

'In high keeping,' Cain said. 'Lord Southern pays the bills, though Belle remains wealthy enough in her own right.'

'You know him?'

'We've shared a gaming table. Prior to him taking up with Belle, we might even have shared the same wenches.'

'Is Belle happy with him?'

'She laughs, she lives.'

'He is good to her?'

Cain shrugged. 'He's a nobleman. Takes what he wants, when he wants it. But for all that, he seems decent enough, though with a temper and a tendency to be petulant, which seems to come with privilege.'

'Not decent enough to marry her.'

'I don't think you – nor I, for that matter – are the ones to make judgement on that score.'

Those words stung. Flynt abruptly turned and walked back in the direction of Henrietta Street. Cain followed. 'Where will you go now?'

'To see Colonel Charters,' said Flynt, his step strong and steady, his mind set as he turned his back on the house on the corner and the memories it held. 'If you are correct, then my arrival will be expected.'

'And if I'm wrong?'

'Then it will be a happy surprise for him,' Flynt said, irony coating his words.

7

As Cain had predicted, Nathaniel Charters was not surprised to see him.

When Jacob Simmons, his old army valet, ushered them into his study, the colonel didn't move from behind his desk. On opening the front door, Jacob had also shown no astonishment at seeing Flynt for the first time in over six years, but then the man was not one to be in any way taken aback by events. Like Flynt, he had been plucked from the ranks by Charters while on active service in Flanders. Jacob had displayed an open contempt for the stupidity of what society called 'his betters' and was being whipped for defying the orders of a brutal serjeant. Charters interceded, took him on as his valet and servant, and earned his loyalty. He was now servant, companion, protector and, on occasion, investigator, for the man never lost touch with old comrades or his links with the streets in which he was born. He wasn't officially part of the Company of Rogues, which was made up of crooks, vagabonds, gamblers, tavern keepers, prostitutes and, yes, even some upstanding citizens, if writers could be termed such, but Charters did occasionally utilise his services for duties other than valeting.

Jacob gave Flynt the minutest of nods, another to Cain, and then led them across the foyer of the townhouse to the study, where Charters waited. He took up a position beside the door, standing against the wall, his arms folded. The colonel stared at them for a moment, giving Flynt the opportunity to study the man who had at one time been both his employer and oppressor. He had aged somewhat. There were circles below his eyes that he had only seen once before, when he had been plagued by nightmares concerning a killer he had allowed to slip through his fingers. He seemed thinner, though Charters was never plump, but his cheeks were hollow. No, not thinner, Flynt thought, faded. His flesh was grey, his eyes dull. His hair, considerably greyer than before, hung loose to splay around the shoulders of his yellow damask dressing gown, a *banyan* Flynt believed it was called. One of the sleeves dangled loosely at his side, wanting of the arm that Charters had left behind at the Battle of Malplaquet. Flynt, in the process of fleeing the carnage, had managed to save the rest of him that day and had cause over the years to both regret and rejoice that particular display of humanity.

'Well,' the colonel said, his lips pressed thin, 'the prodigal returns.'

Flynt didn't wait to be instructed to sit. He dropped into a vacant chair opposite the desk. Charters noted the move but made no comment, though his jaw clamped so much that Flynt feared for the integrity of the man's teeth. Cain chose to remain standing, a display of deference Flynt never thought possible.

'Your return is overdue, by my reckoning, by at least five years, Serjeant,' Charters said.

'I had business in the colonies.'

'And is that business now complete?'

'Not yet.'

Charters grunted. 'It is fortunate that your business intersected with that of the Crown, elsewise I would have sent someone to fetch you back. Mr Cain here, for instance, for he is perhaps the one person in the world who might have succeeded.'

Cain smiled his best smile. 'If only you had, Colonel, for there was a young lady in Nassau with whom I would have enjoyed becoming acquainted again. Remind me to inquire as to the health of Mistress Anne Bonny, Jonas.'

Of course, Charters knew what Flynt had been doing all these years. Captain Woodes Rogers, then Governor of New Providence Island, had first given Flynt the commission to hunt down pirates – a commission he accepted after refusing three times, not only because he realised such official recognition would better serve him well in his more personal business. Rogers would have reported back, though perhaps not directly to Charters, for the Company of Rogues was authorised only to operate within the shores of Great Britain and Ireland. Flynt's voyage to the Indies was a personal matter but one which coincided with a need to gather intelligence on the pirates of Nassau, and so a rule was stretched. Rogers would most certainly have sent regular despatches to Whitehall, may even have surreptitiously ensured a copy reached Charters. When the governor was recalled after three years, to be replaced by a workmanlike administrator without the style or the ruthless nature of his predecessor, those under-the-table reports would have dried up, but one of Charters' many contacts in government would have given him sight.

A flick of the finger to Jacob brought the colonel a crystal goblet of wine. He made no offer to Flynt or Cain. 'So, what unfinished business brings you back to my domain, Serjeant?'

'Daniel Hawke.'

Charters sipped his wine while sitting back in his chair. Hawke would also have been mentioned in the despatches from the Caribbean.

'You were singularly unsuccessful in tracking him down,' he said.

'I nearly had him on a number of occasions.'

Hawke had led a charmed life these six years. There had been at least three encounters when Flynt thought his quest was at an end. Once in a lodging house in Charleston, where Hawke ducked behind a friend just as Flynt fired and made his escape through a window; once in Boston, where he'd left a tavern mere minutes ahead of Flynt's arrival, leaving him watching the carriage conveying Hawke being driven at the gallop down the street; the third on a Jamaican quayside, when interference from a nosy captain of the town's garrison gave Hawke the opportunity to flee.

'Nearly is not mission accomplished, is it?' Charters said. 'Though I understand you did enjoy endeavours that were more fruitful. I have read most avidly of the depredations of Captain John Flint.'

Flynt had no intention of pursuing that subject. 'The imaginings of a Grub Street scrivener. My endeavours, as you'll know, were entirely legal.'

'Perhaps not entirely legal, Serjeant... or should that be Captain now? To be sure, booty liberated from those pirates you brought to heel was returned to the colonial governments for dispersal to rightful owners, but mayhap not all, eh? It be entirely possible that you kept a proportion of it for yourself and your crew, which I understand is made up of cutthroats and sea rogues who would be best employed at the end of a rope, rather than in service of colonial governments.'

Flynt refused to engage in further debate over the rights and wrongs of his actions, nor less the merits of his crew, or lack thereof.

Charters was not to be put off. The glint Flynt recognised from many such times when the man had goaded him returned to his eye. 'Where are they now, by the way? Are they off on their depredations without their captain? That won't end well.'

The *Walrus* was docked in Port Glasgow, the men under the control of his quartermaster, William Bones – Billy Bones, to the men – who was as solid a man and sailor as Flynt could find. Flynt had taken a coach and bounced on uneven roads and uncomfortable seating for over two weeks to reach London. He'd had no wish to place his ship in a dock where Charters might have some sway, though given the city docklands were under the control of an old acquaintance of Flynt's who guarded his domain jealously, that seemed unlikely.

'Daniel Hawke,' Flynt said again, prompting a sigh from Charters.

'You are most single-minded when it comes to this individual, Flynt.'

'I have reason.'

'So I understand. But what makes you believe he is here?'

'He's here.'

Charters' expression told him that this was something he already knew. 'And what do you propose to do?'

'Kill him.'

'Murder him, you mean. I do believe the courts take a dim view of such acts.'

'An eye for an eye, Colonel.'

'For your son.'

'Aye.'

'You have taken a number of eyes in that regard already, I believe.'

'That was work for the Crown. None of those men were responsible for killing Jonas.'

'Hawke killed him?'

'He created the circumstance that led to it.'

'No, Serjeant, you created that by allowing the lad to accompany you.'

Guilt stabbed at Flynt's chest. It was a familiar pain and he had long since grown used to it.

Charters finished his drink, waved to Jacob to have it refilled. They waited until this was done. Again, Charters offered neither Flynt nor Cain a glass.

A Thief's Revenge

'This is a fine Barolo, from the Piedmont region of north-west Italy. It's a robust little wine, not terribly popular here and therefore harder to come by, but I have a friend who owns a vineyard there and he sends me a bottle or two every now and then. He taught me a fine Italian word. *Vendetta* – have you heard of this word?'

Flynt didn't reply.

Charters continued. 'It's born from the Latin *vindicta*, from which our mother tongue derives the words "vindictive" and "revenge". Was it not Mr Milton who said, "He that studieth revenge keepeth his own wounds green, which otherwise would heal and do well"?'

'It was Francis Bacon. And neither he nor Milton had a son murdered before their eyes.'

Charters' lips tightened on being corrected on his literary knowledge. 'Nevertheless, he who seeks revenge at all costs must first sacrifice himself. You have lost all, Flynt, have you not? The woman you love. Your profession. Your country. Your integrity. All in pursuit of this one man. Is it not time to let it rest?'

'I'll rest when he's dead.'

Charters' gaze fixed on him for a moment, then switched to Cain. 'And you assist him in this matter?'

'I loved the boy, too.'

'And if I order you to remain detached from this vendetta?'

'I loved the boy, too,' Cain repeated.

Charters shook his head. 'It is well seen that you are boon companions, for you are both cut from the same block. Stubborn, wilful, unable to see what is best for you.'

'Daniel Hawke,' Flynt said again.

'What makes you think I can assist you?'

'You know where he is.'

'How would I know of his whereabouts?'

'You know everything.'

'Ha! Would that were true.'

Flynt caught a mournful tinge that was entirely genuine. 'I believe he's being shielded by the Fellowship.'

Charters' gaze shifted. Just slightly, but enough to make Flynt suspicious.

'I cannot help you there,' Charters said, a hint of evasion creeping into those few words.

'Why not?'

'The Fellowship is no longer my concern.'

'Why not?'

'I have been instructed to let it be.'

'On whose order would you…?' Flynt began, then made the leap. 'Walpole, correct?'

'Let's say that my belief that the threat posed to the security of this nation by the Fellowship, which, like this Captain John Flint and –' Charters faced Cain briefly – 'an individual known as "the Wraith", may not in fact exist, could have been unfounded.'

'You know that's not the case.'

'If it does exist, then it is little more than a loose confederation of businessmen resolved to increase trade and profits, and if that is the case, then it can only contribute to the wellbeing of the country and is therefore no concern of mine, and by extension my organisation.'

'You know they pose a threat. It's their intention to control governments, to carve the world up to benefit themselves and not any monarch or state, let alone ordinary people.'

'I know nothing of the sort.'

'It was you who told me this in the first place.'

'I was in error. At any rate, there are more serious, more deadly, dangers facing England. *They* are my concern.'

Flynt was shocked to hear Charters talk this way. He had long expressed deep misgivings about the influence the Fellowship had on affairs of state and had, in fact, first set him upon their trail many years before. His position, by its very nature as part of the government, meant he often had to take a pragmatic, even political, approach to some matters but to perform such a *volte-face* and to cleave to this new position with such tenacity was not like him.

'You've sold yourself, Colonel,' Flynt said, bluntly.

'Have a care, Serjeant, with such accusations.'

'You lost everything in the South Sea frenzy. Walpole bailed you out, protected you, saved your position.'

'Yes, the Chancellor of the Exchequer was kind enough to assist me in my hour of need, but—'

'You've been compromised.'

Charters lost patience. 'Damn you, Flynt, you have the nerve to come here, to my home, both of you nothing but cheap thieves and murderers, and accuse me—'

'Cheap thieves we may be, but we are at least self-aware. As for murderers… Well, we have blood on our hands, it's true, but how much of it was spilled in service of you, the Company of Rogues and, by extension, the King and his ministers?'

Charters sneered. 'Please, spare me the sanctimony. Cain is perhaps the most honest between you, for at least he does what he does for coin. You did the same, but you convinced yourself that you were also doing good.'

'Not always.'

'Then you did it out of self-preservation, to save your neck from the noose that I could so very easily have had placed around it.'

'On a bogus charge.'

'Bogus or not, it would have held.'

'But no longer.'

Charters laughed. 'Do you think it would trouble me to arrange another that would be easily proved to the courts' satisfaction?' He flicked a finger towards Cain. 'My God, this one has been killing thieves a-plenty in your absence and raiding their purses, all in the name of Madame de Fontaine's fictional Paladin. Oh yes, I know all about your nocturnal activities, Cain. *All* of your nocturnal activities. But I overlook them because, like Flynt, you are effective in your work for me. But let me warn you –' his finger darted from one to another – 'both of you… If you pursue this matter then I cannot assist you, or protect you. I counsel most vehemently against this course of action. Give it up, Flynt, in the name of God. You have lost everything you hold dear. Give it up before you lose what little is left of you.'

Flynt rose. 'God may or may not exist, but the Fellowship most definitely does and Hawke is part of it. You know it, I know it, Gabriel knows and even Jacob knows it. And now I do wonder if Walpole himself is part of it – James Moncrieff still has his ear, I take it?'

Charters' stiff expression told him he was correct.

'Walpole may have muzzled you, Colonel, but he has no dominion over me. I will have Hawke dead at my feet and I urge you not to get in my way. I saved your life once. I won't do it again.'

Charters glared over his desk. 'You threaten me? You jumped-up Scottish bastard, you threaten me?'

Flynt exhaled in what may have been a laugh as he turned to the door. 'I don't make threats. I make promises.'

Unseen by Flynt, Charters must have given Jacob a signal, for he pushed himself upright and opened the door, his face impassive. If he had taken offence at how Flynt had spoken to his employer, he displayed nothing of it. Flynt didn't look back at Charters as he left the room, Cain at his heels.

In the foyer, Jacob gave a servant a seemingly idle glance as she carried a basket of logs up the stairway, presumably to Charters' bedchamber. He led them to the door, opened it and stepped aside to let them pass. Flynt paused before exiting to the street.

'What happened to him, Jacob?'

'Nothing happened to him, Mr Flynt,' Jacob said in his strong London accent. 'He's the same man he ever was.'

Flynt glanced over his shoulder to the study door. 'You know, I do wonder if you're right about that.'

As Flynt and Cain stepped over the threshold, Jacob said, 'Have a care, gents. Them streets is a dangerous place.'

As they walked away, Cain asked, 'Why did he say that? He knows we are aware of how dangerous these streets are.'

'I think, Gabriel,' Flynt said, his face taut, 'that Colonel Charters has just made a promise of his own.'

8

Flynt declared that he was for his bed, so Cain bade him goodnight after they made arrangements to convene the following day and set off for whatever lady's bed he had arranged to share. Their appointment was for late afternoon, so Flynt assumed his friend expected to be thoroughly debauched and unable to function prior to that.

He walked through the city to Charing Cross. He enjoyed the solitude, even the damp night air. He had known tropical storms and humidity during his time abroad, but for some reason he welcomed the clammy grip of the London autumn. Despite his years away, it was familiar, though perhaps not home, as Flynt was never sure where that might be for him. The truth was, he felt like an outsider wherever he was, even Edinburgh, where he had been born.

At the Golden Cross Inn, Mrs Wilkes greeted him warmly. She had kept his old room for him all these years, the bed cleaned and refreshed even though nobody slept in it. Before he'd left the Indies he had given her a pouch of gold and silver coin, but that would have long run out, and yet she had continued to keep the room free for his return. She was a good woman and he was blessed to have her in his life, even though, prior to his departure from these shores, he had often considered moving on. He had reached the unpleasant truth that too many people had learned where he laid his head, and that knowledge might have put Mrs Wilkes and her husband in jeopardy. His absence would have negated that threat considerably, so he was comfortable lodging there for the duration of his return to London.

She had been landlady of the coaching inn for many years and was well versed in the art of discretion, so she didn't inquire as to where he had been all this time, though she did comment on his tanned skin and beard.

'Suits you, Mr Flynt,' she said.

'Covers more of my face, Mrs Wilkes,' he said.

'Sometimes a beard does that, for sure and certain, but sometimes it just makes the face more complete, if you gathers what I mean.'

Mrs Wilkes was canny enough to sense that he was exhausted, so she led him up to his room, giving him a key. 'We put a new lock on for you, just to be safe.'

He peered through the door she had opened. She had been true to her word. It was as he had left it.

Mrs Wilkes indicated a letter propped up against the washbowl on the sideboard. 'That came for you a day or two ago,' she said. 'Right glad I was to see it, for it told me you was coming home at last.'

'Thank you, Mrs Wilkes.'

'You'll always have a home here, Mr Flynt,' she said. 'You don't never have any cause to worry on that score.'

He felt something burn at his eyes and lodge in his throat. It was as if she had somehow divined his earlier thoughts and sought to assure him that he was no outsider. Now sensing his discomfort, she hurriedly turned away, then stopped, hesitated for a moment before returning to him and giving him a tight embrace.

'You is a good man, Jonas Flynt,' she whispered. 'There's those that say you isn't, but me and Mr Wilkes, we knows the truth. And there are others what knows it, too. You isn't alone. Remember that.'

And then she was gone, leaving him alone in the room, knowing there were many reasons why she was wrong about him. He had good in him, he knew that, but he was not a good man.

He took off his coat, hat and boots, set his weapons close to hand, then locked the door and read the contents of the letter before stretching out fully clothed on the bed. He closed his eyes but knew sleep would be fitful. Too many faces swam from the murk of his mind. The men he had killed, the women he had failed. Too many faces, too many regrets.

But he did sleep, though he didn't know it. For him it was merely an extension of wakefulness, for he slipped so easily from this room in damp London to another in the tropical warmth of the Caribbean.

More faces.

His father, Gideon. His stepmother, Mercy. Cassie. All bound in chairs.

Young Jonas.

And another. A dark visage with bright eyes. A raised pistol in his hand.

Flynt, unbound, knowing what was going to happen, willing his muscles to take life, finally moving forward, desperate to reach them, but he was sluggish, as if battling against an invisible hand, and the voice of the dark man was slow, each word stretched to an impossible degree as the pistol swivelled towards young Jonas, so slowly, so carefully, and Flynt should have had time to reach it but he couldn't get past the unseeable grip and the pistol was aimed at the back of his son's head and Flynt cried out, not a word, just a plea, a warning, the sound of it also elongated...

...and then the report of the pistol, loud, clear, sharp, echoing on and on and on...

...and young Jonas, his head jolting forward, and back, and to the side, his body restrained by the bonds strapping him to a chair, the chair tipping a little, settling...

...and the dark-haired, dark-bearded man laughing...

...and the crack of the pistol still reverberating in the darkness, merging with the laughter and Cassie's scream and Jonas' own guttural roar, on and on and on and on...

9

The following morning, far from rested but used to that and knowing he would still function, Flynt rose early and left the inn without the eagle eye of Mrs Wilkes falling upon him and chiding him for planning to embark without breakfast. Sunrise was little more than a promise that might never be fulfilled, for the sky was iron grey and glowering but it was dry for the moment.

He found a hackney that would convey him eastwards, to Wapping. The man he knew only as 'the Admiral' expected him, for this meeting had been prearranged by letter, the first sent by Flynt before the *Walrus* left New York, another waiting for him on arrival in Port Glasgow from where a third was sent, the mail carriers riding faster than the lumbering coach. The fourth was the one which Mrs Wilkes had placed in his room, confirming arrangements. Despite the exchange of correspondence, Flynt was uncertain what kind of reception he would receive.

The hackney halted near to the tavern at the sign of the Ship and Anchor, close to Execution Dock. In a chamber above the tavern, accessed through a door down a narrow side alleyway and then up a flight of steps, the Admiral was waiting for him. Flynt suspected this would not be an easy reunion, for his actions while away from London would not have sat well with the man. He bade the hackney to wait, but paid him for the round trip in advance. The driver might leave him, but he seemed an honest man and Flynt was reasonably certain he would do as he was asked.

Adjusting his weapons, though he was well aware that they would be of little use to him, Flynt felt his nerves vibrate. His life since leaving Edinburgh had been one of constant jeopardy, alleyways such as this, stairways to be climbed, doors to be opened – lately, ships to be boarded – but he never lost this feeling of dread beforehand. He had scars from when he had been less than fully successful but he still stood. That would not last. He had known that for a long time. Flynt was a gambler and he knew that luck was not a constant. No matter how careful, no matter how capable, one day he would walk down the wrong alley, climb the wrong staircase or open the wrong door. He hoped that today was not that day. He had a mission to fulfil. A promise to keep.

As usual, the Admiral's man Dan Pickett met him at the top of the stairs, where a lamp burned above his head. In many ways he reminded Flynt of Jacob. They were both solid, dependable and loyal. Gabriel Cain was loyal, had proved himself to be dependable, but Flynt knew well he was of a flighty disposition and was perhaps liable to grow bored and move on when the spirit took him. Flynt couldn't condemn him for that. He had done similar in the past, leaving behind people who cared for him.

He handed over his weapons, as was the custom. Under the circumstances he would have preferred not to, but was well aware that access would not be granted as long as Pickett thought him armed.

Flynt made an attempt at courtesy. 'How have you been?'

'I'm well.'

That was all he could expect from him. Pickett had elevated taciturnity to new levels. Before he opened the door, he leaned forward and said, quietly, 'The Admiral isn't alone.'

Flynt nodded his understanding.

The room he was waved into was dim, candles and a roaring fire scaring off the darkness. It was also slightly off kilter, something Flynt had forgotten. It was as if a great hand had pressed against one wall and tipped it a little. Flynt had never entered the tavern below, but he wondered if it was similar. A man who had imbibed a little too heartily in any other tavern might see the world somewhat askew, so perhaps that was the intention behind the angle of floor and wall, to make patrons believe the world around them was as it was, that they would remain sober and thus purvey more liquor.

Feeling as if one leg was a touch shorter than the other, the ancient boards creaking with each step, Flynt walked towards the large desk before a window that looked out upon the grey Thames, the south bank blurred by mist. The Admiral was a large man, his face hidden behind a leather mask with a slit for a mouth and one for the only eye through which the man could see. He had once confided that he had been the victim of a faulty cannon while in battle at sea and had been left badly burned, his lungs scarred by breathing in the heat of the explosion. At that he had been lucky, for the gun crew all perished, including a young powder monkey whose body had shielded his from the worst of the blast. Even now, his desk was positioned as far from the fireplace as possible without losing its warmth.

To his right, at a smaller desk, sat another man, head bent as he scribbled in a ledger. He didn't look up as Flynt approached, just continued to scratch quill upon parchment, the top of his bald head bobbing as he worked.

The sound of the Admiral's harsh breathing reached Flynt before his voice. 'Jonas Flynt, by God. I never thought to see you again.'

There was no warmth in the words. Flynt hadn't expected any. 'I confess, I thought I might never return here.'

The Admiral studied him in the light of the candles burning around the room, his head tilted slightly to favour his one good eye. 'Perhaps you shouldn't have.'

'Circumstances dictated that I must.'

The cyclopean examination continued. 'You've changed.'

'We all change, Admiral. As do the times.'

A liquid grunt oozed from beneath the leather mask. 'They do, and you've had a hand in changing those times, have you not? Your exploits as pirate killer in the Caribbean and in the waters of the colonial seaboard have been most disruptive of illicit commerce. Even transactions that lie on the fringes of illegality.'

Flynt made no comment. There was none that he could make.

The Admiral coughed, a hand reaching for a linen kerchief lying on the desk. He covered his mouth and ejected something liquid. 'This damnable weather is most irritating for my lungs, as you will recall.' He dropped the soiled kerchief onto the desk once more. 'So, do I call you Captain, thanks to your achievements at sea?'

'Jonas will suffice.'

'Very well, though I understand that you have been in the employ of the colonial governors whilst abroad.' The Admiral was very still for a moment. 'You failed to inform me that you were working for the authorities when you asked for my assistance in obtaining passage.'

'Would you have given me that assistance if I had?'

'No. I surmise, therefore, that you had been a government man throughout our acquaintance?'

'Unwillingly. And none of my missions impacted on your business.'

'Until recent.'

Flynt couldn't deny that. 'I didn't molest any of your vessels. Your colours are well known in those waters.'

'My vessels are entirely legitimate. It was trade of a more tangential nature that you disrupted.'

Over the years since Flynt left, he had learned that this man not only controlled all the illicit enterprises on the city wharves, but had interests in the colonies, if not around the world. The fact that pirates respected the colours of his sailing fleet first suggested to Flynt that he had dealings with the Flying Gang, the loose alliance of pirates who ruled the roost in Nassau for some years, until the arrival of Governor Woodes Rogers. 'I regret any inconvenience to your business. That was not my mission nor my intention.'

'And yet you did inconvenience my business. The Flying Gang lies broken, the Republic is no more, their influence shattered, what little remains of their confederation scattered across the oceans, but most be dead. Captain Hornigold lost at sea, Captain Vane hanged at Port Royal, thanks to you, I understand.'

Flynt shook his head. 'I merely took custody of him. His ship was wrecked during a storm, and we found him beached on an island. He tried to pass himself under another name but I recognised him.'

'And Blackbeard?'

Flynt saw again the heavily bearded face, heard the laughter, saw the madness in the man's eyes.

'He died as he lived, violently.'

'He was felled by a sword strike from a Scot, I hear.'

'He was.'

Flynt had killed many men. Some of them necessarily, some of them not. He didn't enjoy talking about them. Even when it was a man like Edward Thatch, the man they called Blackbeard.

'I met him but once,' the Admiral recalled. 'He was a rum cove, and that's putting it mildly. I admit, there was…' He sought the correct word. '…an unsettling air about the man.'

In his mind, Flynt's sword swung again. The blade caught the flesh of the pirate captain's throat. A gush of blood. A look of surprise. Then no look at all.

'And you know that when a man such as I says this, then that impression must have been considerable,' the Admiral continued. 'There are many who find me unsettling. Especially those who incur my wrath.' He took a breath, the phlegm in his throat rattling like impending death. 'Do you find me unsettling, Jonas Flynt?'

Flynt fought the urge to crane round to observe Pickett. He was confident he would hear the creak of at least one board if the man moved. Perhaps confident was overstating it. He hoped he would hear something.

'So tell me, Jonas,' the Admiral said, knowing he was not likely to receive a reply, 'what brought you home and back to my door?'

Flynt glanced at the clerk attacking the ledger as if he were a gladiator.

'Don't mind Albert,' the Admiral said. 'He has become privy to many of my secrets, have you not, Albert?'

The smile the little man delivered when he looked up was so swift that Flynt thought he had imagined it. Then the bald head was lowered again and he continued with his labours.

'So,' the Admiral said, 'what brings you here?'

'I seek a man.'

'Aha, you have not changed that much, then. Who is he?'

'Daniel Hawke.'

Flynt knew the name would be familiar.

'He is no pirate,' the Admiral declared.

'He may not have been, but he and his family made at least part of their fortune from them.'

'As did I.'

'But you didn't have a hand in the murder of my son.'

The Admiral sat back, the mask preventing Flynt from discerning his expression. The single eye revealed nothing.

'I was not aware Hawke was present,' the Admiral said, quietly. Of course, he knew what had happened. Like Charters, he would receive regular despatches from his associates, and the death of young Jonas would have been passed along from mouth to mouth.

'He wasn't, but he was involved. And that makes him responsible.'

'And you seek revenge?'

'Admiral,' Flynt said quietly, 'everything I've done for the past six years has been vengeance upon those who facilitated men such as Hawke, and Thatch.'

'I also have facilitated such men.'

'I bear you no ill will. We were friends in the past and I am friend to you still.'

Flynt had emphasised this in their correspondence, but something hung in the air in this dark room that suggested it had not been accepted. Nevertheless, he had to continue with his course of action.

'I knew Hawke's father,' the Admiral said. 'A scurrilous dog of a man, with whom I rationed my contact.'

'The son is little better.'

'So I understand. What makes you think I know of his whereabouts?'

Flynt shrugged as if the answer to that was self-evident. 'He sailed into the Pool of London. A rat doesn't fart in the docklands without you knowing of it.'

The Admiral accepted that with a slight lifting of one hand. 'He is protected.'

'By the Fellowship.'

Flynt shot another glance at Albert, but he paid no attention to their conversation, the notations on which he worked bearing more import.

'You know of them?'

'I've had experience of them, aye.'

'They are not a group I would recommend irritating.'

'I irritated them long ago. Do you know where he is?'

'I have few dealings with the Fellowship. They go their way and, thankfully, they keep themselves out of mine. Yes, I had heard that Hawke was in the city, but he made no attempt to contact me and given his association with those fine gentlemen of commerce, I have reciprocated.'

'But you do know where he is?'

A slight watery chuckle. 'You credit me with too much knowledge.'

'Will you utilise your connections to help me find him?'

The intelligence he'd elicited in New York regarding Melanie Inglis may or may not ultimately bear fruit. The Admiral's network rivalled that of Charters, at least in London, and if anyone could pick up the trail, it was him.

'I don't believe I shall.'

Given the atmosphere, this came as little surprise to Flynt. 'Why?'

'I thought you a friend, but you betrayed that trust by not disclosing your employer.'

'I didn't betray you.'

'A lie, even by omission, is a betrayal. I believe I once told you that I placed my trust in only two men, Mr Pickett being one, you the other. I should have you killed here and now.'

Flynt glanced at Pickett, who remained as impassive as ever, Flynt's weapons held in one outstretched hand, the other behind his back. Flynt would lay odds that hand held a pistol.

'I've killed men for less,' the Admiral continued. 'But for the sake of our former friendship you shall walk free, but on this occasion only. Should you set foot on the waterside again, for whatever reason, then you will never leave it.' His final words caught on something in his throat and he leaned over the book on his desk. 'Goodbye, Jonas Flynt. Pray to whatever God in which you believe that we never meet again.'

Flynt felt pain lance through his chest as he stared at the leathery top of the man's head. He looked again at Albert, who still paid little heed, and then heard Pickett move behind him. He turned to see him opening the door. The audience was over.

Flynt lingered but a moment, wondering if he should say more. This meeting had always been risky. Despite the content of the correspondence, the Admiral could easily have veered in the other direction, and Pickett would have cut him down where he stood. There was also the possibility that the Fellowship would hear of this conversation and come for him. That was a gamble Flynt was willing to take. Whoever they sent might have further information, or at least be more willing to share, given the correct amount of stimulus. And Flynt had grown very good at applying the correct amount of stimulus.

Outside the room, he accepted the return of the proffered weapons from Pickett's hand. They exchanged a look for a moment, a nod, and Flynt began to descend the stairs. He had reached the bottom of the stairway leading to the alley beside the tavern when he heard Pickett's voice from above.

'Mr Flynt, that young friend of yours, Jack Sheppard.'

Flynt turned.

'Do you know where he is?' Pickett asked.

'I know.'

He had made inquiry after the young man soon after arriving in London. They hadn't parted on the best of terms, at least on Flynt's part, but he had wished to tap into his knowledge of the currents in the city's underworld, just as he had with the Admiral.

'Do you know what happened?'

Flynt continued towards the doorway that led to the alley. 'I can guess.'

10

Jack Sheppard sat in chains, an amused half-grin on his face as he stared at the faces of the gentry. The group of three – two women, one man – peered at him from the doorway of his cell. The Ordinary of Newgate Prison was providing a commentary on Jack's deeds, much of his narrative being exaggerated. The Ordinary was the jail's chaplain, there to do what he could to save the souls of the condemned and the convicted, but he also did his best to make a profit from their misery. After all, was it not often said that God helps those who help themselves? Jack understood that there was no chapter and verse in the Holy Book to strengthen this argument, but over the years successive pastors had reasoned that if God hadn't wished him to bolster his meagre stipend, He would not have placed him in charge of the spiritual wellbeing of men and women who were the object of curiosity by their betters. After all, Newgate Prison – 'the Whit', as it was known to Jack and many others – was an entrepreneurial dream, with jailers, keepers and even inmates all turning coin.

This Ordinary, sitting in for the ailing Thomas Purney, had told Jack all this, by way of either explaining or seeking his permission to turn him into some kind of freak of nature that would be best placed in some travelling show. Jack didn't care what he did; in fact, he gleaned as much enjoyment from seeing the gentle folk in their finery walking among the filth and decay of Newgate as they did from seeing him sitting upon a stool and chained to the floor. Occasionally he would rattle those chains and leer a little, making the ladies press their perfumed linen to their faces and the men puff themselves up like peacocks. The Ordinary, or a keeper, depending on whose palm was being greased, would usher them away, leaving Jack laughing. He had to take what pleasures he could, for there were damned few in this place.

The Ordinary's party had moved on to find some other poor wretch to gawp at when the door to this room, the one they called 'The Castle', opened again and Old Baldy entered. The keeper stared at Jack for a moment, his eyes running over the chains at his wrist, around his ankles and thence to the metal ring embedded in the stone floor. As his title among the prisoners of Newgate suggested, this jailer had a pate that was devoid of strudel, save a few long strands that he flattened across the top of his head as if it could cover his brown-flecked flesh. He was old, certainly, one of the oldest turnkeys in the jail, but he was sharp and he could tell just by that one look that the fetters were secure. With a satisfied nod, he stepped back and allowed entrance to a tall cove with salt in his black mummer. There was something in this bearded man that was familiar, but in the poor light of this room above the gate arch, Jack couldn't quite make him out.

Baldy inspected the coins the visitor dropped into his upturned palm, then produced a timepiece and made a show of studying it. 'You has got ten minutes, no more, no less,' he warned in his now familiar croak.

Jack had eyed that watch ever since he had entered the Whit, named for the former Lord Mayor Richard Whittington, who bequeathed money to have it rebuilt hundreds of years before Jack had been born. His fingers itched to lift it, but Baldy never came near enough for him to do so. Perhaps one day.

'I shall be just beyond this here portal,' Baldy warned, 'what will remain open at all times.'

'That garnish should be sufficient to give us privacy.'

The visitor's voice caused a glimmer of memory to surface in Jack's mind. It was one he hadn't heard for many a year.

'Ain't no garnish what gives you that, not with this here cove. Proper slippery he is and he will remain in my sight at all times.'

Baldy left but stood just outside the door. Jack ignored him to make a closer study of the tall visitor.

'Gawd save us,' he said, softly, 'it's Mr Flynt. I never thought I'd be a-seeing of you no more. I'd heard you was over there in the colonies with all them foreign sorts.'

Mr Flynt took off his wide-brimmed hat and waved it in the direction of the heavy chains. 'I won't ask you how you are, Jack. I do believe I can guess.'

Jack grinned and gave the manacles a little rattle and nodded towards the various padlocks holding them in place. 'These here clinkers ain't nothing, Mr Flynt, though I does wish I could lie down to sleep. They keeps them tight to the leg-irons and the floor, see? So being thus double-slanged, the best I can manage is to lean my noddle against this here wall.'

The turnkey's voice reached them from outside. 'Then p'raps you shouldn't have escaped lawful custody so often, my lad.'

A flash of irritation crossed Mr Flynt's face, but he said nothing as he surveyed the remainder of the room.

'It ain't much,' Jack said, his voice bright, 'but it's home. And I'm better here than down in the Common side, or the condemned hold. At least here I has a bit of space and air, and some sunlight through that window.' He jutted his chin to the barred window high up on the wall. 'I has myself for company without the intrusion of the rats and the lice, not to mention the farting and snoring of those there confined.'

Mr Flynt's eyes were filled with concern. 'You're in trouble, Jack.'

Jack dismissed that with a shrug, making believe that Mr Flynt referred to the chains. 'Nah. It's just a bit of discomfort, is all. It'll ease, and right soon.'

Real pain pierced Mr Flynt's eyes and Jack felt sorry for being so flippant. He hadn't meant to be. He'd meant to reassure him.

'Don't be worrying, Mr Flynt, all will be well.'

Mr Flynt turned away, as if looking in vain for a chair in which to sit, but Jack knew it was to hide the concern that was displayed nakedly in his eyes. It was a little over a week before Jack was due to take the Tyburn walk and he knew the thought of the triple tree haunted his old friend. Or the man who used to be his friend.

'You've led them a merry dance, Jack.'

'And I will again, Mr Flynt. I ain't done yet.'

Baldy cleared his throat, prompting a grin from Jack.

'What happened?' Mr Flynt asked.

Jack's grin faded. 'The upshot is that I should've listened to you and never fell in with that rat bastard Jonathan Wild.'

Mr Flynt had advised Jack against becoming involved with the Thieftaker General, warning that he would turn on him, and he had. Jack had good reason for aligning himself with Wild, though that didn't make his situation any easier.

'What of Blueskin?' Mr Flynt asked.

'He's here, in the Whit, somewheres, awaiting his trial.'

'Don't tell me, Wild betrayed him too.'

'That's the exactitude of it. Old Blueskin, he pulled himself a job, a real sweet crack lay it were, breaking into a…'

He stopped short for a moment, realising he was about to reveal something that Mr Flynt wouldn't like.

'…shop down the Strand. Got me to help him get in, you knows I'm proper nimble with a dub and no lock can beat me. Anyways, he didn't give Mr Wild his garnish and Mr Wild, well, you knows what he is like.'

Mr Flynt nodded. 'I know what he's like.'

'He didn't take well to us pulling no job what he didn't give the nod to in the first place and then not to be given his cut. Had to make an example, I hears is what he said, even if it were Blueskin. Especially if it were Blueskin, I suppose. So he sends two coves called Griffin and Knapp to arrest us.'

'I've already made the acquaintance of Mr Griffin and Mr Knapp.'

'Knapp is a sneaky one, but Griffin? I would steer clear of him if I was you. He's a killer, Mr Flynt, a professional, most certain, but still a killer.'

Mr Flynt said nothing but Jack knew what he was thinking. He was also a killer.

'Blueskin didn't take kindly to it, resisted he did, but Griffin stuck his steel in his shoulder. I ain't never seen nobody move so fast, even you, Mr Flynt. It was like he hardly moved at all. That Toledo of his was in his hand and the tip in Blueskin before anyone knew it. Still, old Blueskin, he managed to get away, damaged wing and all. Not for long, though, for Wild did the job himself a day or two later, him and another two of his men. They'd already nipped me by then.'

'Wild turned you both in because of one job?'

Jack kept his gaze steady. There was another reason, but he couldn't tell Mr Flynt why Wild had turned so hard against him. He daren't breathe a single word to him about that. 'He's changed, Mr Flynt. I mean, don't get me wrong, he was always a rat bastard, you was right about that, always looked out for himself. A few months ago, if you'd asked me about him and Blueskin, I'd say they was as tight as two coves could be, but not no more. But of recent he's become even more mistrustful, of anyone, no matter who it be.'

Jack had nothing more to say on that, so he leaned forward and squinted in the gloom to see Mr Flynt clearer. 'You has changed too, Mr Flynt.'

'We've all changed, Jack.'

'No, you looks bone tired.'

Mr Flynt's smile was wan. 'I'm older, as are you.'

'That's true, I was nothing but a lad when you left. I'm a man now. Bess and me – you remember Bess? – well, her and me, we is married now. Not that we took no vows in front of no preacher or nothing, but we is man and wife for all that. She's not a moll no more, for I was able to earn sufficient to keep her from the streets.'

He could tell Mr Flynt had little interest in Edgeworth Bess, even though Mr Flynt had known Jack had been in love with her for nearly ten years now. He really had been nothing but a lad then, stealing what he could, doing odd jobs for Mr Flynt himself, never asking questions as to why he had to follow a cove or find a cove or get him into a cove's crib. He'd learned about locks thanks to him being apprenticed to a carpenter down Wych Street, again thanks to Mr Flynt, but the life of an honest man wasn't for him. He'd been born to thievery, more or less, learned the ways of the dive in one of Queen Anne's charity schools, learned them so well he could have a silk wipe or a coin purse from a gent's pocket and be away long before the mark knew it was gone.

'So tell me, what makes you come back here to London?'

'I have business, Jack.'

Jack accepted that with a sage nod. Even after the passage of years, he knew better than to inquire as to the nature of Mr Flynt's business. 'It pains me that I ain't in no position to assist you.'

'I regret we didn't part on the best of terms.'

Jack shrugged that way. 'Don't be tormenting yourself about that, Mr Flynt. I did what I did and I should've knowed better.' He paused, wondered if he should say anything further as to why he had taken up with Wild, but once again decided against it. 'More than once you tried to set me on the straight, but it weren't to be. A short life and a merry one, remember?'

He had said that to Mr Flynt once, ironically at Tyburn.

'Anyways, don't be counting me out none. As I said, I isn't done yet. Have some faith. One file is worth all the bibles in this world, ain't that right, Baldy?'

'You keep talking like that, lad.' The jailer's voice drifted from the corridor. 'The day will come when all your bold talk will be choked off.'

Mr Flynt eyed the sturdy chains, the lock on the ring on the floor. Jack knew he doubted his word, but said nothing.

11

Another handful of coin gave Flynt access to Blueskin Blake, who he found squatting on the floor of the ward known as the Master's Side, playing cards with other prisoners. His shirt was ripped at one shoulder and stained with blood. A none-too-clean dressing covered the wound left by Griffin's sword thrust. When he saw Flynt approach, he sat back to lean against the filthy wall behind him, his cards pressed tightly to his chest so that none of the other players might catch a glimpse of his hand.

'Well, the sights you see when you ain't got no barker to hand,' he said. 'Jonas fucking Flynt, as I live and breathe.'

'Not for long, if reports are true,' Flynt said, not wishing to get too close to the ragged prisoners. London as a whole was a city of unpleasant odours, but in this cramped room it was as if all had been distilled here. Unwashed skin, sweat, bodily functions, cheap tobacco, foul breath all merged into one unholy stink. This was supposedly the better accommodation in Newgate. Jack was correct – uncomfortable though he was, he was better off in The Castle.

To his credit, Blake's sneer didn't falter. He was always brave; that was something Flynt admired in him. They had fought each other, Blake had even once saved his life, but Blake didn't like him, didn't trust him, and had said so many a time.

'We live. We die. That's the way of things,' said Blueskin, dropping a card onto the floor between himself and his fellow players.

'If you hadn't been so in the thrall of Jonathan Wild, you might have lived a mite longer.'

Blueskin watched more cards drop. 'I'll admit you was correct in that regard and perhaps I should have listened to you. But you was such a rum cove yourself that I couldn't take your advice.' He raised his head to take Flynt in. 'You're still a rum cove. Never could put my finger on what makes you so, but you is.'

As usual, Flynt could not argue against that point. Instead, he got right to his own. 'Before I left I asked you to look after Jack.'

Blueskin looked down at his cards, studied them as if he was deciding his play, but Flynt sensed his shame. 'I knows it.'

'You said you would.'

'I knows that, too.'

'And now he sits above awaiting the noose.'

Blueskin pushed his remorse aside. 'I did what I could for him. He's a grown man now, not the stripling he were six years ago. I've never seen such a thief. That boy has larceny running right through to his very soul.'

Flynt couldn't argue against that either. He'd long known that young Jack was born to be a thief.

'Why did you engage him on that crack lay? You should have known that Wild would hear of it and take it ill.'

'I didn't believe he would take it so ill, and that's the God's honest. But in the end, that weren't why he had us boxed up.'

'Why, then?'

Blueskin threw in his final card, swore when one of the other players raked in the accumulated coins, and pulled himself to his feet, wincing as he did so, his hand darting to his wound, touching it briefly, then falling away. He stretched his legs, carefully so as not to put any strain upon his shoulder again. No fetters disabled him, as he still awaited trial and in any case, unlike Jack, had never before escaped from custody. Blueskin motioned that Flynt should follow him away from the cackling prisoners on the floor and led him to as quiet a corner as was possible. Flynt continued to maintain his distance, for he swore he could see lice crawling through Blueskin's beard and darting across his flesh. Blake scratched at his chest as if one of the creatures had bitten him, gave his surroundings a close scrutiny to ensure nobody was listening, but still dropped his voice.

'I never believed that Wild would turn on me.'

Flynt snorted. 'All evidence to the contrary.'

Blueskin held up a hand. 'Hear me out. I still believe that he would never have done this to me, even though I did that crack lay without his permission and put him in the hole regarding his garnish. He understands the likes of me, and he would have taken a heftier slice of the takings as punishment. He's done such before, not to me 'cos I never crossed him previous, but coin always calmed him down.'

'Then why didn't he take it this time?'

'Because I wasn't his true target. It was Jack he wanted out of the way.'

'Why?'

'Because he was convinced that the lad was peaching on him.'

'Jack's no informer.'

Flynt injected certainty into his voice, but an idea was already forming in his mind. There was someone who might have lured Jack into his service.

'That's what I spoke exact, but he'd been a-thinking upon this for some time, had Mr Wild.'

'What made him suspect it in the first place?'

'It's my belief that somebody told him.'

Flynt considered this, his suspicions growing. 'To whom was Jack passing information?'

Blueskin scratched the thick stubble on his chin. 'That I can't rightly say. But my speaking up for him was my undoing, for Mr Wild then got the notion into his head that I was working with the lad, him and I being so crony like. So he saw to it that both of us went down together.' Blueskin forced air between his gritted teeth. 'I'll admit that sits on me most discomfortable, that he would believe me to be so disloyal. He should've knowed me better. I had showed him loyalty and good service over the years and he repays me with this. He should've suspicioned less and trusted me more.'

'Joseph,' Flynt said, using the man's given name, 'trust is not in Wild's character. He was always going to do something like this. He will throw all who support him to the wolves when he feels the need.'

Blueskin was silent as he stared at the floor. Then he took a deep breath. 'I knows this, now.'

'If it's any consolation, Wild will stumble and fall sooner or later.'

Blueskin's head came up slowly and a wry little smile raised the corners of his mouth. 'Then let's pray it happens sooner rather than later.'

12

Flynt was certain he saw a face he recognised leaving the prison and joining the throng in Newgate Street. He hurried to intercept, calling out from behind as soon as he was close enough.

'Jacob, what brings you to the Whit?'

When he turned, the man was startled for a brief moment but he composed himself quickly. 'Visiting, Mr Flynt.'

'And who would be of interest to you within those foul walls, Jacob?'

Jacob's smile was unforced. 'I'm here on the colonel's business, to be truthful.' He ducked forward a little and kept his voice low. 'Does you know of a Major Bernardi?'

Flynt recalled the name. 'Not personally.'

'Well, the colonel, he does, but the gentleman's Jacobite sympathies mean he can't come see him personal like, so he sends me to see what he needs in there. As you knows, a little coin goes a long way in Newgate.'

John Bernardi had been arrested under suspicion of plotting to assassinate King William of Orange some twenty-eight years before, but no evidence had ever been produced against him. He had been held since then without trial. That Charters knew him was not a surprise, for they were both military men. That he showed such compassion for one whose allegiance was then, and perhaps remained, to the exiled Stuarts was a revelation. But then, Flynt had learned that Charters was like an onion. You peel off one layer and there is another underneath, sometimes more pungent than the first. As for Jacob's remark that a little coin went a long way, Flynt did indeed know. He'd given Blake some before he left, to allow him to buy some comforts. Soap would have been first on Flynt's list. Blake had contemplated refusing the largesse but then accepted it. Flynt had already given the keeper Jack called Old Baldy some further garnish to ensure Jack's stay was a little more agreeable.

A carter pulled up beside them and climbed down to rearrange his load of cabbages and other vegetables. Jacob gave him a glance, then gestured to Flynt that they should cross the street in the direction of St Paul's Cathedral. When he was satisfied that nobody eavesdropped, Jacob spoke again.

'A word to the wise, Mr Flynt, from one old soldier to another, eh? The colonel spoke most candid last night, more candid than is normal for him, I'm sure you understands that.'

'I knew him to previously be more oblique in his threats, that's for sure, Jacob.'

'That's the thing, though, it weren't no threat. I've been honoured to have his trust these years, as did you, until you left us.'

'With his blessing.'

Jacob grimaced. 'He saw it as a means to an end, and a service to Captain Woodes Rogers, but he didn't think you'd desert him and go a-pirating.'

'Circumstances changed, Jacob, he knows that.'

'And right sorry he was to hear about the young gentleman. You has my sympathies also.'

Flynt doubted if Charters was in any way sorry to hear of the murder of young Jonas. Sympathy was not one of his layers. However, Flynt accepted Jacob's condolences with grace.

'But this is my point, and I hope you will accept it in the spirit in which it's given, Mr Flynt, for you and me has much in common. Pay heed to what he says. Leave this Hawke cove alone. I ain't privy to all that the colonel is about but I does know that he wants him right where he is. And he will take action most drastic to ensure that is the way of it.'

Thoughts of Jack, laden with chains and alone in the dismal room above the gate, made Flynt shake his head. 'I thank you for your concern, but my days of caring over Colonel Charters' wishes are over, Jacob. I will continue to seek Hawke and when I find him I'll kill him. It's as simple as that.'

Jacob exhaled deeply. 'Right painful that is to me, Mr Flynt, for this time you is up against forces what you can't defeat. The colonel is a man what is best to have on your side and not against you, and you seem bound and determined to ensure that is the case.'

'If that's the way it's to be, then so be it,' said Flynt, unaccountably feeling sorrow at saying the words. Then he recalled Jack again and his suspicions. 'But you can take this message to the colonel, if you would be so good. Tell him I will come see him soon, as there is something I must discuss with him.'

Jacob stopped suddenly, his demeanour suddenly both wary and defensive.

'Not to worry, Jacob,' Flynt said, smiling. 'I mean him no harm.'

Jacob's laugh was pithy. 'It ain't something I'd advise, Mr Flynt. I wouldn't even approach him without prior notice, for you know his watchers would not take that kindly. Nor would I. He'll talk to you again, on that you can wager with confidence.'

—

Lincoln's Inn Square was an area of contrasts, as was London itself. Rich and poor rubbed shoulders here as lawyers practised their dark and often obscure arts. The houses might have been grand, but the Londoners milling about beyond their doors, making their way from the fleshpots of Holborn in the north to the watering holes of Drury Lane and the pleasures of Covent Garden were a mix of rich, poor and those in-between. On the far side of the open space from where Flynt stood was the low lying 'bog house', a public privy. It had three doors, slightly obscured by a line of trees, and even at this time of the morning Flynt saw men entering and leaving. They may have been using it for its main function, as a house of office, but others may have been in search of another basic need, that of sexual gratification. London might have been the centre of the civilised world, at least in the eyes of its denizens, but it was also the focal point for pleasure-seekers of all tastes. The square was the embodiment of the city, outwardly respectable, but underneath seethed lust, desire and vice.

He studied the terraces of tall, four-storey buildings surrounding the square, like the Covent Garden Piazza designed by Mr Inigo Jones, suddenly daunted by the prospect before him. It was not long after noon so he had some time before he was due to rendezvous with Cain, and as he was passing the square on his way back from Newgate, he decided this was as good an opportunity as any to find Hawke's lady friend.

He paced the flagstones, occasionally attracting curious looks from passers-by, for he knew he struck an imposing figure in his black clothes, boots and hat. Tact and Diplomacy were concealed under his coat, but he carried his silver cane. It was unlikely he would have cause to wield the slim but sturdy blade concealed within, but in his world the unlikely was never far from becoming likely.

Working on the premise that if you want to gather intelligence, just ask someone, he knocked upon three doors, received no reply from two and a shake of the head at the third when he asked after the person he sought. He stopped some passers-by but nobody knew, or admitted to knowing, Melanie Inglis.

A gentleman emerged from the doorway of the house nearest to where Flynt stood and strode towards him, his own long cane tapping on the pavement. Flynt raised his hat in deferential greeting.

'I beg your pardon, sir,' he said, 'but I wonder if you might assist me.'

The man took him in from head to foot, lingering on the scar. 'I will give you no money, friend. I do not countenance begging.'

'I am no beggar, sir, I seek only information, if you have it. I am looking for a lady by the name of Melanie Inglis, a widow woman who has a house here.'

The man stepped back a half-pace. In that moment, Flynt knew he was acquainted with Mrs Inglis. 'And why do you wish to see this lady?'

'I am recent returned from abroad.' Flynt reached into his pocket to produce a purse filled with coin. 'I have been away for some years but before I left, her husband, her late husband, did me a service for which I am deeply grateful. I heard he died a little time ago—'

'Five years,' the man interjected. 'Spencer has been gone these five years. So you fled the country without making payment, is that the way of it?'

'I paid what I could at the time and pledged to give him further coin when I made my way in the colonies. I have done so, and here I am. I know he left Mrs Inglis most comfortable, but I remain beholden to her husband for his kindness and wish to make good on my pledge.'

The man's gaze darted towards the coin purse, then back to Flynt's face, searching for sign of dissembling. Flynt was a cunning card player, and knew how to maintain an outward semblance of confidence and probity when the flats he held were of a somewhat disorganised nature. He had developed this skill playing the Spanish game of Primero in

Nassau, where one of the objects was to deceive the other players into folding their cards, believing you had the upper hand.

It stood him in good stead here, for the man nodded once and raised his cane to point at the north-eastern corner of the square. 'You'll find Mrs Inglis in the last house on the right.'

Flynt slipped the pouch back into his pocket. 'Thank you, sir.'

The man grunted something and continued on his way. Flynt walked swiftly towards the house in question and rapped upon the door. It was opened almost immediately by a serving girl, who curtsied when he asked for Mrs Inglis and asked who called. He gave her the name Silas Dunne, a snider he had never used before, and explained that he had business with her regarding a mutual acquaintance. She asked him to wait on the step and closed the door.

He waited on the step, watching the myriad of people on the square taking their leisure while the rain was absent. Most were well clothed against the damp chill that hung in the air but others were somewhat tattered, the beggars to whom the man had alluded who congregated in the Lincoln's Inn Fields and here in the new square.

The door opened and the servant girl waved a hand to allow him to enter. He took off his hat as he stepped over the threshold and into the vestibule, where a tall, well-dressed red-haired lady waited for him. She was a few years older than Hawke, but not by much. She carried herself with confidence, as she should in her own home, but her study of him was similar to that of the gentleman in the street – slightly suspicious.

'You are Mrs Inglis?' he asked.

'I am,' she said, 'and how can I assist you?'

'I seek Mr Daniel Hawke.'

It was possible that Hawke had also used a snider with the lady but Flynt had no way of knowing. However, he saw from the tilt of an eyebrow that she recognised the name. 'And what do you wish of Mr Hawke?'

'We're old friends, from the colonies. He told me that you and he were acquainted.'

Her lips compressed slightly, as if she was annoyed with the way Flynt had characterised their relationship. What was more telling, however, was the quick look towards a closed door on the right.

'And what is the nature of your business, Mr Dunne?'

He removed the purse from his pocket again, adapting the fiction he had used in the street. 'We haven't seen each other for some time and I heard he was in the city, so I thought I would repay a debt.'

Another swift glance towards the door. Hawke had to be behind it, listening. Flynt replaced the pouch in his pocket and rested his right hand on the handle of his cane, surreptitiously turning it to loosen the blade, all the while maintaining his easy demeanour, even a smile. That Mrs Inglis knew nothing of Hawke's real persona was made clear to him by her own smile in return.

'Well, as you are old friends...' She made for the door, but it flew open and Hawke thrust himself into the vestibule, a pistol in his hand. He grabbed her, twisted her round and placed the barrel against her temple. Flynt had half-drawn his blade but paused. Mrs Inglis screamed and struggled.

'Another step, Flynt, and I'll blow her brains out,' Hawke said, his voice shaking, his eyes wide and staring.

'You do that and I'll have you, Hawke,' Flynt said.

'You won't let me kill an innocent woman, Flynt. There is too much Galahad in you.'

Hawke pulled the woman towards the still-open street door, where the servant had flattened against the wall, her mouth open as if preparing to scream but her terror so intense that it froze her voice.

'Daniel, what are you...?' Mrs Inglis protested, but he clamped his free hand over her mouth.

'Sorry, Melanie, I truly am, but you and I are going for a walk. Flynt, don't follow, I warn you. You will have this lady's blood on your hands.'

Nevertheless, Flynt followed, step by faltering step. He couldn't allow Hawke to reach the street, for there were too many people there who might get hurt and he could easily make his escape. Mrs Inglis tried to struggle free but Hawke held her fast.

'Let's finish this, Hawke,' Flynt said, his hand reaching under his coat.

Hawke saw the move. 'Ah-ah, don't do it. You touch a weapon and I'll do for her, as God's my judge.'

He dragged his unwilling shield closer to the door, shot a glance outside. Flynt's hand was only inches from Tact, but he daren't draw it, and his sword was useless at this distance. Hawke would shoot the woman, of that he was certain, and doubtless had a second pistol under his coat.

Suddenly, Hawke thrust Mrs Inglis towards Flynt with considerable force, pitching her forward, so that she slammed into him with such power that he almost lost his footing. He caught the screaming woman, righted her, and darted across the vestibule. Hawke had darted out of the door, pulling it shut behind him. Flynt wrenched it open again, then ducked back as he saw Hawke aiming his pistol. When he heard no gunfire, he peered round the door frame to see Hawke sprinting across the square towards the passageway leading to Chancery Lane. He was most fleet of foot, but Flynt couldn't let him enjoy a narrow escape once more.

'Tend to your mistress,' he yelled to the servant, but didn't wait to see if she paid heed. He leaped down the steps to the street and pursued Hawke across the square, ignoring the shouts and cries of alarm from the people he skirted or pushed past. Hawke was halfway across when he looked over his shoulder, saw Flynt pursuing, then raised his pistol into the air and pulled the trigger – a risky move, for what goes up had to return and could easily claim an innocent life. Not that Hawke cared, for the move was designed to hinder Flynt further, and it succeeded. On hearing the gunshot, the people in the square screamed, yelled and panicked, everyone surging away from the source of the confusion. It was Flynt who was now pushed out of the way as they sought safety. He tried to proceed further but for each step forward he was forced two back, giving Hawke liberty to reach the passageway running beside the bog house.

Flynt gave up the chase. From Chancery there were any number of alleyways and passages Hawke could take in order to vanish into the warren that was London. He stood in the middle of the open space that was the square while the final few of the promenaders streamed past him and cursed Hawke's charmed life.

13

In need of a salve for the disappointment of his quarry again slipping through his fingers, Flynt called at the stables near the Golden Cross, where he had left the mount who had served him well during his nights working the heaths around London. She was a fine animal, even though he had never managed to find a name for her. He called her simply 'Horse'. She didn't seem to mind. He had known the animal would be well cared for by the retired army officer who owned the establishment, but he had put off checking on her out of fear that she wouldn't remember him. Everything had changed since he left. Loyalties. Allegiances. Circumstances. Only Gabriel Cain remained a constant.

When the stableboy showed him to Horse's stall, Flynt felt his nervousness rise. He had hoped for some comfort, but it occurred to him that he might only find more disappointment. Damn it, she was only a beast, a means of conveyance. She was an animal, for God's sake. She might not remember him.

But she wasn't just an animal, not just a beast. She had also been a constant. Dependable. And yes, she had saved his life more than once by that constancy, her strength and her loyalty. He would never understand, nor understate, the bond that had forged between man and mare. He was able to communicate with her, not just verbally, though he swore she understood a great deal, but also through subtle shifts of weight and pressure on the saddle, or a simple flick of the reins. Sometimes she knew where he needed her to be, whether through those minute physical directions or by some form of uncanny divination, he couldn't say. She was patient through cold, wet nights as they waited for a coach to rumble their way, remaining stationary for long periods. She was never startled by a pistol crack. She would allow no other person to sit astride her back, which had proved a boon during a sojourn to the north of England, when one man had decided that she would be his to use and abuse as he saw fit. The first time he climbed into the saddle he discovered that she saw matters in a different way. It was a characteristic that Flynt had warned her new keepers about, and the stable owner had assured him that nobody would try. She would be exercised, but led by the reins, he said. Nobody would try to mount her.

'Hello, big girl, somebody is here to see you,' the boy said as he set aside a bag of feed and opened the door to the stall. Flynt stepped round the doorway into view and saw Horse for the first time in six years. She looked immaculate. She had been well groomed, well fed, well exercised. The stall had clean straw and fresh water. The lad poured some of the feed into a trough, but her eyes were fixed on Flynt, blinking slowly. She didn't move towards the trough for the feed.

'Hello, lass,' Flynt said, his voice rough, so he coughed, cleared his throat, spoke again. 'It's been a long time.'

He didn't reach out for her; she had to come to him. If she didn't approach, if she didn't recognise him, then he would leave, for he could see she was in fine condition. He would ensure there were funds sufficient for her care and was confident the stable owner would continue to be solicitous.

Still she didn't move. No twitch of the ear. No swish of her tail.

This had been a mistake, he thought, as an ache spread through his chest. He should never have come to her, not after all this time. With the exception of Cain, nobody seemed particularly pleased to see him. Jack, perhaps, but it appeared he was too late to help him. It was folly to expect Horse, this animal, to have harboured any feelings for him at all. A sorrowful breath escaped his body and disappointment drooped his shoulders. He'd needed a better outcome here and he wasn't sure why. Perhaps because he knew that much of what plagued him now was of his own doing. As a young man in search of adventure he had deserted Cassie, the daughter of a woman his father had brought back from the Caribbean and married, not knowing that she carried their child. He had allowed his family to think him dead on a foreign field while he pursued a life of crime in London, and during his subsequent work for the Company of Rogues. His eventual return to them on a mission resulted in the death of his boyhood friend who, in the interim, had married Cassie and raised young Jonas. His latent feelings for Cassie had come between him and Belle St Clair. He had allowed young Jonas to accompany them to the Indies and then he, too, had died. Cassie bore that regret, perhaps more than he, and he had done his best to live up to a promise to avenge their son's death, but that mattered nothing. He had lost her. He had lost Belle. He had lost Jack. Somehow he had failed them all.

He closed his eyes. He was tired. He had placed too much hope on Horse, but he had needed that one positive, that one moment where nothing had changed and he meant something more in another creature's life than disappointment. Or fear. Or hatred.

He opened his eyes, looked once more at the mare, still immobile, still looking back at him with those big brown eyes, and turned to go.

And then she pawed at the straw strewn on the stall floor.

She whinnied.

He turned back to her.

Her tail swung loosely, easily.

She took one step forward, then another.

He waited.

Closer now.

Come on, girl.

Almost with him.

He reached out, palm up, fingers splayed.

Another step and she nuzzled the hand with her soft nostrils, brought her forelock towards him. He placed both hands against the side of her head, and pressed his forehead against her.

'She remembers you, sir,' said the boy. 'They don't forget who they love.'

Flynt didn't reply. He couldn't reply. If he'd tried, he would have wept. They stood there, man and horse, heads close together, he whispering words of affection and stroking her mane and her neck, she pawing at the floor and snorting softly. The last time he had seen her, the scene had been similar.

Jonas Flynt was glad this, at least, had not changed.

14

He saw Edgeworth Bess as soon as he entered the White Lion. The man at the table with her wore a grey cotton shirt under a short blue jacket, worn and patched at the elbows; his skin was burnished and his hair, tied back in a ponytail, was topped with a weathered leather cap. A Royal Navy sailor, on the town for some fun. Bess had one hand under the table as she spoke, her smile designed to be enticing, and by the jerking of her shoulder, that hand was not resting in any passive way on the man's lap. She had never been of slight stature but she had grown plumper in the years since he'd last seen her, as evidenced by the expanse of breast all but tumbling forth from her scoop top. Jack had told him that she had given up whoring but by this evidence he was deluding himself, as he often did when it came to this woman.

Jack had been besotted with her since he was a boy. At first attracted by those ample charms, the boy had spent what coin he had in order to become more fully acquainted with them. As he grew older, his affection – his infatuation, perhaps – had grown. Flynt, however, had never been convinced that the young woman was good for him. She was a doxy and an enthusiastic one, to be sure, but that was not the reason. Flynt did not judge, unless someone hurt children or animals. He had also been involved with a courtesan, although Belle St Clair was of a considerably higher class than Edgeworth Bess. The fact was, he simply didn't trust her. He suspected that it was Bess who had urged Jack to reject Flynt's protection and friendship and fall in with Jonathan Wild. She had always been chary of him, perhaps ignited when he'd had occasion to threaten her life in order to maintain her silence over an incident she had witnessed. She did everything she could to draw Jack away from his influence and, being of a mercenary bent, would have pushed him towards Wild, believing such an alliance would be more profitable.

He considered confronting her but decided against it. What she did was not his affair. Jack was boxed up in the Whit and Flynt had little doubt that he had become her main source of income, which meant what she was about this day was merely to raise the coin to feed herself and pay the rent. After all, the girl had to live. Instead, he veered away to the corner table where Gabriel Cain already waited.

Before he could tell him how close he came to having Hawke, Cain nodded in the direction of Bess and her gentleman friend. 'You've seen who is pumping at that fellow's roger over there?'

'Aye.'

'You'd think they would have the decency to take it upstairs.'

'Perhaps he has the decency but not the wherewithal to pay for a room.'

'I don't expect Edgeworth Bess to be too pricey.'

Flynt looked to the table again. 'I think she is merely giving him a rub, to entice him a little further. The White Lion is far from salubrious, but I'd expect the landlord might take a dim view of someone boxing the Jesuit in the middle of the tavern.'

Sure enough, the man removed Bess's hand and dropped it on the table, shaking his head. She reached back for his groin but he rose abruptly, his face sharp as he said something short and to the point.

'It appears her blandishments have fallen on deaf ears. Or a limp dick,' Cain observed.

'I think,' Flynt said, 'that, inexpensive as Bess might be, her price has proved too high for a fellow who has probably already spent all his cash.'

Bess watched her potential cull head for the door in that particular swaying fashion of men of the sea, and then surveyed the room for another customer. Eventually, her eye fell on Flynt and Cain at their corner table. At first he believed she hadn't recognised him, for her gaze moved on, then returned, recognition blooming as she took in first Cain, then Flynt, and even at that distance he saw a familiar suspicious glint reach her eye. She couldn't keep the sneer from plucking at her top lip as she rose and headed in their direction.

'Jonas Flynt, by God, you surely does have a nerve showing your face back in these streets, even hidden by that badger mummer on your chin.'

Flynt rose in courtly fashion. 'Bess, it's good to see you.'

She laughed at his courtesy. 'I'll bet.' She gave Cain a disdainful glance. 'And in the company of this one, I might've knowed. You two is like peas in a pod. Dress the same, talk the same.'

'Jack said you had given up the life, Bess,' Flynt said.

She squared her shoulders in defiance. 'What I does or does not do ain't no never mind of yours, Jonas bloody Flynt. Never was, never will be.' Her eyes narrowed. 'You've seen Jack?'

'Just this day.'

'You knows his plight, then?'

'I do.'

'It's your fault, I hope you knows that too.'

Flynt suspected that he was partially to blame, but that was all. 'Jack is a grown man. He made his own way.'

'You deserted him.'

'He deserted me, took up with Wild. Did you try to talk him out of that course of action, I wonder?'

Her sneer appeared as she avoided that question. 'I'll thank you to keep away from my Jack. You has been nothing but heartache for him.'

'He's in trouble, Bess. I'd like to help—'

'He doesn't need no help from you.' Again, her eyes crawled over Cain. 'Nor from nobody what is connected to you. We makes our own help, him and me.'

Cain grew irritable. 'In the name of Christ, girl, you do know what lies ahead of the lad?'

'I knows.'

'And you are content to let him take the walk to Tyburn?'

She opened her mouth to speak, then seemed to think better of it. 'He don't need no help from you,' she repeated.

'I can't let it happen,' Flynt said. 'Jack and I had our differences towards the end, before I left—'

'And you should never have returned back,' she snarled. 'You keep yourselves out of it. We doesn't need no help. Jack can takes care of himself.'

15

Jonathan Wild hadn't changed. The first time Flynt met him was in the room the self-styled Thieftaker General used as an office at the Blue Boar Tavern in Little Old Bailey. On that day he had sported a waistcoat of blue silk and a wig of expansive ringlets, which lay upon the desk before him. The waistcoat he now wore was also blue, also silk, but Flynt doubted that it, and the wig – this time upon his head – were the same ones. Wild was too much the dandy to wear a garment for nearly ten years. His body was perhaps not as sturdy as it once was, but the feeling of strength remained. He had been a manual worker in his youth and he still boasted the remains of the muscle he had developed. He was positioned behind his desk, which Flynt would swear had grown larger. All the better to overwhelm people who called upon him in the room he had grandly named his Office for the Recovery of Lost and Stolen Property. By his right hand rested a silver sword, like his clothes an affectation towards being a gentleman. Most men of Wild's stripe would have favoured a shorter blade, or even a cudgel, if not a brace of pistols. Even Flynt's own sword, encased within a silver cane, was shorter, but no less deadly. However, it was a sign of Wild's office; at least that's how he looked upon it, for as Thieftaker General he enjoyed presenting himself as legitimate, even though the lost or stolen property he presumed to recover was often stolen by men under his orders. When it was then recovered, he received a reward from the true owner. When he made an arrest, he received a reward from the city. At all stages in the process Jonathan Wild had made himself wealthy by turning on his own kind. Cicero, a favourite of Flynt's, had written that even thieves have their own laws, and to an extent that was true, but in the end there was no honour among them. Wild was a living exponent of that. It was said he had a ledger in which he placed a cross against a thief's name when he had him arrested, and then another when he was jailed, transported or executed. Wild was most accomplished in this art of the double-cross.

His smile was almost warm when Flynt and Cain were shown in by a bulging oaf with so many scars on his face that his flesh looked like bare earth that had cracked in a drought. They had refused to part with their weaponry and, surprisingly, that had been accepted with a grunt. On entering the room, Flynt knew why they had gained access so easily. Wild was not alone, for Griffin leaned against the wall behind the door, his arms folded, his expression bored. Knapp's arse was propped against the window ledge behind Wild, his right arm held immobile by a somewhat grubby linen square tied behind his neck. The forefinger of his left hand was at that moment exploring his nose as if he were attempting to scratch an itch in his brain.

'Careful, Knapp,' Cain said, 'you may lose that finger someday.'

Wild gave Cain barely a glance as he rose to walk round the desk. 'Jonas Flynt, by God.'

His tone revealed surprise but Flynt suspected it to be feigned. Wild survived not only through his propensity to besmirch and betray anyone he felt necessary, but also by running his own network of informants throughout the city. In that, he, Charters and the Admiral were very much alike. If they ever joined forces they could rule the world. Such an eventuality was unlikely, for the Admiral and Wild despised each other with such passion that it could heat water, while Charters was not one to engage with partners. At least, Flynt would have believed that until recently, even though Walpole was no partner. The politician was using Charters, and Walpole was, in turn, being used by the Fellowship. Of that, Flynt was certain.

Wild extended a hand and Flynt took it, even though he felt he was shaking hands with the devil.

'Mr Wild,' he said, politely, and received a very slight bow in return.

Wild gave Cain a dismissive look, his tone decidedly chiller. 'Cain.'

Cain didn't seem to mind. He shot back his customary grin. 'Nice to see you too, Mr Wild.'

Knapp had pushed himself from his perch and pointed towards Flynt the finger that had lately been probing the mysteries of his nostril. 'That's him, Mr Wild, that's the cove what interrupted us when we was roasting that rogue Cain.'

Wild's brow furrowed. It was an act, but a good one. 'Be that correct? Did you impede my officers while conducting their lawful duty?'

'I have need of Gabriel, Mr Wild, and I won't have him arrested.'

Wild considered this statement as if it were the Gordian knot he could cut through with his reason. 'It be my understanding that he had robbed and killed two men, the crime being witnessed by my agents.'

Agents. Good God, Flynt thought, but he successfully prevented his eyes from rolling.

'Those two men had been robbing unwary women in that alley for weeks, Wild,' Cain said. 'They were in the process of doing it again when I stepped in. If your *agents* were in any way worth their salt, they would have stopped them before I did.'

Wild didn't even look at Cain; he maintained his attention on Flynt. 'That's not the way my lads tell me it happened. They say he challenged those two, murdered them and then relieved them of their purse.'

Cain laughed. 'I wouldn't stoop to the low toby, and you know it, Wild.'

Flynt suppressed an ironic smile, for committing street robbery was exactly what Cain had done.

Wild's cold stare continued. 'A thief is a thief, Cain, and there is no limit to how far he will stoop.'

Cain's voice was even and friendly. 'You would know all about that, wouldn't you?'

Knapp began to move around the desk. Griffin remained where he was, his eyes lidded, his expression maintaining its lack of interest.

'By God, Mr Wild, will you let this cove speak to you in such a fashion?' Knapp said. 'Griffin and me will roast him immediate, cart him to the Whit right sharpish.'

'That won't be happening, Mr Wild,' Flynt said. 'I saw the incident in the alley. It was as Gabriel described. Those two were about to rob and probably outrage a young woman. Cain saved the courts the trouble of trial and execution.'

'And the robbery afterwards?'

Flynt saw all this as play-acting. The true reason for all this was the money, which was why he had insisted that Cain accompany him. They had work to do and they didn't need Wild breathing down their neck because he had been deprived of a paltry few coins. 'I'm sure Gabriel will donate part of the proceeds towards the costs of your agents.'

Cain opened his mouth to protest but a sharp look from Flynt closed it again. Grumbling, he reached under his coat, prompting Griffin to finally push himself away from his wall and unfold his arms, allowing his hands to rest on sword and pistol.

'Take your ease, friend,' Cain said, slowing his movements and carefully withdrawing a leather pouch from an inside pocket. He tugged the drawstring open and tipped a handful of coins into his palm, which he held out towards Wild. 'Does this satisfy you?'

A flick of the Thieftaker General's finger sent Knapp scurrying forward to scoop up the money. He held it out towards Wild, who inspected the amount and nodded with satisfaction.

'What I gleaned from that doxy makes for a tidy sum, Mr Wild,' Knapp said, a sly grin revealing teeth like rocks in a bay Flynt had sailed into in the Caribbean, widely spaced, jagged and brown.

'She had nothing to do with it,' Cain said, tension creeping into his words.

'Then you should not have engaged her as accomplice,' Wild said, sharply.

Cain made a move towards Knapp. 'You'd best not have harmed her, you weasel.'

Knapp swiftly retreated around the desk, opened a drawer and dropped the coins inside, where they tinkled against those already resting there.

Knapp sneered, emboldened by the presence of Griffin and Wild. 'Swift-Finger Jane is a bobtail, she's used to being ill treated.'

Cain's slightly shameful glance towards Flynt told him that his confidence in her safety extended only to those few moments in that alley. After that, he had cut her adrift.

Knapp's grin widened, his mouth like the opening to hell. 'I tooks my gratifications of her, of course. It weren't so easy with one wing, thanks to you, Cain, but then, it ain't my job to pleasure her, is it?'

Cain's hand inched towards a pistol, but a warning look from Flynt forced him to withdraw it. Instead, he said to Griffin, 'Were you part of this gratification?'

A barely perceptible shake of the head, coupled with a more obvious look of distaste towards Knapp, told them that he had not been. He was a professional. Flynt liked that about him.

Wild cleared his throat and addressed Flynt. 'It is my understanding that your friend has been fleecing many a cove of recent.'

'Well, when you have proofs of further such crimes, then discussion can be had. For now, you have your garnish and be satisfied with it.'

'And if I am not satisfied?'

Flynt felt weariness descend upon him. He was so tired of such discourse, but he had no choice but to keep playing the hand. 'Then we will be in dispute and that would be most disappointing.' He tilted his head to gaze over Wild's shoulder to Knapp. 'For some more than others.'

Fear rippled briefly over Knapp's face, but then a glance towards Griffin saw his bravado return. Flynt doubted that if matters did turn disagreeable, Griffin would be of much assistance. Wild he would aid because he paid Griffin's wages, but not Knapp.

'There be no need for unpleasantness, Jonas.' Wild held up his hands in supplication. 'We're all friends here.'

Cain's barely suppressed snort drew a sharp look from the Thieftaker General as he headed back around his desk while Knapp hurried to his previous position at the window. Griffin resumed his relaxed and inscrutable stance. Flynt noted that Wild's professed friendship didn't stretch to offering them a drink from the bottles lined up on a shelf. Not that he would have taken one, but it was the principle of the thing. Play-acting. Always play-acting. God, he was so wearied by it all.

'So what brought you to my door, Jonas?' Wild asked as he reached his chair. 'Surely not to simply provide me with my garnish.'

'Young Jack,' Flynt said, bluntly.

Wild folded his hands, scarred from his years as a buckle-maker, across his midriff and sat back, pomposity coating his words. 'As despicable a rogue as ever there was. I did my best to guide him, to keep him on the path of the righteous, but his larceny knows no bounds and it was the undoing of him.'

Wild's Staffordshire accent didn't make his sanctimonious words any more believable. Cain let out an exaggerated sigh. 'You wouldn't know the path of the righteous if you had a map and a guide.'

'That makes two of us, doesn't it?' Wild snapped. 'Jonas, our conversation will proceed in a more pleasant manner without this one's comments. I'd be obliged if you would have him await you in the vestibule.'

Flynt groaned inwardly. *The vestibule. Agents. Sweet Jesu, the man's affectations have grown.*

'I'll do that if you do the same with your two companions.'

Wild pursed his lips. He was not a coward – Flynt had seen him face down a baying mob, albeit having been forced to do so – and had tackled many a thief in his day, but he was older and softer now, his years of good living taking its toll. Flynt had also grown older, but he remained lean and fit. Wild would be recalculating the threat risk should they be left alone. If Flynt meant him harm, then he might not be able to defend himself, his silver sword be damned. Without a doubt he had a brace of pistols tucked away in a drawer, but he knew Flynt's reputation. He was a killer and Wild was not. He had other people to do his killing, whether it be Blueskin in the past, Griffin now, or the hangman on the scaffold. All this would have run through his mind in the instant before he continued with the conversation as if the suggestion to speak alone had never been made.

'Your young friend Sheppard went too far, Jonas.'

'I'm told you had it in for him. Wouldn't he pay your garnish?'

'He did, when it suited him, but that's not why he raised my ire.'

'What, then?'

Wild breathed heavily. 'He was informing on me.'

That much Blueskin had already said, but Flynt wished to hear Wild confirm it. 'To whom? The magistrates?'

Wild shook his head.

'Who, then? The Admiral?'

Wild had once sent the boy into his territory to spy on him. It was only Flynt's friendship with the docklands gang leader that had kept him from harm. Had the Admiral decided to return the favour by despatching Jack to spy on Wild?

'That croak-voiced, masked creature of the wetlands? No, he and I have reached an understanding of sorts. He stays down among the rats in his festering Pool of London and I remain on the city streets. No, it was to another man in the game, one of whom I have heard but never encountered.' He paused, unclasped his fingers and leaned on the desk. 'Tell me, Jonas, do you know of a man named Colonel Nathaniel Charters?'

Flynt had steeled himself for the name, having already considered it. Charters had been aware of Jack through Flynt, knew him to be most capable, had commented upon it more than once. He would be ideal fodder for the Company of Rogues. Now the question was whether Wild had knowledge of his own connection to the colonel.

A quick shake of the head. 'How did you hear of him?'

Wild weighed up his response for a moment. 'By way of a business acquaintance.'

'Who would that be?'

'It matters not. Just know that it is someone who would have access to such information. I had heard previous of a cadre of men and women they call the Company of Rogues. Have you heard tell of it?'

It was unlikely that a thief had told him, for Charters ensured that no single member of the company knew another; Flynt had only learned of Cain's involvement by chance. There were few who knew of Charters and the Company of Rogues outside the inner circles of the government. Wild was well connected to the magistrates and the council, but unless his social climbing had led him further up the slopes of power then Flynt suspected there was only one way for him to have learned of its existence. Somehow, the Fellowship had leaked it to him.

Flynt decided that he had to venture a partial truth, remaining unsure whether Wild also knew of his previous involvement with the company. 'A rumour, here and there. I thought it one of those legends of the streets.'

'Did you hear tell of its function?'

'No. If it does exist, I thought it a confederation of thieves.'

'It's more than that, I fear. It's a secret group intent on taking over this city, and by extension, the country.'

Flynt almost laughed. One look to Cain saw that he too fought it down. They both knew Charters to be in love with knowledge, for in knowledge there is power, but neither of them believed that he harboured ambition to rule. He was many things – a manipulator, a womaniser, a liar when he needed to be – but he was also loyal to his country, even when that country did not deserve such faith. No, Flynt's earlier surmise was correct. This was the Fellowship diverting attention from themselves. And Wild was either falling for it, or it suited him to believe it.

Flynt decided to play along. 'And Jack is working for this group?'

'That was my information, yes. You would do well to keep away from him, Jonas. Let the law deal with him.'

'And why Blueskin? He was always loyal to you.'

'Men change. I believe he may have been working in concert with the Sheppard boy. I cannot abide disloyalty.'

If this were not so serious for Jack, Flynt would have laughed at that point. Wild was as loyal as a rabid dog. His mind turned this information over. If Jack was working for Charters, then someone had found out. But how?

More importantly at this juncture, if Jack was part of the company, then why was Charters allowing him to languish in Newgate?

One thing Flynt knew for certain. He was going to have to break the young man out of there as soon as he could.

16

Jack Sheppard knew for certain that he had to get out of Newgate that night. He'd wanted to tell Mr Flynt of his intention but, if he were being frank, he didn't know if he could trust him. Jack's world was one of mistrust and betrayal, and at one time he would have had faith in him, but he'd been gone for years and had changed; Jack saw that right off, and not just because he'd grown himself a mummer. He carried an air of exhaustion about him and he'd aged, yes, but Jack had changed too. He wasn't the wide-eyed lad he'd once been, though he'd been a thief then and he was a thief now, but he'd grown up considerable, had been involved in matters that he'd never thought he ever would.

He waited until it was near nightfall, knowing that most of the turnkeys were otherwise engaged, a number being in attendance at the Sessions House across the press yard. A sturdy dub had been smuggled into him and he'd concealed it in a crack in the flagstones of his cell, itself hidden by the dirty straw that covered the stone floor. He sat immobile for a period, listening for any sounds of movement beyond the doorway and, on hearing none, retrieved the lockpick and began to work on the cuffs around his wrist. They sprang easily, as he'd expected, then he turned his attention to the heavy padlock securing the chains around his ankles to the floor. It was not as easy as the bracelets, but he persevered until it clicked free. The manacles around his leg had been fused tight by a blacksmith. He would need sturdier tools than his dub to loosen them, a hammer and chisel, and those he didn't have, for there was nowhere to hide them. Apart from that, the strike of a hammerhead would be difficult to suppress. Still, there was chain sufficient to allow him to move his legs relatively freely.

He looked towards the door, in case the sound of the clinking metal had alerted Old Baldy, who would still be on duty. The danger would be if the turnkey decided to check on Jack through the judas hole in the door. Luckily, the old man didn't tread lightly and Jack was acquainted with his faltering steps on the stones. Hearing none, he continued with the plan he'd concocted during the days and nights he'd lain here.

His first thought of escape had been to force open the door and make his way out, but there was not only the turnkey to consider but also other prisoners who might catch sight of him and report him in order to curry the favour of the prison authorities, perhaps even have their sentence quashed. The single window set high on the wall opposite the door was secure and, even if he could reach it, was heavily barred. He picked up the loose chains in both hands and hobbled to the fireplace. He'd examined the chimney on the first day he'd been thrown in here. It began wide but narrowed sharply halfway up, where a thick iron bar was set in the stonework. There might have been a time he'd have been able to squeeze past it, but those days were gone, and the chimney beyond was even narrower. Even so, he'd identified that area as the most likely way for him to gain his freedom. But it would take work.

Utilising the uneven brickwork, he climbed up the chimney and positioned himself under the bar, legs splayed for balance, his back propped against one side. Using the padlock's U-shaped shackle, he poked at the crumbling mortar between the large bricks of the chimney breast, scraping it free. Once he had cleared as much as he could, he again used the padlock as a lever to prise the first brick out. It was heavy and it refused to budge, but he continued, the muscles of his wrist and arms straining with the effort. He was rewarded finally with a grating sound as the stone began to give a little, dislodging what remained of the ancient cement. Invigorated, he renewed his labours until he was able to ease the brick free and climb down to set it carefully on the floor. It was a beginning, and with that first one gone, he hoped – God no, he prayed, and Jack Sheppard was not one for praying – that the remainder would be easier to shift. Climbing back again, he worked his way round the brickwork, pulling away the ancient binding until he was able to dislodge the metal bar and create a vertical passageway up to the ceiling. That was where the bar would prove useful.

It was heavy work and he was breathless by the time he'd reached this stage in his endeavours. Placing the final brick on the floor and carrying the bar, he moved carefully to the door, listened, fearful that he might have missed Baldy's distinctive step outside, or perhaps someone else passing by. In addition to the want of hair, Baldy's hearing wasn't so great. The only way he'd hear what was going on in this room was if he was directly outside, just as he was when Mr Flynt was visiting, but that didn't mean someone else whose ears were in better condition wouldn't happen by. Hearing nothing to cause him any alarm, Jack moved back to his escape route.

Tying the chains as best he could around his knees in order to move his legs more freely, he began to clamber up the chimney breast. Balancing on spaces left by the stones he'd removed, he inserted the end of the iron bar into the plasterwork of the ceiling and tore it away, exposing the floorboards of the room above. They called it the Red Room, and it had once been used to hold Jacobite rebels after the 1715 rising. No prisoners had been housed within it since. At least, that's what he had been told, and in the days he'd waited to make this escape he'd listened for footfalls but had heard nothing. So unless someone was in that room and walked softer than a ghost on its tiptoes, he should be safe to do the needful.

He thrust the bar into the spaces between the planks and prised at them ever so carefully, ensuring that he didn't lose his precarious stance. This was no time for him to fall and do himself a damage. The wood was as old as the rest of this building and it splintered easily, but he didn't rush at it. He took his time until one plank was loose enough for him to push it away, taking care not to allow it to scrape or thud, then went to work on another. Like the bricks previous, the second was much easier to budge, leaving a gap wide enough for him to squeeze his shoulders through. Thanking whatever God was in heaven, he hauled himself through the opening into the Red Room, where he lay on his back for a moment or two, his breath laboured, sweat coating his body.

Jack, old son, you is either getting old or you need to cut down on them pies and ale.

He had no time to recline there so, pulling himself to his feet and pausing to tighten the chains around his legs again, being careful not to make any further noise, he hobbled across the room to make a study of the door. It was similar to the one in his cell below, but if it was true that nobody had breathed air in this room for nine years, the lock was likely to be rusted. Still, he had to give it a go. He produced the dub from where he had thrust it in his breeches and, inserting it into the keyhole, began to twist at it. It was a tough job, to be sure, but he thought he felt a slight movement. He took out the dub, spat on it and attacked the lock again. His spit had lubricated the workings a little but it still didn't fully click. It wanted to, he could feel that. Jack had been around locks for ten years, he'd learned of them, fashioned them, built them into doors when he was apprentice to the Wych Street carpenter. He'd sprung more with a dub than any other thief in London, on that he would wager his life. That gave him pause, because that was exactly what he was doing, wagering his life on his skills with a lockpick.

Jack, if you doesn't get out of this here room right sharpish and get to the next part of your plan, you'll be giving the crows a pudding and no mistake.

He peered into the lock, could see through to the corridor where a faint light burned – Gawd, he hoped that didn't mean there was a turnkey out there somewhere tossing himself off or something. Maybe, if the fellow was lucky, having a flourish with some doxy. Jack grinned at the thought of a jailer enjoying a tuppenny upright against the prison wall. 'You takes your pleasures where you can' was his motto, but if there was a turnkey out there with some bunter, or even taking the opportunity to beat his own mutton, then that would put a stop to his plan and he still had quite a way to go before he could even sniff freedom. He couldn't hear anything, though, so he tried again with the dub, this time listening through his fingers as he'd been taught when he was a boy, feeling for the telltale hitch in the mechanism that meant he had caught it at the precise point he needed. After a few tries he found it and the lock turned, not easily, more like an old man rolling out of bed of a morning, stiff and unwilling, but turn it did and the door was open.

He peeped into the corridor, saw a lamp burning a little way down the way, but nobody lurked. Hefting his iron bar – he wasn't a lusty cove but he'd pitch into anyone who tried to stop him now – he moved to the door at the far end of the hallway leading to the prisoners' chapel. He wasn't one for church, not really, though he did have some form of belief in the Almighty, but he'd made sure he was allowed to attend services the Sunday before. He'd needed to see the layout, which he'd studied on the sly, flanked by two sturdy keepers, while feigning prayers and interest in the Ordinary's sermon. Predictably, it was an exhortation against sin. The bolt on the door was on the inside but the brickwork here wasn't any better than it was below – the Whit really needed the tender care of an army of masons, but not till he was long away, thank you all the same – so, wielding his iron bar, he had two of them out without any trouble. This allowed him to stretch his arm in and haul back the bolt. He pushed the bricks back quickly, kicked the rubble into the corner, then stood back to survey his work.

It ain't perfect, but might stand a casual inspection. It'll have to do.

He darted into the chapel, throwing the bolt behind him again. He'd done his best to minimise the noise but by necessity he had made some, perhaps too much, but nobody seemed to have heard. He didn't know what time it was, but he knew he was running out of it.

Holding higher the chains around his knees, he shuffled through the prisoners' pews, which were pens really, delineated by spiked bars. When he'd been here, the public area had been filled with Londoners who had paid the Ordinary a fee to allow them to come and see thieves and murderers. Of course, Jack had known he was the main draw, for he'd seen the eyes on him, all curiosity and judgement. His escapes from the Roundhouse at St Giles – he'd busted through the roof in that one too, even got Bess out – and then the New Prison at Clerkenwell had made him famous. When he broke out of Newgate, thanks to Bess slipping him both a spike to prise open his fetters and a woman's gown as a disguise, he became a bloody legend. He'd enjoyed that notoriety, revelled in it, a bit too much if truth be told, for the Newgate cavalry – turnkeys, even the warden himself, on horseback – caught up with him on Finchley Common and back he went to the Whit. He couldn't make that mistake again, no matter what Bess wanted. She'd enjoyed the attention and had wanted to show him off. She'd need to understand that they would have to keep their heads down this time, even get out of London, as he'd been advised.

He climbed over the spikes, managing to haul one off in case he required another tool, and descended a series of steps to the main entrance to the chapel. This was a more formidable prospect than the two previous doors. It boasted an array of bolts and a pair of thick, strong hinges. The box containing the lock was of stout construction and bolted to the door with two iron straps. He hadn't expected this. He'd been penned up with the other prisoners beyond the spikes and had not seen this door.

The bell of St Sepulchre nearby chimed eight of the clock. He had thought it would be later and that gave him some cheer, even though the prospect of breaching this near impregnable door seemed impossible.

Think, Jack, think. You've come too far to give up now.

He gave the lock box a close study. His dub would do him no good – it had no keyhole, for the door was locked from the other side. The Ordinary would do that at the end of the service, a turnkey then sliding home the bolt on the chapel side. The padlock holding that bolt fast certainly opened easily, Jack had it done in moments, but after his exertions he didn't have the strength to prise open the lockbox. He examined the door frame, which was secured by an iron strap from top to bottom. This fillet was in turn held in place by a lock and clasp. He smiled. There was the weak point. He attacked it with his bar and spike and levered it away from the door and the wall, taking the lock with it. That meant he could then manhandle the door itself away from the frame. It took him some time, and a devil of a lot more din, but finally the door hinges gave way and he was able to squeeze through.

He emerged into a walled courtyard below the parapet. Using the open door as a step, he hauled himself up and climbed onto the roof, where he looked across the city. The clip of horses in the streets, the murmur of voices as people passed the walls, some women's laughter and – yes – the distant sound of music, a fiddler, in some tavern on Fleet Street all reached his ears. *Life*, he thought, *freedom*. If he could only reach it. He peered over the parapet to stare at the nearest rooftop a goodly number of feet below.

He took a moment, enjoying the feel of the breeze on his face, though the night was bitter cold. He considered his next step. He could try a leap of faith, but he ran the risk of injuring himself. Even spraining an ankle could prevent him from making an escape. He had to be nimble, he had to be quick if he was to fully regain his liberty. He stared at the black sky, discerned the ripples of clouds. Daylight was still hours away, but he didn't have hours. At any minute Old Baldy could take it into his head to check on the prisoner in The Castle, only to find him gone. He leaned over the edge again, judging the distance. No, he couldn't chance it. He needed something with which he could lower himself down, at least part of the way.

He had one thought, but that would entail returning to his cell, which was something he didn't relish. Obviously, he could be there and back in a much shorter period of time than it had taken him to reach this point, but it was filled with risk. All it would take was a chance meeting with a turnkey and the jig was up. But he couldn't stand here on this rooftop all night, hoping to sprout wings.

Damn it! I doesn't have no choice.

Leaving his iron bar and spike behind, he lowered himself back into the courtyard, returned to the prisoner's chapel, retraced his steps all the way to the Red Room and then down through the floor to The Castle, where he retrieved his blanket. It was a bit threadbare, but he didn't weigh overmuch and he reckoned it would hold him sufficient to allow him to reach maybe halfway down the wall to the roof below. He could drop the rest with little fear of injury.

He allowed himself a wry little chuckle. *I doesn't have no choice. This here blanket has to take my weight and I has to make that leap after all.*

He was recommencing his climb when he heard a movement from the corridor outside. He dropped as silently as he could, threw himself down on the cold floor, pulling his blanket over him, just as he heard the judas hole flip open. Jack lay perfectly still, even snored a little, hoping that Old Baldy would focus on him and not let his eye wander to the exposed brickwork above the fireplace. It was dark in the cell – Jack had no candle or lantern to ward off the night – so he hoped the shadows would be impenetrable from the doorway, especially if Old Baldy had been sitting in a light somewhere. His eyes would not be accustomed to the full dark.

The flap didn't drop back into place. The old bastard was staring at him. Or had he seen the hole in the ceiling or the rubble on the floor? Jack did his best to remain calm, to keep his breathing slow and easy, even though his heart hammered in his breast and every nerve told him he should look up. He dreaded hearing the telltale thud of the heavy key in the lock and the creak of the door swinging open. If Old Baldy entered, then he couldn't fail to see the bricks and the discarded slivers of mortar strewn among the straw on the floor. All Jack's work, all his effort, would have been for naught, simply because he hadn't considered the possibility that he would have to lower himself from the parapet.

Then, blissfully, he heard the flap slide into place and Old Baldy's limping steps disappearing down the corridor.

Jack immediately leaped up, gathered his blanket and scaled the wall to the Red Room, then on through the corridor to the chapel and out to the courtyard and thence onto the parapet.

The fiddle music was slightly more distinct now; perhaps the wind had changed to carry it further. It was a ballad, one about the blind beggar and his beautiful daughter, and Jack hummed along as he thrust the point of the spike as deep as he could into a crevice in the parapet's stonework. He jiggled it a little, testing it. It felt strong enough. At least, he hoped it was. Next, he took the blanket and rolled it lengthwise as tightly as he could, which to his mind should strengthen the weave, then tied one end tightly around the spike. He'd thought of piercing it with the point and then thrusting the spike into the crevice but he feared the material would rip as soon as he applied his weight. He fashioned the best knot possible and tugged. It seemed tight. Again, he hoped it was.

Then he dropped the free end over the side, staring into the gloom to see how far it stretched. About halfway, he judged. He'd have to dangle down as far as he could while clinging to the end and then drop. He should be safe enough, if he didn't crash through the tiles.

He smiled. 'Nothing ventured, nothing gained,' he'd once heard Mr Flynt say, which Jack took to mean, fuck it, let's go for it.

Still humming along to the ballad, he lowered himself over the edge, very carefully, dangling there for a moment, testing the resilience of his makeshift rope. It seemed robust. It should hold for the few seconds it would take him to descend. He eased his body lower, hand over hand, the blisters on his palm from working the bricks free giving him some discomfort, but he'd had worse. The weight of the chains didn't help. His arms and shoulders felt the strain, even though he wasn't a puff-guts by any means, but he'd been boxed up of recent with no means to keep trim. He resolved again to cut back on the ale and pies. He reached the absolute end of the blanket with little trouble, even though his muscles were screaming most vehemently, and once there he glanced down between his feet to ascertain the distance between him and the roof.

And that was when the blanket gave way.

He was surprised, fearful, panicked even at first, but by luck only a few feet separated him from the roof and he landed relatively easily, if lacking in grace, his feet slipping on the damp tiles and landing on his backside. He froze, hoping that the sound of his fall hadn't alerted anyone, but no alarms sounded, no cries from behind him. The blanket had flapped around him and he wrapped it around his shoulders to ward off the night air as he padded towards the far end of the building, where he dropped to lie flat in order to make a study of the street below. Once again, he was too high to jump and his blanket was not anywhere long enough to help him reduce the distance by any great degree, even if he could trust it again. He craned forward a little. All he needed was a window, preferably open and close enough to the roof to allow him to swing inside, and from there he could steal through the house to freedom. He studied the wall below him from left to right.

There!

A garret window, closed, but even from this distance he could see the wood was rotted and flaked. Smiling broadly, and humming along to a more sprightly tune from the fiddler, Jack Sheppard trotted as nimbly as possible, given he still had to carry the chains between his legs, across the tiles to a position above it, looking forward to tupping Bess. He was never too weary for that.

17

James Moncrieff loved his son. He loved his wife. As he sat in an armchair, the most recent edition of the *London Courant* draped unread across his knee, watching Anne play draughts with Alexander, he felt a contented smile drift across his lips. He was happy – happier than he had ever been. He was more than content at home – not for him the philandering of his father – and business was good. No, better than good. Business was booming. He and other members of the Fellowship had made money out of the South Sea situation and continued to profit from its aftermath. They had all sold their interests in it and the other companies early, helping to generate the bust that came with the boom, but that was the way of commerce. He felt little guilt over those who had either seen their fortunes depleted or lost completely, for they should have been more prudent. What mattered was that the Fellowship did not suffer for their incompetence. He had been responsible for ensuring that Sir Robert Walpole did not invest in anything too risky, and that foresight had proved invaluable, for the man was now back in the favour, if not the entire good graces of His Majesty, and was the head of the government. That was where Moncrieff wanted him. That was where the man could, unwittingly to be sure, do the Fellowship service.

Moncrieff had made one tiny misstep by investing, though not a large sum, in Mr Puckle's machine gun. He had been impressed by a demonstration in which the flintlock revolver, mounted upon a tripod, had loosed 63 shots in six minutes. Moncrieff had long since harboured the belief that there would be many a fortune to be made in armaments and their development, and so had interests in various manufacturers. Mr Puckle had failed to impress the Board of Ordnance and, despite Moncrieff's manipulations, the government had decided against ordering the guns and so the design had never reached mass manufacture. As one critic observed, the weapons wounded only those who held shares. Unfortunately, that included Moncrieff, but it was not a loss he bruited abroad. Thankfully, his successes vastly outweighed that singular failure and he remained convinced that the research and production of weaponry was an area that required further exploration. There would always be wars, even if they had to be manufactured. There would always be greed, for riches, for power, for dominion, and he and the Fellowship would ensure they were in a position to profit from it.

Alexander exclaimed with delight as he manoeuvred his draught piece over three of his mother's. Anne smiled at his victory and Moncrieff suspected she was allowing her son to win. He would overlook it, for they were both happy, but that was not a circumstance he could allow to continue. Even though he was not yet seven years of age, the boy had to learn that life didn't let you win; you had to do so by your own efforts and, yes, sometimes that involved cheating. He had inculcated into Alexander that what mattered was family, and that when he grew to be a man he would have to do anything – *anything* – to protect that family and the family name. His own father, also James, had done his best to sully that good name with his dalliances, and Moncrieff had worked hard to remove those multiple blemishes on their escutcheon. That was one of the reasons he hadn't continued the Moncrieff tradition of naming the first-born James. He wanted Alexander to take the family in new directions, as he had done. Managing to obtain the Fellowship's Grand Mastership had been his crowning achievement so far, a feat his father had never achieved, even though it had taken the assassination of anyone who might have opposed his ascension, including the previous Grand Master, Andrew Wilson. Such decisions had not been taken lightly. He thought them necessary for the continuing existence and flourishing of the Fellowship. Wilson had allowed matters to stagnate. Those who supported him had lacked the vision to see that their confederation could truly guide and shape the world, albeit while hiding within the shadows of politicians and monarchs.

A servant glided into the drawing room and whispered a name in his ear. Irritation flared, albeit briefly, for Moncrieff was most comfortable by his fireplace, watching his wife and son in their childish entertainment. He instructed the servant to show the man into his study, then delayed leaving for a few minutes, unwilling to give up this moment of familial bliss in favour of the demands of business.

Finally, he made his apologies, folded the *Courant* under his arm and left the room. In the study, his visitor stood beside the deep turquoise damask curtains, staring out the window towards the garden to the rear of the Jermyn Street house, one hand absently fingering a passementerie tassel. He turned when he heard Moncrieff enter and dropped the tassel as if it were hot.

'What can I do for you, Hawke?' Moncrieff asked, moving behind his desk. He had detested this man's father and was glad to hear he had died. He didn't much like Daniel Hawke either, but he had his uses in the colonies, though of late that utility had been somewhat limited.

'Flynt is in London,' Hawke said.

'Indeed?' he said, feigning a measure of disinterest. 'And how came you by this intelligence?'

'I have my sources, my lord. And I saw him today.'

Moncrieff also had his sources, but he had not been alerted to Flynt's return, which was not only disappointing but also disturbing. Questions would have to be raised.

Hawke told him of his earlier encounter, ending with a demand to know what Moncrieff intended to do about the situation.

Hiding his annoyance at the man's tone, Moncrieff replied, 'What would you have me do?'

'He intends to kill me.'

'So I understand.'

'Are we not bound by Fellowship law to protect each other?'

Hawke referred to an ancient rule of the confederation that Moncrieff had ignored many times in the past when it suited his purpose. Moncrieff didn't like Hawke, but he was efficient. Or at least, he was until his fear of Jonas Flynt got the better of his nerve.

'Have I not protected you thus far? You still breathe, do you not?'

'The man is a murderous devil. He hounded me throughout the colonies. Tortured associates. Killed them. He killed my father.'

Toby Hawke had been loyal, or as loyal as that man could be, to Andrew Wilson. That meant he had to be removed, and some years earlier, Moncrieff had taken the opportunity to prime Flynt against him. The man hadn't let him down. He was a weapon and Moncrieff had used him.

'He would've got me today,' Hawke continued, 'but I was too swift for the son-of-a-bitch.'

'Perhaps we might be best to ship you back to the colonies,' Moncrieff mused.

Hawke shook his head. 'I won't run any more. We have to end this.'

'We?' Moncrieff found this amusing. God knows he had his own history with Flynt, but Hawke's obvious terror of the man was most entertaining.

'My lord,' Hawke said, earnestly, 'I cannot be of use to you as long as that goddamn bastard haunts me. You know the damage he's done to our affairs in the colonies. The carnage he's wrought. I've tried many times to have him killed but each time he confounded me. I called him a devil and I don't speak lightly. We must end this. Now.'

Moncrieff knew how effective Flynt could be. Their history had led him to make attempts on his life and, as with Hawke's efforts, each time the fellow had emerged relatively unscathed. They had reached something of a truce, that would be strengthened by the apparent neutralisation of Nathaniel Charters' Company of Rogues. Hawke, however, was correct. This charade must end, though perhaps not the way Hawke wished.

'I will deal with it,' he said.

'How?'

Unused to being questioned in such a manner, Moncrieff's anger sparked, but he forced himself to retain his composure. 'I will deal with it.'

Hawke must have caught the heavy emphasis but still shook his head in defiance. 'That's not enough. I told you I've tired of running. I won't stand idly by. You may instigate whatever plan you wish but I'll also take steps. I've got my own people here. Perhaps, this time, between us, we'll achieve the desired end.'

Moncrieff bridled at the obvious disrespect but rather than display his rage, he tucked it away. Yes, for the moment he may need this man, for the Fellowship was expanding its interests in the American colonies. It was a vast continent and there were untold riches to be plundered in the interior. Certainly, such expansion would ultimately lead to war with France and Spain, but therein lay further profit. He would not need this man for much longer. Someone else with the knowledge and contacts with the various elements of the New World would soon be found. And when that day came, Daniel Hawke would go the way of his father.

18

Cain was eager to find Swift-Finger Jane to ensure that Knapp had not hurt her, and God help him if he had, for though he'd broken many a heart he never raised his hand to a woman. Well, not unless they liked that form of sexual endeavour. There had been one lady, Scots-born but with a French name, who he'd met in the course of professional competition, who liked to use a form of the Roman flagellum, a short crop with three leather lashes. She liked to slap it against his buttocks while they rutted, and vice versa. Thankfully, she didn't lay the lash too vehemently, apart from one occasion when she raised quite a welt on his cheeks.

He knew he had provided Jane with coin adequate to keep her off the streets for a time, but wasn't certain she would do that. He trawled the taverns and inns of Drury Lane and Fleet Street, avoiding the buttocking shops as he was certain she wouldn't operate out of any of them. He spoke to the innkeepers and any likely cove or bobtail if they had seen her but none had, or they were unwilling to tell him where she was. After all, she was known for her light-fingered tendencies and he could be a cull out for vengeance after having his pocket dipped. In the Cheddar Cheese on the Fleet, one doxy was forthcoming, especially after he dropped a few coins in her palm, and told him that the last time she'd seen her she was with a cull with one wing in a sling. That had been in the early hours of the morning.

'Where were they?' he asked.

'They was heading back to her crib, up the Rookery,' she said.

'Where up the Rookery?'

Suspicious eyes narrowed and only widened when Cain deposited another silver coin in her hand. 'Up Holborn way, a room beside the Seven Stars tavern. You knows of it?'

He knew it. He thanked the doxy for her assistance and headed for Chancery Lane to take him up to Holborn. The doorway leading to the rented rooms was set in a small alcove near to the tavern entrance. It was open and he climbed the remarkably well-kept stairway to the first floor, where the woman had told him Jane kept a room at the back. He paused outside the door, his impulse being to simply open it but he thought, *what would Flynt do?* His friend was certainly not above springing a lock by kicking it, but in this case he would more likely knock. After all, Jane could be entertaining a cull and he wouldn't wish to interrupt commerce.

He rapped against the panel and waited, listening for movement from within. At first there was nothing, but then he heard shuffling footsteps and her voice asking who was there.

'It's me, Jane,' he said.

'Who's me?'

He hesitated. He hadn't given her his name, of course, and he was unwilling to identify himself. He tilted his head closer to the door and spoke as quietly as he could. 'You know me as Paladin.'

A slight gasp and then a key being turned, and the door opened. She was already stepping back, her back to him, into a dimly lit room that seemed clean and tidy, though sparsely furnished. 'What do you want now?'

'To know of your health.'

She still didn't turn. 'My health? Why would you ask that now?'

'Jane –' he took a step forward – 'did you encounter a man called Knapp? With an injured arm.'

'Is that his name? I know him only as that bastard.'

Cain reached out to lay his hand gently on her shoulder. She flinched all the same. 'Did he hurt you?'

She eased herself away from him. 'Of course he hurt me. He said you sent him.'

Cain's teeth gritted. *The little weasel.* 'I didn't. What did he do?'

She turned and for the first time he saw the rage burning in her eyes. 'Do you want to see?' She began to untie the fastenings of her blouse, pulling it apart to reveal the bruises punctuating her pale flesh, some large, some small, some obviously the marks left by a boot. 'This is what he did. He had his pleasure of me and then for payment he punched and kicked me. He said he'd leave my face, for though it weren't too pretty, he said, it wouldn't do for me to have it marred. He said he was having consideration of my profession.' Her laugh was sharp and bitter. '"Consideration", he said, even while he was laying in at me.' She coughed and moaned, doubling over as she headed for the small straw bed in the corner of the room. Cain proffered a helping hand but she waved it away. 'I doesn't need your help, Paladin, or Cain as he named you. It's your help what has got me in this state in the first place.'

Anger tightened Cain's jaw further. Flynt had been correct. He'd landed this woman in all sorts of trouble. 'I promise I'll make him pay, Jane.'

She laid herself down gingerly, closed her eyes. 'Just go. Just go. You'll hurt him, he'll come back and hurt me, or his friends will.'

'He won't come back, I can assure you.'

She sighed. 'You must do as you wish. You're a man, you will always do as you wish. You did it last night, he did it this morning. Men get what they want and women provide it, whether willing or no.' She began to weep. 'Just go, I beseech you.'

Cain stared at her for a time, unsure what to do. That in itself was a new sensation for him, for he was always so certain as to what step he would take next. But this was different. His conscience was troubled, and that was also a fresh experience for him. At one time, if anyone had asked him if he worried over any of his actions, he would have laughed. Gabriel Cain cared naught for consequences. Even when he recruited Jane the night before, even when he sent her into that alley, he had not considered there would be repercussions. Granted, he had little intention of letting those two rogues escape with their lives, and he later became aware that Griffin was tailing him, but even with that in mind, he had not thought of the ramifications. Now he did.

Christ in heaven, Jonas, you have infected me with something I know not how to handle.

He opened his mouth to speak but no words came. He considered saying he was sorry for what he had brought upon her, but he knew it would be insufficient. He walked back to the door, tarried at a dresser beside it and surreptitiously laid a pouch of coin upon it.

He left without looking back, his chest pierced by a pain he'd never known before. He relieved it by deciding to wreak revenge on Knapp at the first opportunity.

19

Flynt had resolved to find Colonel Charters, but he was not at what was once his usual haunt – White's in Chesterfield Street – nor his home. Perhaps he was paying attention to one of his woman friends for, like Cain, he was fond of the tup and was no respecter of the marital bed. For both men, not to mention the ladies in question, a husband away from home was an ideal opportunity for carnal release. If Charters was indulging in such activity, he could be anywhere apart from the home of the object of his desire at that moment, for walls have ears.

Having no clue as to where he could seek him next, Flynt decided to return to his room at the Golden Cross. Perhaps he would sleep. More likely not.

Too many faces. Too many deaths. Too much blood. Too much loss.

He took off his greatcoat, laid his pistols on the bed beside him and stretched out, as before still fully clothed and wearing his boots. He closed his eyes, his mind on Jack, feeling he had failed the boy. He'd often used his larcenous skills to his own ends, but he'd also tried to protect him, to steer him as much as he could away from the crooked path upon which he'd walked since he was a mere child. Flynt had always suspected that he was destined for Tyburn sooner or later and that prediction had clearly proved correct. Nevertheless, when Jack had first told him that he was working with Blueskin Blake, and therefore for Jonathan Wild, Flynt had cut him off. He shouldn't have done that. He should have stuck by him, but Flynt soon had pressures of his own to deal with that had taken him thousands of miles across the world to the Caribbean. The last time he'd seen him was in St Martin's Lane, when Blueskin had again shown himself to be a somewhat complex individual by coming to Flynt's aid. That was when Flynt, knowing he was leaving the country, had elicited a promise from him that he would look after the boy, and Blake agreed. Flynt thought he'd done the right thing. Now he wasn't so sure. On that occasion, he hadn't spoken to Jack and that pained him now.

The knock on the door was tentative, but Flynt still instinctively reached for his pistols. He knew that anyone who wished him ill would not have knocked, but old habits die hard. It was possible that it might be Mrs Wilkes, so he hid one weapon behind his back, the other concealed by the door as he opened it.

It wasn't his landlady. It wasn't anyone who wished him harm. Nonetheless, he felt a stab of pain when he gazed upon her.

'Hello, Jonas,' Belle St Clair said, drawing back the hood of her cape.

Flynt was not a man easily taken aback, but he was. He stared at her, as usual rendered near breathless by her beauty. Her skin was flawless, her curled black hair long but pinned up on top of her head. Her black cape was of velvet with fur lining and was framed over a mantua of fine satin with lace embroidery. In her hand was a fur muff, for the night was chill.

Her eyes dropped to the pistol that had now appeared unbidden from behind his back.

'You are expecting someone else?' she said, her eyes dancing with humour.

He glanced at the weapon and laid it and its twin on the sideboard beside the door, giving her a sheepish smile. 'Always,' he said, stepping back to let her enter. She hesitated for a moment, then stepped over the threshold. Flynt glanced up and down the corridor.

'You came alone?'

'I have a servant with me who waits in the carriage below.' Belle surveyed the room. 'As spartan as ever, Jonas.'

He closed the door. 'It suits my needs.'

'Your needs are few, clearly.'

He felt awkward, still not sure what to say. At one point they had both come to think there might be some kind of future for them. The arrival of a face from his past ended any such hopes. And then he had left the country.

They regarded each other in silence for a moment or two. 'You've changed,' she said, finally.

'So I've heard,' he said.

'You look...' She hesitated.

'Tired?' he offered. 'Older?'

'Lost,' she said finally.

He could think of no way to respond, so instead he asked, 'How did you know I had returned?'

'Jerome caught sight of you lurking in the shadows of the piazza.'

He had seen Jerome pause as he closed the door to the house. He should have known he would have spotted him. Perhaps he had wished to be seen.

'I understand you no longer live in Mother Grady's house,' he said.

Her gaze dropped a little. 'No, she died. Did you know?'

'I heard. I'm sorry.'

A slight shrug. 'It was the winter after you left. Without her, I felt the house was... oppressive.'

'So you went into high keeping.'

She raised her eyes again and her old defiance returned. 'Yes. Sadie took over the day-to-day running of the house. She is extremely competent. Godfrey had been most attentive following Mary's death. He made the offer of setting me up in new apartments and I accepted.'

'Godfrey being Lord Southern?'

She regarded him quizzically. 'You know him?'

He shook his head.

She understood. 'You've been making inquiries about me?'

He didn't reply, but he didn't need to. She would know the truth. 'He's married, I understand.'

'He is.' Again, she sported a tone that invited challenge. 'His wife remains on his Buckinghamshire estate. She doesn't like London.'

She was daring him to make some kind of judgement, but he had no intention of doing any such thing. However, she seemed to take his brief silence as some kind of comment.

'The arrangement suits me,' she said defensively. His lack of response seemed to irritate her. A sigh escaped her as she wandered around the small room. 'How long have you been back in London?'

'Three days,' he said.

'Why did you return?'

'I have business in London.'

'What sort of business?'

Once again, he didn't reply. He could have lied, concocted some pretence, but he didn't wish to do that. Not with her. She must have discerned something in his silence that told her not to press further, for she nodded as if he had responded. Even after all these years apart, she knew him well.

'How long will you remain?'

'Until my business is concluded.'

'And then?'

That was something he didn't know. He'd left with Billy Bones a letter to be opened if he had not returned to Port Glasgow within a month. In it he'd instructed him to sail the *Walrus* back to the West Indies. He'd also included a map detailing where he'd hidden the fortune he'd plundered from pirates over the years, his garnish for the work, to be dispersed to the crew when Mr Bones saw fit. The remainder of the booty had already been handed over to the various colonial governments. He trusted Mr Bones implicitly, more so even than Barbecue, who remained young and somewhat headstrong at times. Billy Bones would make a fine captain of the ship if the crew elected him as such, and there was no reason why they shouldn't.

'Then I shall see which way the wind blows,' he said.

'That is always the way with you, is it not?'

Again, he had no response to make, for there was truth in what she said.

'I heard of your son,' she said, softly.

He blinked away the memory of young Jonas dying. 'Gabriel, I take it?'

'Yes. I'm so very sorry, Jonas.'

He turned away so she could not see the tears that stung at his eyes. He had long since given up trying to understand this grief, for he had known the boy for such a very short time. In fact, he'd hardly known him at all. And yet, the very mention of him brought back the memory of that shack on the beach and the man with a pistol in his hand and Flynt unable to do anything to save the boy.

'Thank you,' he said, his voice hoarse.

She reached out and touched his arm. The feel of her fingers was both pleasurable and painful. 'Will you see Cassie?'

'I don't think so.'

'Why not?'

He shook his head. What could he say? That he had caused her enough pain, enough loss? That seeing her only heightened his own?

He didn't understand his feelings. He didn't even try. They just existed and he had to cope with them.

Thankfully, she didn't pursue it. She turned away from him, looked for somewhere to sit, rejected the single wooden chair that had seen better days some time around the Great Flood and positioned herself on his bed. There was nothing inviting about the movement. Those days were over. 'Do you wonder why I came, Jonas?'

'Of course.'

'I wished to see you.' She waited for him to say something. 'I missed you.'

'And I you.' The words came easily. He couldn't tell whether it was because they were what was expected of him or because he meant them. Flynt had never been sure of his own feelings and that had not changed with the passage of time. He had thought he loved this woman, but had left her when Cassie had shown up with a plea to help Gideon, his father. He thought he had loved Cassie, but he had deserted her in search of adventure. He hadn't known he'd had a son for many years, and when he lost him he was stricken with rage and grief that had led to him spilling blood. Flynt believed he had a firm understanding of the way of the world, but very little of himself.

They found themselves in an increasingly awkward silence. Flynt could think of nothing to say and wondered if Belle experienced similar. Her eyes moved towards the pistols on the sideboard and a tiny smile began.

'You still have Tact and Diplomacy, I see,' she said.

'They have served me well.'

'They are mere tools, Jonas. It's you who wields them expertly.' She paused, as if considering her next words. 'Will you be wielding them while you are here?'

He contemplated a lie, but she would know it as soon as it left his lips. 'Very likely.'

'This business you speak of demands it?'

'It does.'

'Is it for Colonel Charters?'

Belle and the colonel had met shortly before Flynt left and he had been forced to tell her something of his work for him.

'No,' he said, 'it's personal.'

'You seek Daniel Hawke.'

It wasn't a question. He couldn't disguise his surprise. 'You know of him?'

'Gabriel mentioned him. He is in London?'

Flynt wished to know further of her knowledge of Hawke, but he elected not to pursue it. 'That's my information.'

'And when you find him, you will kill him?'

'That's my intention.'

'You blame him for the death of Jonas.'

'Yes.'

'You seek revenge.'

'I seek justice.'

'Your form of justice.'

'My form of justice is the only one open to me.'

'What about the courts?'

'The courts cannot assist me. Hawke has friends in high places.'

'That's not why you don't pursue it through the courts, though. You want to be judge and executioner.'

'I believe I deserve to be.'

She rose from the bed to stand before him again, her eyes searching his face. 'I said you look lost and I meant it. Revenge has a way of eating at a man, and you have been allowing it to feast for too long.'

'Hawke deserves to die.'

'Only God can declare that with any certainty. You are not He, Jonas.'

'The man with the gun is God. I intend to be that man.'

'And if the situation is reversed?'

'Then I will discover if there truly is a heaven.' He paused, reflected for a beat. 'Or a hell.'

She took that in with a blink. 'Jonas, do you still have feelings for me?' When words failed him momentarily, she jumped back in. 'I don't mean love. We had our moment and we let it slip through our fingers. I loved you, I believe you loved me – in your way, at least – but time and circumstance have a way of making mockery of love. What I ask is if you care about me, about my feelings?'

'I do,' he said, this time without hesitation.

'Then do this for me. Cease this pursuit of revenge before it's too late. Before you are lost completely.'

'I'll do what has to be done. You know me. You know I will always do that.'

'You will not at least consider it?'

'There's nothing to consider. Dan Hawke will pay for his crimes, and his crimes are legion, please believe me.'

She searched his face, looking for any sign of lack of resolve, he thought, but knew she would find none. Tears filled her eyes as she stepped back.

'Or you will pay for yours,' she said. 'For yours also are legion.'

Belle always had a way of striking at him with the truth.

'Is this why you came to see me?' he asked, feeling slightly defensive. 'To dissuade me from my mission?'

'I came to see you because I wished to see you. But also, I came in the hope that I would make you see sense. You are too much the gambler. You have cheated death so often and now you are playing against the odds. One day you will lose.' Tears surged and she wiped them away with the fingers of one hand. 'This will be the final time you will see me. I cannot be around a man who is intent on seeking his own death. Life is too precious to throw away. Mother Grady knew that in her final days. She regretted much. She didn't regret the things she had done but rather the things she hadn't. She had wished to have a child but never had.'

'You became her daughter.'

Belle accepted that with an inclination of her head. 'My point is that you regret both what you have done and what you have failed to do.'

Again, she wielded the truth like a weapon.

'Perhaps it's time to bring a halt to the cycle of death that surrounds you. Only you can do it. Forget this man Hawke. Forget this pursuit of revenge. It will not bring your son back. It will not bring Cassie back.'

He swallowed hard. 'And if I do abandon my quest, will that bring you back?'

'I can't be a replacement for another.' Her sigh was heartbreaking as she reached for the door. 'You're not the only one who is lost, Jonas.'

Before he could say anything further, she left. Her footsteps receded down the corridor but he didn't follow. Sadness weighed heavily upon his shoulders and he slumped against the frame. She had said that he might pay for his crimes. He knew he already had.

20

Flynt was at a breakfast of eggs and coffee in the Golden Cross when he heard from Mrs Wilkes of Jack's escape. She had been most put out when he had left the previous morning without anything in his stomach, and this time she told him that he would not set foot outside the hotel without something hot. She steered him into the small private room she kept aside for special guests and warned him that, should he make any move to leave, she would brain him with the toasting fork she had in her hand.

'He's a proper knacky little scamp, is that Jack Sheppard,' she said, her voice filled with admiration for his ingenuity as she toasted a slice of bread before the fire. 'I mean, I knows he be an unashamed fingersmith and the hemp be a-growing for him down Tyburn way, but Mr Flynt, to escape four times, and twice from Newgate, that is most impressive.'

She outlined what she knew of the escape. Flynt had to agree that Jack's achievement was indeed impressive, but then when someone is properly motivated – and the prospect of what lay ahead at Tyburn was nothing if not motivation – then very little was impossible, even escaping Newgate. He had intended to find a way to break him free, but it seemed Bess had been correct: Jack didn't need his help. Not for the first time he was amazed at the young man's ingenuity. He had thought him too well bound to make egress from that room but, somehow, Jack had managed it.

Good lad.

He smiled, pleased that the lad was breathing free air again, but it was tinged with sadness, knowing that unless he changed his ways he would not be long at liberty. He resolved to do what he could to help him amend his lifestyle. He would also have further words with the man whose use of him he suspected had placed Jack in Newgate's shadow.

Two slices of bread expertly browned and set before him with some scrambled eggs and cheese, his landlady went off to see to other guests of the inn, with a further stern warning that if he didn't eat every crumb then the toasting fork remained an option. He did as he was told, for he had again not slept well, his night terrors this time interspersed with his regrets over failing Belle. He would not get through the day without fuel. He was sipping a second dish of coffee, when Mrs Wilkes poked her head around the door.

'Is you accepting visitors, Mr Flynt?'

He popped a thickly buttered square of toast into his mouth. 'That depends upon who it is, Mrs Wilkes.'

'A tall cove, decent togs, no gentleman by his voice but polite all the same. It was all "if you please, ma'am, and thank you". He didn't give no name, just asked if it were convenient to see you.'

'Armed?'

'Weren't apparent if he was, but I'd hazard by his look and manner that he don't got no Bible tucked away. Shall I send him away?'

Flynt drank some more coffee, considering his response. He was intrigued as to who this man was. He could have been despatched by Jonathan Wild, who might suspect him of having aided Jack in his escape. However, his men usually worked in pairs and would not have been so courteous. Subtlety and manners were not strong points among the Thieftaker General's men. Similarly, if Daniel Hawke or his friends in the Fellowship had sent him – and such was possible, for his return was obviously no secret – the visitor would also not be alone and would not ask politely. There would have been at least two, but probably more, and they would have burst in or lurked in ambush outside. However, he had long since learned that in order to take command of a situation you must first dictate the circumstances. A man arriving at his lodgings and asking for an audience, no matter how courteous he may be, was not something to be taken lightly, given the number of men who might wish him harm. Should this gentleman have mayhem in mind, then Flynt would not wish violence to erupt within Mrs Wilkes' walls.

'Where is he?' he asked.

'He be in the tavern at present.'

Good, he thought, he could work with that. He swallowed the final morsel of toast, generating an approving nod from Mrs Wilkes, washed it down with a mouthful of coffee, then rose. He picked up Tact and Diplomacy from where they rested on the tabletop, thrust them into his belt under his coat, and grasped his silver cane.

'Be so good as to delay returning to him for a few minutes, will you?' he said. 'I'll exit through the kitchens. Then please tell him that I've left for the day and you know not where I'm headed.'

She nodded and ducked away. Mrs Wilkes knew better than to ask any questions. Flynt forked up the last few fragments of his scrambled eggs; his landlady being most skilled with butter, milk and a dash of herbs, it would be a grievous sin to waste her efforts. He wiped his mouth on a linen cloth, then placed his hat on his head and peered around the door to ensure that no strangers lurked in the corridor. From there it was but a matter of moments before he had dashed through the kitchen and into the courtyard at the rear, where a coach was preparing to leave. He followed it through the archway that led out onto the street, opposite the buttocks of the statue of the first King Charles astride his horse as if preparing to charge down Whitehall to reclaim his throne and his head. There were those who said that the Golden Cross coaching inn stood at the arse end of Charing Cross, thanks to that edifice's positioning, but Flynt felt that unfair. The establishment was far from fancy but it was a comfortable enough place to lodge.

The coach clattered onto the thoroughfare but Flynt lingered in the shadow of the archway, leaning against the wall, his thumbs hooked in his belt close to where his pistols nestled. The morning air was damp and, peering at the skies from under the archway, Flynt saw the clouds were dark and full-bellied with rain. Having grown used to the warmer climes of the colonial Americas, it had taken him a few days during his journey to London from Port Glasgow to once again accustom himself to the dank cold of Britain. He had experienced storms in the islands that would have horrified the average Londoner, with winds and rain the creation of which, were he of a religious bent, he might have attributed to a vengeful god. His years at sea had taught him to recognise when such storms were imminent and as he studied the billowed clouds, he sensed something more than rain in the air. There was a storm coming to London.

Mrs Wilkes followed his instruction perfectly, for he waited only a few minutes before the man exited the inn from its main door and walked by the opening to the archway. When Flynt saw his face, he relaxed considerably.

'How can I help you, Jacob?'

Flynt's voice startled him, for Charters' man whirled, reaching for a pistol under his coat before his expression softened into something humorous. He immediately pulled away from the pistol butt and raised the hand in peace. Flynt's own hands hadn't moved.

'I should've expected this, Mr Flynt.'

Flynt stepped closer, knowing there was no threat. 'Such matters are not your business, Jacob.' The man had been a soldier, and was well able to look after himself, but the ways of surviving in the flash world were not within his skill set. 'What do you wish of me?'

'The colonel requests your presence.'

Flynt had already intimated to Jacob that he wished to speak with Charters, but he still asked, 'Why?'

Jacob grinned. 'With the colonel, there's always something to discuss. You should know that, Mr Flynt.'

Flynt returned the smile. There was generally more going on with Charters than appeared on the surface, though his allegiance to Walpole had given Flynt cause to believe that he had been outsmarted by his own greed. 'And if I refuse, I assume you've been ordered to convey me by force?'

'Not at all, Mr Flynt. The invitation is extended, and should you wish to refuse, then I'll be on my way. There's no suggestion that I compel you and, speaking most frank, I wouldn't presume to even try.'

That was true. Had Charters wished to force Flynt to attend the meeting, he would not have sent Jacob. Flynt liked the man. That he had been sent to deliver the invitation was a first, and Flynt sensed there was a good reason behind it.

'Then lead on, Jacob,' he said, with a flourish of his hand. 'It doesn't do to keep the colonel waiting.'

21

Jack couldn't keep warm. The blanket had warded off a certain amount of the night cold, but even now that he was safe in a room that Bess had found in St Giles, a fire in the grate, he still failed to burn the chill from his bones. He'd reached the street without arousing the occupants of the house, for in addition to being nimble of finger, he was also silent of foot when he had to be. He had moved swiftly to put distance between him and the prison, keeping away from busy thoroughfares, dodging down the alleys and back streets he knew so well, hiding when a figure approached or a wheel rumbled his way.

Bess had told him where she'd rented this room in a lane off Carrier Street and he'd reached it long before daybreak. It was on the top floor of a tenement so decrepit that it looked in danger of tumbling down, which was not unknown in this vicinity. To reach it you had to penetrate to the heart of the Rookery and walk a street that even he hadn't been in more than once. The room wasn't large but they had it to themselves, which must have cost Bess a pretty penny because normally it would have housed up to eight people, all crammed into the rickety bed in the corner, or sleeping on the floor. It didn't have any windows, the two that had once allowed entry to at least some daylight having been covered over some time previously to avoid the window tax. He didn't ask how she raised the bunce to pay rent because he knew. She'd done it the only way she knew how. He didn't much like her walking the flesh markets or working the taverns for coin, but they needed a safe crib for him to stay out of sight for a time. With all the jobs he'd pulled, all the purses and pouches he'd dipped, they should have been well flush, but try as he might he never could seem to hang on to the bunce. It flew from his fingers as fast as those fingers could lift it. Blueskin said he was too generous. He'd stand anyone a drink or a meal. He'd gamble without caution. But most of all, he bought Bess clothes and jewellery, the latter being sold or pawned when they were on the flat again, which was always pretty quickly, boom always leading to bust.

You is too proflergate on that doxy's behalf, Blueskin used to say, using a word Jack didn't recognise but one he took to mean too generous.

Can't help it, Jack would say, *I loves her.*

And old Blueskin, he'd laugh and tell him he was soft in the head.

It was the truth, though. He couldn't help himself, not when it came to Bess. She had been cool with him at first, years ago, but once he had grown some and had bunce to spend she had warmed to him most considerable. He knew what she was. Knew she looked out for herself first. But he didn't mind. In this life you have to look out for yourself. Even so, he loved her.

Bess gave the glowing logs a poke with a metal bar, which she then propped up against the wooden fireplace, before giving the contents of the iron pot she had heating over the flames a stir. The sky parlour was small, with a rickety cot in the corner and one chair, in which Jack shivered. It was safe, though. Bess was certain nobody would look for him here – not immediate, anyway.

She ladled some of the stew into a wooden bowl and carried it to him, steam rising from it like mist.

'This'll heat up your bones, my love,' she said. 'You'll soon be back feeling plump current.'

Jack reached out with a shaking hand to take the bowl and the spoon. He didn't feel like he'd ever be back to proper health again. Gawd, the effort of escape had certainly drained the life out of him. He hadn't been fed at all properly in Newgate, even though Bess had told him she'd given Old Baldy considerable garnish to ensure he received extra victuals. Either that skin-domed bastard had pocketed it or…

He didn't want to think about the other option. He loved her too much to believe she'd lie.

The stew was thick with vegetables and beef. He savoured it, enjoying the heat and the sensation of the meat on his tongue. It had been a while since he'd had some beef and this was a good cut, he could tell. She had obviously enjoyed good fortune at the earning.

'Good, ain't it?' Bess said, her eyes dancing. 'Made it my own self.'

He nodded, spooning more into his mouth.

She knelt in front of him, rubbing her hands around his ankles and calves where the fetters had chafed the skin. She'd had hammer and chisel waiting for him and it hadn't taken much effort to free them. Her hands moved up to his thighs. 'You is the talk of the streets, my love. Proper famous you is. A bleeding legend.'

He didn't feel much like a legend. He felt like death.

Her hands edged towards his groin. 'We'll get you back on your feet soon and you can get working again. There's a big city out there and it's ripe for the picking. Blueskin's gone, or soon will be, but there will be many a cove what wants to partner up to the famous Jack Sheppard.'

Pain shafted him at the thought of Blueskin in Newgate. 'I needs to lay low a time, Bess.'

'Of course, a few days most certain, get your strength back.' Her fingers were stroking his roger now and she smiled. 'Though something seems to be back to normal already.'

Despite the pleasure warming his groin and belly, he grabbed her hand and pulled it away. 'We need to leave London, Bess.'

She grimaced. 'Leave London? And go where?'

'Anywhere. The north, out west. Scotland maybe—'

'Scotland? What the hell would we do in Itchland?'

'I don't know, but things is too hot here. We need to get away, start fresh. Maybe go straight.'

She struggled to comprehend what he was suggesting. 'Give up the life? Jack, it's all we've ever known, you and me. What would you do for bunce? Go into service? Become a draper?'

'I thought perhaps working the wood. I had a decent apprenticeship under Mr Owen.'

Bess dismissed this with a plosive noise. 'And what would I do? I doesn't see myself as the type to be keeping house.'

Jack averted his eyes for a moment, feeling as if he'd wandered into some kind of foreign country. He and Bess had never discussed the future. It had always been a short life and a merry one, as he'd said to Mr Flynt. But while he sat in the Whit this time around he'd been thinking about the future.

'I don't know, Bess,' he said. 'I thought, well… maybe we'd have a chit or two and—'

Bess's laugh was like an explosive bark as she stood up. 'Chits! Jack, have you got the Bedlam sickness? You lost your reason? Do you see me as a loving mother? I mean, do you?' She knelt again, began to stroke his thighs once more. 'Jack, this is all a fantasy. Folks like you and me, we don't walk the straight. We lie and we steal and we enjoys what little life there is given to us. You're Jack Sheppard, you're Jack the Lad, cock of the walk. Your name is on everybody's lips right now.'

'Aye,' he said, bitterly, 'including Jonathan Wild, who will move heaven and earth to track me down. That's why we need to leave London, Bess.'

'He will forget you and move on. You can make it up with him by getting out there on the rob. A crack lay, a low toby, a foyst or two what comes up with a sturdy purse, give him his garnish and he will welcome you back in the fold.'

'No, Bess, it's too late for that. He's taken me into a dislike most severe and he won't stop until he sees me on the drop.'

She ceased her ministrations and sat back to stare at him. 'What did you do to him that he hates you so?'

Jack couldn't tell her about being approached by a man with only one wing he'd seen Mr Flynt with on occasion, who said his name was Colonel Nathaniel Charters and offered him a bag of cash to do a service for his country.

I ain't joining no regiment, he'd said, and the colonel had laughed.

Not a regiment, lad, he'd said, *but a company.*

Jack's knowledge of companies was of fat businessmen who thought only of profit, but the one-armed colonel said that a company could also be a collection of individuals who join in a common purpose. This particular company was made of people like Jack, but he would never meet the others, for there was safety in such subterfuge.

And how would I be in service to England with such a company?

I understand you recently did some work for Mr Jonathan Wild in regard to the gentleman of the docklands known as the Admiral, said the colonel.

Jack had been tasked by Wild to glean intelligence concerning the Admiral's operations on the waterside, for the Thieftaker General had cast hungry eyes on the coin to be made there. In the end, Jack didn't learn much.

Nonetheless, lad, the colonel said, *I would have you do similar for me. But this time, the object of your study will be Jonathan Wild…*

'I doesn't know why Wild has taken against me,' he lied, 'but he has. I should've listened to Mr Flynt, for he warned me about falling in with the Thieftaker and his lot.'

Her disdain when he said Mr Flynt's name was very evident. 'Him. He's the cause of all your troubles.'

'No, Bess, I'm the cause of all my troubles. That and life on the streets. Mr Flynt tried to help me.'

'He was at the using of you, and you bloody well know it.'

He shook his head. 'No...' He reassessed for a moment. 'Well, yes, but he give me coin and protection. And he did his best to put me on the straight.'

'He's a bastard and anything he did, it was to his own benefit.' A sly squint crept into her eyes. 'But he won't be doing that no more, I've seen to that.'

Jack felt alarm jingle through his body. 'What has you done, Bess?'

'Let's just say he shouldn't've showed his mug back here.'

Jack gripped her by the upper arms so tightly that she cried out and tried to break free. 'What has you done, girl?'

She jerked in his grip. 'Get off—'

He held tight. 'Bess, tell me what you has done.'

She glared at him with defiance. 'I done what had to be done. He ain't no good for you, Jack—'

His anger snapped. 'Bess, for Gawd's sake...'

'There's people what wanted to know when he returned.'

'What people?'

'I don't know. Not English, though they spoke it. I thought they was coves looking for a double-up tup but they wasn't. They said they knowed I was acquainted with Jonas Flynt and I said acquainted ain't the word, cursed is what I'd say, and that seemed to please them, for they said in that case I wouldn't be against letting them know if I ever sees him on the streets again, and I said that he was in foreign parts and they said they thought he'd return. They give me an address to drop a word to. Send a messenger, they said, and tell him to inform whoever opens the door that the wanderer has returned.'

'And you did this?'

She looked proud of herself. 'They give me some sovereigns with the promise of more if I sees him. There weren't no way I was going to risk not getting my bunce, Jack, so I delivered the message my own self yesterday after I seen Flynt and that bastard Cain in the White Lion.'

He couldn't believe she had done this. 'Bess, you don't know what damage you might've done!'

'I doesn't know and I doesn't care. I doesn't owe Flynt nothing, and neither do you. I mean, how the hell does you think I got the bunce to pay for this place, and that there beef you has been savouring over so much? Because let me tell you, business was slow. You'd think the taverns was filled with them eunuchs, given how often I was declined.'

He threw off his blanket and struggled to his feet, almost knocking her down.

'Where you going?' she demanded.

'Where the hell do you think?' he said, looking around for something warm to wrap himself in, spotting an old coat of his that Bess had obviously retrieved from a previous lodgings.

'You ain't in no fit state to go gallivanting.'

He pulled on the coat. 'I've got to warn Mr Flynt.' He pulled open the door. 'You might have killed him, Bess.'

'And good riddance, is what I says.' She followed him, stood in the open doorway and yelled after him as he descended the stairs. 'I hope they gets him, I really does. I hope he rots in hell, the bastard.'

22

Colonel Charters awaited in the upstairs room of the Black Lion, where they had often met. The tables from the previous night's gaming remained, some still with empty wine glasses waiting to be taken away. On the windowsills plates of uneaten food had been discarded. The room retained the ghost of pipe smoke, liquor and of sweat.

The rain had begun just as Flynt and Jacob reached the tavern on Drury Lane and spat at the grimy windows as if trying to clean them. As he had done so often before, Charters stood in front of the fire that spread welcome warmth through the cold room. He was resplendent in his old army uniform, his empty arm pinned to the shoulder like a badge of honour. He'd lost it not in battle against the enemy but in a struggle with a deranged English soldier while the hell of Malplaquet raged all around them. The soldier had been a full-blooded killer, so Flynt conceded that there truly was honour in it, even though the man escaped. Still, he hadn't seen Charters in uniform since they'd left Flanders.

Charters observed Flynt's noting of the uniform. 'Officers' reunion,' he explained, his voice gruff.

'You wished to see me,' Flynt said, his voice deliberately cold.

Charters caught the tone and gave him a sharp look. 'Unclench, Serjeant. We're all friends here.'

'Really?' Flynt said, doubtfully.

'Yes, really,' Charters said, waving towards a tin coffee pot on the centre table, with three deep dishes waiting to be filled. 'Help yourself to coffee. It's hot.'

Flynt did, more to have something to do other than glare at his former commanding officer. He turned to Jacob, standing by the door, and raised the pot up in a wordless query. Jacob declined. Flynt made a point of pouring one dish only, then took a seat and sipped the thick black beverage. Charters had been correct about one thing: it was hot.

Charters noted the lack of courtesy with a slight grimace and poured himself a coffee, then carried it to the fireplace. The rain was gathering in strength, the individual drops that had earlier spattered the windowpanes now growing into a deluge.

'I have things to do, Colonel, so I'd appreciate you getting to the point,' Flynt said, even though he was glad to be indoors.

A sigh. 'Always so irritable,' Charters said. 'And irritating.'

'Forgive me, but my patience is thin with a man who has allowed himself to be used by the people he is duty-bound to oppose.'

'And also so very gullible.' Charters turned to face him. 'Do you think so little of me that you believe I would allow myself to be so used?'

'So you didn't lose money in the South Sea Company debacle?'

'I did, many people did, but not quite so much as I made out.'

'And Walpole didn't come to your aid?'

'He did. He assisted many afterwards, even some of his political enemies. Of course, some of them are no longer in government.'

'Then you are beholden to him.'

'I am.'

'And he is the Fellowship's man in the government?'

'Not necessarily,' Charters said, sipping his coffee.

Flynt grew exasperated. 'James Moncrieff was, probably still is, his secretary. James Moncrieff is also the Grand Master of the Fellowship.'

'Both true.'

'He'll be manipulating Walpole to the Fellowship's end.'

'Very likely.'

'And Walpole has ordered you to cease any investigation into them, correct?'

'Quite correct.'

'Which you have done.'

A sly smile grew behind the lip of the dish Charters held to his mouth. 'On the face of it.'

'What does that mean?'

'It means that merely because I say I have done a thing, it does not necessarily follow that I have. You should know me better than that, Flynt.'

'So you haven't backed off from the Fellowship?'

'I have not. My investigations of its activities have merely ducked more *sub rosa* than previously.'

Flynt was unsure whether to believe him. Charters could be so devious that his single hand often knew not what it was doing. 'So deeply *sub rosa* that Walpole knows nothing of it?'

'That is also correct.'

'You don't trust him, then? You think him fully under Moncrieff's control?'

'Canny politician that he is, I believe him to be credulous in that regard.'

Flynt watched Charters' expression carefully, seeking the first sign of evasion or falsehood. He saw none, but then the colonel was a master of deception. 'So you believe him to be… what? An innocent dupe?'

Charters' lips twitched. 'As innocent a dupe as any politician can be with the heady scent of self-advancement strong within his nostrils. But he is not of the Fellowship, if that's what you ask, and there remains the possibility that he is, in fact, well aware of what they are and is using them to his own ends.'

'If he is, then he makes the mistake of any man who believes he can control the devil, for the devil will control him.'

This amused Charters. 'You have taken on a spiritual bent in your years away, Flynt.'

'I have met many devils, Colonel,' Flynt said pointedly. 'None were immune to a pistol ball.'

Charters let that lie between them. A wind had grown and rattled the casements, looking for access, finding the chimney and sneaking into the room under cover of a puff of smoke.

Flynt said, 'If all this is true, then why not tell me this before?'

Charters shot a glance towards Jacob, then returned to the table, setting his coffee dish down before he settled in a chair in front of Flynt. 'I believe the Fellowship has someone within my orbit. Perhaps within my household. Perhaps within the Company of Rogues itself.'

Flynt recalled Jacob's suspicious look at the servant climbing the stairs at Charters' home. 'A spy?'

'Yes.'

'Who?'

'That I do not know.'

Flynt considered this. 'Why didn't you mention this when we spoke before?'

'At present the only people I can trust are Jacob and you.'

The colonel's tone was pointed. That meant he mistrusted Cain.

'I'm flattered,' Flynt said.

'Don't be. My faith in you stems only from the fact that you have been abroad for years and you have angered the Fellowship with your activities.'

'How do you know that someone informs against you?'

'I have my own spies within the organisation. They report back to me.'

That didn't surprise Flynt at all. However, he still harboured suspicions as to Charters' motivations. This suggestion of a Fellowship spy who had burrowed into Charters' secret world could merely be a blind to obscure his own capitulation to Walpole. 'Why do you tell me this?'

'I need your help.'

'What manner of help?'

Charters paused to pour himself another dish of coffee, offering Flynt a refill, which he refused. He sensed such civility was merely a means of delaying his reply. Charters sat back in his chair and his gaze rested on Flynt.

'Do you agree that the Fellowship is a danger to this country?'

'It matters nothing to me now.'

'But do you agree?'

'Whether I agree or disagree, they are no longer my concern.'

'They intend to rule the rulers through economic manipulation,' Charters persisted. 'God knows our world is far from democratic, but they would eventually remove all checks and balances. And that is why it is vitally important that we break them.'

'As I said, it matters little to me now.'

'You have disrupted their commerce in the Americas.'

'Inadvertently. Again, Colonel, what is it you wish of me?'

Another pause. 'I wish you to curtail this vendetta of yours.'

Flynt shook his head. 'I will not.'

A sigh as Charters leaned forward, pushed his coffee away and splayed his single hand on the tabletop. 'Serjeant,' he began, then amended. 'Jonas, please hear me. This quest will end badly. Such quests always do. You have committed many questionable acts in the past—'

'Often on your orders.'

Charters accepted that. 'It is a fact that in the protection of a nation we on occasion have to sacrifice right for wrong. In your case, I need you to sacrifice the wrong done to you and yours for a more immediate right.'

'Is that why you threw Jack Sheppard to the wolves?' Before Charters could reply, Flynt continued. 'Was that a right you sacrificed? I know he was working for you, informing on Jonathan Wild.'

A denial built in Charters' eyes before he thought better of it. 'Keeping me abreast of Wild's activities, is all. And he was handsomely paid.'

Secretly pleased that his gut feeling had proved correct, Flynt maintained his attack. 'But when Wild turned on him, you did nothing.'

'The lad knew the risks. As you did when you worked for me.'

Flynt recognised there had always existed the possibility that he ran the danger of capture in the performance of something illegal. Charters had made it clear that if that occurred, there might be nothing he could do for him.

'Jack is different.'

'Why is he different?' Charters said. 'He is a thief, likeable in a rapscallion manner, but still a thief. He was always destined for Tyburn.'

The knowledge that Flynt himself had always believed that would be Jack's final destiny didn't deter him from pressing his point. 'Did he serve you well?'

'He did, that I cannot deny.'

'Then why didn't you help him? You let Wild betray him. It was cruel, Charters. Worse, it was dishonourable—'

Charters' temper burst. 'Damn it all, Flynt, know your place—'

'My place? What in our history has ever made you think that I would know, or acknowledge, my place? I don't recognise these divisions that you and your kind inflict on this world. I don't defer, I don't bend the knee, I don't recognise any right to respect or devotion simply because of accidents of birth. Jack is a human being who served you well and you have deserted him—'

'In the name of holy God, Flynt, will you cease this constant berating of me?' Charters snapped. 'I didn't desert the boy – how in the living hell do you think he escaped from Newgate last night? You think he managed that without external aid?'

That brought Flynt to a halt. He waited for Charters to expand further, which he duly did.

'I greased the wheels with his jailer.'

'The one they call Old Baldy?'

Charters looked over Flynt's shoulder for confirmation from Jacob, who must have nodded. 'That is he. He was paid to ignore any sounds he heard from that cell. I then had a lockpick smuggled to him by that doxy of his—'

'Bess.'

'Aye. A surly bitch, but comely in an ill-bred way. He is to be congratulated upon his taste, if not his wisdom.'

Flynt had no desire to discuss the strengths or failings of Edgeworth Bess. 'Where is he now?'

'I know not. And the truth be that at this juncture I care not. I only hope that he makes himself scarce, which I impressed upon him, for his previous excursions into liberty have been singularly unsuccessful. He remained too open in his movements and somewhat lackadaisical in combating his larcenous tendencies, so he was easily returned to custody. I have informed him that this will be the final time that he could rely on my assistance.'

'You spoke to him directly?'

A shake of the head. 'Jacob.'

Flynt faced Jacob. 'That was why you were in Newgate?'

'It were.'

'And not to see Bernardi?'

'Saw him, too.'

Flynt felt the wind had been sucked from his anger and outrage. His instincts told him that Charters spoke the truth. He had indeed assisted Jack, not once but on other occasions. Each time, the lad's own character had led to him being arrested again. For that continued assistance, Flynt owed Charters a debt. The annoying thing was, Charters knew it.

'Thank you,' he said.

Charters said nothing, no acknowledgement of the gratitude, no display of magnanimity. He simply stared at Flynt, as if waiting for further response. Flynt knew that for which he waited.

'Hawke killed my son,' he said.

'Edward Thatch killed your son.'

'Thatch pulled the trigger but Hawke shares responsibility.'

Charters leaned forward. 'And what if he deeply regrets that?'

Something in Charters' tone made Flynt's breath catch in his throat. This was no idle speculation.

'What if Hawke believed that Thatch meant to kill you, and you alone?'

'You've spoken to him?' Flynt's words were dry, hoarse. He took a sip of coffee. It was cold. As was the feeling in the pit of his stomach.

'I have.'

'And you believe him?'

Charters sat back, considering what he believed. 'I cannot say for certain. He seemed sincere in his remorse. All I do know is that I must ask you to set aside this quest for vengeance.'

'I can't do that.'

'You must.'

'Daniel Hawke is too like his father, who was a deceitful snake, and a brute.'

'You killed his father, I understand.'

'No. I left it to the people he had brutalised and oppressed.' Flynt suddenly stopped, a thought striking him. 'Are you saying that my son's death was the price I paid for my part in despatching the father?'

'Blood begets blood, Flynt.'

Flynt felt his anger rise once more. 'Toby Hawke was a canker on the face of this earth. His son also. Jonas was…' Emotion began to choke him. He had allowed it to break free once before, with Cassie, but not since. He had forced it down for so long but now it was in danger of erupting. He couldn't allow that, not here, not in front of Charters. He swallowed, brought himself under control. 'Jonas was an innocent.'

Charters' expression softened. 'Yes, he was. And even though I have no children, I sympathise with your desire for revenge, I really do. But on this occasion I must ask you to back away.'

'Why?'

Charters held his stare. 'Because Daniel Hawke is working for me.'

23

Jack hurried through the streets, hunched into his coat as deeply as he could, his face buried in the collar, avoiding both the rain that lashed the city but also eye contact from those few Londoners who were abroad in this deluge. He knew walking the streets was dangerous. Yes, there were people who saw him as some kind of hero, and that was adulation in which he could revel. To those who revered him, he was one of them, a lad from the streets who cocked a snook at those who sat in judgement above them. He could drink on it, dine on it, preen with it, but he knew it was all fake. He wasn't any kind of hero. He was a thief who had achieved some measure of fame just because he managed to escape from jails that were none too secure at the best of times. He'd shown doing and wit in making his escapes but he'd needed help, and that had come from one of those coves who was hated by those who lionised him. Jack didn't begin to understand what that Colonel Charters was about. He'd spoken about working for his country, but Jack didn't give a Frenchman's spit for his country. He did what he did for the coin and he knew the risks, knew what Wild would do if he found out. And find out he did.

Two coves looking at him funny made him pick up his pace. He looked back at them, just a quick glance, but they had moved on down Drury Lane, shoulders bent against the rain. He might've imagined their queer look, or they might have recognised him and could be heading for help. Wild and his men would be scouring the city for him, as would the Newgate Cavalry. He was taking a terrible risk being out here in the open, in what daylight there was, given the sky was low and black, but it had to be done. He'd been to the Golden Cross but the lady there said Mr Flynt had left. Now he was heading for the White Lion, where Bess had seen him. If he wasn't there he'd hit every tavern and inn he could. He had to find him, had to warn him about what Bess had done. He didn't know who those coves were that she had contacted, but instinct told him that they weren't interested in Mr Flynt's health. There wasn't much Jack could do to protect him, he was no fighter, but he could at least warn him. He owed him that.

And then he saw someone ahead who would be able to offer Mr Flynt some protection. He didn't much like the cove, but he knew him to be most efficient with barkers and Mr Flynt would need such a man. His blond hair was noticeable as it hung below the brim of his hat, his black clothes the same as Mr Flynt wore. Jack hurried to catch up with him.

'Mr Cain,' he said, and Cain whirled on him, a hand already wrapped around the butt of a pistol in his belt. He relaxed when he recognised him.

'Master Jack Sheppard,' Cain said, his voice low, looking around him. 'The man of the moment.'

'I needs to have converse with you, Mr Cain.'

Cain gripped him by the elbow and propelled him into a doorway, then blocked anyone's view of him from the lane. 'You shouldn't be out here, lad, you're hot property.'

'I knows it, but I has to find Mr Flynt.'

'What is so important that you risk your liberty?'

'I believe there is coves abroad what mean to do him harm.'

Cain laughed. 'That is hardly news for a broadsheet, Jack. There are any number of men who mean Jonas Flynt harm. I've practically made a career out of covering his back.'

'And him you, I would wager.'

Cain smiled. 'Aye. So, who are these men and how do you know of them?'

As the sky above began to grumble, Jack relayed what Bess had told him, seeing Cain's eyes harden as he did so.

24

Flynt was stunned. He had risen from the table and walked around the room while he processed this news. Outside, he heard a faint rumble of thunder. 'You're protecting Hawke?'

'I'm protecting this country, Flynt,' Charters snapped.

'He's a killer.'

'As are you.'

'You said you trusted me.'

'To a point, yes.'

'He's not to be trusted.'

'I don't trust him. But I am using him.'

'And he is willing to betray the Fellowship?'

'He believes the Fellowship betrayed his family, his father. You're not the only one seeking vengeance, Flynt.'

Hawke wasn't wrong in that regard, for Flynt had been in a sense aimed at Toby Hawke by Lord Moncrieff. The reason for it at the time hadn't interested Flynt overly much, as it intersected with his own aims. Flynt moved back to the table. 'I don't care.'

Charters' lips tightened. 'Flynt, you must think on the wider implications, the greater good.'

'I don't give a damn about the greater good. Hawke will die, and at my hand.'

'I cannot allow that.'

'How do you intend to stop me? By force?' Flynt glanced over at Jacob. 'Jacob is a good man but you know he's no match for me. I apologise, Jacob, but you know it to be true.'

'I do that, Mr Flynt,' Jacob said, 'so no offence taken.'

'I have other men, Flynt,' Charters said. 'Two of my best await us downstairs. I'm sure you will have observed them when you entered the tavern.'

Flynt had. There had been times in the past when he had failed to identify Charters' watchers, but this time they had made themselves conspicuous. Now he knew why.

'If you leave here without Jacob at your side, they will know that I'm displeased and will take further steps.'

'Threats now, Colonel?'

'Flynt, I am at war. I am surrounded by duplicity.'

'You are duplicitous yourself.'

Charters accepted that. 'Fire with fire, Flynt. You do not win a war against shadows without first becoming one. You were once part of that shadow, but if you walk through that door, if you again turn your back on me, then you are on your own. I need Daniel Hawke alive. There are matters at stake here far greater than your personal demons. I suspect that what spurs you on this quest is not so much grief, though I don't discount it, but guilt over not being able to protect your family.'

Flynt flinched at that. 'Colonel, I'm going to walk through that door, with or without Jacob, and leave this tavern. If your men attempt anything then their blood will be on your hands. You know me well, you know that of which I am capable. I won't be deterred or deflected from my intention. I'll find Daniel Hawke and I'll kill him. That's the pure and simple of it.'

Charters sighed. 'There is nothing in this world that is pure and simple, and intent to do murder is far from it.'

'It won't be murder, it will be justice,' Flynt said, already walking towards the door. Jacob stepped aside to let him pass.

'One final piece of advice then,' Charters said as Flynt turned the handle. 'Trust no one.'

Flynt pulled the door open. 'Does that include you?'

Charters ignored that. 'This is a cruel world, Flynt. The orbit which is ours is even more cruel and there is no room for friendships. You would be advised to remember that.'

Flynt seethed as he descended the dark stairway to the tavern floor, knowing well to what Charters' final warning referred. Gabriel Cain was his friend and his ally, but there were portions of his past at which Flynt could only guess. He had always been the more reckless of the partnership, willing to take risks on the heath from which Flynt often struggled to dissuade him. The charge of assault and robbery that Charters had held over both their heads in order to utilise their services for the Company had actually been committed by Cain, although Flynt made that discovery much later. At one point Cain had vanished from London – travelling, he said – but Flynt had been told of a man known only as 'the Wraith', who sold his pistol and sword to anyone who needed someone killed. Cain denied that he was this individual, but doubt always remained in Flynt's mind. Had his old friend taken the Fellowship's silver to spy on Charters?

Then there was Jack. He had never mentioned that Charters had approached him, had been happy to let Flynt believe that he had become part of Jonathan Wild's crew, despite his often-stated warnings. Nor had he mentioned that Charters was giving him aid to escape the dual embrace of Newgate and Tyburn. Certainly, Charters would have wanted him not to tell anyone about his affiliation with the Company. Secrets, always secrets. Flynt himself had kept that secret for many years, only telling Belle when it was necessary.

Belle…

She had also urged him to end his pursuit of Hawke. Did she have another reason, other than concern for his wellbeing? Had her paramour despatched her? Godfrey Southern was a wealthy man by all accounts, so it was possible he was of the Fellowship.

That brought to mind another nobleman: James Moncrieff – his half-brother, though neither of them wished that filial connection to be well known. Flynt had attempted to call on him, to urge him to thrust Hawke from his shadow and into the daylight, but he had moved from his last address in St James's Square and the current resident denied any knowledge of his new address. Flynt would have asked Charters for it, for he would know, but it would have been nothing more than a waste of breath. Charters would not reveal it. Not now.

His mind reeling and annoyed with himself for allowing Charters to so easily cause such a whirl of doubts and suspicion, Flynt stepped into the tavern, which was not as crowded as it would normally have been, the inclement weather perhaps dissuading many from taking to the streets. A few idle drinkers dotted the smoky room, others enjoying bread and cheese, one or two sliding back oysters, a doxy or two plying their trade. The glowering clouds outside joined forces with the tavern's soot-blackened windows to combat daylight, so candles were lit around the room, casting a pale yellow light. Normally the room would be a cacophony, with singing and raised voices and a musician providing entertainment for the price of a bottle, but this day it was as if all present had been rendered near-mute by the storm that continued to build. Charters' men had not moved from the positions he had spotted them in earlier. One leaned against the bar, the other at a table on the other side of the room. He knew them not by their garb but by their watchfulness and the way they stiffened when he entered the room, their eyes looking past him to check whether or not he was accompanied. Seeing nobody, they simultaneously laid their tankards down. Flynt would wager the ale was untouched. The man at the bar straightened, the one at the table rose. They wouldn't make any move in the tavern. They would wait until he was outside.

As he threaded between the tables and those few patrons who wandered the floor, he felt a familiar restlessness build in his gut, whether it was caused by fear or the thrill of anticipation he could now no longer tell. He had been in similar situations so often that he had lost count. Walking into buildings with which he was unfamiliar, kicking open doors without knowing what lay on the other side, stalking a man along darkened streets with intent to harm him, encountering others with murder in mind in lonely alleyways. Each time, he had felt this same tingle in his belly that transmitted along his arms to his fingers or an itch at the back of his neck that warned him of impending danger. He had always emerged victorious, but not necessarily unscarred, as the gash on his face proved. But there were other scars that could not be seen. Each time he killed a man, even if that man deserved it, he feared losing a little bit of himself. He grew colder. More distant to the world. Years before, when he had almost professed his feelings to Belle, he had believed – no, hoped – that he might be able to change his life, to move away from this world of blood and death. But then along came Cassie and the need to assist his father in rescuing his wife from the hands of Toby Hawke. That had led to more blood, more death.

In his mind a pistol flashed in the gloom…

A laugh…

The son he had never come to know lying dead…

He forced his concentration back to the two men as they moved with him, their demeanour casual, their limbs loose, monitoring his progress without being too obvious. He widened the flaps of his coat to ensure that access to Tact and Diplomacy would be unhindered. He twisted the catch on his sword cane, knowing the sheath would not free until he pulled it away, but that second's delay in unlatching it could be the difference between life and death. He knew the men would see this tiny movement and understand, but that didn't matter. They were professionals. They would do what was necessary, as would he.

He was almost at the door leading to Drury Lane when he became aware of them coming to a halt and looking back the way he had come. Flynt followed their gaze and saw Jacob approaching him, surreptitiously waving a finger to them in an instruction to stand down. They stepped back, but kept a wary eye on Flynt.

'The colonel wants you to know that this is a warning only,' Jacob said when he reached him. 'Next time he won't be so merciful.'

'He seems very sure of these men,' Flynt said, indicating the two watchers.

'He is, and with good reason, Mr Flynt. I would heed his warning, if I was you.'

Flynt felt his muscles ease. He had been prepared to deal with them. But there was always the chance that he wouldn't have. He was no longer young and the years had taken their toll. Too much tension, too much action, too much blood. Too much loss. Those men were young and fit and capable, and he had nothing against them, though that wouldn't have prevented him from despatching them if that was how the hand played. He would do what had to be done.

'I'm sorry, Mr Flynt, but he says you should leave London,' Jacob continued. 'Go back to the Americas, go anywhere, but don't stay here. London ain't a healthy place at the best of times, he told me to tell you, but for you it could be lethal.'

25

He'd pulled the collar of his coat up, the rain pounding at him and drumming on the brim of his hat before sliding off, the thunder he'd heard earlier growing closer. He headed for the White Lion, where he'd agreed to meet Gabriel Cain. That was another problem. Flynt was of a solitary disposition, to be sure, but that didn't prevent a sinking sensation in the pit of his stomach when he thought that, once again, he might not be able to fully trust Cain. Of course, there was always the possibility that Charters had sown that seed deliberately to undermine their partnership. Or to divert any attention from the fact that Charters himself was, indeed, in the Fellowship's pocket. Organisations such as theirs delight in chaos, in unrest, in confusion, for in such moments there is weakness, and weakness can be capitalised upon.

Perhaps Charters was right. Perhaps he should abandon this pursuit of revenge, return to his life in the Americas. He had sufficient funds now to live well. He could leave that day for Port Glasgow, sail back on the *Walrus*, retrieve the treasure he had hidden on that uninhabited island, live well in New York or Charleston, where there was gambling a-plenty. No more blood. No more killing. No more mistrust. A simple life of pleasure and leisure. What was there for him in London? Belle was lost to him. Even though he was at liberty now, Jack was destined for the noose, he had always known it. And Cain? Cain was ever an enigma – a smiling, seemingly carefree enigma.

And there was Cassie, back in Edinburgh. She was alone now; not completely, but her husband was dead, her son was dead. Another option was that he might return home, attempt to rebuild… what? What was there between them? A love affair that was all fire and the passion of youth. The knowledge that it had resulted in a child. She believed he had deserted her, and he had. And yet, in their final days on New Providence Island he thought there had been something kindling within her, something that had always smouldered in him, but he had been too reckless to understand or recognise. It had burned within him all these years. Perhaps that fire and passion was not all spent. Perhaps a spark still glowed somewhere with her…

He was jerked from his thoughts on Wych Street by the sight of Jack Sheppard, slouched down inside a large coat as if trying to hide, walking swiftly towards him.

'Dear God,' he said, ducking under a mantua-maker's sign, gripping Jack by the arm and pulling him down a lane leading to the carpentry where Jack was once apprenticed. It was a narrow space and the overhanging buildings offered some shelter from the torrent. 'You shouldn't be—'

Jack waved away his words. 'No time, Mr Flynt, I thinks you is in peril.'

Flynt almost erupted in an ironic laugh. It would be more useful to let him know when he was *not* in peril. Before he could ask of this fresh danger, Jack quickly told him about the man to whom Bess had reported his return to London.

'Someone what needs to know you was back can't be good news.'

'Good news is in short support these days,' Flynt said.

'I comes running immediate to find you. Met Mr Cain—'

'Gabriel? Where is he?'

'Gone into the White Lion to await you. I was glad to have met him, for I didn't have no wish to enter that place myself as there might be those what want to claim the reward on my head.'

'You shouldn't have ventured into the streets in the first place, Jack. Though I am grateful for the warning.' Flynt, by habit, was already keeping an eye on the opening to the lane, one hand on Tact.

'Who is these coves, Mr Flynt?'

'I don't know, Jack, but I'll lay money that I'll find out soon enough. You should return to your rooms most swiftly. Take back alleys where you can, keep your face hid.'

Jack gave him a look as if he was teaching egg-sucking to a grandame. 'Don't think hard of my Bess, Mr Flynt. She thinks she has my best interests in her heart 'cos she believes you to be bad for me.'

Flynt had many guilts upon his conscience, but Jack wasn't one of them. He'd done his best to steer him away from the path on which he now knew he was inextricably walking. 'Get away from London, Jack. It's this cesspit that's bad for you.'

'She ain't willing to leave these streets.'

'Then go yourself. I know you ignored my warning regarding Jonathan Wild and I now know why. I bear you no ill-will, and I apologise for my behaviour, but do wish you had trusted me more.'

Jack grew furtive. He was a skilful liar, but around Flynt that talent often deserted him. 'I doesn't—'

'I've spoken to Colonel Charters. He told me he recruited you. I know he helped you escape from Newgate and that he has told you to vacate London. Heed him, Jack. Leave Bess behind, for she will be the ruin of you.'

He could see that the words had hit home as Jack rubbed the rain from his face. 'Ain't so easy.' He took a breath, let it out, took another, and looked away. 'I loves her, you see. I knows what she is, I knows she don't love me in the same way. But I can't leave her, Mr Flynt.' He faced Flynt again, his smile slight but brave. The moisture glistening on his lashes might have been rain but might not. 'If it's the end of me, then so be it. I'll lead them a merry dance before they gets me.'

Flynt wanted to say something further but he didn't have the words. He stared at the young face, seeing through the bravado to the fear beneath. He wanted to take that fear away. In that moment he made a decision.

'I'm leaving London again, Jack.'

'When?'

'Soon. When I do, I want you to come with me.'

'Where would we go?'

'Port Glasgow at first—'

'What? Up in Itchland?' Jack realised what he'd said and had the grace to be ashamed. 'Sorry, Mr Flynt, I doesn't mean to be detrimental about you or Scotland. It just slipped out, from habit like.'

Flynt had heard worse. 'From there we'll take my ship and head to the Americas.'

Jack frowned as he grappled with this concept. 'Leave England entire?'

'Yes. You can have a good life in the Americas, Jack. There are opportunities for bright lads.'

The frown deepened. 'And what about Bess?'

'There's no room for her, Jack. You must leave her.'

'She won't like that.'

Flynt wanted to snap that he didn't give a damn what she liked, but he held back. 'It's for the best,' he said. 'Tell me where you are lodging and I'll send word when we're leaving.'

Jack gave him an address in the Rookery. Flynt committed it to memory. 'Go back there now and stay there until I come to fetch you. Promise me you won't leave.'

A slight nod was all he could expect from the young man as he grappled with this new proposition and the prospect of ditching the woman he at least thought he loved. 'What will you do?'

'I'm meeting Gabriel in the White Lion.'

'That's where Bess told them she saw you. That's the first place they'll look.'

Flynt was already walking back towards the street. 'I know.'

26

He found Cain at their corner table in the White Lion, a tankard in front of him. Flynt surmised the ale was for show only, for though his left hand rested on the tabletop, his right was hidden below it, without doubt gripping his pistol. His eyes scanned the room, watchful, alert. When he saw Flynt enter, he nodded but continued in his study of their surroundings, no doubt looking for anyone who showed more than passing interest in his arrival. Flynt stood in the doorway, ostensibly shaking the rain from his hat but, in reality, giving anyone who sought him the opportunity to recognise him, while also doing the same as Cain.

Aided by the fact that the tavern was as ill populated as the Black Lion, they both recognised the three men in the far corner as those they sought. They were better dressed than the majority of the White Lion's patrons and that on its own was sufficient to set them apart, but what really caught their joint attention was the way they visibly straightened upon seeing Flynt. Two of them immediately averted their eyes, but the third, who was demonstrably younger than his fellows, maintained his gaze while Flynt threaded between the tables. That was the major mistake. Flynt turned his back to them, feigning no awareness of their presence, but knowing Cain would keep them in sight. At least, he hoped he would.

Damn you, Charters.

'I met Jack,' Flynt said as he reached Cain's table but didn't take a seat. He stared at his friend, considering whether to raise Charters' suspicions of a spy in the midst of the Company. He decided against it. There were more pressing matters to deal with and he didn't wish to risk losing Cain's support.

Cain jutted his chin towards the men at the table. 'Do you know them?'

'Never seen them before. But they will have been given my description.' He ran a finger down his face. 'This scar is somewhat distinctive.'

Cain agreed. 'How do you wish to play this?'

'Directly,' Flynt said.

He strode across the tavern floor towards the three men. Cain strolled languidly in his wake so as not to draw too much attention.

Pulling an empty chair towards him, turning the back to the men's table and then straddling it, Flynt gave them a cheerful smile. 'Gentlemen, I feel sure you won't mind me joining you.'

They were all startled by the boldness of the approach and shot each other inquiring, even nervous, glances.

'So,' Flynt said, clasping his hands in front of him, his forearms resting on the top of the backrest. 'I understand you seek me?'

They looked from him to Cain, who stood three paces away, his coat open to reveal the brace of pistols in his belt.

One of them cleared his throat a little. 'What makes you think that, sir?'

'Please, let's not play games. I have business elsewhere and, to be frank, I have little temper to put a crick in my neck looking for you at my back.'

'We don't know what you're talking about. We're here only for some refreshment and relaxation.'

The man's voice was cultured but carried the colonial twang that Flynt had heard so often in recent years.

'You've travelled far?' Flynt asked.

'Far enough.'

'The American colonies, perhaps?'

The man's eyes shifted a touch. 'Perhaps.'

'Dan Hawke sent you.'

Putting it so bluntly must have surprised all three, but it was the young one who reacted. He didn't speak, but his unsettled demeanour spoke volumes.

'I don't know the gentleman,' said the spokesman.

Flynt glanced back to Cain, who shrugged. 'Let's not waste further time, Jonas. Kill them and be gone from this place.'

The spokesman laughed. 'Kill us? Here?' He slowly raised both hands, palm up to reveal that he held no weapon, and spread his arms a little. 'This is a public place for murder.'

Cain's smile might have been construed as friendly if Flynt didn't know him so well. There remained the trace of a chill in his eyes. 'We've done it before. These people are all deaf, mute and blind when they have need.'

The tension in the air rose and hands inched slowly towards weapons.

'There's no need for bloodshed,' Flynt said. 'But you do need to take a message back to Mr Hawke, the man you do not know. Tell him I am coming for him. Tell him it's time to stop running, to stop hiding. He must know by now that he can't run far enough and can't hide well enough to evade me forever. Tell him it's time he and I ended this.'

'I told you,' said the spokesman, 'we don't know him.'

'Tell him anyway.'

Flynt rose, his movements precise, for nerves were stretched and a sudden move might cause at least one of them to misconstrue his intentions. His money was on the youngest one. Flynt carefully swung his leg away from the chair and walked away from the table, leaving Cain to deliver a final smile as he backed up a few paces, then turned and followed.

He caught up with Flynt just as he reached the doorway. 'What do you think?' he asked.

Flynt made no response. He knew this was not yet over.

27

They waited outside, the raindrops firing like bullets at the ground, the sporadic thunder now nearly overhead. Flynt spoke true when he said that he didn't wish to conduct his days constantly looking over his shoulder. This had to end now, one way or another. He would prefer the matter be resolved without blood being spilled, but that was often not an option. White Lion Court was thankfully deserted, the wind sweeping around the narrow space as if hunting for something, picking up detritus, inspecting it and discarding it. The rain rattled on the roof tiles of the tall inn before them and the enclosing buildings on either side. Clogged gutters bled and created waterfalls in miniature. Behind them, from Wych Street beyond a narrow lane, they heard footsteps, voices, the sweep of a broom as a trader attempted to clear the walkway outside his shop of gathering rain, the clatter of a cart on the cobbles, the thud and splash of wheels striking a hole, even the creak of signs caught by the wind. From within the tavern, more voices, more laughter, the rattle of dice in a cup. A groan from one of the upper floors where games of a more intimate nature were transacted.

Little more than two minutes after they left, the three emerged. The young one displayed surprise, but his two older companions did not.

'We had to follow,' the spokesman said.

'We know,' Flynt said.

'Payment has been made.'

'Give it back,' Flynt suggested. 'No amount of coin is worth dying for.'

The man considered this, glancing to his companion to his right, ignoring the young man to his left. 'A contract is a contract. I'm sure you understand.'

Flynt didn't understand, not fully. He was one who, when accepting a commission, did what he had to do in order to get the job done but would never sacrifice his life for it.

'We understand,' Cain said, ignoring Flynt's knowing glance. Cain might deny that he was the Wraith, but his actions often confirmed it. 'Tell me, sir, what's your name?'

'Bartholomew Wyngarde. My friends call me Bart. Why?'

'I like to know who it is I'm killing.'

The young man seemed puzzled. 'You really mean for us to do this here?'

'It's as good a place as any,' Cain said.

'But...'

'This will be over quickly,' Cain said. 'You'll be dead and we'll be gone before anyone can set their ale tankard down.'

'What's your name, boy?' Flynt asked.

'Jed. Jedediah.'

'You needn't stay, Jed,' Flynt said. 'This work is not for you.'

His mind flashed to another situation, nearly ten years before, in a basement, and a young man who was not cut out for similar work. Subsequent events had not gone well for him. Another face to haunt Flynt.

Jed's imploring glance to his older companions was ignored. He swallowed. 'Pa?'

His voice trembled with that single word.

'Go, son,' said Bartholomew, gently.

Flynt felt shock jar his fingers. 'He is your son?'

'He is.'

'And you bring him here for this?'

A shrug. 'He has to learn the trade.'

'He'll learn about the afterlife,' Cain said.

Bartholomew grinned. 'You seem real sure about yourself. Why is that?'

'Experience.'

Flynt stared hard at Jed, willing him to see sense. 'Last chance, Jed, leave. There's no shame in choosing life.'

The young man was clearly tempted, but he shook his head. 'I reckon I better stay.'

Flynt breathed heavily. He didn't want this. Not now. He addressed the young man's father. 'We can part now, Bartholomew, go our separate ways, what do you say?'

'I told you, we can't do that. Word gets out that we failed to deliver on a contract, then we're finished. We don't take the bounty, someone else will.' Bartholomew addressed Cain. 'You seem to know the business. You know we can't do it.'

'I know you can't,' Cain said.

They fell silent at that moment, three men standing at the top of the steps leading to the door, Flynt and Cain in the middle of the courtyard, the noises from the street and tavern all around them, the rain and wind acting in concert with the thunder, which groaned and moaned above them, the flashes of lightning brief. Whatever was to occur had to occur soon, for at any moment someone could happen by. A reveller could spill through the doors, someone could approach from the lane behind them, a face could appear at one of the few windows.

Part of Flynt hoped that someone would come by, because that might defuse the situation. He knew he had instigated this, but only because he wished to dissuade these men from their purpose if he could. In the tavern, had it turned violent, an innocent could have been hurt. Here, at least for the moment, that wasn't possible. Now that violence seemed imminent, he didn't wish it. The knowledge that Jed was Bartholomew's son was the final straw. He didn't know where the mother was, but he didn't wish to deprive her of her boy.

For what seemed like an eternity nobody moved.

And then Bartholomew did.

Pistols were jerked from belts, gunfire barked. A matter of moments only to snuff two lives. Bartholomew was the first to go down, then his companion. Only Jed remained standing, his pistol half out of his belt, obviously bemused by the speed of events. Trying to comprehend what had happened, he stared open-mouthed at the body of his father at his feet, then at the other man, whose name neither Flynt nor Cain had bothered to ascertain. The boy then raised his head slowly towards them, his eyes awash with terror and uncertainty.

'It doesn't need to be like this, Jed,' Flynt said.

The young man looked again at Bartholomew.

'Live your life, boy,' Flynt urged.

Cain touched Flynt's arm. 'We must be away.'

Flynt nodded, his eyes still on Jed, who no longer moved. He was transfixed by the sight of his dead father. Voices rose, approached.

'Now, Jonas,' Cain insisted, already backing towards the lane, thrusting his spent pistol into his belt.

Flynt, who had discharged both Tact and Diplomacy, took a few steps back as he hid them away under his coat, his eyes still on Jed, frozen at the top of the steps. He turned away, took two paces before he saw Cain raising his second pistol, turned back to see Jed hauling at his own weapon, levelling it, managed to cry out a warning to the boy, telling him not to do it, but it fell on deaf ears, for there was a determination in his eyes now, and he cocked the hammer, his finger tightened on the trigger, but Cain fired first, the ball splashing red on Jed's chest, throwing him back, the pistol firing wild into sodden boards beneath his feet, and he tumbled, twisting as he fell, taking such a long time but making no sound, until he landed on his knees, then pitched forward but propped himself up on his hands.

Flynt rushed to kneel by his side. 'Why?' he asked.

Jed's words were halting and blood stretched from his lips. 'My pa…'

Flynt glanced at Bartholomew's lifeless form beside him. 'He should have guided you better.'

'He always did right for me.' The young man coughed, retched, dislodging more blood.

'Where's Daniel Hawke?'

Jed shook his head, the blood frothing at his mouth. He coughed again.

Flynt held him steady. 'Jed, tell me where he is. You must know.'

'I won't tell you. We don't tell…'

And then he slumped forward, breaking free from Flynt's support. He came to rest beside his father, one arm thrown across the body as if in a final embrace.

Figures had appeared in the tavern doorway, peering through the teeming rain at the scene in the courtyard. Cain gripped Flynt by the shoulder to spin him away and propel him into the shadows of the lane, pulling his own hat even lower over his face.

'Did you have to kill the boy?' Flynt asked as they headed towards the street.

'Yes, I did,' Cain said. 'And you should have been prepared to do it, too. Never turn your back on a man who means to kill you.'

28

Flynt had been here before. The sensation had begun in the courtyard of the White Lion. No – it began within the tavern, when he had confronted Bartholomew and his men. How many times had he been in such a position? Engaged in conversation with men who intended him harm? Or waiting for armed men to appear? Waiting to kill or be killed? And now, walking eastwards along the Strand, Cain by his side, mistrust running rampant through his brain, the feeling of his own history repeating itself returning. They had walked this very street, in the opposite direction, years before, when Flynt had suspected that his old friend was the Wraith. Cain had the uncanny ability to be indispensable and loyal, while also harbouring a deceitful nature that often hinted at darker deeds. That he was motivated by profit Flynt had always known and recognised, and it was possible that he had decided to take the Fellowship's coin as well as Charters'. Flynt didn't care about the politics of it, but if Cain was in Fellowship pay, how much could he truly trust him?

Cain seemed unaffected by what had just occurred, but then he never was perturbed by killing. After stating that he'd had to kill the boy, he had immediately changed the subject and asked about the girl he had been tupping on New Providence.

'What happened to Mistress Bonny, Jonas?' he said, as if they had just emerged from a convivial glass of brandy and not just killed three men. 'I confess I have thought of her often, for she shared an enthusiasm for lewd behaviour that matched my own. 'Tis a pity I left, for I do believe we could have enjoyed each other in ways that I dare not consider here for fear of my own enthusiasm becoming apparent and frightening the populace.'

'She wasn't in any way perturbed by your departure,' Flynt said, his voice sharp, for he wished to hurt Cain. 'She soon continued her coital enthusiasm with a gentleman named Jack Rackham, Calico Jack, they called him. They were very active for a time.'

Cain's sigh was more effect than sincere. 'Ah well, it would have been a shame for such libidinous talent to lie dormant. Who was this fellow? And I note the past tense. Are they active no more?'

'Calico Jack was a pirate and he went to the noose.'

'Did you have something to do with that?'

Flynt didn't reply. He had indeed caught Rackham, but he wasn't proud of sending anyone to the gallows. The man was a means to an end, that end being Dan Hawke, for Rackham was in league with him in the disposal of stolen goods. 'Anne Bonny joined him at sea and was as bloody as any man. She developed a fondness for another woman, Mary Read, who also turned pirate.'

'By fondness, I take it you mean...?'

'I do.' Flynt still sought a way to wound Cain's vanity. 'By all accounts they were equally enthusiastic with each other, perhaps more so. Rackham was also involved on occasion.'

Cain grinned. 'By God, I would have greatly enjoyed being part of the menage! Not with this fellow Rackham, but two women. Have you ever been with a brace of ladies, Jonas?'

Flynt hadn't, but was annoyed that his attempt at piercing Cain's veneer had failed.

'There's nothing like it. Most exhilarating.' Cain fell silent as they proceeded through the falling rain, the thunder dissipating. 'And what of Mistress Bonny? Was she for the gallows too?'

'She was, but she escaped it by pleading her belly.'

'She was pregnant to Rackham?'

'No, it was a ruse.'

'Then what happened to her?'

'I don't know. The last I heard she was in prison in Jamaica.'

'And her *inamorata*, Mary Read?'

'Died in jail.'

'Shame.'

Flynt couldn't take the idle chatter any longer. He stopped and faced Cain. 'Damn it, Gabriel, what are you playing at?'

Cain appeared bewildered by the question and Flynt's manner. 'I don't follow, Jonas.'

'The Paladin, working again for Charters – what are you about?'

'I told you, for amusement, for coin, and believe it or not, I have done some good, have helped people. I thought you would wish that legacy to continue.'

'And the money you take?'

'A fellow has to make his way, and as I am resolved to walking the straight, then I—'

'Thieving from thieves is still thieving.'

'So Wild said.' Cain laughed. 'And like him, you would know about that, for have you not been doing similar in American waters?'

Flynt knew the truth of that and didn't try to justify it.

'What's this about?' Cain asked. 'That boy back there? He was about to put a ball in you, or worse, he might have put one in me.'

Flynt half turned, stared down the Strand through the rain. 'Charters believes there's a spy in the Company of Rogues.'

Cain's expression was a mix of surprise and innocence. 'A spy working on whose behalf?'

'He didn't say,' Flynt lied. 'Spain, France, Holland, who can say. England is at peace but that means nothing.'

'Ah, truly, this is a murky world in which we live. Sometimes I long for the solid villainy of the heaths. At least we knew who were friends and who were enemies and we—' The words halted suddenly and Cain frowned. 'By Christ, you think it's me, don't you?' When Flynt again didn't reply, Cain stepped into his line of vision. 'Jonas, do you believe it's me?'

'I don't know. I think it's possible.'

Cain let out an exasperated growl, turned away, swept off his hat, held his face up to the rain. 'Dear God in heaven,' he said. 'We have been this way before, you and I.' He lowered his head, wiped the rainwater away. 'When will you ever trust me, Jonas? Have I not proved to you over the years that I only ever have your best interests at heart? I have defended you, I have supported you, I have killed for you. I could have stolen either of your women, but I didn't. I was a friend to your son. And he needed one, Jonas, because his father was not around. And now you think me traitor.' He scraped the rainwater from his blond hair and put his hat back on. 'I don't know what I can ever do to have your full trust, so you must tell me, Jonas, tell me what I must do.'

Flynt couldn't reply. Cain's speech seemed heartfelt, but he was always a man who could appear convincing. If a man could convincingly fake sincerity, he was capable of anything.

Cain wandered away for a few paces, once again staring up at the falling rain, his back arched as if he was stretching it. When he came back, he said, 'It's not a foreign power, is it? It's the Fellowship, correct?'

'Aye.'

'Is this why Charters says he is not pursuing the Fellowship? Because of this spy? Does he still have them in his sights?'

Flynt had to be careful here. He had blurted out Charters' suspicion without thought. Now he had to consider his words. If Cain was working for Moncrieff, then he couldn't break Charters' confidence regarding his ongoing work against the Fellowship. He owed the man that at least. 'No, he says there are more pressing matters for him to deal with. He truly doesn't believe them to be any kind of threat now.'

Cain was not the only one who could imitate probity when he had to, and seemed satisfied with Flynt's response. 'And what about you? Do you believe them to be a threat?'

Flynt waved back in the direction of Wych Street, wishing he had never began this conversation, knowing he had to tread carefully. Sincere or not, the seeds of doubt had been sown. 'I think that proves they are, at least to me.'

'Hawke sent them, I'll be bound.'

'Aye, but he is Fellowship. They're harbouring him, enabling him to send men such as they.'

'And the fact that I've just aided you in removing that immediate threat doesn't prove my loyalty?'

Flynt remained silent. He could easily have lied, said that it did, and he would have been persuasive, but his friendship with this man, complex though it might be, demanded that he did not. As for the threat being removed, he wasn't so sure. Bartholomew had said that if they didn't collect the bounty someone else would. The way he'd said it hinted there were others out there. There always were.

Cain's face, which had been taut with anger and outrage, sagged and his shoulders drooped. 'Damn you, Jonas Flynt. I grow tired of this. You make being your friend very difficult.'

'I'm sorry, Gabriel, but...'

Cain held up a hand. 'No. Don't. Just...' He searched for his next words but they proved impossible to find, for he gave another little growl – anger, frustration, sadness – and walked away. Flynt watched him stride through the rain and felt anguish churn within. In a matter of days he had been threatened by a man he once thought would never wish him real harm, had sent Belle fleeing from his company, and now wounded the only true friend he had left.

That was quite a feat, even for him.

29

James Moncrieff handed his wet coat and hat to the servant who opened the door, and thanked him, for he had learned that civility towards inferiors cost a man naught. He briefly considered going upstairs to see Anne and Alexander, but the hour was late and they would both be asleep. He had no wish to disturb them and, in any case, he had correspondence to deal with. An hour or two with quill and parchment, accompanied by a fine brandy, would allow him to both catch up with business and relax. He found the scratch of a sharp goose feather against fine paper most calming, despite the stimulation of the liquor.

He crossed the vestibule, unlocked the door to his study and locked it behind him again, for the material he was about to process was not for the eyes of his wife, should she awaken and choose to descend the stairs to find him. She knew his family had wide commercial interests, as did her own people, but she was unaware of his involvement with the Fellowship, even though – again without her knowledge – her own father and brother were members. There was a time, during the early stages of their courtship, when he wondered what Anne would think of the work they did, of the steps they took to further the aims and interests of the organisation and their family fortunes. He wondered no more. Over the years, he had learned that his wife possessed a sense of morality that was quite at odds with the furtherance of commerce. She had a quick wit and a sharp mind, and though the Fellowship did not draw the line at admitting women to its ranks, and some of them were most ruthless in their methods, he knew now that she would not approve of the extreme measures the Fellowship took to both maintain its position but also to protect its anonymity. The Fellowship operated through a mix of secrecy and fear; the majority of mankind knew nothing of its existence, while those who did were aware that to speak of it could result in dire consequences. Moncrieff had been surprised at how easily he had taken to making decisions that resulted in men and women losing their livelihoods, position and lives. So he hid from his dear wife such matters, often locking himself away in his study, as he did now.

He sensed immediately that he was not alone in the room. The shadows were deep, with only a small flame living in the grate. His gaze shot to the open window, where a gauze curtain fluttered against the wind. He clutched his walking stick, ready to wield the heavy silver wolf's head against any attacker.

'You can take your ease, James,' said the voice. 'If I meant you harm, you'd be dead already.'

Taking a deep breath to conceal how unnerved he had been, Moncrieff moved to the fireplace, took a taper from the mantel and ignited it in the fire. He then lit two candles in silver holders on the mantel and turned to face the intruder, who was seated in Moncrieff's own armchair, facing the grate.

'You broke into my home?' Moncrieff's rage stiffened his voice.

'It was an easy thing. You really should make that window more secure. And the gardens to the rear are beautiful in daylight, but at night have many shadows to conceal a man such as I.'

'My servants are most redoubtable men. I could have you beaten and delivered to the magistrates.'

'You could try, but good servants are difficult to find and I would dispose of at least three before they laid a hand on me.'

'Nevertheless, one cry from me and—'

'Oh, in the name of Christ, will you please take your ease? I'm not here to do you harm, I told you.'

Moncrieff knew this man's reputation – indeed, he had made use of his skills many times and even now paid him handsomely for services. Nevertheless, he believed he had no ill intent towards him.

'Then what is so important that you breach the sanctity of my home?'

The man laughed. 'Sanctity. Not a word that springs to mind when I think of you, James.'

The continual use of his Christian name was infuriating, but Moncrieff maintained his outward calm, knowing that this man was doing so purposely to irritate him. 'What is it you wish?'

Gabriel Cain leaned forward in the winged armchair, the candlelight casting a pale glow on his face. 'You sent someone after Jonas.'

'I did not.'

'We had an agreement.'

'And I adhere to it. I didn't send anyone after him.'

'Then your friend Daniel Hawke did.'

'He's not my friend. An associate only.'

'Rein him in, James.'

Moncrieff said nothing as he moved to a table behind his desk and poured himself the brandy he had earlier imagined. 'I don't take orders, Cain.'

'I'm warning you,' said Cain.

Moncrieff turned to face him once again. 'Warning me? You forget yourself, Cain. I am the Grand Master.'

Cain sighed. 'Please, spare me the self-importance. Your position and the organisation you lead mean nothing more to me than a bundle of coin. I'm not like those others in your employ. I'm no zealot and I'll be damned if I do anything for the prospect of your favour. You needed someone to monitor Charters, you offered money and I was available. That's all you mean to me. And thank you, I will have a brandy.'

Moncrieff bridled at Cain's gall, but waved towards the decanter as he took his seat behind his desk. He would not act as the man's servant. 'Help yourself.'

Showing no sign of insult, Cain did so, then carried the glass back to the armchair. 'They were unsuccessful.'

'Who?'

'The men Hawke sent. They lie dead, I know not where now. Three of them.'

'Flynt killed them all?'

'He had assistance.'

'You?'

Cain raised the glass as if in a toast. 'Me.'

Moncrieff considered whether there was advantage to him in this. He could steer the information to someone – a friendly magistrate; Jonathan Wild, perhaps – and have Flynt arrested for murder. It would be an easy thing to pay witnesses to testify against him. It was a tempting thought and perhaps he might act upon it at some point in the future. Not yet, however.

'Have you considered that you may have a spy in your ranks?' Cain stated, casually.

Moncrieff was not taken aback. 'There are spies everywhere, you above all must be aware of that. And who would this secret intelligencer be acting for?'

'I don't know.'

'Charters?'

A shake of the head. 'My own observations suggest he truly has no heart to pay heed to your activities now.'

Moncrieff doubted that. He had never fully subscribed to the belief that the good colonel's interest in the Fellowship had waned. That was why he had recruited Gabriel Cain. The man was hideously expensive but effective, and had kept him apprised of every move Charters made. They did appear to be few in regard to the Fellowship, but Moncrieff suspected that the man made moves of which even he himself was unaware.

'Do you have evidence that I have a traitor within my ranks?'

'I don't.' Cain displayed something that Moncrieff had never seen in him before. Lack of surety. 'The important thing is, Charters believes someone is spying on him.'

This was interesting. 'And what makes him believe that?'

'I would suggest that someone within your camp alerted him.'

'And how did you get wind of it?'

'He told Jonas.'

That made sense. Charters always had trust in Flynt, as much as he trusted anyone. 'And Flynt told you.'

'He's my friend.'

'I thought a man such as you had no friends. Such liaisons are a liability, are they not?'

Cain drained his brandy. 'I confess that being his friend is not easy. He has principles, and for a man such as I that is difficult. Have you heard of the eastern religion called Buddhism?'

'I know a little of it.'

'I spoke to a fellow once, an old sailor who had accompanied Jesuits to the Orient. He encountered these Buddhists. Strange fellows, don't eat meat. At least, the sect he met didn't. So principles and I are like a Buddhist who is also a butcher. It's anathema.'

'They also abhor the taking of life.'

Cain grinned. 'As we both know, I'm not above that.'

Moncrieff did indeed know that. The men Cain said he and Flynt had killed earlier that day were merely the latest in a long line of lives he had ended. Occasionally, once he had been introduced to him as the Wraith, at his behest. Moncrieff had no idea how many murders he had ordered and did not delude himself that being once removed from the act absolved him of guilt. James Moncrieff was a realist, as was Cain. At least, he believed as much, though this bond he shared with Jonas Flynt was troubling. Perhaps it was time to put it to the test.

'Do you think Charters confided in Flynt the identity of this spy?'

'I don't know. I suspect Charters has nothing firmer than a suspicion.' Cain paused, again revealing that break in his confidence. 'Jonas believes it may be I.'

Moncrieff stared across the room at Cain. 'That is not an ideal situation.'

'I agree. I have done my best to alleviate his suspicions.'

'Were you successful?'

'Sometimes with Jonas you never know, but I do believe he cares little. He is focused solely on Hawke and that's why I suggest you let him have him.'

'Out of the question.'

'Jonas has no interest in the Fellowship.'

'So he says. He may have principles but he is not above obfuscation.'

'All he wants is Hawke.'

'He can't have him.'

'Why not?'

'I still have need of him.'

'Nobody is irreplaceable.'

'That is true, Cain, and it's something you would do well to remember. If Charters planted the seeds of your betrayal in Flynt's mind, then perhaps you have outlived your usefulness.'

Cain rose and set his empty glass on the mantel. He seemed amused. 'Threats, James?'

'I merely posit a theory.'

The humour left Cain's eyes. 'That's a theory that could get you killed.'

Moncrieff realised with a surge of nerves that he had allowed his arrogance to speak out of turn. His earlier claim that a single cry would bring his men running meant nothing. This man could snuff his life as easily as he could the candle behind him.

'You have nothing to fear, Cain,' he said, injecting a lightness in the words that his churning guts didn't feel. 'I still have need of you. But if Flynt suspects you, then it's something that must be dealt with.'

'I'll handle Jonas. You just consider Hawke's future. Give him up and Jonas will be out of your way.'

'You're sure of that?'

'He's tired. He's haunted. He wants rest, he wants peace. Give him Hawke and this will all be over.' Cain stooped to retrieve his hat from the floor beside the armchair. 'I know of your connection to him.'

Another thrill surged through Moncrieff's body. 'I have no connection to him.'

'I became friendly with his family, while I was in Edinburgh, before and after the Caribbean adventure. You know that, don't you?' Cain didn't wait for an answer. 'I'm sure you know about Cassie. Flynt's stepsister. The mother of his child. The only woman he ever truly loved. He has a yearning for her that supersedes all others, even Belle St Clair. I know you also know of her. Anyway, she told me about your father and Flynt's mother, how he took her against her will—'

'That's a lie.' Moncrieff's denial was born more out of habit than any true belief. He had long since come to the conclusion that the tales concerning his late father were accurate.

'Come, James, I understand that Jenny Flynt was a most beautiful woman. He wouldn't have been able to help himself. It's well known that the old man was physically incapable of keeping his breeches buttoned.'

Moncrieff winced a little at the crudity. 'That is something you would know very well, Cain.'

Cain grinned. 'I don't deny it. The difference is when a woman says no, I accept it. Your father? Well, he wasn't one to take no as an answer, was he? He ravished Jenny Flynt, left her with child. Jonas. Your half-brother.'

'There's no proof of it.'

'Ah, but there is.'

Moncrieff was desperate to ask what proof existed, but refused to allow Cain to know that he was perturbed. As every nerve in his body raged, his mind turned over Cain's words. What proof could there be?

Where did he find it? Was this some form of artifice? He didn't have long to wait before Cain revealed it.

'Your mother was a tough old girl, was she not? She interrupted the proceedings, in your own parlour, I understand. She was too late to prevent your father's seed from being planted, of course, the existence of Jonas being proof of that. And she denied publicly that anything had occurred. Even after the birth, and Jenny's death, she continued to deny it, spreading word that Jenny was nothing but a common whore. That makes her as guilty as old James. She was a tough old girl but what had transpired preyed on her mind.'

'This is all speculation.'

'No, she said it herself. Did you know she kept a journal?'

Moncrieff frowned. He had never been aware of his mother keeping any sort of diary. There was a book she kept in her chamber, a locked leather volume, but he had never seen her write in it.

'She was something of a Samuel Pepys, was Lady Moncrieff. She wrote everything down. Household accounts. Gossip from her friends. Her pride in your accomplishments. Her husband's infidelities – those she knew about, at any rate, for his dalliances were plentiful. I admit I am in awe of his libidinous capabilities. It embarrassed even me.'

Moncrieff searched his memory for sight of a journal among his mother's effects. 'These are lies, Cain, there is no journal.'

'There is and, guess what? I have it. It was found among her papers after her death and an astute lawyer decided it was better in his possession than that of the family.'

'Nonsense—'

'Lawyers can be as venal as you and I. Perhaps even more so. I bought it from him. The lock was still intact.'

Cain waited for this to penetrate. Moncrieff struggled not to react. The point about the lock could be a feint, a guess, for many people kept their journals private.

'Of course, he could have been lying when he said he didn't have the key. No matter, the lock is broken now. And a very entertaining read it was, too.'

Moncrieff's patience snapped, whether due to anger or fear he could not say. 'Get to your point, man, for I tire of your voice.'

'Just this. Leave Jonas alone. Give him Hawke. If you send anyone else, if you continue to protect the man, then you and I will be in dispute. I don't wish it, for I am most comfortable taking your money and what little Charters gives me. But in the end, I can make coin elsewhere and neither of you mean a fart to me. But Jonas Flynt does. Remember that.'

Cain moved past him to the window, leaving Moncrieff concentrating on ensuring the hand resting on his desktop didn't tremble. He refused to allow this hired killer who had no morals, no beliefs, no principles, to intimidate him. Moncrieff had many sins to his name, but he did have morals, unlike his father. He had beliefs, perhaps not in a God but in the power of the Fellowship and the great work on which it was embarked, a work that could transform the world, bring prosperity and perhaps even peace. He also had principles, which was why he had agreed never to pursue Jonas Flynt. He had decided some years before that his half-brother was no threat to his position, while even his moves against the Fellowship in the past were of little concern. However, he could not countenance being delivered an ultimatum in his own home by a subordinate.

Cain was halfway out of the window when Moncrieff spoke. 'Think on this...' He twisted in his chair to face Cain, who had paused with one leg in the room, the other over the sill. 'If Colonel Charters does focus upon you, if he does come to believe you are the viper in his nest, then he will take action. And who do you think he will entrust with such a task? There is only one man I can think of. And his principles might not take kindly to such a betrayal.' Moncrieff turned away again. 'Should that day arrive, then you would find yourself with Flynt on one side and the Fellowship on the other. A far from ideal situation, wouldn't you say?'

Cain's slight laugh was mocking. 'Should that day arrive, James, I'll come looking for you first. And you know I'll find you.'

Cain was gone before Moncrieff could speak again. He rose from his chair and peered into the garden but saw nothing move within the shadows. He slid the window down, and pulled the drapes. He stared at the turquoise damask for a moment, forcing his breath to ease and the beating in his chest to still, his mind flitting to his dinner companion earlier that evening. He had assured Cain that he had taken no action against Jonas Flynt. But that didn't mean he hadn't encouraged someone else.

30

'Damn you, Jonas Flynt. Damn you to hell. And I am just the fellow to do it.'

He was a tall man, muscled under his fine clothes, his features even, his jaw firm, his cheekbones sharp. His simmering anger was expressed in a hardness of his eyes and a tautness in his voice. Flynt had been threatened many times before, so many times he couldn't count, so he knew which was bluster and which sincere. During the discourse with this gentleman, there had been some bluster for sure, but at this point, he meant what he said.

Having left Cain to his own devices, Flynt visited Jack Sheppard to ensure he had returned to his room in the Rookery safely. Thankfully, Bess was not present; Jack had no idea where she had gone. Flynt was able to repeat his offer of taking the young man away from London and emphasise heavily that life in these streets was at an end without her customary interjections. Jack was receptive but Flynt feared the later influence of Edgeworth Bess, should the young man feel the need to tell her.

The rain had ceased as he walked back to Charing Cross, leaving the air curiously fresh, if still slightly charged following the thunderstorm. The torrent had washed away much of the muck from the streets, dousing the city stench, for which he was thankful, for he had not yet grown accustomed to it again. Such a reprieve would not last, he knew. The capacity of city dwellers to contaminate the very ground on which they lived was endless, and soon the streets would be filled with detritus: droppings from livestock being driven to market, from the horses on which men relied for transport, even those animals that had died, and human waste tossed from buckets and pots. Colonists had most certainly left their unwelcome mark in the Caribbean and the Americas, but the decks of a ship provided a welcome haven from the reek of humanity, even if below decks was a different matter. He missed the sea, missed standing on a quarterdeck staring at the wide expanse that seemed to stretch forever. Lately though, he'd begun to feel that he would never return to it.

The carriage was a fine one, slightly out of place outside the entrance to the Golden Cross. The coaches that called here were utilitarian, sturdy constructions built for the bump and grind of England's roads, but this rig was of a more delicate appearance, designed to display the position of its owner. The door sported a coat of arms featuring two rampant griffins beside an elaborate shield featuring the motto *Nemo nos insultet* – Let no man insult us. That door opened as Flynt approached and a man stepped down and into his path, studying him from hat to boot.

'Do I have the displeasure of addressing Mr Jonas Flynt?'

As a conversation opener it left Flynt under no doubt that this was a man who was vexed. His voice was deep, cultured, coated with disdain. His hand rested on the hilt of a somewhat ornate sword. The muscles of his jaw flexed and extended as if he was masticating upon something extremely tough and distasteful.

The coach driver watched them with utmost care, the reins held easily in his left hand while his right was buried in the folds of his coat, without a doubt holding a pistol out of sight. To the rear, a footman had alighted from the hind footboard, both hands behind his back. He would also be armed.

These men were not about to ask for directions. Flynt sighed inwardly, guessing who this gentleman was.

'Don't deny your identity, sir, for you have been well described to me.'

Flynt had no intention of denying it. 'I'm Jonas Flynt.'

The man pulled himself up to his full height, towering over Flynt by almost a foot. 'I am Lord Southern.' He waited for a reaction, then pressed on. 'I suspect you know of me.'

'I've heard your name.'

'I'd wager you have, sir, yes indeed I would. And I would win that wager, by God.'

Flynt felt a weariness creep over him that had nothing to do with the stresses of the day. 'How can I help you?'

'Help me?' Southern looked up at his driver. 'D'you hear that, Benson? This damned cur asks how he can help me. By God, sir, I should box your ears immediate, and I would, sir, were I not after a more meaningful punishment.'

'Punishment for what?'

'For what, he asks. I'll tell you for what, sir, for besmirching the honour of a lady and delivering a great insult to me.'

Flynt decided he was in no mood for this and took a step around him. 'Mr Southern, I am fatigued and in no mood for this.'

Southern stepped in his path. 'You will address me as "my lord", if you please.'

'And if I don't please?'

His flat voice and steady gaze gave Southern some pause. He glanced at Benson, then at the footman, as if ensuring they were still there. But he wasn't intimidated, for a mocking smile teased his lips, if not his eyes. 'You do not scare me, sir, most certainly you don't. I know of your reputation and of your belief that men such as I are but a waste of good oxygen. Nobleman I may be, but I am not one to be afeared of you, I assure you of that most ardently.'

'Then I suggest you state your business,' Flynt said, even though he already bore a suspicion.

'My business is the matter of Miss Belle St Clair, sir,' Southern said. 'You received her in your rooms in this very establishment. My man Benson here delivered her, and reports that she was alone with you for some considerable time.'

Flynt gave the driver another look and was instantly irritated by the man's smirk. If Belle had believed she could trust him, that trust had been misplaced. 'Your man is wrong.'

'You deny that the lady made visitation upon you?'

'No, but she didn't spend considerable time with me. It was a matter of minutes.'

'Long enough to bruise her honour, sir. Long enough for that. And mine, too.'

Flynt almost laughed. 'No honour was bruised. Belle and I are old friends. She had heard I was returned from the colonies and wished to say hello, that's all.'

'And you think it acceptable that you accept her in your rooms in this –' he waved a dismissive hand towards the inn – 'place, without a chaperone.'

The laugh built in Flynt's throat. 'As I said, we're old friends. She was quite safe in my company and nothing untoward took place. Now, if you will excuse me…'

He tried to walk around the man again, but was once more impeded. 'No, sir, I will not excuse you. I will not excuse your actions and I will have satisfaction.'

This time the laugh broke through. This was ridiculous. 'Good God, you're challenging me to a duel?'

'I am, sir, by God I am.'

Southern's voice had dropped now and there was a determination steeling his eyes that caused Flynt to amend his first impression of him. Until that moment he had thought him a typical English nobleman, full of sound and fury that signified nothing more than hot air, but there was a quality in his demeanour now, in his tone, that told him he was more than that.

It was at that point that he damned Jonas to hell, and followed it up by swinging his open right hand to strike him across the face. Flynt's instinct was to strike back, but he controlled himself. 'If you believe I'm going to pander to your madness, you're wrong. I have no time for such inanities. Nothing occurred between Belle and I, you have my word.'

'Your word, sir? You expect me to take the word of a common thief?'

Flynt wondered who he had been speaking to. Belle would never have described him as such, and there was the matter of how Southern knew what he looked like, as well as knowledge of his low opinion of the nobility.

'I expect nothing of you, but that doesn't mean I don't speak the truth.'

'I would wager that the truth and Jonas Flynt are ships that pass in the night. Yes, I have heard the stories, sir. I know you to be a most dangerous man.' His voice dropped even further. 'But I, too, am a dangerous man, as you will discover if you choose to meet me at Tothill Fields tomorrow at nine of the clock.'

Flynt stepped back two paces and allowed his coat to flap open to reveal the butts of his brace of pistols in his belt. 'Why wait? Why not resolve this now?'

He didn't expect the man to agree and was rewarded by a thin smile. 'You think I am some street ruffian? I have no need of going abroad armed.'

'No, you let your men do that for you, don't you?'

A grunt that may have been a laugh. 'I will not brawl in public with you. Even though you are no gentleman, we shall dispose of this matter as though you were. If there lives any honour under this ragtag exterior, then you will meet me at the prescribed hour and we shall settle the matter once and for all.'

He turned back to the coach, the footman springing forward to open the door, the pistol he had held behind his back now in full view.

'And if I don't choose to attend?' Flynt asked.

Southern settled himself into the coach, but held his hand up to tell his servant to keep the door open. He paused for a moment, as if contemplating his reply. 'Then it will go badly for Belle. She already regrets her actions.'

Before Flynt could retort, a flick of a finger saw the door slammed shut and the servant leaped onto the hind footboard just as Benson jerked the reins to set the horses in motion.

31

Cain arrived at the Golden Cross while it was still dark the following morning, looking as though he had been dragged out of bed just moments before.

'I am here, though God knows why, for this is an unearthly hour of the day for any decent fellow to be abroad. This had best be important, for I've not had my morning tup, and my landlady was looking especially alluring as I rose. I didn't have the heart to disturb her slumbers, even though my priapic urges were particularly energetic.'

The night before, Flynt had Mrs Wilkes find him a messenger to despatch to Cain's lodgings with a request that he attend at seven of the clock. He had not explained the need for his company; duels were illegal and though the legislation was not strictly enforced, it wouldn't do to provide a street lad with such knowledge. He placed his faith in the fact that Cain would realise that such a summons was unprecedented and therefore not one to be ignored.

Flynt conveyed the gist of the conversation with Southern. Cain listened, stirring some sugar into the coffee Flynt had poured for him.

At the end of the story, he sighed. 'Why do they insist that such affairs of honour be completed before any civilised man has had at least a breakfast, if not a morning tup?'

Cain's words conveyed levity, but his tone did not.

'Perhaps they prefer to get their bloodletting out of the way early so as not to spoil a whole day.' Flynt studied his friend for a moment. 'I take it Southern is not your usual foppish aristocrat?'

'I would say not.'

'You said he seemed a decent enough man.'

'And he is, as far as I know.'

'I sense a "but" there.'

Cain's smile was slim. 'There is another side to him.'

'I assume I'm not the first man he has challenged to a duel.'
'You're not.'
'And judging by the fact that he remains hale and hearty, he is most accomplished in the art.'
'He is.'
'Swords or pistols?'
'Both. And he be extremely proficient.'
'Has he ever killed a man?'
'There is rumour that he has despatched at least two, but the deaths were quickly covered up.'
'And the law took no interest?'
'The law has interest only in the transgressions of the poor, Jonas. You know what these affairs of honour are like. As long as the rules are observed, the law turns a blind eye, unless someone in the dead man's family raises their voice.'
'And the families of these men did not?'
'If they did, I haven't heard about it. Southern is obscenely rich, both personally and through marriage. He might have made a payment to the families.'
'Blood money.'
'Aye. The rich have their ways, have they not?' Cain poured himself more coffee, spooned another two heaps of sugar and stirred. 'You're not considering answering the challenge, are you?'
'He hurt Belle.'
'He implied it.'
'That's sufficient for me.'
Cain toyed with his cup.
'You don't believe it?' Flynt asked.
'It may have been an attempt to force you to attend. A suggestion that he has hurt Belle, a promise of further if you don't show, would prove effective.'
'You don't think him capable of harming her?'
'Any man is capable, but this particular man, I know not. But consider this, Jonas. You had the feeling that someone had primed him about you. The fact that he knew of your appearance, of your past. We both know that would not be Belle's doing. Whoever it was would be aware that you are not a man to be lured into defending your honour

in this manner. Other stimuli would be required. Your knight errant tendencies would provide that.'

Flynt mulled this over, then said, 'What if you're wrong?'

'And therein lies the rub. No actual harm needs to be done to Belle, just the hint that there had been and will be further. Whoever lies behind this no doubt had Southern's ear and riled him up about this. As I said, he's something of a hothead and it would be no difficult task to kindle his ire.'

'Who do you think did that?'

Cain smiled, but there was no spirit to it. 'It's you, Jonas. There are any number of candidates.'

32

They found Southern by a copse of trees, their branches stark against the sky, to the south-east of Tothill Fields, beside a stream that gurgled towards the Thames. To the north-west lay the Westminster Bridewell, to their rear was the steeple of Westminster Abbey. Beneath the marshy ground lay the bodies of plague victims, as well as over one thousand Scots brought here to die after fighting for a king who cared little for them at Worcester in 1651.

The morning was grey and cold and misty rain seemed to hang over the fields, rubbing away the starkness of the prison walls some distance away. Above them, gulls and crows wheeled and banked, their cries like warnings. Southern had brought friends, a considerable crowd for this inclement morning. If Cain was correct in his brief history of the nobleman's activities, then this would be a scene with which they would be familiar. Flynt searched for sight of Belle, but she was not present, unless she was being held captive within the confines of Southern's coach, which waited nearby.

Flynt and Cain dismounted from their respective horses and fastened the reins to a low-lying branch of one of the trees. It was good to be on Horse's back once more and he hoped it would not be the last time. He had no wish to join his countrymen under this sod. Cain's mount, hired from the stable owner, was a handsome black gelding that had snorted and bucked all the way to the fields. Cain stretched his back and rubbed his buttocks as they walked towards the waiting group.

'I'm out of practice with the saddle,' he said. 'My arse feels as if it's been pummelled. And not in a pleasurable way.'

'Too much soft living,' Flynt said, knowing that Cain was deflecting his attention for what lay ahead and grateful for it. He scanned the faces of the men clustered around Southern, searching for one he recognised, perhaps the one who had provided the nobleman with his description and lit the fire under his anger, but none was familiar. On the ride from Charing Cross he had considered who this might be. The hand of Charters – literally, given he only had one – suggested itself, possibly as a means of keeping him from seeking retribution against Hawke. However, Flynt thought not. Charters was cunning, and though Flynt had the feeling that the colonel was playing some sort of game with him, it wasn't one that would see him dead. At least, not through anything Charters arranged. Not yet, anyway. Hawke himself was also a candidate, but again he was not the type of man who would have the ear of a man such as Godfrey Southern. There was one other name that suggested itself.

James Moncrieff.

He was of equal rank, which would add credence to his words as far as Southern was concerned, which was another reason for rejecting Charters. The colonel was upper class, he was a retired officer, but he was not of noble blood, and that sort of thing mattered to men like Southern. So, unless there was another player in the game, then Flynt would lay coin that Moncrieff was behind this oblique way of removing him from the picture, at the very least having him wounded and rendered *hors de combat*, and thus protecting Hawke. When this was over – and he fully intended to make every effort to walk from this field both alive and unbloodied – he would renew his efforts to seek his half-brother's new address.

As they neared Southern and his friends, Cain whispered, 'If he is victorious, do you want me to kill him?'

'That would be unsporting.'

'The shedding of blood is not a sport, Jonas. Sometimes it's simply a necessity.'

Southern stepped away from the others. 'I suspected you wouldn't show, Flynt. A common criminal you may be, but it appears there be some vestige of honour in you.'

Flynt ignored the snide tone. He had no intention of debating what honour he had or had not. 'I would see Belle.'

'One last glimpse, eh?'

'To ensure she is well.'

Southern inclined his head to his friends. 'I regret Mistress St Clair is indisposed at present.'

Mindful of Cain's suggestion that his implication that Belle had suffered harm was a means of goading him, Flynt searched Southern's expression and demeanour for sign of dissimulation. However, he detected no such indicator. Southern was confident, arrogantly so, and the snigger from his companions suggested they knew something at which Flynt could only guess.

Southern turned his attention to Cain. 'And this is your second? A man of your own stripe, I'll hazard, a gutter waif with pretensions to something higher. You may dress a man in something akin to a gentleman, but that doesn't make him one.'

'A king can make a lord, but only God makes a gentleman,' Cain said. 'And I believe He missed the mark with you.' He smiled. 'My lord.'

Southern's own supercilious smile slipped a little. 'I will deal with you after this one.'

Cain gave him a little bow. 'I look forward to it.'

Southern glared at him for a moment, then turned away, already stripping off his coat. 'Then let us proceed. The morning wears on and I have need of a hearty breakfast.'

His friends laughed dutifully as Flynt turned away to remove his own coat. 'Was that necessary?'

Cain took his coat. 'No, but it was pleasurable. And I've angered him. And what is it you always say about an angry man?'

'That he is a careless man.' He glanced back at Southern, who was flexing and extending his arms. 'He doesn't look terribly careless to me.'

Cain had to agree. 'It was still enjoyable, though. Perhaps you should prick at him further. He has a temper, remember.'

Southern ceased his preliminary exercises. 'Come then, sir, let's not dawdle. Let's be at it.'

Flynt, with Cain at the rear carrying his coat and weapons, stepped closer.

'I'm the offended party,' Southern shouted, 'so I will have the choice of weapons. Do you agree, sir?'

Flynt shrugged. 'Swords or pistols, it makes no difference to me.'

'A sword is a gentleman's weapon, sir, and as we have already stated, you are no gentleman. Pistols it will be.'

Southern crooked a finger to a distinguished-looking gentleman in a sombre brown coat and breeches and carrying a mahogany case. The man stepped forward, cleared his throat. 'Gentlemen...' He paused when his eye fell on Flynt, perhaps reconsidering, but decided to continue. 'I am Dr Mortimer Brown and I shall oversee the proceedings, and of course treat any wounds, or pronounce life extinct should that occasion arise, which I sincerely hope it will not.' As he said those final words he stared directly at Southern, who waved a hand as if he was bored. The doctor opened the case to reveal two fine pistols nestling in felt lining.

'These are mine, Flynt,' Southern said. 'They are perfectly balanced, and are superior weapons in every way. Both are primed and ready. You are welcome to use one, or your own, whichever you prefer.'

Flynt held out a hand to Cain behind him. 'I'll use my own weapon, if you please.'

Southern obviously cared little either way. He removed one pistol and took a few paces away. Cain handed Tact to him unloaded, knowing Flynt would wish to perform that function himself. Gideon Flynt had told Jonas as a boy that a man should be responsible for his own load, whether in a weapon or in life. Flynt had adhered to that stricture as well as he could. Until he found out that he had a son he never knew. He now carried that load, but it was comprised of grief and rage. And guilt. Charters had been correct in that.

Dr Brown handed the case containing the remaining pistol to Southern's servant and took up a position between the two combatants. 'You each have one shot only. No other weapon will be wielded. If either combatant attempts to do so, then he will be forcibly restrained by my men here.' He indicated two burly men to his rear.

'I shall have no need of a second weapon,' Southern said, confidently.

'Whoever draws blood is the winner,' Brown continued.

'Whoever remains standing,' Southern amended, causing the doctor to look sharply at him.

'I did not agree to the death, my lord.'

'I don't give a damn what you agreed to. This man besmirched the honour of my lady and he will pay dearly for it.'

The doctor looked at Flynt, as if searching for a way out. 'Unless, sir, you would wish to apologise in this public place for the transgression.'

Flynt was about to reply, but Southern interjected. 'I would accept no apology.'

'And I make none,' said Flynt, 'for there was no transgression requiring an apology, Mr Southern.'

'"My lord", damn you! I will have respect for my position from you, you Scottish bastard.'

'Respect is earned, not simply bestowed through an accident of birth. My Scottish father taught me that.'

Flynt was following Cain's lead in trying to anger the man. And given the mottling of his flesh spreading from his neck to his face, he had succeeded.

'Begin the count, Brown,' Southern ordered.

'Sir, I beseech you,' Brown said to Flynt, 'make an apology. Avoid this unpleasantness.'

Flynt gave him a brief shake of the head but did address Southern. 'Tell me this, Southern. Tell me Belle is unharmed, assure me, and I will walk away and that will be an end to it.'

Southern's eyes narrowed. 'That is something you will never discover.'

'I will,' Flynt assured him, with a confidence he didn't fully feel. 'And I tell you now, if she is in any manner harmed, then you shall regret that you had ever listened to James Moncrieff or heard of the Fellowship.'

He said the name purposely, to see the reaction. It was a guess only, but he had proved correct, for Southern's face blanched. 'How did…?' He caught himself in time, tried to cover his surprise. 'I know not what you mean, sir. Get on with it, Brown.'

'He told me he was going to speak with you,' Flynt continued before Brown could begin. 'He's not pleased with you.'

The nobleman was visibly shaken; nevertheless, he sneered. 'You're lying, sir.'

Flynt struggled to remain casual in his demeanour, but in reality he was stumbling around in the dark. He risked a glance at Cain to his left, well out of the line of fire, and saw his frown. This was for his benefit as well as Southern's.

Flynt returned his attention to the man opposite. 'How would I know he had spoken to you, then? He pushed you into this, didn't he? Suggested that a man such as I dishonoured a lady just by looking at her. He didn't give me chapter and verse of your conversation, but that was the thrust of it, I'm sure. Now, why would he do that, I wonder? Could it be he wishes rid of you?'

He let that thought lie. Southern turned it over, without doubt replaying what he recalled of the conversation. Finally, he shook his head. 'No,' he said, 'you try to distract me with your lies. I shan't have it, sir.' He waved his pistol towards Brown. 'Proceed, doctor. We linger too long in this place.'

Brown gave Flynt a puzzled look and stepped back a few paces before raising a kerchief of white linen. 'I shall make the count of five,' he said, 'and will then let this kerchief fall. Then, and only then, can you fire. And may God have mercy on your souls.'

He looked from one to the other, then…

'One…'

They were about ten feet apart, pistols raised, muzzles to the air, their bodies presenting as slender a target as possible.

'Two…'

Flynt was unaccountably anxious. He had been in many situations where he might have fallen victim to a ball from a pistol or cannon, or the thrust of a sword.

'Three…'

The day before, he and Cain had stood in the streaming rain, waiting for those three men to emerge from the White Lion. He had known that would end with either the deaths of the men or their own.

'Four…'

He had walked through darkness as black as pitch in alleyways or stairways, not knowing who hid within them. But there was something deeply unsettling about facing someone in the grey morning light, while a crowd of onlookers held their breath and a learned man made the count. This was unlike anything Flynt had experienced before. This was…

'Five.'

The linen slipped from the doctor's fingers, fluttered a little in the slight breeze as it fell…

Even though Flynt was expecting it, he was still taken by surprise, and reacted slowly – too slowly…

…Southern had levelled his pistol, taken aim, but he moved too quickly, for deliberation was everything…

…but there remained a danger that his aim was true, so Flynt trained his weapon – too late, however…

…for Southern pulled the trigger and the ball was flying…

…Flynt still hadn't discharged his weapon, and all he could hope was that his ruse had been effective…

He felt it: the pistol ball.

It grazed his left arm, ripping the sleeve of his shirt, carving a furrow in the flesh of his upper arm. The pain was sharp, intense, burning, and he grunted, his shoulder dropping as he reflexively clasped the fingers still wrapped around the butt of his pistol to the wound.

Around him he heard a collective moan, as if there was surprise, even some measure of disappointment, that Lord Southern's shot had missed its mark. Cain made to rush to Flynt's side, but he waved him back and looked across the ground to Southern, who was as stunned as his friends that he had missed. One or two of those companions began to move towards him but were halted by Flynt's voice.

'Last man standing, you said. We both remain on our feet.'

Silence fell. The breeze breathed over the grass and through the naked branches of the trees.

Flynt raised his pistol, took aim. Southern looked around him, as if for aid, but remained rooted to the spot. He was panicking, but he had the good grace not to flee. He was arrogant, he was insufferable, he may have hurt Belle, but he had courage. Flynt took a deep breath, held it while he steadied the muzzle.

'Belle – is she harmed?' he asked.

A desire to refuse an answer built in Southern's eyes, but then slid away and he shook his head.

'You lied, then?'

A nod of the head, but there remained defiance.

'And Moncrieff?'

Southern's resolve hardened and he shook his head. 'I shall say nothing of my Lord Moncrieff.'

Moncrieff had primed the man for this challenge, of that Flynt was certain. That he was happy to run the risk of sacrificing this man suggested that he was either of no further use to him or he wished him dead for some reason. Flynt had allowed himself to be used once before by him, but only because their intentions overlapped. He would not do so again.

He dropped his arm and fired into the ground.

'Not today, Southern,' he said. 'And if you take my advice, you would do well to ensure that we never meet again, for if I find that you lie to me now and you have hurt Belle, then I will come looking for you.'

He turned away, the pain from his wound lessening but still smarting. Cain dropped into step beside him, handing him his coat and weapons, giving the arm a quick study. 'I've bled more while shaving.'

Flynt was considering a retort when a shout from behind caused them both to turn. Southern had darted to the servant carrying the mahogany case and wrenched it from him to free the second pistol.

'My lord, no!' Brown yelled, as the two men he had indicated earlier rushed forward, but Southern was already bringing the weapon to bear on Flynt. It was Cain who reacted first, his own pistol already drawn but held unseen by his side. He fired, the bullet catching Southern in the chest. He crumpled, the weapon slipping from his grasp.

Silence fell again.

The doctor knelt alongside Southern, placed his fingers on his wrist, then the flat of his palm on his chest. His head drooped for a moment before he rose laboriously to his feet. Flynt glanced to Cain, who shook his head in silent reproach. 'You never learn.'

Another cry, and men on horseback galloped towards them from the north-east.

'I don't like the look of this, Jonas,' Cain said, as he broke into a run towards their horses. Flynt lingered, straining to make out a face among the approaching horsemen, finally recognised Jonathan Wild, heard him call out for them to stop. The crowd dispersed hurriedly, some impeding the Thieftaker's party as they attempted to reach Flynt and Cain.

Cain was in the saddle, holding out Horse's reins. 'In the name of Christ, move! They're not here to clap you on the back.'

His foot in the stirrup, Flynt sprang onto Horse's back, followed Cain as his horse leaped over the stream, and then they were both galloping hard westwards away from the city.

33

They evaded Wild and his men easily. Flynt and Cain knew the country beyond the city well, having both worked it as highwaymen, and used it to avoid capture. They circled northwards, finally taking their ease in a coaching inn on the Oxford road. They had exchanged few words as they fled, making directional changes only, but now they were at a table, bread, cheese and ale before them, their horses being rubbed down and fed in the stables to the rear.

'How came Wild to be there, do you think?' Cain mused.

'He was sent, I'll wager.'

'By whom?'

Flynt had been pondering this as they rode. 'I'd hazard Moncrieff.'

Cain's lips tightened. 'How do you figure that? And what made you mention him to Southern?'

'A guess, a gamble. Someone had primed him before he challenged me, and to my mind Moncrieff was the ideal prospect.'

Cain exhaled heavily. 'He wanted you out of the way, to protect Hawke.'

'Aye, but perhaps also because of our shared past, and as punishment for disrupting Fellowship business. I don't know. I wasn't sure, so I threw the dice. If I was wrong, or if Southern had been a more astute player, he would have professed innocence more convincingly.'

Cain sat back, following Flynt's line of reasoning. 'So you believe Moncrieff's thinking was this: Southern, an accomplished duellist, would either kill you or you would kill him, and Wild, also primed by Moncrieff, would arrest you for murder. Either way, you were neutralised.'

'That's the way I see it. You said it yourself: they turn a blind eye to duelling because it's the province of the rich. Had Southern been victorious, then Wild would have remained hidden. Or transacted a sum of garnish.'

'And you are certain that Moncrieff is the architect of this?'

'I can't be certain, but who else would be so devious? And have cause?'

Cain thought of this. 'So you believe Southern was Fellowship?'

'Again, another thrust to the unknown.'

'It hit the mark.'

Yes, it did, Flynt thought, and that realisation brought up another possibility that merited pursuing. He sipped his ale, cut a slice of bread and slapped some cheese on it. 'We'll stable the horses here for now and then we'll head back to the city. There's a coach due in shortly.'

'Back to London? Are you soft in the head?'

'My main business there remains unfinished.'

'They're looking for us, Jonas.' Cain sighed heavily. 'This thirst for vengeance will be the end of you.'

Flynt made no response. He still wished Daniel Hawke dead at his feet, but there was more going on here than that. His jibe regarding Moncrieff had indeed struck home and he intended to confront his half-brother. There was also the fresh possibility to be explored. But first he had to be certain of Belle's condition. And to do that, he had to use someone whose knowledge of the streets surpassed even that of him and Cain – someone who could navigate the city without being seen.

34

Edgeworth Bess was not pleased to see Flynt and Cain at her door. Her face transformed into one of exquisite hate. 'I thought we'd seen the last of you, Flynt.'

She made no move to welcome them into the single-roomed hovel, so Flynt barged past her. 'It wasn't for the want of you trying, Bess.'

Jack was seated in the same ragged old armchair in which Flynt had last seen him. He was pleased to find him at home, even though he was about to request that he break the promise he'd made the day before not to leave this room.

'Here,' Bess protested, reaching out towards Flynt to pull him back, 'you ain't got no right to just walk in here without a by-your-leave.'

Cain gripped her arm and hauled her back. 'Jonas has business.'

'I don't care what business he has.' She wrenched her arm free. 'This here is our home. It may not be much, but that still don't give him the right to just walk in and—'

'It's all right, Bess,' Jack said, sounding weary as he rose from the chair. He seemed troubled. 'If Mr Flynt is here, it must be important.'

'It is, Jack.' Flynt ignored Bess's continuing protestations. 'I'm afraid I must utilise your services.'

Jack seemed to brighten, as if the act of simply sitting around this room with Bess had sapped his spirits and now the prospect of some action had revitalised them. 'Whatever you requires, Mr Flynt.'

'Don't you bloody dare, Jack Sheppard.' Bess strode quickly to stand between him and Flynt. 'You wouldn't leave this room when I asks, to go out and have us an ale or two, or to eat, to have us a good time now that you is at liberty to do so, so had me cooking over that there pot like some kitchen waif. Now one word from this here bastard and you is ready to go God knows where.'

'Mr Flynt wouldn't ask if it wasn't important, girl.'

'He's at the using of you, can't you see that? He's always been at the using of you.'

'Mr Flynt has always taken care of me.'

'And for why, has you ever stopped to wonder?' She gave Flynt a disdainful glance over her shoulder. 'Why would a cove like him want to help you? You knows what he is, what he's done. He's hushed people. He's spilled more claret than a drunken lord.'

'Bess…' Jack's voice was strained. They'd had this conversation so often before. Flynt had been party to many of them. The world had changed but everything remained the same.

'He's at the using, Jack, for Gawd's sake, can't you see it? And no good will come of it—'

Jack snapped. 'Bess, be quiet, will you? Let Mr Flynt speak without you sticking your conk in, right?'

Flynt had never seen Jack so ill-tempered with her, and he wondered whether he was beginning to see that she was a liability. Or perhaps his enforced time within these walls, albeit only a day, had frayed his nerves.

Bess's mouth clamped shut and she glared first at Jack, then at Flynt, then looked to Cain, who lounged against the closed door, his arms folded, a small smile playing on his lips. Her breath whistling through her nostrils, she whirled away and snatched up a shawl.

'I won't be staying here to watch you throw everything away, Jack Sheppard. You has the choice, here and now, to make, between me and him.'

Jack's eyes closed and his narrow chest heaved. 'Bess…'

'No, no…' She glared at him, catching her breath. 'For too long I've stood and watched you waste your life working for this man. I thought all that was over, and we was together, proper like, without him in the middle, pushing me away and pulling at you with his jobs and his favours. You had yourself a good thing with Mr Wild but you threw that away, Gawd knows how, and made him enemy instead of friend. And even though this bastard here weren't around, I suspects somehow he had a hand in it, p'raps through this one here.' She jerked her thumb towards Cain. 'So choose your pick, my lad, and make it a wise one, for elsewise I'll take my leave and you and me won't be a-bothering each other no more.'

Flynt rescued Jack from making any decision. 'I'm afraid we can't let you leave, Bess.'

'What does you mean, you can't let me leave?' When he didn't reply, she threw the shawl around her shoulders and marched towards the door 'We'll see about that, we shall.'

When Cain stepped forward to intercept her, she cursed as she swung a blow that would have been impressive had it connected, but he ducked under it and gripped her around the waist. She snarled a few more choice words, calling into question not only his parentage but also his sexual preferences and abilities, at the same time twisting in his hands, trying to jerk her elbow into his face, but Cain avoided it easily.

'I'm sorry, but I can't trust you,' Flynt said, then looked to Jack. 'You know I can't let her go, Jack.'

Jack nodded his acceptance, prompting a flurry of insults and abuse to flow from Bess's mouth. 'Be still, girl,' Jack said. 'What does you require of me, Mr Flynt?'

'Cain here will tell you of a Piccadilly address. You won't be recognised there, don't worry. I need you to seek Belle St Clair there and glean as much as you can regarding her condition.'

Jack had met Belle more than once. He frowned. 'You think she's been harmed?'

'That's what I wish to know. If you manage to speak to her, and her alone, don't trust this next part to any servant, ask her to meet me at her house.'

Cain, still holding back a squirming, cursing Bess, looked up. Flynt guessed the question in his eyes but left it unanswered for now.

Jack was already hauling on his coat. Flynt held out some coins. 'Take this in case it's needed.'

Jack dropped the money in his pocket, asked Cain for the address, and turned to the door, Bess still screaming abuse at him. He stopped beside her and Cain. 'Sorry, girl,' he said. 'But this is something I has to do. Mr Flynt, he's my friend. That's the beginning and the end to it.'

Cain hauled her to the side, leaving Jack free to open the door. As soon as he was gone, all the fight seemed to leave Bess and she began to cry.

'I'm sorry it has to be this way, Bess,' Flynt said.

Tears streaked the grime on her cheeks as she glared through them. 'You'll be the death of him, Jonas Flynt.'

He hoped she was wrong.

35

It was not an ideal afternoon for a stroll in St James' Park, it being damp and overcast, but Moncrieff had arranged to take such a constitutional at this time, and as he was desperate for the news the man brought, he kept the appointment. That things had not gone according to plan he already knew, but he wished details of how matters had progressed so badly and what was being done to make up for it.

He didn't blame Griffin, of course. He was not the organiser of the operation that might have removed Flynt from his path. That dishonour fell to Jonathan Wild, a man Moncrieff had met a mere handful of times, generally at official receptions where he had witnessed the so-called Thieftaker General's breathtaking ability to swagger and grovel simultaneously. He was a most distasteful creature and yet he had his uses in furthering the aims of the Fellowship – and by extension, Moncrieff's – as long as he was kept at arm's length, of course. And preferably somebody else's arms, in this case Mr Griffin's.

To a casual observer, they were little more than two gentlemen who happened to be walking in the same direction, Griffin a foot or two to the rear and to Moncrieff's left. Far enough to suggest there was no connection, but close enough for a terse conversation. The weather had kept all but the most hardy of promenaders indoors, which worked in their favour.

'Wild botched the job, I take it?' Moncrieff asked, keeping his head down so that his hat covered his face sufficiently to hide the movement of his lips.

'I suggested he wait to make the arrest in a place we could more easily contain them, but the magistrate wished to make a show of it.'

Moncrieff stifled a curse. All he'd wanted, at least ideally, was Southern dead and Flynt in custody. He liked to leave the fine details of such matters to men of aptitude, like Griffin, but that occasionally led to situations such as this, where men of lesser ability had to take the opportunity to prove themselves.

'The magistrate, not Wild?'

'Wild demurred, but not with any great force. He wished Flynt, and particularly Cain, in his hands, but he also had no desire to offend the magistrate.'

Swagger and simper. It would be his undoing one day. As for Cain, he regretted the possibility that he might lose him, but their discourse the previous evening had given him cause to doubt his loyalty. He knew that the man could be bought – most men could be – and his willingness to betray Charters and the Company of Rogues was proof of it, but when it came to Flynt it had become clear as crystal that money was not enough. Had Moncrieff thought him dependable, he might have suggested that he make himself scarce and unavailable to assist Flynt. As it was, he made himself fair game. Though the fact that he had also avoided capture was disconcerting. He would have much preferred the knowledge that Cain was safely tucked up in a Newgate cell, loaded down with chains.

Moncrieff halted at the side of a field and studied the grazing cattle. 'And what steps have been taken to find them?'

'I've called at Flynt's lodgings, forced my way into his room against the protestations of the landlady, but he wasn't there. Similarly, he had not been seen at the whorehouse.'

'Mother Grady's?'

'Yes. The house bully also attempted to prevent me from gaining access and I was tempted to teach him a lesson, but thought that, given the station of the clientele, you would not wish anyone present to be disturbed.'

Moncrieff inclined his head slightly in agreement. He had no use for the services of courtesans but many of his acquaintances, and government ministers, did and it would not do to disturb them in their endeavours. In any case, he doubted Flynt would be there. He knew the woman Belle was no longer in residence. Nevertheless, it was advisable to be careful.

'You have the brothel under surveillance?'

'Yes.'

'Front and rear?'

'Yes.'

'Dependable men?'

Griffin's expression twisted a little. 'As dependable as possible given the pool I have to draw from.'

Moncrieff understood what he meant. Wild's forces were made up of the dregs of the underworld. He would have preferred using his own people, but he had to maintain that arm's-length approach.

'We'll get them, my lord,' Griffin assured him.

'Of course you will. I have every faith in you, Griffin.'

The man was confident. Moncrieff less so. His own watchers had informed him that the St Clair woman was not to be found at the apartment in Piccadilly. She had been his weakness, his liaison with her the beginning of Moncrieff's lack of faith in the man. He could never trust someone who was not true to his marriage vows, and Southern had been until that creature managed to dig her claws into him. It meant he was open to manipulation, and the Fellowship could not have that. When he seized the position of Grand Master – he no longer pretended that he had been voted into the chair – he had ensured that every man and woman on the Fellowship council was steady and without blemish on their character. They were all married and faithful to their spouses and families. Moncrieff only feigned adherence to the Kirk but he believed in its strictures against infidelity, the result perhaps of a childhood listening to the exhortations of Presbyterian ministers. Or of his growing horror over the extent of his father's faithlessness. It showed a lack of character. It showed a lack of dependability. It showed a lack of resolve.

Moncrieff scanned the dark clouds. 'Flynt will go to ground. He knows the city, as does Cain. They know where to hide so completely that even Wild's scum couldn't find them. But he will reveal himself eventually. He still wants Hawke.'

One of the things he admired about his half-brother was his doggedness. He wouldn't remain hidden for long.

He began walking again, his cane tapping abruptly on the pathway. He was anxious to reach home before the rain fell. His scheme had partly failed, which was annoying, but it mattered little. Over the years he had seen many of his schemes fail. It was part of life, especially when he had to depend on men of lesser ability to carry them out.

All the same, something within him was glad that Flynt had survived. He could use a man such as he.

36

They'd had little fuel in the attic room, so Cain had left Bess and Flynt alone for a time while he found some. Flynt was glad of the opportunity to question the young woman. He knew she would resist his probing, so he would have to become the man she despised and he didn't wish an audience to that, not even Cain. She sat by the fire, staring into the flames with a dreamy look, as if enraptured by their movement, but looked up when he stood before her.

'You reported my presence in London, correct?'

Defiance hardened her eyes. 'I did, and I'd do it again.'

Of that he had little doubt. 'I want the address.'

A sneering smile curled her lip. 'I'll bet you do.'

'Tell me what it is, Bess.'

'I shan't be telling you.'

He pulled her from the chair by both arms. 'You will tell me, girl.'

First there was fear, then hatred and a bravery he hadn't expected to find. 'And you'll do what, Jonas Flynt? Threaten me? You did that before, years ago. Beat me? You won't be the first bastard what has laid hands on me and I'm damn sure you won't be the last. But then, you won't do that, will you? Jack wouldn't like it. And you needs him, you does, to help you in your dirty work.'

She had assessed him perfectly. His guts churned at even this level of manhandling. There was no possibility of him taking it further, not because of Jack, though that was a consideration, but because it wasn't in him. He didn't much like Bess, but he would not see her harmed.

He set her free with such force that she fell back into the chair again. Crossing her arms over her chest to rub where he had gripped her, she glared at him, triumph now in her eyes. He turned away, more disgusted with his actions than annoyed that he had not gleaned the information he'd wanted.

When Cain returned, laden with wood he'd obviously prised from a stairway or banister in one of the derelict buildings nearby, he clearly sensed something between them but limited himself to a brief glance at Flynt with eyebrows raised. Flynt shook his head, and Cain accepted that whatever had occurred was not to be discussed and set about bolstering the flames in the grate.

It was mid-evening before Jack reappeared, breathless and soaked through. Belle wasn't at the Piccadilly apartment, he told them.

'But I speaks with a young servant girl,' he said, a familiar twinkle in his eye, which drew a surly look from Bess sitting by the fire. 'This girl tells me that her mistress, Miss Belle, left early this morning.'

'How was she when she left?' Flynt asked.

'She said she was healthy, Mr Flynt, I doesn't think you has any worries on that score.'

'No visible bruises?'

'Not what that girl sees.'

This failed to satisfy Flynt. If Southern were an abuser of women, he would be adept at striking at points of the anatomy that were unseen. As Cain had told him, even a gutter rat like Knapp knew how to do that.

'She didn't limp, or wince, or show any signs of discomfort?'

'No.'

'Did you ask that directly?'

'I did, on my honour I did. I knowed you would be wishing to have the complete picture and the girl was most accommodating.'

Bess snorted. 'You didn't tup her then. She'd've been right disappointed after that.'

That brought a roll of the eyes and a sly grin from Jack towards Flynt. 'You ain't had no complaints, my girl.'

Another scornful grunt. 'None that I has spoke.'

'Did the girl know where Belle was going?'

'Just that she intimidated that she wouldn't be returning for some time.'

Flynt considered the information. Perhaps Southern had indeed been using a lie concerning having abused Belle in order to provoke Flynt further. But perhaps not. He wouldn't know for certain until he found her. He picked his hat and coat up from where he had left them on the floor.

'Where do we go now, Jonas?' Cain asked.

'You stay here. I need you to keep watch on Bess.'

'I doesn't need no husher of men to protect me,' she sneered.

'It's not to protect you, but me,' Flynt said. 'As soon as we're out of that door you'd be off to your friend Jonathan Wild, and I can't have that.'

He expected Jack to defend her but he remained silent. It seemed he had begun to see the light regarding Edgeworth Bess. Flynt's old friend, guilt, scratched at him, but he told himself it was best the young man see her for what she was.

'Why can't Jack look after her?' Cain asked.

'I have another errand for him.'

That generated a sharp, mocking laugh from Bess, which they all ignored.

'I need you to use whatever channel you used to contact Colonel Charters,' Flynt said, drawing another sharp look from Cain. Thanks to Charters' rule never to reveal the identity of members of the Company of Rogues to anyone, he wouldn't have known that Jack was working for him. 'Tell him that I must see him tonight at our usual place.'

'Is this wise?' Cain asked.

Flynt donned his coat and hat. 'I have questions.'

'Need I remind you that we're being hunted?'

'I'll be careful.'

'The boy is also wanted, Jonas. You put him at risk.'

Jack bristled a little at being called 'boy' and delivered Cain a heated look, but Flynt replied before he could take issue. 'Jack is the most accomplished man I've ever met at staying hid while in the open.'

'He'll get you killed, Jack Sheppard,' Bess said, her voice low. 'And when he does, don't expect me to grieve. In fact, when you comes back here – if you comes back here – I'll be gone. All it will take is this one to take his eyes off me for an instant. You ain't the only one what can vanish in the streets.'

Jack took a few slow steps towards her. 'No, Bess, it'll be you that gets me killed one day. I knows that now.' He looked at Flynt, then at Cain, suddenly embarrassed at what he was about to say. 'Gawd knows I loves you, always have and probably always will. But it's like a love a cove has for the gin and the wine. He needs it but some day it'll take him. You ain't good for me, Bess, I sees that now, and I ain't good for you. So maybe it's best you ain't here when I comes back. Best for you, best for me.'

Bess stared at him as if he'd slapped her. It was obvious she hadn't expected that from him. 'What? You mean that?'

'I does.' He turned away from her and moved swiftly to the door without looking back. As he left the room, one hand surreptitiously rose and wiped something from his face.

The room was in silence for a time, broken only by a sob from Bess that was so faint that Flynt thought he had imagined it. He risked a glance at her, knowing full well that if she caught him doing so, she would without a doubt snarl at him. She stared at the fire, but in profile her lower lip and chin trembled. For the second time that evening, he felt shame. It was easy to forget that under that sneery, callous exterior there lay a young woman who perhaps had dreams of a life so much different from the one she was dealt. It was possible she saw in Jack a means to change, even though she had never made sufficient effort in that regard. Her anguish at his leaving, and his final words, had hurt her. He knew Jack loved her, or at least the idea of her, but now he saw that she returned that love but lacked the ability to display it openly. And that was something Flynt understood. He wished to console her, but such a move would be rebuffed. Too much had passed between them this night and in the years previous.

He motioned for Cain to follow him into the hallway. 'Take care of her,' he said when he was satisfied the door was fully closed behind them.

'That one? She can take care of herself.'

Flynt thought of Cain's attitude towards Swift-Finger Jane that night in Saffron Hill, but decided against using it in response. 'Keep her safe for now, ensure she doesn't leave. When I return we'll give her some money and send her on her way.'

'The boy is well shot of her.'

Flynt saw again the heartache that had creased her face. 'He is, but he was the best thing in her life and now he's gone.'

'You know she'll report us as soon as we let her go.'

That was why he hadn't named the meeting place. 'I know.'

'And you will still have me free her?'

'By the time she reaches anyone, we'll be long gone from this place, as will Jack. She's hurting and she has every reason to hurt, thanks to me.'

Cain displayed little interest in Bess's sorrow. 'Going to the city is folly, Jonas.'

'They won't be searching the city,' Flynt argued. 'They'll have checked our respective lodgings as a matter of course, but they will reason that I would not be so careless as to walk into their domain.'

'Careless is not the word I would use. Stupid. Ill-considered. Remarkably dim-witted. They all better describe this course of action. As for Wild's men having any kind of reasoning abilities, I have severe doubts.'

Despite their predicament, Flynt smiled. 'I know my way around London, Gabriel. I can move without being seen. I can handle Wild's men.'

'You've been away for years. The city has changed and you're not as young as you were once. And you can't handle Griffin, believe me.'

'Gabriel, when did you become such an old woman? You were always the one who advocated taking the fight to the other side.'

'At least let me accompany you.'

Flynt was already moving down the stairs towards the street. 'No, we are better travelling solo. They're looking for two men. It's not much of a subterfuge but it will have to do.'

'You're a damned fool, Jonas Flynt.'

Flynt laughed. 'Thank you, Mother, and I love you too.'

37

Flynt spotted Wild's man with little difficulty. There was only one, which was lax; had he been leading the hunt, there would be three men at least and more in surrounding streets, and they would have ensured they were not easily identified. He wasn't dealing with members of the Royal Society, though. Wild's men were thieves and villains and, Griffin perhaps apart, lacking not only in reasoning powers, as Cain had said, but also subtlety. Of course, it was always possible that others were more skilful at concealing themselves, but that was a chance he would have to take. He had to gain access to the house. He had to know if Belle was there.

What helped him was that this particular watcher was known to him. Flynt was glad that Cain had not accompanied him, for he might have taken more direct action against Knapp, who leaned his good arm against a pillar at the piazza, cupping a clay pipe between his lips, his gaze drifting around him in a bored fashion. Having heard what he had done to Swift-Finger Jane, Flynt would also have liked to mete out some punishment, but the piazza was busy and another way to divert the fellow had to be found. The way Knapp's eyes occasionally lighted upon one of the girls who earned their living in these streets provided the answer.

Flynt sauntered around the square beside the church, keeping his hat low, even though Knapp paid very little attention to anyone wearing breeches. Finally, Flynt crooked a finger to one woman, not young, not old, but one who would have the experience he believed was required. He whispered a few words in her ear, surreptitiously indicating Knapp, who had his back to them, and then slipped a coin in her palm. She was at first bemused by the request, but one look at the half-crown told her this was no time to question. Flynt withdrew into the deeper shadows of the piazza and watched as she eased her way up to Knapp but walked past him, then came to a halt and looked around her. She sighed impatiently and glanced back at him; Knapp was by that time admiring her behind. She caught his look and smiled, turning around to step closer. She said something to him and he shook his head. She said something further and he shook his head again. Perhaps Flynt had misjudged the man. Perhaps his lusts were not as powerful as he had thought. Perhaps looking at and, in Jane's case, forcing himself upon women was all he could manage.

The woman Flynt had engaged was not to be dissuaded. She moved even closer, so close that her breasts brushed Knapp's coat, and one hand slid down the front of his breeches. She said something else, Flynt had suggested she offer him a free tup, and smiled her most inviting smile. What her approach lacked in delicacy it made up for in effectiveness, because Knapp did nothing to remove her stroking fingers and this time, when his head shook, it was less adamant than before. She leaned into him, her lips to his ear, obviously whispering something Flynt hoped was sufficiently arousing that it would break through what was left of Knapp's defences.

Whatever it was she said, it worked, for when she tugged at his arm, he followed, glancing only once at the door to Mother Grady's house. He had other things on his mind.

Flynt waited a few minutes after they had vanished from view, making a final scan of the perimeter for watchers he might have missed, but seeing none. Knapp would be missing for some little time, for he had requested that the woman take him somewhere a goodly few streets away and there detain him for as long as she could. He suspected she could engineer that for some considerable period.

Taking his time, for a man in a hurry was a man to be noticed, he crossed the square to the steps leading to the front door. It was Jerome who opened the door almost immediately, quickly overcoming his shock at seeing him, then, casting his eyes around the square and piazza, ushering him inside.

'Thou is taking a chance coming here, Mr Flynt,' Jerome said glancing up the stairs as he guided him towards the private parlour at the rear of the house. 'Two men called earlier inquiring as to whether I had seen thee.'

'Wild's men?'

'They identified theyselves as such. One were tall and silent with watchful eyes, the other more garrulous, smaller, and carrying one arm in a sling.'

'The latter is a man called Knapp and he was outside just now, keeping an eye on the house.'

'Did he see thee?'

Flynt suppressed a smile. 'No, he is currently otherwise occupied.'

'Right unpleasant, he were. T'other fellow—'

'His name is Griffin.'

Jerome checked the parlour was empty and closed the door behind them. 'Aye, that were how he introduced hisself. He were more polite but his courtesy were a mask only. They wished entry to search, but I refused and casual like dropped into the conversation that we had two powerful men doing an overnight and they wouldn't thank them for the disturbance. The smaller one, he were all set to force his way in, but it were my luck that Lord Samuelson took that moment to wander down the stairs in search of a midday tightener. He took them to task, told them there were no fugitives from justice in this house, and sent them on their way.'

Samuelson had been a regular at Mother Grady's when Flynt was more or less resident. He was one of the few nobles that he had any time for. He also had the ear of not just the King but also the Prince of Wales, or at least he had back then. The political fortunes of the rich and powerful tended to fluctuate.

Without asking, Jerome poured Flynt a brandy from the decanter on a table behind the door and handed it to him.

Flynt sipped it, grateful for its warmth. 'Is Mistress Belle here?'

'Nay, not seen her today.'

'Have you heard from her?'

'Not a word.' Jerome caught something in Flynt's voice or expression that made him frown. 'Is there summat amiss, Mr Flynt?'

'I hope not.' Flynt took off his coat and gave him a brief but accurate description of the day's events. Jerome's broad features darkened at the suggestion that Belle might have come to harm at the hand of Southern.

'I can send one of the kitchen girls to fetch her,' he suggested.

Flynt swallowed what remained of his brandy. 'She's not at the Piccadilly apartment. I've already sent someone.'

Jerome's gaze fell upon the blood staining Flynt's shirt. 'Thee is hurt.'

Flynt looked at the rip in the arm of his shirt as if he'd forgotten about it. It had bled copiously but the pain had long since numbed. 'Southern's bullet found me but thankfully not too well.'

'That needs tending to.'

'It's fine, Jerome, honestly. I…'

But Jerome was already gone, leaving Flynt alone in the parlour he had once known so well but which now seemed alien to him. The furniture looked different – perhaps it was – and the decor had been smartened. But that wasn't what seemed so unfamiliar. It was something intangible, something just out of reach. He felt like an intruder.

Jerome returned with a basin of hot water, some gauze, linen and a tub of salve, all of which he set on the floor beside a winged armchair by the fire. 'Sit thysen down, Mr Flynt, we'll have that wound cleaned right sharp.'

Flynt did as he was told while Jerome fetched him another brandy. He then ripped open the sleeve in order to see the wound more clearly. 'It cut quite a furrow in thy flesh. I'd say thou were lucky, a little more to the left and it would've breached muscle.'

Luck certainly played its part. It always did with Flynt. One of these days it wouldn't.

Jerome tore the gauze into strips, soaked one of them in the water and began to tenderly dab at the gash. 'Does thou really think that Lord Southern has hurt Mistress Belle, Mr Flynt? He seemed to care for her most tender.'

'Sometimes men can appear to be something they're not, Jerome.'

Jerome's grunt conveyed his agreement. As the house bully, he saw all kinds of men walk through that door from the piazza.

'Tell me how they met, Mistress Belle and Southern,' Flynt said, finally getting down to the reason for his visit. He hadn't expected Belle to be here, though he had hoped for it. 'Was he a cull of hers?'

'Nay, she had left such work behind, as thou knows, Mister Flynt. She were owner, pure and proper, looking after girls most careful like, tending to business. But his lordship, he come here with friends, never dallied with the girls, though, but he took a shine to her, he did, began to pay attention, just talking at first, you know, as a man does to a woman when he is interested, not like a cull to a courtesan.'

'And Mistress Belle responded?'

'Aye, though not at first but later, of a sudden like, I'd say she did, begging thy pardon for such an admission, as I know thee and she were... Well, you know...'

'That's all right, Jerome, I need to know. What there was between Belle and me ended a long time ago.'

Flynt winced.

'Sorry, Mr Flynt, but this here salve will bite a touch.'

That wasn't the only reason he'd winced. It was the truth of what lay between him and Belle being over. 'So she was cool to him at first?'

'Aye.'

'How quickly did she become more receptive?'

Jerome had to calculate. 'I'd say p'raps a month or so. Just with friends, as I say, and they'd play cards and have a drink or two, but he never took up with any of the lasses.'

'And you say her interest was quite sudden?'

Jerome seemed embarrassed. 'Aye. Thou has to understand, thou had been gone for such a long time and...'

'I understand, Jerome.' He did and he didn't; that was the damnable part of all this. He had no reason, not to mention any right, to feel the envy he felt now, but that didn't prevent it. He forced himself to focus on what he needed to know. 'Now, please think back. Can you recall if Mistress Belle instigated the connection in any way?'

'You mean if she began it?'

'Aye.'

Jerome's brow furrowed. 'I don't rightly recall.' He set the tub of salve down, stared at the wound but perhaps not seeing it. 'Now that I come to think upon it with me mind, I do believe it were Mistress Belle who approached him.'

'She knew who he was, correct?'

'Mistress Belle made a point of knowing who all the culls were. Mother Grady taught her that. Know the men well, she used to say, for in knowledge there is power. A house like this can only exist through such power. The power of the women and what they know. That's what she used to say.'

In that way, Mother Grady was similar to Charters, Flynt thought. Jerome had paused, thinking of his aunt, the woman who brought him down from Yorkshire when his mother – her sister – died, who gave him a home and a job, looking after the women of the house.

'And had Mistress Belle paid such close attention to any cull before this?'

'Nay, she always kept it professional like.'

'So Southern was different?'

'Aye. But truth be told, Mistress Belle wouldn't be the first to be smitten by a man such as Southern. I've seen it mi'sen, working both ways, a girl falls for a cull and t'other way about.'

Flynt had heard of such stories but rejected it in this case. Belle was too sharp to fall for a cull just because he was fair of face and rich. She saw the former as nothing but facade, while the latter would not interest her. The house was prosperous. There had to be another reason.

'Why him, Jerome?'

Jerome carefully dried the wound, now free of crusted blood, clean and coated with whatever concoction he'd smeared over it. He took up the linen and wrapped it around Flynt's bicep. 'Not for me to say. P'raps she was tired of this life and saw a way of bettering her circumstances.'

'She'd had many opportunities to better her circumstances, even before she inherited this house. Many rich culls took an interest in her, suggested that they place her in high keeping, am I correct?'

'Aye, there were one or two. Thou too, if I recall correct.'

Flynt had made an offer to buy her out from Mother Grady but had been refused. She would make her own way, Mother Grady had said, and didn't need any man to help her.

'And she rejected every one, true?'

'Aye, gently, mind, for she had no desire to hurt their feelings, but she was of the belief that her circumstances couldn't be much bettered. I mean, this here house is most comfortably appointed.'

'She was happy.'

'Aye... Well, she mourned Mother Grady something fierce for a time. And...' Jerome squirmed a little, suddenly ruffled. 'Well... she missed other people...'

Flynt shared his discomfort, knowing that he was those 'other people' to whom Jerome referred. He stood up, made a show of flexing his wounded arm as a means of covering his unease. There was a stiffness and a pang of pain but he knew both would ease. Jerome's dressing was most expertly administered.

'That's a good job, thank you, Jerome.'

'Me mam taught me how to do that, back on't farm in Yorkshire. We had many an accident there and in other farms. She said skill with gauze and linen would never go amiss.' He paused, busied himself with dropping the bloodied materials into the bowl of water. 'I'll say this, though.' Jerome's words were hesitant at first, as though he thought better of speaking further, but strengthened as he continued, determined to say his piece. 'I were right surprised when she told me she was leaving the house. She'd always said that of all the men she had known, there was only one who she would even countenance establishing anything deeper than a tup. But he was gone.' Jerome gave him a pointed stare. 'Thou hurt her, Mister Flynt.'

Flynt's shame caused heat to flush to his face. 'I know.'

'Did thou have to leave?'

'My father, my stepmother, were in peril.'

'Aye, but did thou have to stay away for so long? I saw her, Mister Flynt, standing at the window of her chamber, watching the crowds on the piazza, looking for one face that never showed. I said she were happy here, but that weren't exactly true.'

Flynt couldn't find the words. He looked around the parlour, remembering nights when he and Belle simply sat here and talked and laughed. When he felt at home here. He remembered her chamber, her bed, their bodies intertwined. With her he had been as close to being happy as he had ever been. And yet, the shadows cast by his life, and a longing for another woman, had been too deep. His leaving had been an imperative, his continued absence perhaps a choice, thanks to his desire to find Hawke. He thought that by doing so he was sparing Belle from the dangers his life presented, for he seemed to attract danger like flies to honey. He now feared that he had already introduced her to those dangers and had left her to deal with them.

He pulled his hat and coat back on. Jerome rose from his position beside the chair. 'Will thou find Mistress Belle?'

'I'll find her,' Flynt said, confidently. What he'd heard tonight helped strengthen his suspicions.

'Bring her home. This is where she belongs, not out there.'

Flynt nodded but paused in the doorway, a thought striking him. 'Jerome, do you have a shaving razor? And some clothes I could borrow?'

38

Flynt had taken the precaution of approaching the Black Lion's private room by the rear stairway but had still been challenged in the alleyway by Charters' watchers. That had pleased him, as it meant his appearance had been amended sufficiently to make recognition impossible by all bar those who knew him well. Even so, Colonel Charters was startled when he saw him in the doorway.

'My God, man,' he said, waving the watchers away, 'I confess, had we passed in the street I might not have realised it was you right off.' He studied him from head to foot. 'And those clothes are... well... not particularly becoming.'

Flynt had chosen the plainest garb he could from Jerome's limited wardrobe. He passed no judgement on the quality or even the sparseness, for he only possessed at most three shirts, all of white linen, three pairs of black breeches, a similar number of waistcoats, also black, and three pairs of dark hose. He laid the bundle containing his own clothes on the table and rubbed the bare flesh of his chin and cheek, no longer feeling the chill that had met him on leaving the house earlier. Jerome had shaved him himself and had done an admirable job, the sharp straight razor cutting the hairs but not the skin. When Flynt had studied himself in the mirror, he was distressed to see that the flesh that had been covered by the beard was now noticeably white compared to the sun brown of the remainder of his face. Apart from the scar, of course. Jerome had snapped his fingers and fetched a jar of dubbin, which he mixed with some soot to create a dark sheen on his exposed chin. The smell of the tallow and oil in the dubbin was thankfully not too overpowering and the effect passed muster to all but the closest of scrutiny, which Charters now gave it, peering into Flynt's face and sniffing.

'You smell like Mr Hines' candles,' he said. 'I wouldn't get too close to any naked flame, or you'll go up like a firework. Boot black, I presume?'

'Mixed with yellow ochre to lighten the colour.'

Charters studied the disguise further, grunted his approval, and turned to the table in order to pour two glasses of wine, one of which he held out to Flynt, who accepted it without thanks. Flynt noted that a third glass remained unused.

'You've been busy making trouble, Serjeant.' Charters sipped his wine and took a seat at the table. 'Though I'm glad to hear that you haven't lost your talent for mayhem, I do wish you hadn't been so public about it. Three men shot in a courtyard off Wych Street.'

'What makes you believe that was me?'

'Witnesses saw two men flee, both dressed in black coats and black hats. They could furnish no further description, but as soon as I hear of such slaughter, my thoughts automatically turn to you. And Mr Cain, of course.'

Flynt kept his own counsel, knowing it was always best never to admit anything.

'And then there was this morning's excursion to Tothill Fields,' Charters added.

'It wasn't my choice. Southern had his heart set upon it.'

'Yes,' Charters conceded, solemnly. 'My Lord Southern could be something of a firebrand.'

Flynt decided to get right to the point. 'Where's Belle?'

'Mistress St Clair? Why should I know of her whereabouts?'

'Because you make a point of generally knowing the location of everyone you recruit to the Company of Rogues.'

Flynt had expected him to deny it, but the colonel merely stared back at him, sipping his wine. The silence stretched for a considerable time. In that space, the fire crackled, the candles fluttered as a breeze caught them. Below them the tavern continued on its merry way. Singing, laughing, murmuring.

Finally, Charters set his glass down. 'I think perhaps you should reveal yourself, my dear.'

A footfall caused Flynt to turn. Belle stepped from behind the screen that concealed the gentleman's offices. She held her head high, refusing to avoid Flynt's eyes.

'Jonas,' she said.

'Belle,' he replied, giving her a slight bow, glad to see that she showed no sign of harm.

'How did you know, Serjeant?' Charters asked.

Flynt kept his gaze upon her as she walked past him, her skirts brushing against the rough-hewn wood of the floor. 'I didn't know at first for certain, it was a suspicion only.'

Charters rose to pour wine into the remaining glass, which he handed to Belle, who thanked him politely and lowered herself into a chair, smoothing the folds of her dress over her lap.

'And what first raised that suspicion, I wonder?' Charters asked.

'The roots were planted when Belle visited me and tried to dissuade me from pursuing Daniel Hawke.'

'That was genuine, Jonas,' she said. 'I was... am... concerned for your wellbeing and such pursuits eat at a man.'

He inclined his head to show he accepted that. 'However, it seemed just a little too coincidental that you would urge me to give up my search so soon after the colonel here had threatened me. But, as I say, that was just the first glimmer.' He paced the room, feeling the need for movement. 'It was later, when Southern had challenged me to the duel, that I began to put things together, but still I remained unsure of my reasoning. His informant, the servant who conveyed you to the Golden Cross, would have told him that you were with me only a short while.'

'Benson disappointed me,' Belle said. 'I thought I could trust him.'

'The man still had a duty to his employer, who no doubt tasked him to report your movements. If we are correct, then Benson would have been aware that we were together nowhere near long enough for anything to have passed between us but words.'

'Unless the fellow lied,' Charters suggested.

'What would he gain from that? Southern was too outraged for such a petty transgression against his honour.'

'My Lord Southern was easily outraged,' Charters observed.

'Especially when someone fanned the flames of his anger.'

Belle looked up. 'You don't think I—'

'No, not you. And not you, Colonel. I believe Moncrieff was behind it. Southern himself confirmed it, more or less.'

'He said as much?'

'He failed to deny it with any great fervour. And someone told him exactly what to say in order to goad me. Moncrieff knows of our history, Belle, and his tongue would have dripped poisonous words into Southern's ear.' Flynt fixed his eyes on Belle. 'And then there were the circumstances of how your relationship began. You had never before been interested in being in any man's high keeping, even when it might have suited you. But now that you have the house?' He shook his head. 'No, I didn't believe that.'

'Life changes us, Jonas,' she said. 'You, above all, should know that.'

'I know this, Belle. You would never put yourself in the position of being in the keeping of any man. And you had no interest in Southern until, all of a sudden, you began to pay attention to him. Something changed, and I believe it was you, Colonel. You suggested that Belle become close to him, because Southern was Fellowship and men speak more openly between the sheets.'

That drew a sharp look from Belle, and Flynt instantly regretted his words. They had pained them both. 'I mean nothing by that, Belle, you must believe me and forgive me. But you know it's true. What was it Mother Grady used to say? The bed chamber is more powerful than the confessional.'

'Not for all men,' she said softly.

He let that pass and addressed Charters again, who watched and listened with a half-smile that could signify entertainment or mockery. 'You recognised how intelligent and resourceful Belle was, and her house is frequented by many men of influence. You knew Southern was connected to the Fellowship, I take it?'

Charters nodded. 'His name had come up.'

'You wished information on the Fellowship and it was highly likely that Belle would be able to glean it over a period of time. And so you urged her to flirt with him, to accede to his attentions, to gain his trust. He was an easy target, in many ways. He was quick to outrage but also susceptible to Belle's charms, as any man would be.'

'Again, not every man,' she said.

'Any man with sense.'

'And without baggage.'

He let that pass, too.

'All very intuitive, Flynt,' Charters admitted. 'What confirmed these suspicions?'

He focused once more on the colonel, who still sported that half-smile. 'When Belle walked out from behind that partition. Up until that point it was conjecture, an amalgam of guess and circumstance. You brought Cain back into the fold, you recruited Jack, it was a mere stretch to come to a conclusion that you had also drawn Belle into your world.'

Charters didn't try to deny it. 'You had created quite a network of agents, Serjeant. It would have been remiss of me not to make use of it in your absence. Cain is most useful in many ways, as long as he is paid. The lad Sheppard is a veritable wellspring of intelligence concerning the underworld of this fair city, while Belle proved herself to be highly effective in gleaning information from those men of power who frequent her establishment. Mrs Grady was most perspicacious in her observation. Some men do indeed find themselves garrulous in the extreme while they are at the tup.'

'You put her in danger by placing her with Southern.'

It was Belle who denied this. 'I was never in any danger from Godfrey. I told you he was a decent man and I meant it.'

'Even though he was part of the Fellowship? You know what they are, correct?'

'Colonel Charters has educated me, but even though he was of their number, he was not a true believer.'

'That's what made him an easy target,' Charters added. 'Thanks to Mistress St Clair, I learned a great deal about the Fellowship and its workings.'

'Enough to bring it down?'

'Not yet, but enough to cause Lord Moncrieff some distress should I choose to use it.'

'And when will you use it?'

'When I'm ready. There is more yet to glean, and I'm afraid you cut off that particular source.'

'Ultimately it was his choice.'

'Aided by Lord Moncrieff, if you are correct in your analysis.'

Flynt chose not to respond. That was something he would discover for himself. 'You still have Daniel Hawke on the inside?'

Charters didn't hesitate. 'Yes, I do.'

'And he can bring you no closer to finding the cuckoo in your nest?'

Charters glanced towards Belle, then gave Flynt a warning look. 'That is not a subject for discussion at this moment, Flynt.'

Flynt continued anyway. 'Surely if he is so valuable an asset to you, then he must be able to aid you in such a matter.'

Charters' teeth gritted. 'Like you, I have my suspicions.'

'Do you care to share?'

'No.'

'Come now, Colonel, are we not all friends here? You surely don't suspect Belle, for she has been most effective, has she not? And I've been away for six years, so it can't be me. Jack might have proved himself useful but he is unlikely to be the spy, especially as you have aided him in his escapes.' He saw Belle's eyebrows raise. 'Didn't you know that the colonel here was most gracious in assisting him flee Newgate? He always says he won't help any of the Company should they get into difficulty, but he did so for Jack.'

'I like the boy.'

'We all do. And he is too valuable to lose, correct? It's most certainly not Jacob. I'm sure Mr Hines down below knows little of the Company's workings beyond what you tell him. The same goes for all your other agents, am I right?'

Charters' voice was tight. 'You know my methods.'

'I do. But that leaves one other who I would identify as a candidate, so long as Moncrieff pays him enough. Someone who had the wit to discover as much as he could, if there was coin in it. Someone you would use more regularly than your other recruits.'

Charters didn't reply but his expression revealed the truth. Cain was the suspected spy. Flynt had been making further conjecture, but now he knew he had hit the mark.

He placed his untouched glass of wine down and picked up his bundle. 'That's all I needed to know.'

'Where will you go?' Belle asked.

'I still have unfinished business.' Flynt faced Charters. 'Hawke. I don't suppose you would tell me where he is.'

'I wouldn't,' Charters replied, his voice harsh, 'even if I knew. Your despatch of his comrades has sent him to ground. But even so, I remind you that my stricture remains in place. Leave the man alone. That's an order.'

Flynt was already making for the door. 'I was never one for orders, Colonel, you should know that.'

'Flynt…'

Something in Charters' voice made him stop and turn back. The colonel had twisted round to face him, his expression devoid of its usual playfulness, his eyes hard. This was the face Flynt had seen when Charters ordered someone's death.

'Do not test me,' Charters said.

They stared at each other across the room and the years and all that had occurred between them. This was the man whom Flynt had dragged from a battlefield. This was the man whose life he had saved. Now he threatened his. Flynt decided not to respond and broke the eye contact.

Belle rose and met him by the doorway. 'What I said the other day still stands, Jonas. You should put this need for blood aside.'

He looked at his hand upon the doorknob. 'I can't, Belle. I have to finish this.' He opened the door, then stopped as she laid her hand on his arm. Even through the material of Jerome's rough clothing he could feel her touch.

'Did he love you?' he asked, not daring to look at her.

She didn't ask who. 'I believe he did.'

Flynt took a breath, not wishing to pose the next question but knowing he had to. 'And did you love him?'

When she took a moment to reply, he raised his eyes and saw the tears forming. 'Love is not for the likes of you and me, as I believe I've said before. It merely complicates and confuses matters, does it not?'

He nodded, accepting the truth of that, and opened the door.

'He was a decent man,' she said.

'You said that.'

'I cared for him as much as I could care for any man.' She paused. 'Almost any man.'

Charters remained seated at the table. To his credit, he had turned away from them, giving them this brief moment of what passed for privacy.

'He was good to you?'

'He was.'

He stepped onto the top landing beyond the door, letting her hand fall away from his arm. 'Then I'm sorry for your loss. I truly am.'

He hurried down the stairs to the rear exit as quickly as he could, feeling his throat constrict.

39

Flynt sensed the shadow.

Walking through the night-darkened streets, the cold and what they called in his homeland a smirr of rain hanging around him, he felt the presence, but saw nobody paying him the slightest bit of attention. He was either imagining it or whoever was behind him was an expert at concealment. He had felt their presence almost as soon as he emerged from the alley behind the tavern into the main thoroughfare of Drury Lane. His first thought was that Charters had sent his men after him to mount an attack. He slid his hand into the bundle and gripped the butt of one of his pistols, then turned left on Long Acre, surreptitiously looking behind him for anyone following suit. There were people about; there always were. The doxies, the culls, the drinkers, the gamblers, the link boys guiding travellers to their destination, or a robbery down some deserted lane, honest citizens hurrying to hearth and home or harlot, all avoiding the filth of the street, but all he perceived in his wake was a drunken man being propped up by an equally drunken woman. He stopped, made a study of them as they approached, ready to move if they made any attack, but they weaved around him without a second glance, then vanished into an open doorway. He trod carefully after them in case they lurked in ambush, but as he approached he heard them labouring to climb a flight of stairs, his muffled curses and her laughter echoing down the passageway. He waited until he heard a door close and then looked back along the street again. Nobody stared at him, nobody had stopped to feign some innocuous movement. But someone was there, he was sure of it. He had a sense for such things, and it had served him well in the past.

He walked the length of Long Acre, passing the various coach- and carriage-makers' yards that had set up home there, until he reached St Martin's Lane, where he turned left again, once more attempting to spot anyone making a similar turn. Again, he was aware of no person of note duplicating his journey.

Perhaps he imagined it. Perhaps he was letting events play with his mind. Perhaps...

The big man stepped out in front of him. His thick beard was level with Flynt's eyes and his hand, large enough to cradle a baby comfortably, gripped Flynt's shoulder to prevent him from proceeding further. Flynt attempted to twist free, but the grip held firm. His other hand – Flynt saw it was made of iron – was poised to strike should Flynt decide to make an issue of the situation. Flynt had no wish to make an issue of the situation. He'd survived previous entanglements with this brute only by the skin of his teeth.

'Gregor,' he said, injecting affability into his voice, even though he was nervous. 'How delightful to see you again.' He indicated the beefy paw on his shoulder. 'I see you have lost none of your social skills.'

The big fellow grunted, which was his usual manner of communicating. Flynt peered around the man's girth to search behind him, knowing that where Gregor was, his mistress was bound to be near. 'And where is the lovely Madame de Fontaine?'

'I'm here, Jonas.'

The familiar voice, its native Scots still evident, came from behind him. In that moment he knew that it had been her he had sensed behind him, while Gregor had used another, more circuitous, route to intercept him.

'Impressive work, Gregor, on catching up,' he said, the compliment sincere. 'You're remarkably nimble for such a big laddie.'

'Oh, Gregor is extremely nimble,' said Madame de Fontaine, coating her words with a heavy layer of suggestion. Flynt had never known for certain if she and the big Russian had ever been lovers, but knowing her appetites, there was certainly a history there.

'Gregor must have veered off before I turned down St Martin's,' he said. 'How did you know this was the route I would take?'

She compressed her lips and delivered a patient look as if she was talking to a child. 'You were predictable, Jonas.' She wagged a finger. 'You really should take more care. When you left the Black Lion, I suspected your plan was to return to the Rookery and your friends – yes, I know of them and their whereabouts – but I knew you had an inkling that someone was following and wouldn't risk leading anyone to the disgusting rat trap. In reality, I was ahead of you. I had taken a gamble on Long Acre. You're not the only one who will wager, Jonas. I truly believed you would turn left on St Martin's, so I lingered in that little alley yonder while Gregor waited here to intercept you. And here we are.'

'And if I had turned right on St Martin's?'

'If you did, then there was no harm done. I knew where you'd be.'

Making a note to take her advice and be more careful in the future, Flynt did what he could to retain his aplomb. 'So, Madame, what brings you back to London?'

'Formality, Jonas? After all we mean to each other? Surely you can call me Christy.'

He jerked a thumb towards Gregor behind him, who continued to hold him. 'Suspended as I am in this vice, I feel no inclination to be less formal.'

A quick nod from her resulted in Gregor releasing him. Flynt swore he dropped an inch or two to the ground. He fixed his clothing and surreptitiously rubbed his shoulder, still feeling the impression of those hairy fingers.

Christy seemed concerned, reached out to gently caress his arm. 'Oh dear, did he hurt you?'

'Of course he hurt me, that's what Gregor does, is it not?'

A sly little smile teased her lips and eyes. 'Not all the time. Although sometimes it can be fun.'

Flynt couldn't hide his own smile. He was unable to do anything other than like this woman, even though he trusted her about as far as he could throw Gregor. She was without doubt the most sexually liberated female he had ever met, and that included Belle, who had been raised within the confines of a bordello since a child. For Belle, sex had become a profession and not through choice. For Christy, it was both a leisure pursuit and a weapon.

'You didn't say why you're in London, Christy,' he repeated.

'Well, let's say that it was best I make myself scarce from Paris.'

Christy de Fontaine, though Scottish by birth, was often – but not always – an agent for France. She had married a rich French merchant who, when he died, left her a fortune and a route into the highest echelons of Gallic society. That eventually led to her talents being recognised by the intelligence services. Christy, however, being of a mercenary bent, discovered that she could further bolster her fortune by hiring herself out to other nations and agencies, including on occasion the Company of Rogues and even the Fellowship. Like Cain, she harboured no patriotic or political motives for the work she did. She was influenced solely by coin and a desire to enjoy herself as much as she could. Along the way she met Grigori Vasilovich, who had once been a member of the *Streltsy*, the Russian praetorian guard, who had become so powerful that the Tsar Peter believed them a threat to his own dominion and had them disbanded. Just to make sure they fully understood they were no longer required, he'd had hundreds slaughtered. Grigori left the country to put his fighting – and, to be frank, murdering – skills to use as a soldier of fortune, along the way joining forces with Madame de Fontaine, who called him by the Scottish version of his name, Gregor.

'You're out of favour again?' Flynt said. 'What was it this time?'

She gave him a little shrug accompanied by a smile that managed to be both coy and suggestive at the same time. 'It was a matter of an intimate nature involving one of the king's ministers. It became something of an embarrassment for him.'

'You had an affair with a member of Louis' inner circle?'

'No, not him, his wife. Hence his embarrassment.' She laughed when she saw Flynt's eyebrow raised. 'Don't look so shocked, Jonas, she is a most becoming woman and you know I take my pleasures in whatever way I wish.' She sighed in a wistful manner. 'And there was a great deal of pleasure but it ended when her husband discovered us *in flagrante*.' She affected a tiny frown. 'Took it quite personally for some reason. Anyway, I had to make myself scarce for a time. Thankfully, I had a commission here in London to attend to.'

Flynt hadn't been shocked. Nothing Christy de Fontaine could do would shock him. 'And for whom is this commission undertaken?'

She waved a finger at him and tutted. 'Now, now. To paraphrase the words of Mr William Congreve, you know I'm not a lady to kill and tell.'

Flynt gave Gregor another glance. 'You're here to kill somebody?'

She laughed. 'A figure of speech only.'

That she had killed before, Flynt had little doubt, and she didn't always have Gregor do the deed. It was rumoured that she began with that rich husband, giving him a helping hand in his final steps towards eternity. The thing about Christy de Fontaine was that she liked to tease Flynt, not just with her innuendo but also with whatever mission she was on. The first time they had met, he and Gregor had grappled and she would have left him for dead on a bare wooden floor in Southwark. However, he managed to best the Russian, not without difficulty, but it had been close and even now he could feel the grip of that false hand – wooden, then – on his throat. After that, she seemed to take an interest in his welfare, assisting him with oblique statements and hints, recruiting him on one occasion to assist in the freeing of a Scots nobleman from the Tower of London, but always with the promise that one day their relationship, whatever it was, could turn loving, interspersed with the threat that it might become lethal. One thing he knew for certain: she didn't seek him out on this night just for some badinage.

She reached out and stroked his cheek. 'I think I prefer you with the beard.'

She had seen him before he'd had Jerome shave him. That meant she had been watching him.

She appraised the rest of him with a practised eye. 'You were never fashionable, Jonas, but I would suggest you have a meaningful conversation with whatever tailor you use. This apparel simply does not suit you.'

'What is it you wish of me, Christy?'

She brushed her body across his. 'What I always want, Jonas. You. Me. A night of passion.'

Flynt's eyes darted to Gregor behind her, who watched them, his eyes impassive. 'What would Gregor say to that?'

'Well, I didn't think you'd want to make it a threesome, but I'm open to it, if you are.'

That made him grin. She could always do that. 'What does Gregor think of you propositioning other men?'

She detached herself from Flynt to stroke his chest. 'Gregor understands I have my peccadilloes, as does he. We're very accommodating of each other's pleasures, aren't we, my big Russian bear?'

He made a noise in his throat that might have been an affirmative, it might have been a warning; Flynt had no way of telling. 'As talkative as ever, I see.'

'Gregor is a man of few words.'

She had once told him that the Russian did talk, but Flynt had never heard him utter much more than a grunt.

'Christy, the night wears on and I have places to be. State your business and let me be on my way.'

She gave him a reproving look. 'Why are you always so brusque? Can't two friends take a moment or two to enjoy each other's company, to reacquaint themselves after being so long apart? You've been a very busy boy in recent years and I've missed you. Your few days back in London have not been uneventful. You've upset some people it would be best not to upset.'

He felt he was reaching the true agenda behind this meeting. 'And who would that be?'

'Please, Jonas, you know I won't tell you that, professional courtesy, *et cetera et cetera*. But I am here to help you, or at least offer some advice.' She reconsidered. 'Well, to repeat some advice I gave you some time ago. Don't you remember? Concerning the intricacies of a timepiece? I was very proud of it.'

'Yes, you were, for you've had occasion to remind me of it previously.'

'And I do again, for though you are a worldly man, Jonas darling, you remain something of a *naïf*. You would do well to take to heart my eternal warning to you regarding the intricacies of the life we lead.'

He remembered it well, for he had indeed thought of it often over the years, and when he did it generally proved to be extremely accurate. It had first been delivered in a dark street not unlike this one, but many hundreds of miles north, on another cold night and Christy stood as near to him as she did now.

The dial is merely the public face of the clock, she said. *The maker needs you to know only what he believes you must know, that is the time of day, and so will have you look at the face alone where all is straightforward. One hand marks the minutes and in turn moves the hour hand. But to understand how it all works you must look below the surface. There are cogs and ratchets and tiny little wheels... so tiny it is a wonder the watchmaker can operate them at all, and they all work in harmony while at the same time working against each other. One may turn this way, another that, but together they make the timepiece tick...*

'Wheels within wheels,' he said aloud.

'You do remember, I'm so pleased.' She did sound genuinely delighted.

'And that's what's happening now?'

'That is what is always happening in our world, Jonas, you should be aware of that by now. Nothing is ever as it seems. Take your young friend Jack, for instance.'

'What about him?'

'Who was it, do you wonder, who alerted Jonathan Wild to his true employer, our mutual friend Colonel Nathaniel Charters?'

That had puzzled Flynt too, but he'd not had the time to pursue it. 'I take it you know?'

'Of course I know, because it was me.'

Anger stirring, Flynt stared at her for a long time, then at Gregor, who remained as still as ever. He had to control his temper. He was cold and tired and he had not the inclination, nor less the energy, to attempt to tackle him. 'Why would you do that, Christy?'

'Not out of malice, of that I can assure you, and I hope you accept that. It was business only.'

Malice or business, she had still endangered the lad, and for that he wouldn't forgive her. 'What sort of business?'

'Wrong question, darling. What you should be asking is whose business.'

He considered this. 'The Fellowship?'

'No, try again. Think closer to home.'

Flynt mulled it over again. *Closer to home. What did that mean?*

She tutted. 'Very well, I'll give you a hint. You've recently been in his company.' Her brow crinkled as she became pensive for a moment. 'Both personally and by employment, now that I think on it.'

Personally and by employment.

'Charters?' He was genuinely shocked, but only for a moment. Of course it was Charters. He'd just left him and he'd once been part of the Company of Rogues.

'He wanted the lad out of London, for he had business for him elsewhere,' she explained. 'How else could he do that other than by making life too difficult in the city? So he had him arrested and then assisted him to escape from Newgate.'

He should have known the colonel hadn't assisted Jack out of affection, recognition of past service, or charity. There had to be something of benefit to him. That is, if what she said was true.

Wheels within wheels. Always wheels within wheels.

'What is the nature of this business elsewhere?'

'Alas, I'm not omniscient. That is something you would have to glean from the man himself. But he had me steer the information to Mr Wild, who has forgiven me for my play-acting when we first met.'

She had posed as a noblewoman seeking the return of an incriminating letter, which in reality was a document being sought by her employers — in that case, the Fellowship using Moncrieff's father as an intermediary, as well as Colonel Charters, which in turn saw Flynt becoming involved. It had led to the struggle with Gregor in Southwark and from there to this curious relationship, which Flynt had to confess had brought dividends in the past. At this confession his anger rose but subsided. Rage at this woman made no difference. She was what she was, just as he was.

'I made it seem as if I had made a slip of the tongue,' she said, 'though my tongue seldom slips in that way. Other ways, perhaps, more pleasurable ways.'

Though his anger had vanished, Flynt had no time now for her coquettish behaviour. 'Wild might have killed the boy.'

'That is not his habit,' she said, confidently. 'There is no profit in killing. Much better to arrest him, claim the reward and see him on the road to Tyburn.'

Flynt saw the sense in her reasoning, but even so, it was a risky stratagem on Charters' part. 'So Charters is your employer?'

'Then, yes.'

'But not now?'

'Ah-ah,' she chastised. 'Rules are rules.'

'God damn it, Christy—'

'Don't be angry with me, Jonas. I was offered another commission and I took it. It's my profession.'

'It's your nature,' he snapped. 'You care little for the welfare of others.'

Christy took a step back, obviously hurt. 'How can you say that when here I am, warning you that your own life is in danger.'

'My life is always in danger. That's my profession.'

'But you are also being used.'

'By whom?'

She shook her head. 'That's not how I operate, Jonas, you know that. All I will tell you is that there is a watchmaker at work here and you are one of the cogs in his creation. My advice is to leave London tonight. The longer you tarry here, the greater the danger grows.'

'Be more specific.'

She began to back away, Gregor standing his ground in case Flynt decided to pursue. 'No, *that* is not in my nature. Please heed my warning, Jonas. It will be the only one I will give. I would hate to see any harm befall you.'

'Daniel Hawke,' he said, knowing he was throwing this out but not wishing to give her the final word.

She paused, her head tilted to one side, her smile returning. 'You took your time asking me about him.'

'You know I seek him.'

She gave him an overtly patient look. 'Jonas, how long have we been friends?'

He didn't reply. He was never sure if they were friends.

'You must know that I make it my business to know all I can about you,' she said.

'Then you'll know where he is.'

She closed the gap between them again. 'And if I did, why would I tell you?'

'For friendship's sake.'

Her face turned slightly to the side to regard from the corner of her eye. 'Oh, that is a foul blow.'

'To quote Mr John Lyly – the rules of fair play do not apply in love and war.'

Those lips twitched. 'And what is this, love or war?'

His own smile returned. 'A bit of both.'

'Mmm,' she said. 'I do believe I'm wearing you down.' She took a breath, as if she was reaching a decision. 'Very well, I can give you an address, but I cannot guarantee that he remains there. You killed his men and he would be a fool if he has remained *in situ*.'

Flynt was certain Hawke would indeed have moved on, but if he had his last location, he might at least glean some further information. She gave him an address in Coventry Street. This time, before she moved away, she raised herself up, clasped his face with both hands and kissed him. Her lips were soft and cool, the tongue that darted between his teeth enticing. His body reacted; he was human, after all, and this woman carried with her an allure that he found hard to resist. His hands reached out to her waist in an instinctive, unconscious movement, but she skipped away.

'Another time, darling,' she said. 'Perhaps when you have regrown your beard. I do believe it would tickle me in a most exciting way.' She backed away, blew him another kiss and wiggled her fingers at him. 'Oh, and when you next see Mr Cain, please do send him my love. And inquire as to the health of his hind parts.'

Flynt had no idea what she referred to but knew one thing: she and Cain had shared their mutual love of carnality. That surprised him not at all, for they were well suited to each other. Gregor remained motionless. If he felt anything about watching Christy kiss Flynt, or refer to her connection to another man, it didn't reflect in those deep, dead eyes.

Flynt gave him a goodbye nod. 'Nice beard, Gregor.'

With a final guttural noise rumbling from the depths of that facial hair – it might have been a thanks, it might have been an insult; Flynt couldn't tell, for he didn't speak grunt – Gregor followed Christy.

40

A light burned in the lower window of the house on Coventry Street. It was one of the few buildings on this narrow roadway connecting Leicester Fields with Haymarket that was residential, the others being given over to houses for gaming and sex. Flynt recognised that any hope the presence of that candle meant Hawke remained in residence was a slim one. He had been on his trail for a long time and if he had learned one thing about the man, it was that he had the ability to move at a moment's notice and had always managed to keep himself at least one address ahead of Flynt all these years. Charters had said he'd gone to ground, like an animal in flight. Nonetheless, Flynt would follow the trail, for he might yet sniff something in the wind that would force Hawke to break cover.

He rattled the somewhat ornate knocker, then stepped back down the two steps to the street. He didn't know who would open the door, whether an innocent or someone not so innocent. If the former, he didn't wish to appear intimidating. If the latter, then some air between them was always recommended. Nevertheless, he had already drawn a pistol, which he hid behind his back, holding his clothing bundle across his torso with his other hand. It afforded at least some protection if the person he now heard drawing back locks on the door was armed.

It was a young man who opened the door. Big, burly, his hands showing the slight nicks and scabs that came with manual labour. He carried a lantern in one hand, a cudgel in the other, and he peered down from the top of the steps at Flynt with wary eyes.

'Who knocks at this here time of eve?' he asked, the sound of the country heavy on his words.

'I mean no harm, friend,' Flynt said, ready to reveal the pistol if the young man decided to wave that club. 'I seek a man by the name of Daniel Hawke. He rooms here, or at least did.'

A woman appeared at the man's shoulder, one hand on his upper arm, pushing him gently out of the way. 'He ain't here,' she said.

She was situated in that curious middle age in which Flynt would find himself before he knew it. In fact, he realised, he was already in it. She had been making herself ready for bed, her head wrapped in some kind of material that Flynt could not distinguish in this light, one hand clutching the neck of her robe.

'Is he out for the evening or…?'

'He moved on,' she said, her accent similar to the young man's; Flynt presumed he was her son. 'His friends, too, though I didn't see them carrying their traps out the door. They seemed nice fellers, for colonials.'

Flynt forced a charming smile. 'May I have the pleasure of your name, madam?'

'I don't know if it be a pleasure or not, but it be Elizabeth Jelly, Mrs Elizabeth Jelly. This be my lad. And who might you be, as we're being so familiar?'

If Hawke was gone, he saw no reason for subterfuge. 'My name is Jonas Flynt.'

'Be you friend to Mr Hawke?' She added an *r* into her pronunciation of the name.

'Aye,' he said, 'from the Americas.' He raised his bundle a little, as if it were his traps. 'Just newly arrived. He'd sent me this address, told me to meet him here.'

Mrs Jelly regarded him with caution. 'You doesn't sound like them other fellers, and they was from the Americas. You sound more Scotch.'

Her voice was even enough, but her expression suggested that judgement was deferred on his blood.

'I've been there only a year or more. The Virginia colony. Bart has lived there for many a year,' he said, thinking fast, 'and his own tongue was watered down by the many different tongues that reside across the water. The boy was colony-born.'

'I does reckon that would explain it,' she said, still wary. 'Jim were the boy's name, if I recall correct.'

'Jed,' Flynt corrected, unsure whether it was a genuine mistake or some kind of test. 'Short for Jedediah.'

She nodded, his knowledge of their names convincing her that she knew them. 'That be right. Both names from scripture. My own boy here is Amos, named after the prophet.'

Flynt bobbed his head in the young man's direction. 'It's a good name.'

'That it be,' said Mrs Jelly.

'Jonas is derived from the Holy Word, too.' He hoped that might play well with her. 'From Jonah, he of the whale.' He couldn't tell whether he had somehow ingratiated himself further so he pressed on. 'So, Mr Hawke. Did he leave any forwarding address? Or any indication at all as to where he was bound?'

'Not a word. He packed up his traps, settled his dues like a gentleman, even if he were a colonial, and then went off.'

'By foot, horse, carriage?'

'I didn't pay no never mind. As soon as he were out the door I went up to ensure he'd left the rooms above in proper order. Which he had. As I said, a proper gentleman.'

'For a colonial,' Flynt added, receiving a look that told him she had doubts whether anyone from north of the border could lay claim to being a gentleman.

'I ain't reletting the rooms right now,' she said. She stopped abruptly, and he wondered if in her mind she had completed the sentence with *not to a Scot*.

'I reckons that Mr Hawke be right popular, Mam,' said Amos.

'Why do you say that?' Flynt asked.

'Youm be the second feller what come by asking after him. Come by earlier this eve, he did.'

'I didn't see him, Amos,' said Mrs Jelly.

'You were out, Mam, down at bookseller's. Sometimes I think you might be best moving in there.'

'This fellow.' Flynt eased him back to what interested him. 'Can you describe him?'

'Tall feller, he were, easy as tall as youm be. Well spoke.'

'Young, old?'

'Didn't pay no 'tention to that. It were already grown dark and he kept hisself down in street, like youm. I didn't bring this here lantern, then, not like now.'

'I've told you never to answer door after dark without a lamp, Amos,' his mother chided.

'I had me stick, Mam.' He displayed the cudgel. He paused, then added, 'There were one thing I noticed right off, though.'

'What?'

'This feller, he only had one arm. His sleeve be as empty as Satan's heart.'

41

The Sessions House stood to the south of the prison of Newgate, on the Old Bailey. It was a fine looking three-storey building, its design in the Italian style complete with Doric columns, and had been built to replace a wooden construction, itself erected to stand in for the old Elizabethan courthouse that had succumbed to the Great Fire of 1666. The prisoners were shuffled in chains from the Whit nearby to be penned like sheep awaiting the slaughter in a noxious mix of odour, profanity and even disease in the bail yard outside. They huddled together, a spray of rain covering them, some giving the brick wall behind them a furtive glance, perhaps gauging whether they could scale it, overcome the sharp spikes that lined the top, and so gain their freedom in the street beyond. A few with the garnish to purchase it were allowed to stand apart, with some meagre shelter.

The courtroom itself was open to the elements. The judges, the lawyers, the nobility preferred the cold to the possibility of contracting jail-fever. Lice and fleas carrying the typhus contagion could easily spread from the filthy, bedraggled souls who gathered to hear their fate. For that, Flynt was grateful. Visiting the prison out of necessity was one thing, but to sit within a closed courtroom for what might be hours and being enveloped by the stench and possibly in danger of becoming afflicted with the fever was another. That said, the various perfumes utilised to obscure the body odours of the gentry and the general public viewing proceedings from the two galleries above the courtroom could also be overpowering. With only the weak light afforded by the grey skies, reliance was placed on the tallow candles to illuminate the proceedings, and the reek of the melting animal fat drifted with the brown smoke.

Among the ordinary spectators who had paid to observe the panoply of life and death below them were a few faces Flynt recognised, for criminals made a point of attending when they could to pick up tips for their own defence when the time came. If there was one constant in the criminal life, it was that sooner or later they could face the consequences of their crimes, either at the hands of justice or another crook, or be found dead in some hovel or gutter through an excess of alcohol and the debilitating effects of daily life in the underworld. He kept himself slumped as far down in the hard wooden seat as he could, the hat he had borrowed from Jerome kept low, hopeful that his years away would have dimmed their recollection of his features. Thankfully, though hats were not allowed in the actual court, gentlemen in the upper galleries were permitted to retain them, so he didn't look out of place.

Below him the U-shaped court faced the open air, all the better for the judging panel to reap the benefits of the breeze. The judge, dressed in a robe and stole of scarlet offset by a black scarf and two linen ribbons tied at the neck, sat between the Lord Mayor and an alderman, both in their official finery, in an elevated position facing the raised dock, where the accused would stand with his back to his fellow prisoners waiting outside. The jury, a collection of property owners, tradesmen and merchants, were seated on either side of the room, while between the bench and the dock were the lawyers and court officials and a special area for witnesses to give their testimony.

Flynt watched the proceedings below rumble on. Crimes, both petty and serious, were disposed of with an efficiency that was impressive. Though some of the charges were dismissed, fines, imprisonment, branding, burning, whippings were all dished out, while the ultimate punishments were saved for extremely serious crimes. Legislation regarding sentencing had been expanded the year before to allow more offences that could attract the death penalty or transportation to the colonies. In his travels in the Americas, Flynt had met many a man who had been despatched from England away from his family and all he'd known in life for what might have been seen as a petty offence. British society saw property as more valuable than human life, especially if that life belonged to someone from the lower classes, and that meant the lifting of a trifling sum could be deemed grand larceny.

That didn't mean that justice prevailed, for there were the straw men to contend with. They lingered outside the courts, recognised by a straw stuck into the buckle of a shoe, who were willing – for a fee, of course – to provide perjured testimony for either side of a case. Flynt had seen a few of these professional witnesses as he entered, and a number of the cases being heard that day fell thanks to them providing an alibi for the accused. Then there were those crimes which evaporated after the accused managed to get word to the defendant that they were willing to compensate them for their loss. This left the court docket riddled with holes. Justice was indeed blind to the many injustices that occurred under this roof, for its machinations were powered by money, from the rewards offered by victims and the city, thence giving rise in the thieftakers, to the jails and then the courts.

Flynt's attention was fixed on one particular branch of the justice industry. Jonathan Wild sat behind the dock, his mouth fixed in a prim little smile as he watched men and women for whom he had been rewarded for bringing to trial being dealt with by the justices.

When he had returned to the room in the Rookery the night before, Flynt found Bess already gone and Jack and Cain anxiously awaiting him. They left immediately, for Flynt and Cain each agreed that Bess couldn't be trusted not to strike back at them by informing. Flynt had watched Jack carefully while this was discussed. He had not voiced an opinion either way, but he was clearly torn between wishing to defend his love and his recognition of her flaws, whether such insight was newfound or had been suppressed until that day. However, he didn't protest when they moved on, even assisted in finding a new room in a building even more derelict than the one they had left. The new lodging was smaller than the first, with a single unblocked window that looked out onto a back yard that was more mud and pig filth than it was firm ground, and Flynt resolved never to venture in that direction, if he could help it.

It was once they were settled into the new accommodation, if straw mats thrown on the floor and no other furniture apart from a three-legged stool by the fireplace could be called accommodation, that Flynt announced his intention to speak to Wild the following day.

'Dear God, Jonas, you'd be better advised to call upon the good doctors at Bedlam,' Cain had said. 'You're displaying a distinct decline in faculties that is quite alarming.'

Flynt had once before visited Bethlehem, the hospital for the mentally afflicted, and frankly, risking all with Wild was preferable.

'I want to clear the air with him,' Flynt lied. The truth was, he had questions for the Thieftaker General.

'Cast your mind back to him and his men pursuing us from Tothill Fields. You won't clear the air, he'll clear you off the streets.'

'I won't let him.'

'You have a mighty high opinion of your abilities, Jonas. Don't ask me to come with you, for I will not.'

'I wouldn't expect you to.'

'Yes, you bloody would.'

Under normal circumstances, that might be true, but not this time. If Cain was in the pay of Moncrieff and the Fellowship, he could not be certain exactly how much of his loyalty could be purchased, and by extension, how far his betrayal could go. His gut told him that Cain would not break faith with him, but good sense demanded prudence. For that reason, Flynt's questions for Wild were not for Cain's ears.

He was not the watchmaker Christy had referred to; of that Flynt was fairly certain. Cain was too impulsive, too swift to boredom, to be a plotter. His principal aims in life were pleasure and profit, but he could easily be one of the wheels Christy had mentioned. Wild was a candidate. He was ambitious, he was venal and corrupt, he was intelligent. Charters' mind was circuitous, as was that of Moncrieff. The very nature of the work performed by both men required their thinking to be convoluted and yet single-minded. The result was more important than the means employed, or the sacrifices made, in order to achieve it.

Between his spiralling trust in all around him, the dreams and the scratching of rats somewhere in the decaying accommodation, Flynt slept little. And so there he sat, fighting sleep as witnesses droned and the accused thieves, coiners and murderers pleaded and the justices judged in the gathering gloom. He had to seize the first opportunity to speak to Wild, preferably without the two men who sat on either side of him. He recognised that might prove difficult, if not impossible, but it was worth the time to see if he could catch him alone, perhaps if Wild left the court in order to empty his bladder. Unfortunately, that particular organ seemed to be made of Toledo steel, for he didn't move from his seat behind the dock.

Eventually, Flynt feared that he had remained too long and that this enforced inactivity was causing his overall weariness to worsen. Surrendering any hope of succeeding in his aim, he rose to leave the gallery, when a face he recognised was led into the dock from the holding area and he decided to remain a little longer. He wished to hear this.

Blueskin Blake scowled at Wild and his two men as he stepped into the enclosed dock. The crime of which he was accused was announced, namely, that in the company of one Jack Sheppard he did gain entry by means of stealth to the premises of Mr William Kneebone in the Strand and thence did steal 108 yards of woollen cloth to the value of £36 and sundry other goods.

When he heard the name, Flynt was startled. Kneebone was a good man and had once taken Jack in. Treated him well, too. Jack hadn't mentioned it was him who they had robbed. That was a matter he would take up with him later. He listened as the merchant stated that his premises had been robbed and accused Blueskin of being involved along with Jack Sheppard.

'And where is this fellow Sheppard?' the judge asked. 'Is he in custody?'

An official rose from the well of the court. 'He was, Your Honour, but he escaped from Newgate not two days since.'

'And he remains at liberty?'

'He does, Your Honour.'

The judge's lips tightened in disapproval and he scribbled something in his ledger.

The two men with Wild then both gave evidence, stating they had been with the Thieftaker General when they arrested the accused. No mention was made of the first attempt, when Blueskin was wounded but still managed to retain his liberty.

'It was I what did beat upon his chamber door, demanding access,' said the first, whose name was announced as Quilt Arnold, 'and informing him that I was accompanied by Mr Jonathan Wild, Thieftaker General, who had decided to honour us with—'

The Lord Mayor coughed, irritation threading his voice, though glaring at Wild rather than Arnold. 'Yes, yes, never mind that, we know of Mr Wild's involvement. Get on with it.'

Flynt wondered why he was annoyed with the Thieftaker General. Was it the unofficial title that he had bestowed upon himself that had vexed him? Flynt studied Wild once again, his head dipped, refusing to look in the Lord Mayor's direction. Was there a rift there?

Arnold's head bobbed in apology. 'The accused person, Blake, did swear that he would not allow us entry, and using colourful language what I won't besmear the hallowedness of this place with, promised to hush the first man what comes through the door.'

The judge gave Blueskin a stern glare. 'Did he, now?'

'That he did, Your Honour.' Arnold straightened. 'It was me what forced that door open and did make entry first, where I was confronted by the accused person, Blueskin... I mean, Joseph Blake... brandishing a knife. "Deliver that blade," demands I, "for if you do not we shall chop off the arm that holds it," I promises. Seeing that we was armed and prepared to spill claret if we had to, he threw the knife to the floor and was apprehended by Mr Wild, all due and right and proper.'

Arnold grinned at his own bravery and Flynt doubted very much if that was how matters had progressed, especially when the other man – Abraham Mendez by name – also implied he'd been first through the door when he took the stand.

'Come on, lads, you couldn't be both through first,' Blueskin shouted, causing some laughter in the gallery and a few voices calling into question the veracity of the thieftaker's men.

The justice ordered silence, though there remained some muttering, and Mendez continued with his testimony, stating that they returned the accused Blake to the Strand where they showed him the premises of the prosecutor, William Kneebone.

'Right off, Blake admitted his crime. I heard him utter, "Say no more, Mr Wild, for I know I am a dead man, but what I fear is that I shall be carried to the Surgeons' Hall and anatomised."'

'And by that he means to be dissected, as laid down by statute regarding the bodies of the condemned following execution,' the judge said, to clarify for anyone in the court who didn't understand the meaning of the word 'anatomised'. He then looked down towards Mendez. 'And did Mr Wild make any reply?'

'He did, Your Honour, sir. He said that he would take care to prevent the surgeons taking a blade to his dead cadaver and would in fact give him a coffin, out of respect of their past friendship. It was an uncommon show of decency on the part of the Thieftaker General, if I may make such comment.'

The Lord Mayor cleared his throat again. 'No, you may not, sir.'

Blueskin had sneered throughout the evidence of both men, turning constantly to glare at Wild, who remained ramrod-straight and stared straight ahead. His only movement was when Griffin entered the court and whispered in his ear. Wild smiled, nodded and muttered something before Griffin left again. Flynt would dearly have loved to know what was said between them, but he was too far away.

Next to speak was a receiver of stolen goods called William Field, who had been accused with both Jack and Blueskin. He stated that he had been with Blake when they met with Jack Sheppard on the night of the robbery, and all three then travelled to the house and shop in the Strand. Once there, Sheppard used his knowledge of locks and the interior of the premises to lead them to the goods, which he helped carry, but saw nothing more of them, nor received a share of the proceeds. It was his conscience that compelled him to report the matter to Mr Jonathan Wild.

'You do not face charges in this court for this offence,' the justice observed.

Wild then rose. 'If I may speak, Your Honour.' The judge waved a hand, giving permission. The Lord Mayor visibly sighed and folded his arms, an obvious signifier as to his antagonistic attitude towards Wild, who fixedly ignored any eye contact with him. 'Mr Field was most courageous in coming forward and agreeing to give evidence against this man. I suggested to Mr Kneebone, the prosecutor, that justice was best served by not bringing charges against him.'

As spectators jeered, the judge accepted Wild's explanation, but the Lord Mayor continued to glare at Wild. 'Tell me this, Mr Wild, as you are on your feet. Is this Joseph Blake not a confederate of yours?'

Wild was unperturbed by the query. 'He was one of my agents for many a year, My Lord Mayor.'

'And he turned thief.'

'He did, much to my chagrin.'

'Was he not thief previous?'

'Before he joined my strength, My Lord Mayor, he had been such a miscreant, but I truly believed I had led him to the path of righteousness.'

The Lord Mayor allowed this to sit between them for a beat before he grunted. 'I'm sure you led him somewhere.'

Yes, Flynt thought, *there's a rift there.*

Blueskin denied everything, interjecting at every turn to call each of the witnesses a liar, in Field's case a goddamned piece of pus – provoking further cheers from the gallery – but there was nothing he could do. Flynt had heard testimony such as this before and it mattered nothing how much the accused claimed it was a falsehood. Blueskin's life was forfeit and his head sunk low, as if he was in prayer.

Wild stood up then and leaned into the dock. 'You're a dead man, Blake. Make your peace with God.'

But Blueskin wasn't praying. With a hoarse bellow, he leaped over the low partition separating him from the rest of the court and lunged with his manacled hands at Wild, a small knife clutched between his fingers. Wild tried to leap back, but he was too slow and the blade sliced at his throat. He screamed, his fingers clutching at the blood streaming through the gash, as Mendez hauled him away, Arnold hiding behind the bigger man, while two officers seized Blueskin and held him down.

As Wild was carried away to a side room, the call going out for a doctor to attend, the justice regained his composure and gave Blueskin Blake a stern look.

'By God, sir, you are a bold fellow to attempt murder in this hallowed place.'

Blueskin's lip raised. 'This place ain't hallowed – it's the doorway to hell. I is sorry only for not having achieved my aim, for never did such a rogue as Jonathan Wild live and go unpunished for so long by you good men and true. Would that I had brung me a better blade with which to cut off his lying head and throw it to the Sessions House yard to be used as a football by the rabble.'

'You will hang, sir!' the judge thundered.

'And I would go with pleasure if that viper had gone before me.'

'Then may God have mercy on your soul.'

Blueskin laughed, but there was a flinty edge to the sound. He was still laughing as they dragged him from the courtroom. It echoed and faded as he was taken across the yard to the prison. By that time, Flynt had descended from the gallery to the courtroom proper and made his way towards the side room into which they had taken Wild. One of his men, Mendez, was outside, looking flustered.

'You called for a doctor?' Flynt said, the ruse occurring to him only at that moment. It was a risk – there might already be a physician within – but his entire life was one of risk. A fresh one would make no difference.

Mendez gave him a quick study. 'You don't look like no doctor.'

'Ship's doctor, recently arrived from the Indies.'

Mendez continued to examine him, seeing the tanned skin, but doubt remaining in his eyes.

Flynt hardened his tone. 'Look, Mr Mendez, was it not?' He nodded, but surprise splashed at the use of his name. 'As we dither here, beyond that door, Mr Wild's exsanguination could prove deadly.' Flynt hoped the use of the word would strengthen his ploy. 'Now, you can let me pass and I will use my skills to assist him, or you can continue to judge me by the clothes I wear and let his blood ebb away.'

Mendez delayed only a moment further, then opened the door and stood back to let him pass. 'Fetch me some water,' Flynt ordered, 'preferably hot, and for God's sake make sure it's clean, and some linen, also clean. And be swift about it.'

Mendez nodded and beetled off, leaving Flynt to enter the room unaccompanied. He was already drawing a pistol from where it was concealed under the brown woollen coat Jerome had given him, and as he closed the door with his heel, aimed it at Quilt Arnold, standing over Wild as he sat upon a desk clasping a far from pristine kerchief to his wound, his face drawn, his flesh waxy, blood staining his fine coat. When he saw Flynt enter, he was at first confused, then as recognition dawned, his eyes widened.

'Be so good as to step aside, Mr Arnold,' Flynt said, jerking the muzzle. 'I have no argument with you unless you wish to make one. Oh… and best unburden yourself of that pistol in your belt.'

Arnold allowed the pistol to fall to the floor without hesitation.

'Now, clasp both hands behind your head, face the wall and drop to your knees.'

Once again, Arnold followed the orders without a moment's delay. Wild watched, his initial astonishment at seeing Flynt having passed, his breath ragged, his jaw clamped, his eyes narrowed with pain.

'You are a brazen fellow, Flynt,' he muttered through his teeth. His voice was as frayed as his breathing, as if Blueskin's knife had lacerated it as well as his throat.

'I would have a word, Wild.'

'Another time perhaps,' Wild said, and pulled the kerchief from his neck. 'At this moment I have other matters with which I must contend.'

Keeping his distance, Flynt leaned over a little to examine the wound. 'It's nothing much. Blueskin's aim was wanting. It must have been the lack of sustenance in the Whit.'

'I gave the man a purpose,' Wild said, bitterly, turning the kerchief to find a spot that was not sodden with his blood. 'And this is how he repays me.'

'Perhaps you shouldn't have manoeuvred towards these circumstances. He was loyal to you but you were too insecure to see it.'

Wild sneered that away. 'State your business, Flynt, for I feel certain you're not here to plead Blake's case.'

'Jack Sheppard.'

Wild nodded, expecting it. 'I'll have him, soon enough.'

'Who told you he was informing Colonel Charters about your activities?'

Wild clasped the kerchief to his throat again. 'What is it to you? You abandoned the lad, did you not? To Blake's care, no less. You abandoned a lot of things when you left.'

'Who told you of his connection to Charters?'

'None of your business.'

With a glance at Arnold, who hadn't moved, Flynt swung the pistol in Wild's direction. 'Don't make me ask again.'

'You'd shoot me? Here in the Sessions House, with Newgate not a rat's fart away from us?'

'I would.'

Wild stared at him, trying to decide how sincere he was. Eventually, he shrugged. 'It makes no difference. It was a lady, Madame de Fontaine, though she isn't a Frenchie, but a blasted Scot, like you. She seems a saucy mare. I feel sure you and she are related, like all of your breed.'

Flynt had wanted Christy's version confirmed. Her facility for twisting alternative truths to suit her needs was one of her less admirable traits.

'Who told you about the duel with Lord Southern?'

Again, Wild didn't answer at first. Flynt guessed he was playing for time, hoping someone would come. Such an eventuality had occurred to him, too, so he took a brisk step forward and with his free hand delivered a powerful backhanded blow across Wild's cheek. He grunted, his head jerking to the side, the sharp movement generating another cry of pain.

'Damn you, Flynt,' he groaned, pressing the kerchief tighter against the neck wound. Arnold had half turned but, upon a stern look from Flynt, faced the wall once more.

'Who told you about the duel with Lord Southern?' Flynt repeated.

'Why should I tell you?'

'Because if you don't, I'll finish the work Blueskin began.'

'You'd do murder?'

'Why not? I've done it before.'

Wild swallowed, looked to the door, then to Arnold, then back at Flynt. 'Griffin.'

If Moncrieff had encouraged Southern to challenge him, and then sent word to Wild about the hour and location of the duel, he was unlikely to do so himself. Moncrieff liked to be insulated from such matters. Griffin might only be the first layer of that insulation, although given the speed of events, Flynt doubted it.

'Where can I find him?'

Wild's laugh was weak but mocking. 'You expect me to tell you?'

Flynt reached out with his free hand, batted the kerchief away from Wild's neck and jabbed a finger into the wound to hook the ruptured flesh. Wild struggled, screamed, but Flynt jammed the barrel of his pistol into his mouth, cutting the sound off. He had little time; the screams would alert someone. 'Think carefully, Wild. You know me. You know of what I am capable. Don't give me an excuse to end your pitiful existence. Where can I find Griffin?'

He removed the barrel. The Thieftaker General groaned before he rasped, 'You're too late, Flynt.'

Flynt removed his finger from the slash, wiped the blood onto Wild's already stained coat. 'Too late for what?'

'Griffin. He makes his way to the Rookery.' Despite his pain, triumph rose in Wild's eyes. 'To arrest Jack Sheppard.'

Flynt recalled the brief conversation he had witnessed in the courtroom and began to back away towards the door.

'You're done, Flynt, you do know that, do you not?' Wild sneered, holding the kerchief even tighter against the wound. 'Jack's done, Blueskin's done, you're done. You've led a charmed life, until now. The word is out. Jonas Flynt dies. You'd be best to surrender yourself to it.'

Flynt was eager to be on his way, but he gestured with the pistol towards the still bleeding neck. 'Take that as a warning. Blueskin was your most trusted lieutenant and you turned him against you. How many men such as he have you betrayed? How many remain at liberty? Who can you trust now? Nobody. Not completely.' He recalled the Lord Mayor's obvious antipathy towards Wild. 'The tide is turning against you. Your days of strutting these streets will soon draw to a close. Mark me, you'll be dead long before I am.'

As he ducked out of the door, he saw something cross Wild's eyes – something he thought he'd never see: a look of resignation, as if he, too, had sensed the end of his days. Flynt might have taken some comfort in that if he didn't share a similar sensation.

42

Continuing to ensure his face was as concealed as he could, Flynt rushed from the Sessions House, not knowing for certain if Wild had spoken the truth but not willing to take the chance. Griffin, of course, was nowhere to be seen, so he ran towards Snow Hill in search of a carriage or a chair to carry him. The hill bustled with foot traffic and he paused between St Sepulchre's Church and the Saracen Head Inn, searching around him, seeing no sign of any form of transport, and was about to take off on foot along Holborn when a voice stopped him. He turned to see Cain following behind him.

'What are you doing here, Gabriel?' he snapped.

'Fine way to thank a fellow who came to help you.'

'You left Jack alone?'

'He's a grown man, Jonas, he doesn't need me to look after him. I told you that before.'

'When did you leave?'

'No more than fifteen minutes after you. I regretted my words and set off, but kept my distance in the Sessions House. You said they'd be looking for two men so I thought it would be best to remain apart. I followed you to that little room, and delayed that fellow Mendez when he returned, led him away to give you time. I assume you were questioning Wild?'

Flynt didn't reply. That meant Jack had been left to his own devices all morning and much of the afternoon. Flynt turned away, throwing his words over his shoulder. 'Griffin is on his way to take him into custody. They think they know where he is.'

Cain hurried to catch up. 'Already? How in hell's teeth could they have found him so quickly? Christ, I barely know where that room is and I just left there.'

It was possible that Wild's claim was little more than feint, a means to distract Flynt, but he didn't believe so. Flynt had seen too many men lie to him, either at the gaming tables or as they begged for mercy, and he was skilled at spotting it. He wasn't always correct, but this time he felt certain he was. If they truly had tracked Jack down, he suspected the means of that discovery.

'Bess,' he said.

Cain dismissed this with a wave of one hand. 'We moved quickly. She didn't know where we had relocated.'

Flynt had waved a carriage down, opened the door, thinking this over. If there was one person who knew the Rookery better than even Jack, it was Bess. It was possible she might have found him, but he thought it unlikely – not in such a short time. He climbed into the carriage. 'We'll go to the room she knew about and take it from there.'

Jack couldn't help himself.

He had to see her, to explain, to make her understand why he had said what he said, maybe even convince her to come with him and Mr Flynt, though he reckoned that was not on the cards. Bess was London to her very marrow, and something in her would die if she wasn't breathing the stinking air and walking the dirty streets. But he had to try.

He couldn't help himself.

Gabriel Cain leaving the room so soon was a regular godsend. Jack had been thinking on how he could slip away, but then was given the opportunity on a plate. He'd made a show of trying to talk Mr Cain out of following after Mr Flynt, knowing he wouldn't make an impression, and then waited a few minutes to make certain he was well clear of the building before he took his own leave. He didn't lock the door. There was no key and, anyway, there was nothing in the place to steal.

The thing about Bess was that she stuck close to her habits. She didn't like anything new, preferring the familiar. That meant there was only a few places that she would be and he could get round them easy. But he didn't want to run the risk of being recognised, so he took some precautions. He stepped out the back door of the tenement and lifted a handful of mud. It stank to high heaven but he didn't care; needs must, he reasoned. He slapped it over his hair, darkening his fair locks, then smeared some over his face. There were many in the streets with dirty mugs. It weren't much but it would be sufficient to fool any idle glance. A not so idle glance might mean he'd have to have it away on his toes, but he'd deal with that if and when.

It helped that it wasn't a pleasant day and so people were more intent on their own business than paying attention to him. All the same, he affected a limp, turned his right foot inwards a touch and bent his back a little – not too much, not so much as to draw particular attention but enough to further throw anyone off that it was him. There were plenty of coves what were crump-backed, but he wished he had a lifter to tuck under his arm. There weren't nobody what would think Jack Sheppard needed a crutch to get about.

He poked his head through the doors of some of the taverns in the Rookery, then headed down by Seven Dials, where the gin shops were, but there weren't no sign of her. He stood for a moment at the dials. It was beginning to rain – not much, but it did make him fear for his disguise, for it might wash off the dirt. He looked up at the ever-darkening clouds, his mind racing around the possibilities. She could have gone up Holborn; she could have headed down Westminster way through St Martin's Lane; she could have walked to Drury Lane, stationed herself in any one of the taverns down there. A few faces turned in his direction, perhaps wondering why he was so still like. He couldn't linger here. He had to make up his mind, which way to go.

Come on, Jack, think. Where would Bess go to spend some of the bunce Mr Flynt and Mr Cain had given her? She wouldn't need to do no trade, not for a while yet, so she wouldn't be frequenting none of the flash houses. She'd want somewhere she maybe weren't known so well. Somewhere that she ran less of a chance of running into an old customer.

He felt a spasm of jealousy at the thought of her working. He had understood why she had to do it and had long accepted it, but it still pained him to think of another man laying hands on her.

He couldn't help himself.

No, Jack, where would she go where she might not be recognised, where she runs less of a chance of meeting someone of her acquaintance, somewhere you know for a fact she has never traded in.

He could think of only one establishment nearby, and even though it was not one he relished visiting, he limped off in the direction of St Giles High Street.

43

The coachman took Flynt and Cain as far as Seven Dials, where he stated he would go no further. The Rookery was not only dangerous for him, it being a lair for thieves and rogues, but many of the streets were too narrow to navigate. They paid him and set off at a run just as the rain began to intensify, their boots splashing in swiftly topped-up puddles.

They found Knapp waiting in the lane off Carrier Street. They peered at him round the corner as he huddled in the doorway, attempting to shelter from the downpour.

'I would have words with him,' Cain breathed.

He would wish to punish the man for his treatment of Swift-Fingered Jane, but Flynt blocked his way with one arm. 'We need to know where Griffin is.'

'They had a head start, Jonas. They would be aware by now that we no longer occupy that room above. I would hazard that Knapp here was left in case we return, while Griffin searched elsewhere. He'll know where.'

It made sense and though Flynt desired caution, he was aware that they didn't have such leisure. It was time to throw the dice and see where they landed. 'Give me a count. I'll skirt around to the other end of the alley and approach from there.'

'How long?'

Flynt made a calculation. 'Fifty.'

Cain's eyebrow raised. 'That long?'

'As you said, we're no longer young.'

He moved quickly along Carrier Street to the first left turn, all the while maintaining the count in his head and hoping that Cain wasn't so intent on delivering hurt to Knapp for what he did to Swift-Finger Jane that he missed out a few numbers. He had already got to forty before he reached the second left turn, another narrow lane, and he picked up the pace, reaching fifty as he found the alley he sought. He took off his hat and squinted around the crumbling brickwork to see Cain already striding purposefully from the opposite end. Knapp, still hunched in misery in the doorway, became aware of his approach almost too late. He fumbled for a weapon with his free hand, his other still in a sling.

'We have business you and I,' Cain roared, pointing his finger like a pistol.

In his terror, Knapp found he couldn't pull his gun free in time, so decided that discretion was the better part of duty. He stumbled from the doorway and splashed through the gathering rainfall and ordure that littered the ground in a bid to escape, his head looking over his shoulder in panic. Cain didn't break his stride, nor quicken his pace, nor draw a weapon. He kept walking, his hands now in the pockets of his long coat, his head slightly tilted forward to allow the rain to run off the brim of his hat, so his eyes burned towards the fleeing man under the brim with an intensity Flynt had never seen in him before.

Flynt waited until the panicked Knapp was almost upon him before he stepped into his path. The man reeled back against the far wall, his head jerking from Cain to Flynt and back again.

'I is here on official business,' he said, his Adam's apple bobbing as if it were afloat. 'If you does me harm there will be consequences most serious. I has a man above awaiting in the room, and all it would take is one call and he will come to my assistance most immediate.'

Cain's smile was humourless as he came closer. 'Only one man? I'm happy to take that chance.'

Flynt had no way of knowing if Knapp spoke the truth, but it was possible that Griffin had left only the two here, having guessed that they had vacated the room. Flynt knew his friend was intent on vengeance for Jane, but he had more pressing matters. 'Where's Griffin?'

'Gone.'

'Where?'

'On official business.'

Cain drew his knife from his pocket. 'Remember this, Knapp?' He pressed the tip against Knapp's shoulder. 'You still carry its mark.'

Knapp flinched and edged away, but Flynt blocked his progress.

'So say official business once more,' Cain said, digging the tip into the material of the man's thick coat. 'Please.'

Knapp swallowed, gave Flynt an imploring look. 'If I tells you where Griffin has gone, will you let me go unharmed?'

'Happy to,' Flynt said.

Knapp studied his face for sign of a lie. Finding none, he gave Cain another look, before returning his attention to Flynt. 'Does I have your word of honour?'

'You do.'

That seemed to satisfy him. 'Very well. I doesn't owe Griffin nothing. He ain't no friend to me.'

Having seen Griffin's expression in Wild's office, that much Flynt had already surmised. 'Where is he?'

'He's gone to The Crown on St Giles Broad, you heard of it?'

'Also known as The Angel or The Bowl?'

'That be the one.'

'Is he stricken with a devilish thirst of a sudden?' Cain asked.

'That's where the girl said she'd be.'

Flynt asked, 'Who?'

'That moll, Edgeworth Bess.'

Flynt's head jerked in the direction of the building behind them. 'It was she who told you of this place?'

'It were.'

Flynt shot Cain a glance. 'And why has Griffin gone to meet her?'

''Cos Sheppard ain't here, is he? That bitch, she played us false, she did. He weren't there, and neither were you. She's up there in that tavern awaiting her reward.' Knapp felt confident enough to smirk. 'She'll get her reward, right enough. She'll get what she deserves, that deceitful slattern.'

Flynt began to walk away but Cain remained, his knife still poised at Knapp's shoulder.

'You gives me your word of honour that you would leave me unharmed,' Knapp pleaded.

'He did,' Cain said. 'But I didn't.'

Flynt didn't look back when he heard the man squeal. At the doorway leading to the apartment, a man appeared and peered towards the sound, but a shake of the head from Flynt sent him shrinking back into the corridor. Knapp clearly had few friends. He had reached Carrier Street and had turned towards St Giles Broad before Cain caught up with him.

'He still breathes,' Cain said eventually.

'You're growing soft in your old age.'

Cain gave him a sideways look. 'Not that soft. His features are even less pleasing than previously.' He held up his hand to reveal an object nestling in his palm. 'And I told him he'd lose that some day.'

He dropped the severed finger into the street. Flynt felt no pity for Knapp. He had assaulted Swift-Finger Jane. He was an odious individual. He worked for Wild. For all three he deserved some punishment.

'So,' Cain said as if they had just enjoyed a hearty breakfast. 'Do we head for this tavern then?'

Flynt would have wished to go alone, for he had questions to which he didn't wish Cain to be privy, but he doubted Griffin would work solo. He would have expected to find not just Jack, but also him and Cain, so Flynt might need his friend's skills. 'We do.'

'And if Griffin decides to arrest us too?'

Flynt strode onwards. 'Nobody is arresting me. Not today.'

44

The Angel Inn, sometimes known as The Crown, was over 200 years old, dating back to when the monasteries were brought tumbling down by the eighth King Henry, including one in St Giles. When a gallows stood nearby, before public executions were moved to Tyburn on the Oxford Road, it was customary for a nearby leper hospital to give the condemned a bowl of strong ale to smooth his way to eternity. That tradition continued after the leper hospital went the way of the monastery, and the inn became one of the stopping points on the road from Newgate to Tyburn to allow those set to ride the three-legged mare to take refreshment. Sometimes the condemned were dead drunk before they were dead. This traditional service saw the establishment known by many as 'The Bowl'.

It was for that reason that Jack had never set foot in this establishment. All his life he had been but one step away from the Tyburn trail, and he'd never wished to reduce that gap by frequenting any of the drinking stops. But Bess was not known there – he knew that for a solid fact – and so he had to see if this was where she had taken refuge in order to drink away the bunce, it being close by the lodgings.

He saw her right off, as soon as he entered, over in a corner table, staring into the tankard of ale in front of her as if it were the fountain of youth that Mr Flynt had once told him about. She didn't see him until he was standing right before her. She gave him a quick glance, not recognising him in the gloom of the tavern.

'I ain't doing no business,' she said, her voice more tired than he had ever heard before. *No*, he thought, *not tired. Beaten.*

'It's me, girl,' he said, taking a seat and leaning in closer.

She examined him for a second or two. 'Gawd's truth, what you done to yourself, Jack?'

'Never mind,' he said. 'We need to talk, you and me.'

She sneered. 'Ain't we done enough talking? You did some rattling last time we talked, if I recall correct.'

'You was speaking out of place, Bess.'

She looked away from him. 'Well, you certainly put me in my place, didn't you?'

'I come here to speak with you, Bess.'

'So you said.'

'But we can't do it here.'

She looked back at him. 'Why not? You too good for this tavern, or something?'

He kept his voice down. 'I'm on me toes, Bess, you knows this. I'm taking a terrible chance just being here.'

'Nobody's making you stay, Jack Sheppard.'

'For Gawd's sake, keep your voice down.'

'Why? It ain't no never mind to me if you is arrested.'

'You don't mean that.'

'Don't I? Then tell me this… If I doesn't mean it, then why did I tell the Thieftaker's men where they might find you?'

That made Jack sit back in shock. 'You didn't.'

'I bloody did, and when they catches you, I'm in for a bundle of bunce. I'll be right well set up and…'

She stopped talking as her eyes fixed on something over Jack's shoulder. He craned round to see a tall cove in decent togs making straight for them. He had never before clapped his peepers upon him, but he knew him for what he was: a Thieftaker's man. Others in the tavern also recognised him, for there were nudges and nods and winks and some muttering, one man even draining his tankard before legging it out of the door. But the cove ignored all this, for his eyes were fixed firmly on Jack, who cast around him, looking for another doorway.

'Don't flee, Sheppard,' the man bellowed. 'I have men to the rear. You can't escape.'

Jack had half risen from his chair, but when he saw the futility of escape, he sank back down again. He should have listened to Mr Flynt. He should have stayed in that room. Now, he was nabbed again.

'Oh, Bess…' he said, his voice cracking.

She didn't reply. Her head sank as she avoided his gaze. He liked to think it was shame, but it was only because she herself had been caught.

She would have much preferred that he be pinched elsewhere and that she didn't have to face him.

'Lucky for you, my girl –' the man was now standing beside the table – 'that this rogue is here, for I was coming to chastise you. This fox was not in his lair.' He dropped a pouch weighty with coin on the table. 'Your reward in full, even though we've not yet the men Flynt and Cain in our custody.'

Jack maintained his stare at Bess, who hadn't reached out to touch the purse. 'Why not take it, girl?' he said. 'Twenty pieces of silver. That's the price of it, ain't it?'

Her eyes flashed at that. 'You ain't no messiah, Jack Sheppard. You is just a cheap thief, no more.'

The man laughed. 'Well said, my girl. You have performed your civic duty and deserve the recompense. On your feet, Jack lad. And don't even consider making a run for it, for I'll bring you down.' To emphasise his words, he drew a pistol from under his coat.

Jack looked at it and then around him, seeing the faces of the patrons darken. Although anxious at the sight of the pistol and the unyielding look in the cove's eye, he forced himself to appear relaxed, sitting back in the chair. 'You ain't never been in this here lush crib, I'd say.'

The man appraised the nature of the surroundings. 'That's true, I've not had the pleasure, but it's much like any other.'

'On its face, that be right, but it ain't like any other in one respect. This here crib is on the Tyburn trail.'

'A trail you will become acquainted with come next hanging day.'

Jack ignored that, though he did feel a shudder surge through him. He had to play this very carefully, for it might be his only chance.

'Maybe so, Mr Thieftaker's man, but take another peep around you. The coves what come here, they don't take kindly to the likes of you. There's a reason why those destined for the deadly nevergreen makes a stop here, and it ain't just because of the St Giles Bowl. The folks here is sympathetic to them.'

He was glad to see something a little less than confidence creep into the man's eyes, but it was only momentarily, for he soon displayed his previous casual contempt. 'This lot? They are nothing but rogues and sluts.' He raised his voice. 'And if one of them, I care not if man or woman, attempts to impede me in the performance of my lawful duty, then it will not go well for them.'

Jack saw the door open and he couldn't help but smile. 'You sure and certain about that?'

45

Flynt had never entered the establishment before, so was unsure what to expect. However, he should have known it would be just like any other tavern in London: gloomy, smoky, raucous. At least the dingy light would assist in hiding his features. He didn't linger in the doorway, stepping aside from the dim light, for he would be too easily identified by Griffin and, thus framed, would make an easy target. He saw him at a far table staring down at Jack and Bess, a pistol in his hand. Jack appeared to be very relaxed as he reclined in the wooden chair, his legs stretched out before him and crossed at the ankles. Bess, however, was not at her ease. She was slumped in her chair and, with a shaking hand, began to raise the pewter tankard before her, then seemed to reconsider, so set it down again, her attention falling on a money pouch on the table.

Griffin's voice reached him. '...if man or woman, attempts to impede me in the performance of my lawful duty, then it will not go well for them.'

Jack's smile was cheeky and he said something that Flynt didn't catch, but whatever it was, it made Griffin twist round. It took him a moment to process Flynt heading his way, but then he began to raise his pistol. Jack was already out of his chair and wrapping his arms around Griffin's waist, knocking him over, the pistol triggering harmlessly into the floor. Flynt had Tact in his hand and aimed at Griffin's head as he lay on the dirty boards. Around him, chairs scraped and curses were uttered as patrons fled the scene.

Jack got to his feet. He looked filthy and a smell rose from him that made Flynt's nose twitch. Seeing him take in his matted hair, Jack grinned again. 'I had to pull me a disguise. Slapped some mud on my strudel to hide the colour. Smeared it on my phizog also. Reckons there must be some pig squirt in there 'cos it don't half stink.'

A quick glance at the remaining patrons reassured Flynt that none were likely to come to Griffin's aid.

'He says he's got some coves round the back,' Jack said, understanding Flynt's reconnoitre.

'Gabriel will take care of them, if true. His blood is up so I hope for their sake they don't choose to tackle him.' He flicked Tact's barrel upwards. 'On your feet, Griffin.'

Jack was edgy. 'We should be off, Mr Flynt.'

'Soon, Jack. I wish a word with this gentleman.'

Griffin rose, being careful not to make any sudden moves. 'You're a dead man, Flynt.'

'That's been said before and yet, here I am.' He motioned him towards a quiet corner. 'Over there, and don't reach for the sword. I've heard you're most skilful with the blade and I have no desire to discover if it's true. I'll drop you at the first twitch.'

Griffin was wise enough to understand that was no idle threat, so kept his arms slightly open as he walked. Once in the corner, he calmly took a seat and crossed his legs.

'Fold your arms, too, if you please,' Flynt said.

Griffin did so. 'Now, what do we have to talk about, you and I?'

Flynt wasted no time, for he didn't have it to waste. 'Did Lord Moncrieff warn you of the duel with Southern?'

A very slight rising of both eyebrows confirmed it, but Griffin still tried to brazen it. 'I don't know this gentleman.'

'Yes, you do. Come, Griffin, you're a professional, let's not waste time.'

Griffin's eyes became hooded. 'And if I do wish to waste time, what will you do? Kill me? Here, with witnesses? Your thieving little friend there may believe that there is no love for thieftakers in this establishment, but I would hazard they would draw the line at murder.'

'I'm already wanted for murder. Another will make no difference.'

Griffin's lips pursed slightly. 'I see your point.'

'I have no argument with you, Griffin, just those above you. Now, was it Moncrieff who told you of the duel?'

Without hesitation, Griffin said, 'Under the circumstances, I see no reason to deny it.'

'So you do serve the Fellowship?'

This time he did hesitate, but then nodded.

'And what was Moncrieff's purpose in so doing?'

'He wished you out of the way, one way or the other – and the way you discombobulated Southern ahead of his shot was masterful. Congratulations.'

Flynt shrugged that away. 'So either Southern would kill me or Wild would have me jailed, is that correct?'

'That's my understanding. My Lord Moncrieff is not in the habit of explaining himself to me. I'm a mere employee, not a member of the Fellowship council.'

'Why does he wish me gone?'

'Again, I'm not privy, but I make the assumption that you have become troublesome, here and abroad.'

'Because I seek Daniel Hawke?'

'I know of no Daniel Hawke.'

'So you don't know where he is?'

'I truly have no knowledge of that gentleman, or his whereabouts.'

Flynt believed him. Like the Company of Rogues, Moncrieff would keep the identities of Fellowship members secret. 'Where does Moncrieff now live?'

Griffin laughed. 'You expect me to tell you that? My life would be forfeit.'

'He won't know you told me.'

A wry laugh this time. 'He has a way of knowing things, much like your master, Colonel Charters.'

'He was never my master but, in any case, I no longer work with him.'

Griffin considered the veracity of the statement. 'I do believe you speak the truth.' His head tilted as he pondered further. 'And if I give you the address, what will you do?'

'Lord Moncrieff and I will have an open and frank exchange of views.'

'You will kill him?'

'I didn't say that.'

'It's what you do. Kill your enemies.'

Not Moncrieff. Flynt had no argument with him, even though he had tried to arrange his death. They shared blood and he had no desire to spill it. Not if he could help it. 'I wish information.'

'Concerning this Daniel Hawke?'

'Yes.'

'And you will not harm him, I have your word upon that?'

'Does it matter to you?'

Griffin sighed. 'As you said, I'm a professional. I work for coin. If you kill him, then that revenue source might be sealed.'

There was a convincing timbre to the words. 'You have my word that I have no intention of harming him. We shall talk only.'

Griffin paused to examine him for sign of deceit. A door to the rear opened and Cain entered, giving him a grin and a wave. Griffin saw this and visibly deflated, knowing that Flynt had not been lying about him being out the back. If Cain was here, then Griffin's men had been somehow rendered *hors de combat*. Flynt hoped he hadn't killed them.

'I'll take your word, then,' Griffin said, with a deep sigh, 'but if you break it, I will come looking for you. I like my life and Lord Moncrieff helps me fund it. You shall not gain the upper hand with me a third time.'

'So be it.'

Griffin gave him an address in St James's, not far from Moncrieff's former residence. Flynt thanked him politely, then said, 'Be so good as to remain seated until Jack and I have left. Don't pursue us. Cain has already punished your friend Knapp for his treatment of Swift-Finger Jane. He won't be so swift-fingered now. Don't give him an excuse to punish you.'

'Knapp is scum. Wild sends him with me, I believe, to keep an eye on me.'

'He doesn't trust you?'

'He doesn't trust anyone – not me, not Knapp, nobody. He uses us all to keep an eye on each other. But go, I won't follow. I believe I'm done with Jonathan Wild. It's dirty work.'

'And the Fellowship isn't?'

Griffin smiled. 'Perhaps, but the pay is better.'

Cain and Griffin. Both were cut from the same block of wood, both motivated solely by money but both possessing a curious form of honour.

Cain waited by the table at which Jack and Bess sat, she still staring at the money Flynt presumed had been dropped there by Griffin. He indicated that they should leave and Cain followed him.

As Jack rose, Bess mumbled, 'I'm sorry.'

He paused, gave her a quick glance, then turned away. 'So is I, girl, so is I.'

46

The Jermyn Street house was modest for one such as Moncrieff, Flynt thought, but then immediately reassessed his judgement. It was impressive in a reserved way, unostentatious. Much like its owner. His half-brother was prone to keeping to the shadows, to be the man who wielded power behind the man who thought he wielded power. This three-storey, plain brick terrace in the middle of a narrow little street between St James's Square and Piccadilly was just what Flynt would have expected from him. The house he had previously owned was far from what might be called grand, it being of plain brick much like this one, but by dint of it facing the gardens in the square – even though they were not what they might be – it seemed somewhat grander.

Behind James Moncrieff's ability to shrink into the background was a mind so convoluted that it rivalled that of Colonel Charters. He had once concocted a scheme to lure Flynt from London to a village in the north, where a deranged nobleman was ready to murder him. To ensure his plot succeeded, he had retained the services of a professional killer.

It was during that interlude that Flynt first began to suspect that Cain was also of that profession. Despite their friendship, Flynt had had cause to question Cain's attitude to violence. Flynt was well aware that he carried a ferocity that troubled him, but Cain could rejoice in it. When they were active in the highwayman trade, he'd had to rein in Cain's enthusiasm for unnecessary brutality on a regular basis. On the other hand, time and time again he had displayed his loyalty and on many occasions had saved Flynt's life. Being his friend was a complex business, and he hadn't informed him where he was headed. He had left Cain and Jack in the new lodgings, as confident as he could be that they were safe from the attentions of Jonathan Wild, at least temporarily. Griffin had expressed an intention to cease his employment; Knapp was out of the game, and it was doubtful that the Thieftaker had men on his strength who would be willing to scour the Rookery. Jack had told him of the stratagem he'd taken with Griffin in the tavern, and it was not all a ruse. The streets and alleyways and cramped rooms of St Giles were filled with men and women who had little love for Wild and his men. It would be a brave one who set foot among them and asked questions.

He didn't fully believe that Cain would betray him to Moncrieff – if, indeed, he was in his pay – but he was best to take no chances. He didn't enjoy doubting him, just as he didn't enjoy the way his mind still reeled regarding Christy's claim of someone directing proceedings with the precision of a watchmaker. It could be either Moncrieff or Charters. It could be nobody at all, for Christy was known for playing games. The Paladin had been her concoction, after all: created both to amuse herself while she was bored playing court politics on behalf of Walpole, and to undermine Flynt by making the deeds he performed in secret a little more public.

And then there was the suggestion that she had another purpose for being in the city. She was not in these streets for her pleasure, much as she took them whenever she could. She had a purpose, and Flynt wondered if he was that purpose. Had she been engaged to kill him? If so, why had she not done so? She – or rather, Gregor – could easily have taken him in the street. Was this another of her games? Was she toying with his mind, just for the sheer pleasure of it?

He had to thrust such suspicions, such reflections, to the back of his mind, for dwelling upon them made his reason swirl even further. He needed as sharp a focus as he could to complete the task in hand.

He stood in the narrow street for some time, staring at the green front door. There would be a garden to the rear, of that he was certain, and it would cause him little trouble to gain access and from there enter by a rear door. His lockpicking skills were highly advanced, having been taught many years before by an ageing thief called Tom and honed from that time to this. No, he thought this was a time to be more forthright. Moncrieff was a man who liked the side streets and back lanes of plot and counterplot, and by taking a bold, more open, approach, Flynt hoped to catch him off guard.

So he marched right up to the door and rattled the cast-iron knocker, then waited, twisting round to watch the people pass by: the well dressed, the fashionable, the not so fashionable, the purveyors of goods and wares who came to hawk their fruits, vegetables, pots, pans and clothing. Servants emerged to shoo them away, others to light a lamp above the doorway even though it was not yet nightfall, for the skies scowled with the threat of another downpour. Further along he could see the red brick of Sir Christopher Wren's St James's Church, the corner dressed in white Portland stone, but its spire obscured by a terrace on the other side of the road.

The door opened and a hawk-faced servant appeared, his eyes narrowing as he took in the black coat, hat and boots Flynt had changed back into before setting off from the Rookery lodgings. The time for disguise was over. He had to become Jonas Flynt again.

'Yes?' In that single word the servant conveyed disdain. The slight curl of the lip and a delicately arched eyebrow helped.

'I'm here to see Lord Moncrieff.'

Another look up and down. 'Do you have an appointment?'

'No.'

Yet another look. 'His lordship is not receiving at present.'

'He'll receive me.'

The ghost of a mocking smile. 'I do so doubt that. His lordship is not in the habit of receiving men such as...' He waved a long, tapered finger at Flynt. 'Not without an appointment. I suggest you make one with his secretary.'

When he attempted to close the door he found it impeded by Flynt's boot.

'Remove your foot, you rogue,' he ordered. 'This is a respectable house and well manned with servants. You shall not succeed in any mayhem without suffering consequences yourself.'

Flynt jutted his face closer. 'Tell him Jonas Flynt is here to see him. I guarantee he'll admit me. I also guarantee that if he hears you've denied me entrance, he'll be far from pleased.'

The servant's haughty manner melted in the face of Flynt's firm tone and steady gaze. He swung back a little as if to escape it, glanced at the boot still blocking the door.

'Ask him,' Flynt said amicably, taking a chance by withdrawing his foot. 'I promise I'll wait here until you return.'

Bewildered by Flynt's sudden change of attitude, the servant closed the door, the lock turning solidly. Flynt leaned against the wall at the side of the door, folded his arms and crooked one leg in front of the other, the toe of his boot resting on the top step. He wished to appear relaxed and confident in case Moncrieff viewed him from a window. He was neither relaxed nor confident, however. Yet again, he was gambling. He had no way of knowing for sure if Moncrieff would see him, but he hoped the man's curiosity – no, his arrogance – would win through. Behind him, the street traffic continued on its way; more lamps were lit outside doorways to ward off the gathering gloom.

Within minutes the lock clicked again, the door swung open and the servant waved him in, keeping well back as Flynt passed into the vestibule. It was a well-appointed house. Ahead of him a staircase curled up and to the right. Under it was a doorway, which without doubt led to the servants' quarters below stairs. To his left he glimpsed a parlour through a slightly ajar door.

The servant gestured to the right. 'His lordship would be pleased to receive you in his study.'

The servant's tone suggested that he, personally, was not so pleased. Flynt gave him a courteous, near imperceptible, bow. The man opened the door before stepping aside to allow him to enter, then closed it behind him.

He'd expected Moncrieff to have summoned at least two of the staff – two of the burliest men – but he was alone. He sat behind a large desk, a window facing the garden to his rear, a somewhat plain wooden chair sitting before it. To Flynt's left was a wall lined with books leading towards a blazing fire, in front of it a winged armchair and a small table beside it carrying three further volumes. Beeswax candles fluttered in silver sticks at either end of the mantel with two on the desktop, bathing Moncrieff's face in a yellow glow. Both hands rested palm downwards, close to two pistols.

'I'm not here to harm you,' Flynt said.

'I won't provide you with the opportunity,' Moncrieff said.

Flynt shrugged and wandered the length of the bookcases, studying the titles. 'You have read all of these?'

'Not all.'

'An impressive collection.' Flynt pulled out a volume of Cicero and flicked through the rough-edged pages, quoting from memory, '"If you have a garden and a library, you have everything you need."'

'You have read Cicero?'

Flynt replaced the volume. 'You seem surprised, brother.'

'I am not your brother,' Moncrieff said, as if by rote.

Flynt ran his finger along the spines of the shelf. 'Please, let's not deny it any longer. We share blood. You know it. I know it.' He turned away from the shelves, jerking a thumb over his shoulder towards the book he had been leafing through. 'As old Marcus Tullius said, "Any man is liable to err, but only a fool persists in error." If it helps, I'm not particularly happy about it either.'

Moncrieff breathed in sharply, then out again, before inclining his head. 'Let us agree to disagree, then.'

Flynt dropped his hat onto the armchair, then wandered towards the desk, looking around the room with an appraising eye. 'You have a nice home, James, but why did you move from St James's Square?'

'I grew tired of the condition of the square's garden. Too many vagrants. It was too much a receptacle for offal and cinders and dead cats and dogs from all over Westminster. It was not the atmosphere in which I wished to raise a child.'

'You have a child?'

'A boy. Near eight now.'

It was possible that Moncrieff told him this in case he truly did have violent intent.

'You haven't called him James, have you?'

That brought the hint of a smile. 'No. Alexander.'

'A name fit for a king.'

There had been three rulers of Scotland named Alexander, but Flynt was unsure if the child was named for them or for the Greek conqueror. He wasn't inclined to ask. He couldn't believe they were standing here as if they were old friends. Moncrieff soon dispelled that feeling.

'What do you want, Flynt?'

'You know what I want.'

'I'm afraid I leave the prescience to the tricksters and the cartomancers.'

'Daniel Hawke,' Flynt said.

Moncrieff sighed and rose, turning to the table behind him carrying decanters. 'I forget my manners. Would you care for a refreshment? I have brandy, but perhaps you would prefer some of the fine Highland whisky from home?'

Flynt accepted the latter. He was not one to drink to excess, but he hadn't had a taste of a genuine whisky for some time. There was liquor a-plenty in the colonies but the Scottish *uisge beatha*, the water of life, was in short supply. Rum, beer, cider, and what wine and brandy was brought from the Old World, and a few farmers made a spirit out of rye, but precious little true Scottish whisky. Moncrieff poured two measures into fine crystal glasses and held one out. Flynt took it and lowered himself into the chair facing the desk. Moncrieff returned to his more comfortable chair, sipped his drink, savouring the flavour. Flynt did the same. They sat in silence for a moment or two.

'My interests in the colonies have been somewhat disrupted of late,' Moncrieff said, eventually. 'Thank you for that, by the way.'

'It was my pleasure, but not my intent.'

'Nevertheless, by your actions, by this quest, you have succeeded in denting revenues both personal and those of the Fellowship. I have need of Mr Hawke to help repair the damage and to assist us in opening fresh revenue avenues.'

'You had no further need of his father, elsewise why would you refer me to him?'

'The father is not the son.'

Moncrieff's gaze was steady as he allowed the words to sink in. Flynt understood his meaning. James Moncrieff was not the man his father was, just as neither of them were like the man who had sired them. They both had come from the same wellspring, but each of them flowed in different directions away from the source.

Flynt sipped his whisky again, feeling the fire course through him. It reminded him of home. Of Edinburgh. Was that home? Or was it now the *Walrus*? He no longer knew.

Focus, Jonas.

'You trust him, then?'

'As much as I trust any man.'

Flynt gave it a moment. 'You shouldn't.'

'What do you mean by that?'

'I think you know.' He held up the glass. 'A fine drop of the water, by the way.'

Moncrieff didn't acknowledge the praise for his whisky. Flynt waited, again gambling that by remaining somewhat opaque, he might appear to be more certain than he actually was concerning this stratagem.

'I'm afraid I don't know,' Moncrieff said, his voice casual, but in the flickering candlelight Flynt perceived tension in his jaw. He had hit something; of that he was certain.

Flynt decided to go all in. 'You have a spy in your midst. Someone is reporting back to Nathaniel Charters. Someone is telling tales. I believe you have suspected it for some time.'

Although Moncrieff tried to hide it, Flynt knew he had hit his mark. It had been a guess that Moncrieff knew he had a traitor. If Charters knew there was one in his ranks, then it was highly likely he was aware of it too.

'And you claim this turncoat is Daniel Hawke?'

'Not a claim. I state it as fact.'

'How do you know?'

'Charters told me.'

No guilt at betraying this confidence stirred his conscience. He was intent on one thing and one thing only: finding and killing Daniel Hawke. Only then would he have a hope of finding something resembling peace.

Moncrieff asked, 'Why would you tell me this?'

Flynt decided on truth. 'So that you will cut him loose.'

'You could lie for that very reason.'

'I could, but I'm not. I will find him sooner or later, you know me well enough to know that. You won't stop me, no matter who you send to impede me. It was you who aimed Southern like a weapon, was it not?'

Moncrieff gave him a little shrug. 'A word or two in his ear, perhaps. A nudge. He was most susceptible to suggestion.'

'You should have been more direct in coming for me, instead of...' Flynt stopped when he saw Moncrieff's smile, suddenly understanding. Wheels within wheels. 'You had another reason for doing it, didn't you?'

Moncrieff, his smile still in place, pushed one of the pistols on his desk with a forefinger. 'Do you give me your word that you mean me no harm? I do so dislike having these things in plain view. You are a man of violence. I am one of thoughts and words.'

'If I'd meant you harm I wouldn't have come through the front door.'

'I understand you have kicked in many a door and left carnage in your wake.'

'You're not my quarry.'

'Not at the moment, anyway, correct?'

'I'm done with that. I'm finished with the Company of Rogues.'

'But is it finished with you, I wonder?'

With that thought hanging between them, Moncrieff opened the middle drawer of his desk and placed the brace of pistols inside.

'You wanted Southern out of the way,' Flynt said. 'He had lost your trust somehow, am I right?'

'For the sake of brotherhood, although I continue to dispute that, let us speak hypothetically. It might be that someone had shown a distinct lack of judgement in forming an alliance with an individual whose background and former connections were not conducive to retaining my complete faith.'

Flynt's mind ticked over as he worked out Moncrieff's references. 'Belle St Clair.'

Moncrieff's lips twitched in acquiescence.

'You didn't like him having her in high keeping?'

'I thought it unwise.'

'Why? You must have many gentlemen in the Fellowship who keep a woman in such a way.'

'Actually, I don't.'

'You are a wholesome group, then?'

Moncrieff smiled. 'I think you know we are not. But I do like probity.'

'Then you were unhappy with him because he was unfaithful to his wife?'

'And the fact that he was involved with the former paramour of an enemy.'

'I'm no longer an enemy.'

'I can't be certain of that. But there was more. She'd also had contact, through you, with Colonel Charters, and even if I could countenance the lack of moral fibre, I could not ignore that.'

'So provoking him into challenging me was a way of disposing of him? He would kill me or I would kill him, and either way you were rid of one of us.'

'If it means anything, I had the utmost confidence in your abilities, but whatever direction events took, I had a secondary plan to take care of the victorious party.'

'That was why you tipped Wild to the duel.'

'Normally he would not have troubled himself over an affair of honour, but when he heard it was you involved, he jumped at the chance, I understand. He doesn't like you much.'

'That's a shame, for I have nothing but the utmost respect for him.'

'It was suggested to him, through an intermediary, of course—'

'Of course.'

'...that should you lie dead on that field, then it was highly likely Lord Southern would pay a princely sum to keep himself out of the courts.'

'But it was Southern who died.'

'And therein lay the beauty of the plan, for you were now a hunted man, for murder.'

'Even though it was not I who killed him.'

'A minor detail.'

'Had I been caught, I would have been for Tyburn.'

Moncrieff waved that away. 'No, I would not have allowed that.'

'You would have prevented it how?'

'A word here, a suggestion there. The exchange of funds for legal services rendered.'

'Or subverted.'

'Indeed.'

'And then I would be in your debt.'

'Perhaps. You must understand this, I merely saw your return as a threat that had to be dealt with. I did not wish you actual harm.'

'Brotherly love?'

'As I say, I do continue to dispute the claim, but I will concede that the passage of years has given me a more benevolent view regarding your presence on this earth.'

'Even though I remain a threat?'

'Threat is perhaps too strong a word. Annoyance is perhaps closer to the nub of it.'

'Is that why you have Christy de Fontaine at my heels?'

Moncrieff frowned. 'I don't understand.'

'Come, James, we're being open and frank, in a hypothetical manner. Madame de Fontaine has worked for the Fellowship in the past and she is here in London, working again.'

'I did not retain her services. I didn't even know she was back in England. The last I heard she was in France.'

Flynt studied him, searching for sign of a lie but detected none. That meant nothing. Like Colonel Charters, lies, deceit and half-truths were James Moncrieff's meat and wine.

'Daniel Hawke,' he said again. 'You would be best to cut him loose before he can inform Charters further.'

'Do you have anything to corroborate this allegation?'

Flynt paused as if unsure what he should say. But he wasn't hesitant; he merely wanted to give it added weight. 'You have a man within the Company of Rogues.'

'Do I?'

'Yes.' Flynt paused again, now unsure he was correct in doing this, but he had played the hand; he must finish it. 'Gabriel Cain.'

Moncrieff covered it well, but there was a slight tightening of the jaw as he swirled the remainder of his whisky in the crystal. 'I know of him, of course. I know you and he are friends. Why would you implicate him?'

'I'm not implicating him.' Flynt also had to adopt a nonchalant attitude even though disappointment gnawed at him. He'd harboured a hope that he was wrong. 'You already know he is your man.'

'And you had this from Colonel Charters also?'

'No. He suspects he has a traitor but he knows not who. I've deduced this myself. The Company of Rogues is riddled with men and women who would betray their own mother for a sixpence, but none have the wit to betray Charters at this level. Gabriel is the most likely suspect.'

Moncrieff turned this over in his mind. 'And how does this deduction of yours strengthen your claim regarding Hawke?'

'Because I haven't shared my belief with Charters. If I had, you would no longer have your wolf in his fold.'

'And why would he take your word?'

'He trusts me. And he wishes to have me back within that fold.'

He watched Moncrieff take this in. He didn't expect him to admit anything, or even to accept at this stage what he said was true, but could only hope that he would at least successfully plant a seed of doubt. That might be enough to have Moncrieff set Hawke adrift.

Moncrieff threw back what remained of his whisky, then rose to refill his glass. He raised the decanter in a wordless invitation for Flynt to have another, but he laid his palm over the rim of his own crystal.

'There are those who see you as a blunt instrument, Jonas,' Moncrieff said as he poured. 'A brace of pistols, a cunning blade, a propensity towards violence. I take another view.' He turned back but remained standing. 'You have the reputation of being a man who does what has to be done, and I respect that. In order to do so, you must often employ deceit, and a subtlety beyond the bark of a firearm. I believe you are employing that skill at this moment.'

Flynt threw back what remained of his whisky, hoping the warmth of the Scottish water of life would help ward off the damp that awaited outside.

Moncrieff took his seat again. 'It is those skills that I would see working on my behalf.'

Flynt almost laughed. 'You expect me to work for the Fellowship?'

'Why not? We are not the devils you may believe. We are businessmen, and women, but more than that – we are visionaries.'

Flynt's laugh burst through.

'We see a world that is forever on the verge of chaos. Countries, religions, castes, all vie against one another – wars, disputes, destruction.'

'From which you profit.'

'Yes. But we – I – also wish to bring everyone together. And you know what will do that? Trade. For in profit there is power, and with power comes the opportunity to make change. Think of it, Jonas… An international web of like-minded individuals whose focus is not on what God you pray to or what flag you salute, what king you kneel before, but on trade, international trade that knows no borders, no boundaries. And with that we can unify, strengthen, set aside those petty differences and take us to a stable future.'

'With you at the head, of course.'

'No, we would still have governments and monarchs and popes.'

'Figureheads.'

Moncrieff shrugged. 'That is putting it strongly, but as I said, whoever controls the profit has the power. You can join me, Jonas. I need someone like you. Strong, resolute, dependable. Honourable. Too many of those on whom I depend have none of those qualities. Your Mr Cain being a prime example. You have built up contacts, relationships, in the New World. You could assist me in opening up the new territories for business, while also overseeing our existing interests.'

Flynt made a show of considering the proposition. He rose, paced around the room, studied the spines of the books again, then turned, shaking his head. 'I have no interest in your activities in the New or the Old World, nor those of Gabriel Cain.'

'He is your friend.'

'He is.'

'Yet you condone him betraying Charters? If indeed he is.'

'I don't condone it. It matters nothing to me.'

Moncrieff was reading him carefully. 'You reject my offer?'

'Let's say I cannot consider it at this moment. I have one aim and one aim only, and that is to kill Daniel Hawke.'

Moncrieff was disappointed. 'You walk a bleak path. It's my understanding that you have left a trail of death behind you, and not just connected to this vengeance you seek. You have known a great deal of death, Jonas. In so doing, you have become death yourself.'

Flynt retrieved his hat from the armchair. 'You've been responsible for the loss of lives yourself, James. Keeping the commission of it at arm's length doesn't protect you from the stain of guilt. We have both become death, James. In that manner, we are truly brothers.'

47

After his meeting with Moncrieff, Flynt knew he would be forced to be open with Cain, so when he returned to the Rookery, he invited him out for a drink, choosing the Rat's Castle as the venue. The patrons of The Crown in St Giles Broad were averse to the authorities, or those who adopted authority, but those in the Rat's Castle were positively antagonistic. This establishment made the meanest of city taverns look like a palace. It was of three storeys and offered vice on every level. If it was drinking and debauchery a person sought, then the ground floor was enough, for the bar was never closed and offered an abundance of liquor for sale, if not of the highest quality. But then, the denizens of the Rookery didn't seek quality, just quantity, for life was something to be endured and then blotted out for a period by being rendered insensate through an overindulgence in spirits. If the customer felt the need to disperse tension by means of physical exercise, then the upper floor offered music and a convivial atmosphere in which to dance or to make connection with the opposite sex. If that connection should lead to matters of an intimate nature, whether through mutual lust or a more businesslike arrangement, then for a small fee the top floor provided beds of straw in which to recline in whatever position was preferred – or positions, if the alcohol imbibed below had not dampened excessive ardour. This level also boasted a series of wooden pillars against which participants could enjoy a perpendicular diversion, known as the tuppenny upright.

Although not exactly a liberty zone, which offered limited protection from certain offences like debt, the Rat's Castle's independence was fiercely defended and the landlord had a strict set of rules. There would be no arrest made within its walls. There would be no fighting within its walls. There would be no killing within its walls. What occurred outside the walls was not the landlord's concern. These strictures were enforced by a group of men who wandered around the various rooms, armed to the teeth and unafraid to use them, including the teeth. Flynt had once flouted those rules, but had got away with it and he hoped the passage of time would have dimmed memories.

He and Cain ensured their weapons were well concealed as they ordered ale and carried them to a table, as was their habit, in the far corner where they could observe the arrivals and exits.

Once they were settled, Flynt decided to get right down to it.

'I saw Lord Moncrieff earlier this evening.'

Cain remained relaxed. 'By chance or design?'

'I paid him a call at his home. In Jermyn Street. But I suspect that is something you already know.'

'Why would I know that?'

Flynt maintained a steady gaze. 'Because you're in his pay.'

Cain forced a laugh. 'What makes you—'

'Don't deny it, Gabriel. You're his man in the Company of Rogues.'

Cain was about to deny it further, but thought better of it. His mouth snapped shut and he allowed his eyes to wander around the room. He wasn't looking for anything in particular; he was simply avoiding Flynt's scrutiny. Too late, though, for Flynt had already seen the truth in his eyes.

'Time is not our friend, Jonas. You said as much yourself. We grow old. A little slower. Bit by bit, day by day, week by week. And in our profession, that can be lethal. It's not happened yet, but I can feel it. The years, the tension, the work, they take a toll. So of late I've had to make consideration for my future. I have no family fortune. I have no skills apart from my acuity with pistols.'

He fell silent. Flynt sipped his ale, letting him speak, understanding how he felt.

'You were away, Jonas,' Cain said, eventually. 'For so long you were away and I thought you would not return. So I took Charters' coin and Moncrieff's coin and any other coin I could find. Where's the harm?'

Flynt didn't reply. Cain obviously didn't expect one, for he continued speaking.

'These matters, of the Fellowship, of the Company of Rogues, of the State, these are not matters for the likes of you and I. We are rogues, thieves...'

'Killers,' added Flynt.

Cain paused. 'Yes, and killers. I've killed for money. So have you.'

'Never for money.'

'Please, Jonas, let's not delude ourselves. You have indeed killed for money, whether it was for Charters or pirate-hunting for Woodes Rogers. How many of the old Flying Gang did you have a hand in sending to the gallows? At least I am honest enough to admit that I did it solely for the coin. You dress it up as something noble.'

'I'm not noble,' Flynt said, quietly.

'Then don't judge me for doing what I do.'

'I don't. I don't care what you do in that regard. You will follow the money, that is your nature. I just needed for us to be open about the situation.'

They fell silent again until Cain said, 'I've never betrayed you, you must know that.'

'I do know that.'

'I never will betray you.'

'I know that, too.'

But as they sat together, Flynt knew that he didn't know that. Cain had never let him down in the past, but there might come a time when he would be made an offer that was too good to allow to pass.

He decided to lighten the mood. 'Madame de Fontaine sends her regards. She inquires after your health.' He narrowed his eyes as if puzzled. 'Particularly your buttocks.'

Cain was never embarrassed by his sexual adventures. 'That witch! She took a riding crop to me. Left a few stripes. It seemed to spur her on to greater enthusiasm.'

'And you?'

'After the initial shock, I must confess it was something of an aphrodisiac.'

Flynt couldn't imagine the inflicting or receiving of pain during lovemaking as being any kind of stimulant for a normal person, but Christy and Cain were not normal.

'So she's back in London,' Cain said, a calculating gleam in his eyes. His earlier melancholy had dispersed, as was his way. His fears of impending seniority had not impinged on his libido.

'She is.'

'For what reason?'

'She wouldn't say.'

'I would imagine she wouldn't. She keeps things very close to her breast, that woman. And what a breast it is.' He fell silent, without doubt recalling Christy's charms. Then he sighed. 'Well, whatever her reason for being here, I can say this without hesitation. She's the ill wind that blows nobody good.'

'Oh, I don't know. She seems to have done you some good.'

Cain laughed. 'I still bear the marks, and fine piece though she be, I have no burning desire to open those old wounds.' He sighed again, as if he regretted that decision. 'So what is next for us, Jonas?'

'We remain cautious and we wait.' Flynt's mood darkened. 'We're reaching the endgame, Gabriel. I've rolled the dice for the final time, I think. They will either come up in my favour or I will lose all. I've planted a seed in Moncrieff's mind that I hope will blossom. Only time will tell.'

48

The hoarse roar of the lions was unusually loud to Moncrieff's ear, but then he had little frame of reference. The previous night's rain had thankfully dried and there was even the promise of some blue sky behind the grey, but that could well prove to be a false hope. England's weather was mercurial in the extreme, and often the hint of a change for the better could be nothing more than a ruse, as if God himself was making sport of his creations, promising one set of conditions but then, like a magician, delivering another in the blink of an eye. He considered whether the lions, born to warmer climes, were in fact complaining over the changeability of the elements native to their enforced home. Or perhaps they merely wished to be fed.

He had lain in bed all night, his wife sleeping by his side, staring at the ceiling. How often had he done that over the years, he wondered? Whenever he had an issue with which to wrestle, a decision to make, an unpalatable order to give, he would lie there, willing himself to sleep, wishing to sleep, but finding it just out of reach.

Flynt's claim regarding Daniel Hawke troubled him, not just because he was unsure if it was true but because if it was, then the man had duped him. Part of him urged action. Another part suggested caution. Flynt had his own reasons for wishing Hawke set free – he had been open about that – but Moncrieff couldn't shake off the feeling that his half-brother was sincere in his assertion regarding Hawke's infidelity. It was no mere attempt to nudge Moncrieff into giving him access to Hawke; he truly believed what he said.

Moncrieff had long suspected he had a spy in the Fellowship's midst. Some elements of the Fellowship's enterprises had been compromised recently: nothing major, certainly, but enough for him to consider the possibility that someone was talking when they should be mute. One or two of these breaches *had* occurred since Hawke had arrived from the colonies. Hawke's own father had betrayed the Fellowship by siphoning off profit that should have reached them. That, and the fact that he had supported Moncrieff's predecessor as Grand Master, had meant he had to be dealt with. It was possible that Daniel Hawke was as untrustworthy as his father, though he had to confess he had not thought so. Until now.

Moncrieff had feared Southern was speaking out of turn to his whore, which was why he had used Flynt again. Gabriel Cain had been another suspect, but he had rejected him. He paid him too well, far more than Charters could or would, and Cain was enslaved to money. Moncrieff recognised that coin was the only way to keep a man like him faithful. He had no ambitions beyond his own gratification, whereas Daniel Hawke perhaps harboured dreams of self-advancement, possibly even becoming Grand Master, although Fellowship rules precluded a non-Scot from holding such a position.

He tried not to toss and turn too much, for fear of disturbing Anne, but eventually he had to rise and repair to his study, where he sat until dawn's grey fingers crept over the windowsill. By then he had made a decision and he despatched two messengers, one to an address only he knew, the other to Mr Griffin's lodgings.

He breakfasted and dressed before his wife, and even his son, had awakened and, upon the arrival of Griffin, set out to meet Daniel Hawke at the wharf by the Tower of London, where it was almost pleasant and where the lions of the menagerie were particularly vocal. He made a note that he should bring Alexander to view the beasts of the wild that had long been kept behind the citadel's walls. He himself had not visited for many a year, but well recalled looking in amazement at the lions, leopards and even eagles kept for the delectation of visitors. As he had gazed upon them reclining or pacing behind the bars of their cages, he felt sorrow, for they were as much prisoners as the traitors and rebels housed in the cells. That said, he still believed his son would enjoy seeing such exotic creatures.

Mr Griffin maintained a watchful distance as around them the work of the docklands continued. Porters carried bales and baskets and bundles. Sailors sporting a variety of garbs sauntered or called to one another in a babel of tongues. On the masts of ships moored nearby, men laboured at ropes and sheets, while on the decks below them their shipmates caulked and sewed and cleaned.

Below where he stood was Traitors' Gate, by which those political prisoners traditionally gained access. Many of them never left again. When he spied Hawke walking in his direction he realised that the location of their assignation might well have been an apt one.

Hawke was alone, for he had lost all his men at the hands of Flynt and Cain. Nevertheless, Moncrieff was glad he'd brought Griffin along, for what he was about to say might provoke Hawke's ire. Moncrieff carried a pistol but had only once felt the desire to discharge it, and even then had failed to properly hit his mark. He was more likely to be successful with the heavy silver wolf's-head handle of his cane, but the thought of actually delivering violence himself was unpalatable. Flynt was correct: when such business was deemed necessary, Moncrieff conducted it by proxy.

He wasted no time on pleasantries. 'I believe it is time for you to vacate these shores, Mr Hawke.'

Hawke was disconcerted with the bluntness of the words. 'You're sending me back home?'

'I am,' Moncrieff said.

'That'll solve nothing. Flynt remains at large, and sooner or later he'll discover that I've sailed and will follow. He'll continue to disrupt my work, our work, in the colonies.' His voice rose. 'Damn it, Moncrieff, I've told you before that you should take direct action against that son-of-a-whore, and it must be done now.'

'That is not on my agenda, Hawke,' Moncrieff said, sharply. 'And I would suggest you moderate your tone when speaking to me. Also, you will address me as "my Lord" in public, "Grand Master" in private.'

Hawke's face remained taut but he lowered his eyes. 'I apologise, my Lord.'

Moncrieff waited a moment before speaking again. *These damned colonials often forgot who were their betters.* 'I have no intention of taking direct action against Flynt. I may have use for him in the future.'

Despite Flynt's refusal, he continued to harbour an intent to have his half-brother work for the Fellowship.

Hawke's eyes rose again, the defiance still evident. 'And you've no use for me, is that it?'

'I didn't say that. Your utility to me lies across the Atlantic, not here in London.'

The truculent cast to Hawke's eyes transformed as he sensed something behind Moncrieff's words and shifted uneasily on his feet as he tried to pinpoint the source. Treacherous he might have been, but he was no fool. That was why he was of use to Moncrieff's work — or rather, had been.

'You're sacrificing me,' Hawke declared.

'Not at all. I will ensure that Flynt is detained in London for a considerable time. Who knows, perhaps he will give up the hunt.'

'He's been after me for years, for something in which I had no involvement. I can't see him relinquishing it. It's what keeps him alive.'

'Perhaps, perhaps not. Nevertheless, I would suggest you prepare to leave immediately. I cannot guarantee your safety in London much longer.'

Hawke's suspicions were not assuaged. If anything, they were even further inflamed. Moncrieff didn't care what the man thought, for he had made his mind up. He couldn't be certain if Hawke was indeed betraying Fellowship secrets, or if it was a feint by Flynt to flush him out. It was that uncertainty that forced him to cut Hawke loose, for he couldn't abide ambivalence in his own mind. This way, he was taking action. If the man was true, then he would continue to do his work in the colonies. If he was not, and if Moncrieff felt that no further operations at home had been compromised in his absence, then it was an easy matter to have him punished, even on the other side of the world. The Fellowship's reach was vast, and it would be very easy to steer Flynt, or Cain, towards Hawke. Just as Moncrieff had done with Hawke's father and Southern.

Of course, there was always the possibility that Flynt would get to Hawke before he left London. That would certainly cure his uncertainty.

'Why can't you make such a guarantee?' Hawke demanded.

'Because I have an apostate in my ranks.' Moncrieff saw no reason to create any illusion. 'Someone is carrying tales regarding the work of the Fellowship. That person may well discover your whereabouts and see fit to inform others, including Flynt. So you see, it is for your own safety that I urge this displacement.'

'When you had me moved to that filthy hovel on the waterfront you vowed I'd be safe. Flynt wouldn't dare set foot in the docklands, you said, because to do so would place him under a sentence of death at the hands of the Admiral. You said all this, my lord, and you seemed certain. What's changed?'

'I do believe Flynt would find himself unable to resist taking that gamble, should he learn of your presence there.'

'And if I don't agree to leave?'

'Then, my dear Hawke, regrettably you will be on your own.'

Hawke stared beyond the masts of boats moored nearby, and those in the centre of the river, past the water boatmen rowing steadily against the currents of the grey water chopped by the breeze. His gaze fixed on the southern bank, as if seeking sanctuary. The river was a living thing, a wonder to behold. It snaked through the city, dividing it in two, but it was what bound the disparate parts together. For that which made London the booming heart of commerce flowed through here, in and out: silks and spices and porcelain from the East; tobacco and furs and timber and silver and sugar and rum from the West; wine and cloth from the Continent; slaves and exotic materials from Africa; coal and iron and tallow from ports in England and Scotland. There were riches here: goods that connected ports and countries and colonies together. Trade was what made the world turn, and right where Moncrieff stood was the centre of it. That was why he was in the process of ensuring that the Fellowship took control of these docklands. There were revenues to be had, here and abroad, and he would have them. He had gleaned a great deal of knowledge concerning the Admiral's interests, and in time would be in a position to make his move. The masked man who at that moment controlled the docklands could either relinquish his hold or be swept aside.

'And what if I end this myself and take my chances with Flynt, here in London?' Hawke said, suddenly turning back to face him. 'For I'm done running, you know that. I can't live my life looking over my shoulder.'

Moncrieff was blunt. 'Then you will die, for you are no match for him. He is a seasoned killer of men.'

'I've killed. I can kill him.' He paused. 'I can have him killed.'

Until he knew for certain one way or another if he could be trusted, Moncrieff had no desire to allow the man to throw his life away. 'Many have tried, all have failed. Jonas Flynt possesses an aptitude for dealing out death that is near supernatural. And your last attempt was far from successful.'

'There are others who are more skilled.' Hawke pointed towards Griffin. 'From what I understand, he is proficient in that regard.'

'Mr Griffin has other tasks and, I say again, I have my own plans for Jonas Flynt.'

'And what are they?'

'They need not concern you.'

He had no idea if Flynt would ever join forces with the Fellowship. He had made the offer, but was astutely aware that Flynt would not countenance such a move until he had completed his work.

'So, that's the way of it, then?' Hawke said.

'That's the way it must be. Arrange passage, Daniel, but tell me nothing of it. If I do have a renegade within my ranks, then it's best I don't know. Flee these shores, and flee them soon, for Flynt is close.'

He turned away, leaving Griffin to ensure that Hawke didn't feel it necessary to stop him.

Within the high Kentish ragstone walls of the tower, the lions still roared. Moncrieff became acutely aware that he had just sent this particular Daniel into the den of another – if figurative – lion.

49

Word regarding Hawke reached Flynt two days later.

They were in the dismal room in the Rookery, though they had a fire burning and Jack had managed to find some little bits of furniture: a moth-eaten armchair, another couple of wooden chairs, some pots for cooking, and three straw mattresses that they laid out on the floor. The accommodations remained somewhat sparse but at least they offered a little more comfort than before. Jack had even found some books, upon which Flynt fell voraciously. Cain became restive after a time. He abhorred being confined in this small space and on occasion left Flynt and Jack alone to walk the streets. Flynt didn't try to dissuade him. He had cautioned him to take care, to not draw any attention, and he trusted Cain to do so. Occasionally, Flynt accompanied him and they enjoyed some ale in a back alley tavern where they were not known.

The messenger delivering the letter said it must be handed only to Flynt. Its seal remained intact, and Flynt was satisfied that it had not been in any way tampered with. He gave the lad a shilling, which caused him to smile broadly and declare profuse gratitude before he darted downstairs.

'Who knows we are here?' Cain reclined on a mattress, reading a copy of Mr Defoe's *Moll Flanders*, but Flynt didn't enlighten him, even though he knew who had sent it before he even opened it. He snapped the seal, unfolded the paper and scanned the contents.

'Jonas, who sent the message?' Cain asked.

'Who sent it doesn't matter.' Flynt folded the note and tucked it away inside his waistcoat. He retrieved his coat from where it was draped over the back of a chair, and his hat, which lay on the floor beside it. 'What it contains does.'

Cain put the book aside and pushed himself upright. 'News of Hawke?'

Flynt thrust Tact and Diplomacy into his belt and retrieved his silver stick from where it was propped against the chair. That was all the answer Cain required. He rose from the straw and proceeded to prepare his own weapons, obviously energised by the prospect of action. 'He is in motion?'

Flynt was already at the door. 'He is.'

Cain hauled on his coat. 'Where?'

'He has passage booked on a vessel heading to the colonies. He sails from the Pool tonight. Jack, I will have need of you.'

50

The rains had moved on. The night was clear, the moon a half-crescent, its reflection glistening on the undulating surface of the river as if trying to hook a fish. The docks at Wapping bristled with the masts of ships either having arrived recently from far-off lands, or about to leave. One of the latter was the *Prince Frederick*, a brigantine packet ship bound for New York, lying at anchor in the centre of the Thames, a dark mass bedecked with lights. It had only one passenger on its manifest, and Flynt was going to ensure that he never set foot on board.

The wharf heaved with traffic, for there was much to be done before any vessel could sail. Cargo was being transported by wherry from the dockside, and dockers and sailors were busy loading and carrying large bundles of coloured cloth. The mail to be taken to the colonies would already be aboard. Boatmen bustled to and fro across the dark water, their lamps bobbing and weaving in the dark night, their curses and calls drifting with the wind back to land.

Flynt, Cain and Jack Sheppard hid themselves in the shadows of a large stack of timber, Flynt's gaze never moving from the steps leading to the small boat that would carry Hawke to the brigantine. The thrill of the chase surged through his flesh. It would all end tonight. And then, finally, peace.

A dock worker carrying a basket of fruit passed their hiding place and looked in their direction, but moved on without breaking stride. Jack shifted nervously on his feet.

'We is exposed here, Mr Flynt,' he said.

'I'm aware, Jack,' Flynt said without turning.

'Jack's right, Jonas,' Cain said. 'We should perhaps find ourselves a better vantage point.'

'This suits us well.' Flynt gave them both a smile. 'Put yourself at ease, lads. The *Prince Frederick* sails in an hour. Hawke will be here presently.'

He resumed his surveillance. Cain stared at his friend for a moment, then at Jack, who shrugged and continued to nervously watch the movement on the wharf. Cain, for what seemed like the tenth time since they had arrived, ensured his pistols were primed.

Flynt tensed and drew back a little further. 'As I said,' he whispered, 'we didn't have long to wait.'

Hawke dropped his sack and stared down the steps leading to the wherry, seemingly arguing with someone at their foot. He gestured angrily towards the *Prince Frederick*. Flynt couldn't see the boatman, but given the amount of gear and small cargo that he had witnessed being loaded while they waited, his small vessel was full. *Good*, he thought, *that gives us time.*

'Jack, take Mr Hawke a message. Render him Lord Moncrieff's compliments, and tell him that he would be obliged if he would meet him in the East India Company warehouse by King Edward's Stairs. Then you beetle back to the Rookery. Don't linger, is that understood? As you say, we are exposed, and you are a valuable prize for someone with the gumption to report back to Wild.'

'Lord Moncrieff, East India Company warehouse at King Edward's Stairs, then back to the Rookery,' Jack repeated. 'But what if he refuses?'

'He won't refuse. Off now. And be careful.'

It was obvious to Flynt that Jack was grateful for the chance now to be active, for he gave him his cheekiest grin. 'I is always careful, Mr Flynt.'

Aye, lad, that's why you ended up in chains in the Whit.

Flynt and Cain watched as Jack approached Hawke and delivered the message, pointing away from them in the direction of the stairs Flynt had specified. Hawke asked a question. Jack replied.

'What do you think he's saying?' Cain whispered.

'Whatever it is, Jack will convince him. He has a way with him. If he told me I'd meet myself in that warehouse, I'd believe him.'

Hawke seemed to sigh, looking out to the wherry, which had just shoved off from the dock and was in the process of being rowed towards the *Prince Frederick*. He reached into the pocket of his coat and handed Jack a coin, then hefted his sack again and started into the darkness beyond the guttering torches around the loading dock. As he passed, Jack gave Flynt and Cain a salute and a swift grin, flipping the coin.

Flynt returned the salute, then he and Cain stepped out of their hiding place to follow Hawke along the dockside.

'How do you know this warehouse will be empty?' Cain asked. 'It's owned by the East India Company, for God's sake. It's likely to be manned at all hours.'

'They don't own it, they rent it,' Flynt said. 'And it will be clear.'

'How do you know?'

Flynt walked ahead. 'Research.'

51

It was a hulking timber building, not in the best of repair, situated at the very end of a pier. Beyond it was a dock leading to a boatyard. In the middle of the river they saw the lights of a large merchant ship, but there were no smaller vessels alongside the quay nor scurrying back and forth. The thrill of finally reaching the end of this hunt filled Flynt's body, gave him fresh purpose. He sensed Cain's confusion, but he didn't ask any further questions.

They maintained their distance, ensuring they made no noise. Hawke didn't look behind him, so confident was he that he was about to make his escape. Flynt was pleased with that, too. An overconfident quarry was one apt to make errors of judgement. In fact, in responding to the counterfeit message delivered by Jack, he had already made one.

Hawke found an open doorway and vanished into the darkness beyond. Cain stopped and laid a hand on Flynt's arm. 'What the hell goes on here, Jonas? An empty warehouse, an open door?'

Flynt kept walking. 'Providence, Gabriel.'

Before he entered the building, he drew both Tact and Diplomacy. Cain produced his weapons from under his coat, muttering something incomprehensible, but which without doubt amounted to an expression of the need for caution as well as questioning the tenacity of Flynt's grip on sanity. Flynt paused, closed his eyes for a moment and breathed deeply, then exhaled. He was prepared for this, but he still felt that tremor of trepidation, as he always did. He filled his lungs again, held the breath for an instant, then released it. The tremor stilled. He was ready. He nodded to Cain, who was scanning the gloom ahead with narrowed eyes.

They were in a short corridor that led to another open door, after which it opened up to a larger space: a wooden cavern piled high with goods in bales or bundles or casks or crates. Flynt had no way of knowing if some of it had recently arrived from that merchantman moored in the Thames or were to be loaded onto it. The East India Company had grown into a powerful force as it attempted to milk the great Moghul Empire of its riches. There might even be weapons among them, for that milking was often not a peaceful process. The trade goods were stacked in rows, creating a canyon through which they walked warily, both listening for any sound ahead and watching for another sight of Hawke, who had vanished. Somewhere, water dripped, the heavy rains of late having penetrated the timber roof. The odour of dampness, of fetid standing water, reached them. The lap of the dirty river against wooden pilings beneath the warehouse reminded them of how precarious this structure was. It was aged – it might even have been standing when Queen Bess ruled – and the floorboards felt somewhat springy.

And worse, he detected the scratch of rodent claws as they scampered unseen in corners and between the rows. He shuddered. Rats filled him with a fear that no man could.

'Jonas,' Cain whispered, and in that one word Flynt heard a warning, at first believing it related to the instability of the surface below their feet. But it didn't. Cain had turned, his weapons swaying back and forth as he searched the darkness that had folded behind them as if he had heard, seen, or at least sensed something within. 'Do you feel it?'

Flynt maintained his forward gaze but growled an assent. Something was amiss here. It tickled the back of his neck and agitated his gut. However, he had come too far to turn back. And anyway, he had a plan.

He took a few careful steps, pistols at the ready, the boards seeming to bend. Cain lagged behind a moment, still staring into the blackness, before walking backwards in Flynt's wake. They edged forward in this way for a time, keeping their breath even and silent, occasionally swinging their weapons upwards to scan the towers of goods on either side in case someone had found a vantage point among them. The steady drip-drip-drip of the water somewhere in the darkness kept time with the groan of the floorboards and the soft lick of the river below.

They reached the end of the canyon of goods and found themselves in an open arena, where two lamps burned upon a table. And beside them stood Daniel Hawke, two pistols levelled in their direction.

He sneered. 'You didn't believe I'd be so stupid, did you?'

Flynt edged into the space, both pistols trained on Hawke, Cain behind him, surveilling the perimeter, but beyond the pool of brown light cast by the lamps there was only darkness. Flynt was aware there was somebody nearby, but didn't know exactly where.

He trained both pistols on Hawke. 'You're here, are you not?'

'I am –' Hawke tilted his weapons a little – 'but not the helpless prey you expected.'

'We're two to your one, Hawke. One of us is bound to take you down.'

Hawke smiled. He was confident, feeling secure, knowing something Flynt didn't. Flynt was not overly concerned by this turn of events. He still had his plan.

And then Hawke played his hand. 'Are you certain of that, Flynt?'

A movement behind them caused them to whirl as Christy de Fontaine and Gregor emerged from the gloom, both armed. Flynt retreated a few paces from them, twisting his aim back and forward from them to Hawke. Cain maintained his focus on Hawke.

'Hello, Gabriel, darling,' Christy said. 'How are the buttocks?'

'Christy,' Cain said, his eyes never leaving Hawke. 'Nice to see you again.'

'And you, my sweet.' She seemed to notice Flynt for the first time. 'Don't be jealous, Jonas, my darling. If you deny me your pleasures then I must find them elsewhere.'

Flynt had no time for badinage. He now knew for certain he was her target. 'You've been in Hawke's pay, I take it?'

'I have, of recent,' she admitted. 'And have followed you all evening. You really have been most remiss in watching your flanks.'

Flynt glared at Cain. It had been his job to maintain a watch for anyone following. Cain shrugged an apology. Flynt mentally accepted it, for he knew how well this woman and her Russian consort could avoid being detected. When you have so much darkness in your heart, then it is easy to become one with it. Even so, this complicated matters.

'I knew that son-of-a-bitch Moncrieff had betrayed me,' Hawke snarled. 'You thought to trap me, Flynt, but I've snared you.' He moved closer. 'I told Moncrieff that I'd end this.'

'It's not over yet, Hawke,' Flynt said.

Hawke laughed. 'You really are an arrogant son-of-a-bitch, you know that? You think you're immortal, is that it?'

Another voice chimed in – one that wheezed – from the darkness beyond Hawke. 'Yes, Jonas, do you believe yourself to be immortal?'

All eyes turned to a passageway between the goods on the far side, pistols still aimed in all directions. Two figures emerged, both tall, one dressed in a heavy seaman's coat, a cocked hat perched above his masked face, the other with his head bare, a pistol in each hand.

The Admiral came to a halt, one hand in the pocket of his coat, the other leaning on his cane, Pickett at his side, his aim falling on Hawke and Flynt. Behind him, Flynt heard Cain breathe a curse that might have been a prayer.

'I warned you not to come to the waterfront, Jonas,' the Admiral rasped.

'I know.'

'I told you what would happen.'

'You did.'

'I did this before witnesses. Mr Pickett and my clerk, Albert.'

'They were there, yes.'

'And yet, here you are.'

'Yes, here I am.'

Hawke lowered his pistols. 'My name is Daniel Hawke, Admiral.'

The Admiral didn't look at him. 'Yes, I know who you are, Mr Hawke.'

'I got reasons of my own for wishing this man dead.'

'I know that, too.'

'I know of your warning to him, that if he ever set foot in your territory then you would kill him. I'm happy to have my people step aside and let you finish him.'

The Admiral now faced him, scanning him from head to foot. 'Thank you, that is very kind of you. When I issue a directive I do expect it to be obeyed, for failure would undermine my authority. If word were to get out that Mr Flynt here had flaunted my order, then it would be most upsetting.'

Hawke was pleased, even relieved. 'Then I'm glad I was able to lure him here.'

'Yes,' the Admiral said thoughtfully before a cough racked his body. He brought his gloved hand out from his pocket and pressed a linen square to his mouth. When the cough subsided, he returned the kerchief to his pocket. 'I apologise. The night air and the dampness in this accursed building have irritated my lungs. It should have been razed years ago, but it was the first warehouse I ever bought and I hold a soft spot for it.' He looked up and around him, as if inspecting the property. 'It's far from a thing of beauty, but it's good enough for the East India Company, the rapacious bastards.' He lowered his face to stare hard at Flynt, then at Cain, then back to Hawke. 'The question remains, Mr Hawke, as to how you came to learn of my ultimatum to Mr Flynt.'

Hawke's brow furrowed. 'I don't understand.'

'As I said, apart from Jonas and me, there were only two others present – Mr Pickett and my clerk. I have not mentioned it to anyone, I doubt if Jonas has. Am I correct?'

Flynt smiled. 'You are, Admiral.'

'So, it raises the question, how did you hear?'

Hawke floundered. 'I... I mean... I was told by Lord Moncrieff.'

'Ah,' was all the Admiral said in reply.

'You were correct, Admiral,' Flynt said. 'Your man Albert is in the pay of the Fellowship.'

'Indeed,' the Admiral said, his voice tinged with regret. 'He will be dealt with presently, I'm afraid. Such a shame, he was the best clerk I could find, having lost my previous bookkeeper to murder, as you are aware, Jonas. But unlike his Huguenot predecessor, who was exceeding dextrous with figures, Albert was open to corruption. When such venality works in my favour I welcome it, but not when it breaches my confidence.'

Hawke was at first confused, then realisation dawned. Cain leaned closer to Flynt and said, 'What is this, Jonas?'

'The Admiral's displeasure with me was exaggerated,' Flynt explained. 'We'd had correspondence before my arrival, and he informed me that he suspected he had a spy in his midst.' He gave Cain a knowing wink. 'It appears there are a lot of them about.'

'Yes, we are all keeping watch on one another,' the Admiral said. 'The Fellowship on me, I on the Fellowship and Jonathan Wild, Colonel Charters on everyone. I swear, with all the spying and tattling going on, I don't know how we get things done. When Jonas wished to find Mr Hawke here, I saw a way of winkling out the worm in my decks. So we devised a little drama for Albert's benefit.'

'We knew you would flee at some point, Hawke,' Flynt added. 'And it would be from the Pool of London. Nothing comes in or out without the Admiral knowing of it. On the waterfront, he is God.'

The Admiral's chortle was loose with liquid. 'Please, Jonas, I pretend to be no deity. King, perhaps, but not God.'

'He informed me as soon as he knew you were ready to sail.'

'Yes, I regret I did not discover where you had been berthing this past day or so until too late,' said the Admiral. 'But you really should not have booked passage under your own name. Granted, you believed that my feigned enmity for Jonas would act as some form of defence, but prudence should have dictated the use of a soubriquet.'

Hawke raised his pistols again, one on the Admiral, the other on Flynt. When both Flynt and Pickett took one step forward, he swung them wildly between them. 'He damaged your business in the colonies!'

'Not as much as I claimed,' the Admiral said. 'In truth, I am annoyed with him for not telling me of his past connections with the Company of Rogues, but that's all water under the bow. I am content that he didn't inform Colonel Charters concerning any of my enterprises. Good friends are hard to find in this life, as I do believe you are beginning to realise, Mr Hawke.'

Hawke turned a little towards Christy and Gregor, who had during the interim separated and moved a little further into the space, both hands filled with pistols. Christy had one aimed at Flynt, the other in the vague direction of Pickett; Gregor had a bead on Cain and the Admiral. 'Damn you, woman, do something about this!'

Christy smiled. 'What would you have me do? We seem to be at an impasse. We have six shots between us, they have six shots. I don't like being so even-matched.'

Hawke, seeing his plan falling apart, grew irritable. 'You're the goddamned expert at such situations. At least, I was told you were the best. So far I've seen nothing to support that. Defend me. Kill them all. That's what I've paid you for.'

Christy tilted her head in thought, giving Flynt a saucy smile. 'Well, about that...'

She swivelled the pistol trained on Flynt towards Hawke. Gregor also shifted his aim from Cain.

Hawke's eyes blinked furiously and he tried to say something, but all he could come up with was to repeat, 'I paid you!'

'You did,' said Christy. 'But someone paid us more.'

Hawke's anger rose. 'What? Who the hell...?'

'That would be me,' said Cain. Seeing Flynt's querying glance, he continued. 'When you told me that Christy and Gregor were on your tail, I tracked them down and discovered this bastard had recently hired them to kill you.'

'You tracked them down? How did you manage that?'

Cain shrugged, suddenly a little boy. 'Professional secrets, Jonas. You know what I mean.'

Flynt knew. In that moment he'd admitted to being the Wraith.

Christy looked sorrowful. 'I don't usually disclose my employer's name but, in my darling Gabriel's case, I think it fell under the aegis of professional courtesy. I do apologise, Mr Hawke, but I couldn't bring myself to fulfil the contract.' She blew Flynt a kiss. 'You see? I really do have a soft spot for you, Jonas.'

'It helped that I made them a counter-offer,' said Cain.

'Which I accepted.'

Hawke stared at her, his blinking ever more agitated. 'You can't... You took my money...'

Christy's shame was entirely fabricated. 'And I apologise for my breach of etiquette. But in my defence, given your background, your own activities, did you really expect good faith from someone like me? I am the first to admit that I really cannot be trusted.'

Hawke swore, loudly and fluently, calling Christy's parentage and her honour into question, and condemning her to everlasting torment. She merely shrugged it all away, and agreed that all were true.

'Finish it, Jonas,' Cain urged.

'Yes, Jonas, do what you came here to do and let us be done with it,' the Admiral agreed, his kerchief once again employed at his lips. 'This place will be the death of me.'

Flynt moved towards Hawke, who immediately dropped his pistols on the table at his side and held his hands before him. 'I'm unarmed, Flynt. You kill me, it'll be murder.'

'That would require witnesses and there are none here who would testify to that,' Flynt said, still moving closer. 'And my son was unarmed when he was murdered.'

'That was not my doing.'

'It was the result of a situation of your creation.'

'I did not wish it... Your boy...'

'Jonas,' Flynt said, his tone dead, still advancing, slowly, steadily. 'His name was Jonas. Say it. Say his name.'

Hawke swallowed, took a half-step back. 'Jonas. I didn't wish his death. That was Thatch, it was all Thatch. He suffered a distemper of the mind.'

Flynt halted at the far end of the long table. 'Thatch paid the penalty and the turbulence of his mind is now at peace. Now it's your turn. But I'll give you a chance denied to Jonas.' He lowered both pistols and laid them on the table. 'I've recently learned the gentleman's way of such matters. I'll make a count of ten, at the end of which we will both reach for our weapons and fire.'

'Jonas, for God's sake,' Cain said, slightly exasperated, but Flynt merely held one hand up to silence him.

Hawke looked to his weapons, just within reach, but shook his head. 'I won't.'

'Then you'll die, for whether or not you reach for your weapon, I will.' Flynt positioned his feet so that he was balanced correctly. 'One...'

Hawke lowered his hands, a flickering glance cast towards the pistols. To Flynt's rear, the Admiral and Pickett moved away from the line of fire. In the pale glow of the lamps Flynt focused on Hawke: on his face, on his eyes. If the man decided to beat the count and reach for the weapons before ten was called, he would see it there before the command reached his fingers.

'Two...'

Despite his best efforts, his mind turned backwards. To the small shack on the golden beach.

'Three...'

He saw Thatch, his black beard making him more threatening. His eyes ablaze.

'Four...'

He saw young Jonas, tied to a chair. Thatch raising his pistol. Firing...

'Five...'

Cassie's eyes brimming with tears. *Find him. Find him and kill him*, she said. *It's what you do, so do it now.* It wasn't Hawke she meant, though. He had killed the man she meant. But he'd continued to kill.

'Six...'

Belle's voice. *Revenge has a way of eating at a man.*

'Seven...'

You have become death. Moncrieff this time.

'Eight...'

He who seeks revenge at all costs must first sacrifice himself. Charters' words.

'Nine...'

Of a sudden, weariness draped itself over Flynt as he realised that he had allowed his thirst for vengeance to consume him. He'd often believed that every time he killed a man, a piece of him died along with him, but how much of him remained? Would one more death be the end? He gazed at Hawke, watchful, waiting, nervous, wondering if he could pluck the pistols from their resting place before Flynt. Perhaps he could let him do so. Simply call ten and not move, allowing Hawke to reach them. Perhaps it was time to end all of this, because after this, what did he have left to him? He'd lost Cassie. He'd lost Belle. Had he lost himself?

The drip of the water counted the seconds. He knew all eyes were on him, all ears awaiting that final number. Hawke edged a little closer to the table. Flynt didn't move. He didn't speak.

'Finish it, Jonas.'

Cain. His voice hushed. Urgent. Hawke's eyes darted instinctively in his direction, then back to Flynt. His hands moved, his fingers flexing, clenching, then flexing again. Flynt knew it would be so very easy to best him. The man's nerves were too stretched, his body too tight. He might reach his weapons first, but Flynt would still take him. Flynt knew this as fact. It would be so very easy. Finish the count, take up Tact, put a ball in Hawke before he had even raised his own pistol.

Another death: another piece of him dying with him.

It's what you do...

There had been a challenge in Cassie's voice, but also a sadness. What was it she said to him when he had returned to Edinburgh?

There's a darkness that follows you... You carry the stench of death...

He knew he did, but until that moment, all those years ago, he had never heard it put into words. And there had been so many deaths since then: friends; enemies; people he hardly knew; people he didn't know at all. He saw a young man kneeling on the deck of a ship, thousands of miles away, waiting for the shot that would end his life. He saw a woman who had helped him beaten and bloodied on a cot. He saw the life bleed out of Rab, the man young Jonas called 'Father', as a bitter snow fell on a Scottish hillside. He saw these and more, all in the instant before he was due to complete the count.

He shook his head and turned away. He was done with killing. Done with his life. He didn't want to lose himself completely. He should end the cycle now. He began to turn away…

It was Hawke who ended it. Perhaps his nerves had shredded; perhaps he'd sensed something in Flynt's demeanour that made him think he had the advantage, but he moved.

'TEN!' he screamed, lunging for a pistol, his fingers wrapping around the butt, his left hand cocking it, raising the weapon, bringing it to bear…

'*JONAS!*'

Cain's voice merged with a shot, but Flynt was only dimly aware of both. Neither was he aware that he had also plucked Tact from the table, palmed back the hammer and fired. It was all instinctive, as if his muscles had taken control of his reason, and he looked at the weapon as if someone had placed it there without his knowledge.

He was dimly aware that before he fired, Hawke had jerked to one side, a wound glistening at his shoulder in the lamplight. Flynt's ball caused a little round hole to ooze red above his right eye, and Hawke slumped but remained on his feet, his pistol slanted to the side, his finger still tightening on the trigger, sending the shot into the darkness. He leaned over, taking a faltering step that served no purpose because he was already dead. His body struck the edge of the table, tipping it over, sending the lamps crashing to the floor, the oil spilling and erupting, enveloping him.

'Douse those flames!' The Admiral's scream was filled with horror as he retreated. 'For the love of mercy, douse them!'

Flynt knew how he had become disfigured, knew why he was so terrified, so moved quickly to wrench some heavy burlap from a loosely tied bundle and proceeded to beat at the fire before it spread too far. Gregor also leaped to assist, stamping on flames while Pickett swiftly pulled off his coat and used it to smother a streak of fire that raced along the spilled oil. Breathing heavily with the exertion and tension, they beat and stamped and fought before the blaze took hold of the aged wood and spread to the bales of cotton and linen. The Admiral kept his distance, but continued to scream, his body writhing as he relived past terrors.

Finally, they had it under control, the damp condition of the wood proving a boon, and stepped back to survey the scorched boards surrounding the smoking, charred remains of Daniel Hawke. The smell of roasted flesh was overpowering.

'The fire,' the Admiral said, a little calmer, but his voice more hoarse than usual. There was insufficient light for Flynt to see, but he knew his single eye would be wide and staring at a conflagration that raged only in his memory. 'The fire,' he said again. 'It burns...'

'All is well, sir,' soothed Pickett. 'The flames are doused. All is well.'

Flynt heard Christy calling his name. A split second before he heard her voice, he had realised that someone hadn't assisted in fighting the flames. And in that split second he knew.

He turned, not slowly, but it seemed so.

And his world tilted.

Christy had Cain's head in her lap, stroking his blond hair. His hands were laid across his chest, as if trying to hide the blood. Flynt dashed to his side, dropping to his knees, his fingers hovering over the wound.

'No,' he whispered.

Cain coughed, managed a weak smile. 'Never... turn your back... on a man who means to kill you.'

Tears welled. Flynt attempted to blink them away. They broke through. He gave Christy a glance, an appeal, as if she could make this right.

'Hawke's ball went wild,' she said. 'Gabriel caught him on the shoulder, but...'

No, Flynt thought, not wild. It found a mark, but the wrong one. It should have been him.

Cain coughed up black blood. 'Never been shot before. It's not... as painful... as I thought.'

'Don't speak,' Flynt said, clasping Cain's hands in his.

A small laugh, causing another flood of blood. 'I don't think... it makes much... difference...'

'We'll get help.'

A slight shake of the head. 'Won't help... Too late...' His hands suddenly gripped Flynt's as if they were a lifeline. Then he groaned, and relaxed again. 'I was... wrong... about the pain,' he said.

Pickett had led the Admiral to them. His breath remained harsh, his posture tense, his masked face continually turning towards the smoke hanging over the site of the blaze. Gregor stood to the side, as impassive as ever. Flynt looked at them all, wishing they could do something. But all they could do was watch. All he could do was watch.

Cain managed another smile. 'At least I'm… dying… with the touch of a beautiful woman.'

Flynt was surprised to see tears welling in Christy's eyes. Surprised and pleased. She could kill without a second's thought, was duplicitous in the extreme, but she still had some measure of humanity. As had Cain. He was the most dependable undependable man he had ever known.

Cain's fingers tightened again as another spasm strained him. 'Good times and bad times, Jonas,' he said, his voice strangled.

Flynt's voice broke. 'And those in between, Gabriel.'

His muscles relaxed again. 'I wonder which this is,' he whispered.

His hands slipped away, his blue eyes gazing at nothing as if in wonder, then losing focus. His entire body loosened.

Silence. Even the Admiral had forgotten his terrors. Flynt willed his old friend to wake up and tell them it was all a jest, that he was fine, that he had smeared something on his chest. But he didn't. Flynt's vision smeared; his throat and eyes burned.

Another friend gone. Another dead because of him. He should say something but couldn't find the words, so instead he roared, the sound deep, primal, filled with fury and grief and helplessness. It echoed around the cavernous warehouse before it died somewhere in the dark, leaving an even deeper silence in its wake.

'We can't leave him here.'

Pickett speaking eventually. Ever the pragmatist.

'We'll carry him out,' Christy said.

'No,' said a gravelly voice Flynt didn't recognise. 'I will do this.'

And then Gregor gently raised Cain from the floor and carried him away, the rest following like a funeral cortège.

Behind them, smoke drifted from the black boards and the charred remains of Daniel Hawke. Flynt became aware again of the water that dripped.

Dripped.

Dripped.

Tears for a dead friend, that would never end.

52

Droplets of rain spattered the grimy windows of the upper room at the Black Lion as if working in concert with the sparking of the logs in the fireplace. Colonel Charters was expressing his condolences and they might even have been sincere, but Flynt couldn't tell. He never could with Charters, so he let them fade to a murmur.

'He was a good man,' Charters said.

Those words registered. 'No, he wasn't. He was a rogue. A thief. A killer. That's why you used him, just as you've used me. He wasn't a good man, but he was a good friend. He was my friend.'

And he died because of it. Like so many others had died because of him. And yet he still lived.

'It was his choice, Serjeant,' Charters said. He was trying to be helpful, Flynt recognised that, but he was failing.

'I shouldn't have continued hunting Hawke. You all tried to warn me, even Gabriel. But I realised too late.' He stopped to reassess. 'No, I should have killed Hawke outright, but instead I gave him a chance. I left it to luck, to fate. And Gabriel paid for it.'

Like giving someone else your money to play with...

'You did what you had to do,' Charters said.

That finally hit home. 'That's the issue, isn't it? That's what you all say, isn't it? Jonas Flynt – he always does what has to be done. I've had a lifetime of doing what had to be done. I had to leave Edinburgh, seek adventure. I had to see action. I had to drag you from that bloody field. I had to thieve and gamble and lie and cheat. I had to walk away from Cassie, from Belle. I had to watch my son...' He stopped, swallowed. 'I had to pursue men and kill them. I had to betray your trust to force Moncrieff to set Hawke adrift. I had to do all that, and in the end, what have I got? You tell me, Colonel. What have I got?' When Charters didn't reply, Flynt indicated his weapons on the table. 'I have two pistols, a sword and a horse and that's it. I have no life, no real home, no future, no friends left, apart from Jack. And all because I did what had to be done.'

Charters, sitting opposite him, maintained his silence for a few moments.

'You didn't betray my trust,' he said eventually.

'What do you mean?'

'Regarding Hawke. You didn't betray my trust. He was not my man within the Fellowship. Though I knew of him, I never met the man.'

Flynt was confused. 'But you called upon his lodgings? I had a description of you from the landlady's son.'

Charters shook his head. 'That was Jacob, one arm tucked away under one of my coats.'

'Why?'

'Because I knew you would trace those lodgings eventually, and I wished you to believe that I was in contact with him.'

'Again, why? To protect him?'

Charters sighed. 'Good God, Serjeant, must I spell it out for you? I needed you to believe that he was my spy. I knew that, if you had to, you would use that knowledge to your advantage. And mine.'

Flynt picked away at this information, sifted it, tried to comprehend what it meant. 'You used Hawke as a decoy.'

'Finally, dawn breaks.'

Staring at the tabletop as if the solution was written there, Flynt pieced it together. 'You knew I'd tell Moncrieff, that's why you told me.'

'Yes.'

'And you did this to protect the real spy.'

'Though it did me little good.'

Understanding hit Flynt hard. 'Gabriel.'

Charters acknowledged with a slight inclination of his head and rose to pull a tray with a decanter and two glasses closer. 'Mr Cain was most accomplished in the art of subterfuge. Moncrieff believed that he was his man in my ranks, and we fed him some inconsequential details regarding the operations of the Company of Rogues to convince him.'

'But Moncrieff has the ear of Sir Robert Walpole, who is privy to all the Company does.'

Charters poured himself a sherry. 'There are many facets of our work that I keep from the politicians. Do you care for a glass? It really is rather good.' When Flynt shook his head, he continued. 'Politicians come and go, fall in and out of favour, can be inconsistent with their loyalties and values. I tell them only what I need them to know.'

'You used me.'

'Yes, I did. We feared Moncrieff had begun to suspect Mr Cain and we needed to throw him off the scent. You did that, though, ultimately…'

He left the thought unexpressed.

'Did Gabriel know of this?' Flynt asked.

'It was his idea. As I said, he took well to the world of subterfuge. And profited from it.'

Flynt had already considered that. Diverting Christy from her original commission would not have been cheaply bought. She said she was fond of Flynt, but that didn't mean she wouldn't have completed her task. After they had placed Cain's body in a cart provided by Pickett, she had vanished along with Gregor. No farewell. No final flirtation. They had melted into the night as if they had never been there.

Like wraiths.

Wheels within wheels.

Flynt stood, stared at his weapons.

'Where will you go?' Charters asked.

He shrugged, making no attempt to reach for Tact and Diplomacy. They had been his first line of defence for many years. They were fine weapons, hand-made, finely balanced, and had never failed him. But even the finest weapon is only as good as the person who wields it. And he was very good at that.

'You can always come back to the Company,' Charters suggested.

Flynt, the knuckles of both hands resting on the table, shook his head.

'There is work yet to be done,' Charters said. 'The Fellowship remains a threat.'

'You'll never defeat them.'

A slight jerk of the head told Flynt that Charters recognised that. 'They are powerful, it's true, and well established. But I can monitor them, impede them when they grow too arrogant. You can assist me.'

'I care nothing for the Fellowship, or the Company, or the stability of the State. I'm done with it.'

'What, then? A return to piracy?'

Another shake of the head.

'What is it you seek, then?'

Flynt considered his reply. 'Rest.'

Charters' lips thinned in a wry smile. 'Something we all long for. May I suggest as a first step that you try to exercise some measure of forgiveness?'

'For whom? Hawke is dead. Blackbeard is dead. Gabriel is dead.'

'For yourself, man. Begin with that, at least.'

Flynt was unsure if he could do that, but he considered whether he could at least try. If he couldn't come to terms with his failings, how could he expect others to? One other in particular?

He picked up his hat and walked to the door.

'Serjeant, you've forgotten your weapons.'

Flynt opened the door leading to the alley, but didn't turn around. 'No, I haven't.'

53

Flynt tightened the girth on Horse's saddle and gave her a gentle pat on the neck. He hooked the sack containing his few clothes and possessions to a strap on the flap and took hold of the reins to lead her from the stall. He'd fetched her and Cain's rented gelding from the stable near the Oxford Road where he and Cain had placed her when evading Wild's men.

Jack stood in the weak light in the stable doorway. The light rain had ceased, but it wasn't far away. Flynt looked for his traps but he was empty-handed.

Jack noticed the direction of his gaze and divined his thoughts. 'I ain't coming with you, Mr Flynt.'

Flynt was not surprised, but he was disappointed.

'I appreciates the offer and all,' Jack went on. 'But going to sea? All them hot places? It ain't me.'

'I know, Jack,' said Flynt.

'So I reckons I'll be staying here, where I knows who I is and where I is.' He hesitated before adding, 'And where I has Bess.'

'She'll be the death of you.'

'I knows it. But...' He sought the words, and when found spoke them almost shamefully. 'I can't live without her. Her and me, we is... Well, it's her and me. When it's just me, it don't feel correct. Does that sound wrong-headed?'

Flynt didn't confirm or deny how it sounded. He'd been wrong-headed most of his life and now sought a way of making it right.

'They'll come for you,' he said. 'And this time they'll ensure they keep you. Colonel Charters won't help you again.'

'I reckons that's the way of it. I knows it, I always knowed it. So did old Blueskin, Gawd rest him.'

Blueskin was dead. He had gone to the gallows that morning. With him, the power of the Thieftaker General was nearly broken. Jonathan

Wild continued to suffer from the effects of Blueskin's attempt on his life, while his star with London's authorities was in the descendent. Griffin had been true to his word and had left his employ. Knapp was no threat.

Suddenly Jack smiled. It was bright and bold and filled with life. 'But I will lead them a merry dance, on that you can be sure and certain.'

'Yes, you will. On that I am sure and certain.'

He held out his hand and Jack, surprised at first, took it. He looked at their clasped hands for a moment. 'You has been a good friend to me, Mr Flynt.'

'I haven't, but you've been a better friend than I deserved. But thank you for saying it.'

Jack nodded and walked to the door again, then stopped and turned back. 'I was never too fond of Mr Cain, you knows that. But he did good in the end, didn't he?'

'Yes, he did,' said Flynt. 'He always did.'

Jack was about to leave when he stopped again. 'I almost forgot.' He bent over beyond the door and brought out a leather pouch, which he handed to Flynt, along with a letter. 'A lady give me this to give to you. Fine looking, she were, Scottish, like you…'

Flynt hefted the pouch, which was weighty with coin, set it at his feet and broke the seal on the letter. It was only a few lines and he read it quickly.

> *My darling Jonas,*
>
> *It doesn't feel proper to keep Gabriel's fee. After all, I do have my doubts as to whether I would have fulfilled the commission, even though Daniel Hawke paid me handsomely, as did Colonel Charters, who commissioned me to keep watch upon you in the first place and report your movements. He also ordered me to let you know why young Sheppard was betrayed to Wild. As I said, wheels within wheels, and the good colonel was the maker of them, all to propel you to his ultimate aim. He is a most underhand individual in pursuit of those aims and, even though I am not without my devious ways, I confess I was most confused in the end as to whose interests I represented, Hawke's, his or Gabriel's. In the end I sided with what was in your best interests, for I really am very fond of you.*

> *I believe Gabriel would have wished you to have this coin, for you were his only true friend.*
> *I will not say goodbye, for that has too final a ring to it. Instead, I will say au revoir. Till we meet again. Some day.*
> *Know that I am your true friend,*
>
> *Christy de Fontaine*

When he looked up, Jack was gone. Although there was regret over the lad's decision to remain in London, for Flynt knew that would end only one way, there was an underlying relief. He had suggested that Jack come with him to the *Walrus* and thence to the Caribbean, but he would not be returning there. Mr Bones would follow his instructions and set sail, keeping the treasure map well hidden until the time was right.

He thrust the pouch into a saddlebag, led Horse from the stall and through the door into the yard, where he hesitated. He had considered seeing Belle once more, but they had said all that needed to be said. Or at least, all that could be said between them. He had hurt her too often and too well. He had hurt himself too often and too well. It was best he take his leave without further goodbyes. There had been too many of those, some unsaid but permanent.

He raised himself into the saddle and sat still for a moment, unsure whether his chosen plan of action was the correct one. He couldn't remain in London. He had no desire to return to the colonies. He could travel, but he'd done enough of that. He had never known where home was, but he was intent on discovering it. Or rediscovering it.

He spurred Horse into motion, taking her easy. They had a long way to go and a lifetime to do it.

Once through the gates of the stable yard he headed for the Great North Road. He didn't know if Cassie in Edinburgh would welcome him, but he intended to find out.

Historical Note

This is a work of fiction, but many of the events regarding Jack Sheppard, Jonathan Wild and Joseph 'Blueskin' Blake are (more or less) accurate. As before, the characters I assign to these historical figures are mine, and I have played a little fast and loose with chronology to suit my storyline.

Jack did indeed escape from Newgate in the manner described, although I have taken a few liberties for dramatic purposes. He and Blueskin were arrested for breaking into Mr Kneebone's shop on the Strand, and the testimony provided by Mendez and Arnold, both of whom arrested Blake along with Wild, was (again more or less) what they said at the time. Fields was also involved and informed against them, though his testimony changed between providing it against Jack and then Blueskin. The court saw little problem with that.

Jack, however, was captured again and this time he didn't escape. He went to Tyburn on 16 November 1724. He was twenty-two years of age. He was buried in the churchyard of St Martin-in-the-Fields.

Blake did attack Wild in the Sessions House, badly slashing his throat. He was executed on 11 November and buried in the churchyard of St Andrew on Holborn.

Jonathan Wild's star was indeed in the descendent. In 1725 he was arrested and tried for theft, and himself suffered the doom to which he had condemned so many others on 24 May. According to *The Newgate Calendar*, in jail he tried to take his own life by overdosing on laudanum, but it only succeeded in rendering him insensate. Jack Sheppard was treated as a hero on the Newgate Trail. Wild was not, being insulted and pelted with stones and dirt. He was still suffering the effects of the opium, so perhaps he knew very little about it. He was buried in St Pancras churchyard but his body was later dug up and, presumably, anatomised. His skeleton was later discovered in the possession of a

Windsor doctor and put on display in the museum of the Royal College of Surgeons.

Although he was said to keep a ledger with crosses beside the names of thieves, it's unclear whether this was the derivation of the term double-cross. It didn't enter popular usage until the following century. Obviously, I like to think it began with him.

The Puckle Machine Gun did exist. Patented in 1718, it was a manually operated flintlock revolver, mounted on a tripod. There may only have been two actual weapons made, though there were designs for two different types: one, firing conventional bullets, was for use against Christian enemies; the other fired square ammunition, said to inflict more pain, and was intended to be used against non-Christians.

Major John Bernardi, whom Jacob visits in Newgate, did exist. He was a Jacobite who fought at Killiecrankie in 1689 and was implicated in a plot to assassinate King William III. He was thrown into Newgate in 1696 without trial, though no convincing evidence was presented against him. In 1712 he married in prison and fathered ten children. He was never released, never tried, and died in 1736, having spent forty years in Newgate.

The collapse of the South Sea Company, and the mania for investment it had helped create, did shock society and caused the loss of fortunes. Like today's investments, it was a form of gambling, and many people lost. The political fallout did assist Sir Robert Walpole back into power.

The Sessions House as I describe it was (once again, more or less) accurate. The straw men mentioned were also known as affidavit men, and did linger outside the courtroom awaiting to be hired to help deliver a 'not guilty' verdict.

Most of the public houses mentioned existed, the use of 'Lion' in the names being prevalent. The Golden Cross was also real and stood in what is now Trafalgar Square. The bog house on Lincoln's Inn Square also existed.

As for what happened to John 'Barbecue' Silver, Israel Hands, Billy Bones and the fortune Flynt had hidden…?

Well, that's another story.

Acknowledgements

Thanks are, as ever, due to all at Canelo for giving this series life, especially my editor, Craig Lye, and my copy-editor, Steve O'Gorman, for guiding this particular story to its finished form, and to Kate Shepherd for getting the word out about them!

Also my agent, Jo Bell, for her unwavering support and guidance.

My wife Sarah made sure that I finished this one, even though she faced incredibly difficult circumstances. I publicly declare my love for her.

Elizabeth Jelly won a competition at a book launch for my friend Gordon J Brown (aka Morgan Cry) to have her name included in our next works. I hope she's happy with the completely fictional character to bear it.

Thanks to Gary McLaughlin for looking after Mickey and Tom (my dog and cat) when Sarah and I have to be away for book events.

And thanks to the readers, booksellers and organisers of those events for their continued support.